Praise for bestselling author
ANIA AHLBORN

BROTHER

"[A] visceral, nihilistic thriller. . . . Ahlborn's impressive writing and expert exploration of the psychological effects of systemic abuse elevate what could have been the literary equivalent of a slasher flick, and the twist in the final act is jaw-dropping. This relentlessly grim tale is definitely not for the squeamish, but it's nearly impossible to put down."

—*Publishers Weekly* (starred review)

"This story of brotherly love/hate will crush you to the core. . . . *Brother* delivers horror on all fronts. . . . The writing is so good, so precision perfect, that *Brother* may be this year's sleeper novel, certainly of the *Gone Girl* caliber, that deserves all the praise and accolades it will definitely receive. . . . An instant classic. . . . This is one book you need to get in your hands as soon as possible."

—*This is Horror*

WITHIN THESE WALLS

"Terrifyingly sad. . . . *Within These Walls* creeps under your skin, and stays there. It's insidious. . . . The book's atmosphere is distinctly damp, clammy, overcast, and it isn't all the Washington weather: its characters' souls are gray, dimmed by failure. Ahlborn is awfully good on the insecurities that plague both aging writers . . . and over-sensitive young girls . . . which leave them vulnerable to those who . . . know how to get into their heads. So grim."
—*The New York Times Book Review*

"Cruel, bone-chilling, and destined to become a classic, *Within These Walls* is worth the sleep it will cost you. Some of the most promising horror I've encountered in years."

—Seanan McGuire, *New York Times* bestselling author

"A monstrous Russian nesting doll of a book, holding se-crets within secrets; the plot barrels headlong toward one of the most shocking climaxes you're ever likely to read. This one's going to wreck you."
—Nick Cutter, national bestselling author of *Little Heaven* and *The Troop*

"Ania Ahlborn is a great storyteller who spins an atmosphere of dread literally from the first page, increasing the mental pressure all the way through to the terrifying, chilling ending."

—Jeff Somers, acclaimed author of
The Electric Church and *We Are Not Good People*

"Ever-mounting terror and a foreboding setting make for pure storytelling alchemy. . . . Ania Ahlborn goes for the gut with surprise twists that will stay with you for days. Not a book, or an author, that you'll soon forget."

—Vicki Pettersson, *New York Times* bestselling author

Also by ANIA AHLBORN

Brother

The Pretty Ones (novella)

Within These Walls

The Bird Eater

The Shuddering

The Neighbors

Seed

THE DEVIL
CREPT IN

ANIA AHLBORN

G

Gallery Books

New York   London   Toronto   Sydney   New Delhi

G

Gallery Books

An Imprint of Simon & Schuster, Inc.
1230 Avenue of the Americas
New York, NY 10020

First Gallery Books trade paperback edition February 2017

GALLERY BOOKS and colophon are registered trademarks of Simon & Schuster, Inc.

For information about special discounts for bulk purchases, please contact Simon & Schuster Special Sales at 1-866-506-1949 or business@simonandschuster.com.

The Simon & Schuster Speakers Bureau can bring authors to your live event. For more information or to book an event contact the Simon & Schuster Speakers Bureau at 1-866-248-3049 or visit our website at www.simonspeakers.com.

Manufactured in the United States of America

5   7   9   10   8   6   4

Library of Congress Cataloging-in-Publication Data

Names: Ahlborn, Ania, author.
Title: The devil crept in : a novel / Ania Ahlborn.
Description: New York : Gallery Books, 2017.

Identifiers: LCCN 2016037375 (print) | LCCN 2016045706 (ebook) |
ISBN 9781476783758 (softcover) | ISBN 9781476783802 (ebook)
Subjects: LCSH: Missing persons—Investigation—Fiction. | City and town life—Fiction. | Missing children—Fiction. | BISAC: FICTION / Horror.|
FICTION / Family Life. | FICTION / Suspense. | GSAFD: Suspense fiction. |
Mystery fiction. | Horror fiction.
Classification: LCC PS3601.H556 D49 2017 (print) | LCC PS3601.H556
(ebook) |
DDC 813/.6—dc23
LC record available at https://lccn.loc.gov/2016037375

ISBN 978-1-4767-8375-8
ISBN 978-1-4767-8380-2 (ebook)

And then the child ran into the wood.
To find his friend where the devil stood.

—Anonymous

Because I feel that, in the Heavens above
The angels, whispering to one another,
Can find, among their burning terms of love
None so devotional as that of "Mother."

—Edgar Allan Poe

PART ONE

PART ONE

1

———

JUDE BRIGHTON WAS missing. Stevie Clark stood at the edge of the woods, his small hands clasped together, watching people comb the trees for his friend.

Jude had disappeared that Sunday, after he and Stevie had spent hours ransacking the backs of buildings for broken two-by-fours. Their fort was almost complete. All it needed was a couple more boards and a replacement set of ladder stairs. The ones they'd nailed to the tree trunk were treacherous, like climbing up Sauron's tower. But they both liked the danger—clinging to splintery planks with their bare hands, comparing scratches and scrapes once they got to the top, nearly breaking their necks climbing down from the turret every single time. Because *Life is no fun without the risk*, said Jude. And if Stevie knew anyone who sought out peril, it was definitely his cousin. His best friend. Now vanished like a ghost.

Stevie had been sitting on the couch, watching TV, when his aunt Amanda knocked on the front door. "Is Jude here?" she'd asked, wearing her usual glass-fragile smile. But there was something in her voice that put Stevie on edge, something festering, like a scourge. "It's time to come home," she said. "Dinner is in the oven."

Stevie loved his aunt Mandy. She was a pretty lady despite her exaggerated features. Her face was long and her eyes were huge. *She's got a horse face*, his stepdad, Terry, had guffawed. *Horse face Brighton. We should enter her in the Kentucky Derby and win us some dough.* Terry Marks was a giant asshole. Stevie hated him, probably more than he hated anyone on earth.

And yet, despite loathing "The Tyrant" for being such a dick, Stevie occasionally found himself resenting his mother even more; partly because she didn't defend Aunt Mandy when Terry insulted her, but mostly because she let him detonate their lives. She'd worn a black eye for the better part of two weeks once. *Walked right into the corner of the kitchen cabinet*, she had said, laughing. *I swear, if my head wasn't screwed on . . . You know how it goes.* Yeah, Stevie knew. The whole town knew, despite the ruse.

It was why Aunt Mandy was on edge whenever she came over. Terry wasn't exactly what you'd call hospitable. It was a wonder she let Jude play at Stevie's house at all. Luckily, she did, because her house gave Stevie a headache. It smelled pink, like flowers. That, and he was pretty sure there was a snake living in her toilet. He'd seen it, regardless of whether or not Jude swore he had imagined the whole thing.

"He's not here, nope," Stevie said.

The fact that Jude hadn't come to hang out that afternoon or that he had yet to make it home didn't seem like that big a deal. Jude played by his own rules. If he wanted to hang out in the woods all day, he would. If he felt like missing dinner, he did. There wasn't anyone who could stop him, especially not his mom. But Aunt Mandy's thinly veiled panic assured Stevie that, despite Jude being a rule breaker and the old saying that *boys will be boys*, this was much more than her son being his usual, defiant self. This was something different. Far more serious than missing a curfew. Aunt Mandy's wavering smile fractured into a thousand shards of worry.

"Do you know where he is?" she asked.

"Nuh-uh." Stevie supposed Jude could have been at the fort, but that was a long trek, one that was boring if made alone. That, and the fort was top secret. With a single park and a half-mile drag of shops making up Main Street, Deer Valley wasn't exactly a hip and happening place. They'd spent all summer building that citadel, had discussed building another one—bigger and better—after the first was complete. They fantasized about installing a zip line fifteen feet in the air; just another way to kill themselves when they weren't shooting foamy Nerf darts into each other's eyes or lobbing water balloons at each other's heads. If they were lucky, they'd locate a pipe at the scrap yard long enough to make a fireman's pole. These were all upgrades they'd thought of after the fact, far too late to implement into their original design. Stevie wasn't about to squeal their secret just because Aunt Mandy was a little worried about Jude being late.

For any kid other than Jude, there would have been places to suggest. He could have been hanging out at a friend's house across town. There would have been neighboring houses to visit, parents to call. But Jude didn't have friends. Not in the facetious *He's such a loner* way, but in a genuine *Nobody likes Jude Brighton* way. It could be said that the only reason he'd spent hundreds of hours building a tree house with Stevie, a cousin two years his junior, was because his reputation preceded him. Kids didn't like Stevie because he was weird, because he had fingers missing off his right hand. Their distaste for Jude was simpler: they didn't like him because he was a jerk.

Parents, on the other hand, didn't like Jude because he was trouble. He used words like *goddamn* and *shit* and *asshole*, even around adults. Once, he'd dropped an f-bomb for no reason other than to use it; just threw it out there to make conversation more colorful. Stevie had heard words like that blast through the walls of his house on the regular. His big brother, Duncan, would let an occasional curse fly. And Terry had quite the vocabulary, one he didn't mind the whole neighborhood hearing. But Dunk was in high school and Terry was a full-grown man; Jude was only twelve. Hearing the sharp edges of that curse word come from a kid had left Stevie's nerves fizzing like a bag of wet Pop Rocks.

Jude was tough, unforgiving. He'd been that way since his dad—Stevie's uncle Scott—had died. Nothing scared him. Two summers ago, while playing in the creek, he had shoo'd off a snarling coyote; skinny, probably starving, ready for a mid-afternoon snack. But Jude just grabbed a downed branch and ran at it like he was going to skewer it through, bellowing a battle cry as he blasted toward the animal, leaving Stevie to stare wide-eyed at his ballsy brother-in-arms.

"Jeez," Stevie had said after Jude came trudging back. "What if it had attacked you instead of running off?"

"Then it would have ended up dead instead of scared," Jude had said, as though killing coyotes with his bare hands was no big deal. When the coyote had found them, Uncle Scott hadn't been gone for more than a year. Jude had been ten, but his rage was big enough to fill a man twice his size.

. . .

By the next morning, there were already rumors that Jude had up and run away, and the theory wasn't hard to believe. Everyone knew Jude had issues. He was Deer Valley's problem child; a menace, always getting in trouble. And Amanda Brighton wasn't exactly a stern or assertive woman. She had tried to take Jude to therapy, but it only seemed to intensify his furor. Giving up after a couple of tries, Jude had been allowed to run wild.

More than a few times, he'd gotten busted by the cops for petty stuff like shoplifting. There were counts of vandalism and trespassing, though that infraction was just on someone's bazillion-acre farm. The owners hadn't posted signs to keep people out, so it was a total bogus charge, if anyone asked him. But the police, like everyone else, didn't like Jude, so they gave him hell.

The worst of it had come when Jude was caught wielding a plank of wood—rusty nails crooked and jutting out like a medieval mace—taunting one of Deer Valley's countless strays behind one of the Main Street shops. The sickly-looking cat had scrambled up a tree in search of safety. Meanwhile, Jude swung the two-by-four convincingly enough to have the shop owner call for help. Stevie was pretty sure Jude had only been trying to help the dumb animal down, but nobody cared about what he thought. Jude ended up with a warning for attempted animal abuse. One more slipup and he'd get full-blown probation, maybe even end up in juvie thirty miles outside of town.

Somehow, Aunt Mandy managed to talk her son out of each and every infraction. There was a lot of pleading and explaining involved. Lots of Aunt Mandy having to relive the death of her husband while telling the tale of how the loss of Jude's dad had hit her only child hard. Assurances were made: Jude was a good boy, just lost and angry, struggling to cope with his grief. And honestly, sometimes that made *Stevie* mad, because he was pretty sure he'd rather have a dead dad than Terry Marks looming over his each and every move.

But this wasn't about Stevie.

Less than an hour after Aunt Mandy left his house, the cops were next door, taking a report. Stevie had watched enough investigation shows to know the first forty-eight hours were crucial. After that, the chance of finding a kid became next to impossible. And no matter how much Jude grandstanded and wanted to believe he was an adult, he was still a kid. What Stevie's mom referred to as an overgrown baby and his stepdad called a no-good little shit.

First thing Monday, there was a report on the early-morning news: Jude Brighton, age twelve, had taken off. To those who didn't know him, it was as good an explanation as any. Stevie, however, knew it was a load of crap. Because Jude didn't keep his mouth shut about anything. When he had a wise idea, Stevie was the first to know.

By that first morning, bored reporters were trying to get interviews with anyone who would talk. Stevie's mom demanded he stay away. He watched through the windows as neighbors leaned into microphones—those people didn't even know Jude, yet there they were, giving statements all the same. *Oh, that Brighton kid. Just a whole lot of trouble, if you ask me.*

Aunt Mandy was hysterical. Stevie's mom was preoccupied with trying to keep her sister from losing her mind, and so— left to his own devices—Stevie shoved a granola bar into the back pocket of his shorts and hiked out to the fort, just to check that Jude wasn't there. Not a single loose board or nail had been disturbed. There was no sign of him.

Pivoting to face a different direction, Stevie stared through the forest toward an altogether different destination, their other secret: the *house*. Did he dare? No. He turned tail and booked it back home, because that house was a place neither one of them went by themselves. Not ever. No way.

. . .

Tuesday morning. Stevie was up with the birds, and he'd just about made it out the door when his mom caught him by the arm. "Where are you going?" she asked, looking dubious as usual.

"To h-help look for Jude." But all that got him was a tug away from the front door. Nicole Clark confiscated his little spiral notebook and mechanical pencil—the stuff he used to take field notes—and slid them on top of the fridge. Unless he scaled the counter or dragged a chair across the room, he wouldn't be able to reach them. She sat him down at the table and fixed him a Pop-Tart as though a breakfast pastry was an appropriate alternative for aiding in the search for his missing best friend. "You need to stay here," she told him. No explanation. Just a command.

"But why?" Stevie asked. If he wasn't allowed to look for Jude, he sure as heck wanted a better reason than *Because I said so.*

"Because . . ." Terry's voice cut through the conversation. He filled the kitchen's doorway, his square shoulders blocking out the sun that filtered in through the front-room window. A second later, he entered the kitchen with his hulking gait. "No one needs a funny-farm nutcase hanging around while they're trying to get shit done, that's why." He shot Stevie a stern, reproachful look. Then again, every look seemed hateful from eyes as deep-set and narrow as The Tyrant's. He was as ugly as he was mean with his high, shiny forehead and his sandy-brown mullet. But it was that mustache that grossed Stevie out the most—an ugly upside-down *U* that crawled down the sides of his mouth like a dying caterpillar.

"Oh, Ter." Stevie's mom. "Leave him alone." Except she didn't mean it. If The Tyrant decided to lay into Stevie then and there, she'd quietly shuffle out of the room.

Stevie looked down at his paper plate and glared at his Pop-Tart. Other than dinner, every meal was served on disposables. That's what happened when the dishwasher broke and, no matter how much Stevie's mom pleaded, it didn't get fixed.

"So, if I don't help they'll find him *faster?*" That seemed pretty unlikely, especially since the cops weren't asking many questions. Those guys hardly seemed to be worried at all.

His mom sighed. "Stevie . . ."

"Maybe," Terry said. "And maybe if you don't ask so many stupid fucking questions, you won't piss me off this morning." Terry wasn't the least bit affected by Jude's disappearance. He would have cared more if someone's dog had taken a dump on their weedy front lawn. Except that nobody had dogs in Deer Valley. Cats, neither. When Stevie was younger, his mom convinced him that there were no pets around because they were germy and not allowed in town. When he deciphered that bullshit story, she explained that, after the "incident" with Dunk's dog, there would be no more pets for the Clarks, end of story. She never did elaborate on what that incident had been.

Stevie glared at his plate, then dared to look up at his mother. Of course, her back was turned. She was busying herself at the counter, as though not hearing a word of his and Terry's exchange.

He sat there, unmoving, until The Tyrant gulped his instant coffee and scarfed down the doughnut in front of him—glazed chocolate that made Stevie think of a crumbly old tractor tire. He kept his eyes averted, silently ticking off the seconds inside his head—*one, two, ten*—until his stepdad pushed away from the table and stepped up to the counter where Stevie's mom continued to loom. Stevie didn't look, but the sounds coming from next to the sink accompanied the pictures in his head: Terry pressing himself against his mom's backside, his giant block-like hands gripping her hips, jerking her backward toward his crotch. Sometimes, he'd slide his hand down her front and between her legs as she stood frozen and unresponsive, like perhaps she was scared or even secretly grossed out. And then, without so much as a good-bye, Terry Marks detached himself from Stevie's mother like a pilot fish releasing a shark, grabbed the keys to his giant pickup, and left.

Dunk liked to say that Terry's truck was big because his dick was small.

Stevie didn't want to know a damn thing about that. All he knew was that he sometimes thought about sabotaging his stepdad's stupid truck or poisoning his food, but had yet to go through with any of those grand, homicidal plans. Because that was the thing about Stevie. He was a chicken shit. A pain in the ass who had tough thoughts but did nothing in the end.

"I know it's hard, sweetheart." His mom's voice cut through the stifling silence that Terry had left in his wake. Her uncanny ability to pretend as though Terry existed in some parallel universe never failed to creep him out. One second, she was being mounted by a horndog, and the next she was asking Stevie if he wanted grilled cheese for lunch, as though pet names like *sweetheart* and *honey* made up for the fact that she let a grown man beat on her and her kids.

But that was the thing about Terry: he had a decent paying job. And ever since Stevie's real dad had bailed, bills were hard to pay.

"I know you're really interested in all this investigation stuff," his mom was now saying, "but just sit tight."

Stevie almost scoffed at her reasoning. Yeah. Sure. He wanted to go look for Jude because he was into "investigation stuff," *not* because Jude was his only friend; a friend who very likely could have been lying dead in the forest somewhere.

"The police will find him," she said. "He'll be back by dinner."

Except Stevie didn't believe that for a second.

Jude Brighton was gone, like he'd never existed; vanished, as though he and Stevie hadn't spent their entire lives stomping the pavement of Main Street and living their summers in those woods. To them, the ferns were landmarks. Each bend in Cedar Creek, a compass. If someone had chased Jude through those trees, he would have outrun them. If they had dragged him deep into the wilderness, he would have broken free.

2

STEVIE STAYED IN his room all day to make his mother happy. But his thoughts veered in different directions. What if Jude really *had* run off? Maybe he was sitting in some seedy diner a hundred miles away, divvying out what little cash he had stolen from Aunt Mandy's purse, waiting on a bus to take him west toward Universal Studios. He'd always wanted to go there. *Disneyland*, he said, *is for dumb-ass babies. Universal Studios is where they've got Jaws and the* Psycho *house. It's cool*. And when it came to Jude, cool was the golden rule.

Or it could have been that Jude was the next Max Larsen. Dunk had told the tale a dozen times, probably more. A kid goes into the forest and never comes out. Two weeks later, his body is discovered. Mangled. Half-eaten. Swelling up like a balloon. The cops called it an animal attack, but everyone knew it was the work of a madman. A psychopath as bad as Albert Fish, maybe worse. A cannibal who loved the taste of kids.

And the story was true. It was on Google and everything. Dunk had showed him. The adults hardly ever mentioned the Larsen kid, as if afraid that a single utterance of that long-lost boy's name would bring evil out from the forest that surrounded the town. But all the kids knew the story. A dead boy found on the side of the road wasn't a secret a place as small as Deer Valley could keep, especially not from the eager ears and dark imaginations of its youth.

Stevie found it weird that none of the adults ever talked about Max Larsen, as though not bringing him up would somehow erase him from the past. Once, having evoked the name while his mom grilled chicken legs on the backyard barbecue, he watched her expression shift from benevolent to shocked. *Where did you hear that name?* she demanded. *Was it Duncan? Is your brother telling you stupid stories again?* It had, in fact, been Dunk who had laid down the gruesome tale—a fable that big brothers impart on younger siblings in hopes of birthing a well-spring of perpetual nightmares. The first time Stevie had heard it, it had been just a story, something that had happened in the past and would never be repeated again. But now he couldn't get Dunk's word pictures out of his head; innocuous phrases made debilitating by what they referenced. *Shredded beef. Buzzing flies. Cries. Dies. Dies.*

• • •

That night, unable to sit still and driving his mother nuts, Stevie went to a movie with Dunk. The outing was a result of their mother's pleading, probably with some sort of bribe attached—because, unless she gave Dunk some kind of incentive, or unless Dunk was swatting at the back of Stevie's head or telling him scary stories to keep him up at night, Duncan Clark hardly acknowledged his kid brother's existence. And despite Stevie coming unstrung over Jude, it was nice to get out. He needed it. Because his stuttering, his word salad, his rhyming problem, were starting to creep back into his brain, and that was never good.

Duncan's girlfriend, Annie, met them at the ValleyPlex. She was pretty, and didn't seem to care that all Dunk ever wore was basketball stuff. She didn't even mind his stupid haircut, which was shaved on the sides with a poof of longer hair flaring out at the top like a soft-serve swirl. He was dead-set on getting a design buzzed into his hair by the end of the summer. Their mom said no way, but as one of Olympia High's star basketball players, Dunk was determined to have all eyes on him . . . especially Annie's, which were as big and round as the bottoms of two soda cans, like a girl in one of those Japanese cartoons.

The ValleyPlex was a whopping two-screen cinema that could afford only one mainstream flick every three months. Screen two always played stuff Stevie hadn't heard of but made his mom and Aunt Mandy sigh like they were in love: *Pretty in Pink, St. Elmo's Fire, Say Anything* . . . Whatever those were.

Inside the ValleyPlex, Stevie settled into his crummy seat— the armrest so wobbly he had to hold his drink between his knees. The cold of the cup roused phantom pain in the missing tips of the pointer and middle fingers of his right hand—both cut off at the first knuckle, ground to bits, the remnants floating around in a sewer somewhere. He curled his fingers into a fist to keep them warm and tried not to notice Dunk's hand drifting across Annie's leg and up her pleated skirt; tried to ignore it when she slouched and placed the empty tub of popcorn in her lap, Dunk's right hand missing in action, his left tugging at his jeans as though his pants were suddenly way too tight. With popcorn now out of the question, Stevie tried to focus on the velociraptors—his favorite dinosaur—as they caused chaos all over Jurassic World. He almost forgot what was going on back home until Dunk kicked his sneaker as the credits rolled.

"Get your ass up," he said.

By the time they reached the parking lot, Stevie was drowning in worry once more.

When they pulled into the driveway, Dunk flattened the same right hand he'd stuffed up Annie's skirt against Stevie's T-shirt to keep him where he was. "You didn't see shit, did you, Sack?" Duncan gave Stevie a warning look, heavy with the promise of a brotherly beating if Stevie mentioned anything to their mom about Annie and her popcorn tub. Stevie grimaced both at the hand against his chest and his brother's use of his least favorite nickname. Stephen Aaron Clark's initials added up to a harmless S-A-C, until the *k* of his last name was tacked on to the end. That's when Stevie became Sack, or Sackboy, or Ballsack, or Sack of Shit, or—when the threat of having his ass kicked came up—Hacky Sack.

"I just saw dinosaurs," Stevie murmured. "J-just seesaw dinos . . ." He diverted his attention from his brother's hand to the portable basketball hoop—nothing but a rusty rim and a crooked backboard inches from Dunk's front bumper. Dunk's future. His life.

Duncan appeared satisfied with Stevie's answer and pulled his hand away. "You gonna go look for the Jewd tomorrow?"

Sack was a shitty moniker, but Jude had Stevie beat in the unfortunate nickname category. Jude wasn't Jewish, but that didn't matter one iota to a guy like Duncan. Sack and the Jewd, like peas in a crappy pod.

Dunk's question threw Stevie for a loop, not only because Terry and his mom had specifically forbidden him to aid in the search for his cousin, but also because he couldn't remember the last time Dunk had asked him a question he actually expected Stevie to answer.

"Mom said I can't," he said.

"Mom." Dunk rolled his eyes. "Because *she's* someone who should be giving out life advice. But I guess it's for the better."

Stevie squinted at the scuffed-up knees of his jeans. He'd need a new pair soon. One squat too many and they were liable to bust like a birthday piñata. He only hoped it wouldn't happen at school, in the cafeteria, where all the jerk-off fifth-graders would see it happen and never let him live it down. Once, a kid had tripped with his food tray and gotten mac and cheese all over the front of his shirt. It had looked a little like vomit, so that's exactly what they called him all year long. Another kid had taken a tetherball to the face during recess, fallen backward, and wailed as blood spurted from his nose. That kid was henceforth dubbed Ballface Gusher. For how stupid the fifth-graders were, they were pretty creative when it came to being total dicks, and the last thing Stevie needed was another clever nickname. He was already Sack at home; Schizo Steve-O, Stuttering Stevie, and Screws-Loose Magoose at school.

"For the better how?" Stevie asked.

"You know . . ," Dunk said. Stevie kept his eyes diverted, but he could hear the smirk in his brother's voice. "Nobody wants a loony running around the goddamn woods." He pulled the keys out of the ignition and patted the steering wheel as if to thank his old Firebird for her service. It was a rusty heap, but Dunk loved that car. When he wasn't shooting hoops or losing his hand up Annie's skirt, he was nothing but a pair of legs, his top half swallowed by the engine compartment of his faithful steed. "Now get out," he said, "and you better lock the door behind you or I'll bust your goddamn face."

Stevie crawled out of the car that smelled faintly of cigarettes, French fries, and sweat, hit the lock, and slammed the door shut behind him. Dunk retreated into the house while Stevie was left staring at Jude's place directly next door to his own. All the windows were lit up, casting long, sorrowful rectangles across an unkempt lawn. But Aunt Mandy's yard— no matter how weedy—wasn't nearly as bad as their own. For the great Terry Marks had a taste for collecting random crap, and his junk had spread from the backyard to the side of the house—stuff he'd find at local wrecking yards and recycling plants that he wanted to fix up and sell because *Idiots will buy anything off of the Internet.* Except that Terry never posted anything online and a garage sale was out of the question, too much goddamn work. So the stacks of crap just kept piling up. But now, with Jude gone, Aunt Mandy's house looked sadder than usual, possibly even more so than Stevie's, despite The Tyrant's overwhelming hoard.

Aunt Mandy's single-story Craftsman had a sagging, moss-covered roof that Stevie's mom swore would cave in and kill both her sister and nephew one day. All it would take was a bad storm, a high wind, some hail. But Aunt Mandy didn't have the money to fix it, and Terry sure wasn't going to climb up there and reinforce it out of the goodness of his heart. He couldn't be bothered to look at the dishwasher in his own kitchen, after all.

The house's paint job was just as bad as the roof; giant white strips of the stuff peeling from the clapboard siding like dirty old bandages that had lost their stick. Aunt Mandy's once-preened rosebushes now grew in chaotic brambles of white, fuchsia, and pink. Not so long ago, she had toyed with the idea of joining the Oregon Rose Society. She talked of entering her flowers in competitions and dreamed of winning silk ribbons and shiny trophies that she could proudly display on her mantel for everyone to see. Stevie had pictured her standing up on a stage, holding a golden two-handled cup, beaming as wide as if she'd won the million-dollar jackpot, flashbulbs lighting up her face. *Pop, POP!* He'd even cleared off a spot for that very photograph on his bookshelf, sure of his aunt's destiny. But after what happened to Uncle Scott, Aunt Mandy never bothered to clip another bloom. Both houses—his and Jude's—had been built around the same time, but Stevie's mom managed to keep theirs in decent shape. Meanwhile, grief ruled next door.

Standing in the dark, Stevie wanted to venture over to check on his aunt. Sometimes, when Terry took to his belt and Stevie's mom went temporarily blind, he was sure he loved Aunt Mandy more than anyone. It was yet another thing that made Stevie angry when it came to Jude acting out. Sure, Jude was upset about losing his dad, but Aunt Mandy was just as hurt. What gave Jude the right to act like an idiot, to be disrespectful, to make his mother's life more difficult than it already was? It would have been nice to live next door where there was no danger of being cornered by an angry man; where, regardless of tragedy, there was compassion. Openheartedness. Love. It was why Stevie hoped that Jude *hadn't* run away. Because if he had, man was he stupid. Dumber than a bag of rocks.

A stray cat meandered across Aunt Amanda's front lawn, stopping in a square of window light. It was sickly looking, just like all the strays around town, of which there were many. There were more cats than dogs, but that didn't matter. It was a perfect reason for Stevie's mom to deny him the pet he'd always wanted anyway. Deer Valley residents had a bad habit of letting their animals run wild. And then there was the expense: food and vet bills. The cat on Aunt Mandy's lawn looked like it hadn't seen either of those in a long time, if ever. Little more than skin and bone, its patchy fur hung off its frame like an oversized mink on a rich old lady's feeble frame. Momentarily frozen, the animal met Stevie's gaze, then broke its stasis to scratch an itch. A tuft of fur puffed out from where it stroked its coat, leaving a clump of orange and white on the brittle, dying grass.

Stevie wrinkled his nose and turned toward his own home. It was probably too late to visit Aunt Amanda tonight anyway; she was more than likely already in bed. That, and that cat made his skin crawl. He'd never been a fan of felines. Dunk said they had parasites; bugs that found their way into their owners' brains, turning them into mindless slaves. No way he was getting close to that thing. It wasn't worth the risk.

He made his way up onto his own porch one weary step at a time. He considered asking his mom to let him stay next door; a sleepover. Aunt Mandy would undoubtedly appreciate the company. Nights must have been hard, and Aunt Mandy shouldn't be alone. Stevie would feel better if he were sleeping on her couch, just in case Jude *did* come home. But even if his mom considered the overnight, The Tyrant would never allow it. It was a power thing. He didn't give half a damn about Stevie's well-being, but when it came to being lenient, Terry was a dictator. This, however, was a special case. Maybe he'd make an exception, since Aunt Mandy's house was just a few feet away.

But Stevie stopped just shy of his front door, catching movement from the corner of his eye. There was something out there, lurking around the side of the house near Terry's piles of junk.

"J-Jude?" The name escaped his throat before he could tamp down his hope. And the thing was, when he spoke, whatever was hiding out in those shadows moved, crouching behind one of Terry's many leaning towers of crap, as though waiting for Stevie to notice it; or just waiting for him to move on.

But Stevie was ten years old, and even if he *had* been a full-grown adult, he wouldn't have been able to shrug off his curiosity. He tiptoed across the porch planks toward the side railing, not wanting to scare away that mysterious shifting shadow with a sudden move, all the while assuring himself that he was a grade-A idiot. The strays around here had been marked an official village problem. People talked about it at town meetings. Solutions were occasionally proposed in the weekly *Deer Valley Gazette.* Terry's junk was the perfect spot for hiding. Just last summer, Stevie discovered a litter of kittens living along the interior of an old truck tire, hungry and soaked by the rain. Suddenly, even the boy who didn't like cats was begging his mom to keep one, even if it was just outdoors. Those kittens were too cute to abandon. But The Tyrant put the kibosh on that possibility before Stevie's mom ever had the chance to say no. He tossed those kittens into a rain-warped cardboard box, threw the box into the back of his truck, and that was the end of that. Stevie only hoped that his stepdad had taken them to the Humane Society and not dumped them off somewhere along the side of the road.

Then again, maybe he had, and that sad-looking feline in Aunt Amanda's yard was one of the exiled. Stevie imagined it waiting all night for Terry to come outside. And when he did? *Whoosh!* A flying leap. *Fwoomp!* A perfect landing on The Tyrant's stupid face. *Hiss!* Claws out, slashing at that ugly caterpillar 'stache. If Stevie bore witness to such an event, he'd adopt every stray cat in town, brain worms and all.

Deer Valley wasn't just crawling with cats and the occasional dog. There were raccoons as well. Dunk nearly had his face torn off by one while playing basketball late one night.

And sometimes, while he didn't like to admit it even to himself, Stevie saw things that probably weren't there. Like the snakes that crawled out of the cracked plaster ceiling above his bed. Or ants in the sugar bowl. Bugs coming out of electrical sockets. Shadow people standing in empty rooms, there one second, gone the next. Maybe that's what he was seeing now—a whole lot of nothing.

All of that reasoning, however, escaped him as he crept to the balustrade, his dirty sneakers silent upon the old wooden boards. He slowly bent at the waist to get a better view of the side yard. Whatever was lurking out there had moved again, retreating farther back along the property.

"H-hello . . . ?"

A rusted-over truck fender—apparently a great thing to sell online, if you asked Terry the Online Entrepreneur—shifted among the mounds of stuff. It was the real deal; bigger than a cat or a raccoon. Stevie supposed it could have been a coyote, but those weren't exactly known for being sneaky. And if it *was* a dog, he was pretty sure the thing would have shown itself by now. Either that or made a run for it, knocking over a bunch of junk and putting the whole neighborhood on red alert.

It wasn't that he really cared what was hanging around out there. Why should he, to protect Terry's gold mine of crap? But not allowed to search for Jude, he was buzzing with pent-up energy. He could at least investigate the noise along the side of the house. He threw a leg over the porch banister and hopped the two feet it took to get to the ground.

Something bumped against the dented-up fender again.

"Who's there?" *Nightmare,* his mind replied. *Prepare the Lord's Prayer. Beware.* Suddenly reminded of an episode of some news show he'd seen a while back, he hesitated. There was a possibility that it was a homeless person, like the one who had been living in a fancy city apartment, hidden above the closet and behind some secret hatch. Except that Deer Valley didn't have much of a homeless population. Folks who couldn't afford their own houses lived with people they knew. After Stevie's dad had left them high and dry with no money to pay the gas bill, that winter had been horrible. When the lights finally got shut off, Stevie, Dunk, and his mom moved in with Aunt Mandy and Jude for a while.

But the town *did* have its share of drunks—guys who spent every night getting hammered at The Antler. Every so often, Terry was one of those guys, bumbling and loud and driving after a six-pack too many. It was possible for one of Terry's drunky friends to have stumbled over and gotten lost in Terry's hoard. Hell, The Tyrant coveted that useless crap so much, it wouldn't have been surprising if he talked those piles up as being worth their weight in gold. One of his pals was probably hard up for money, and a night of intoxicated stealing was right up his alley. But drunks were about as stealthy as half-starved dogs. If it *was* one of the guys from The Antler, he'd be falling over stacks of bicycle parts and broken kitchen appliances by now, not hiding in the dark.

"I—I know you're there, you know . . . ," Stevie said. He wanted to yell it, but didn't want to rouse The Tyrant from his La-Z-Boy in front of the TV. But he couldn't act like a chicken standing right next to his own house, either. Because what if it really was a burglar? What if it was some creepy guy peeking at Aunt Mandy through her windows as she waited for Jude to come home? "You better get lost before I call the cops, Pops."

Scripted TV lines rolled off his tongue. It was instinctual, a security blanket. If it worked for people on television shows, it was bound to work now . . . right?

And yet, he was still apprehensive, not wanting to venture farther into the dark. But he steeled his nerves and somehow forced another handful of forward steps from his feet, refusing to succumb to his own fear, to be the crazy chicken-shit fingerless kid Dunk and Jude and the whole school thought him to be. He gritted his teeth, coiled his hands into fists, and continued to move ahead. But he made it only a few feet before he stopped, startled by the sideways tumbling fender, the thing falling against the house with a crash.

The noise gave Stevie's heart an electric jolt, like a jumper cable sparking against a corroded battery bolt. He careened backward in self-preservation, his left foot jamming between the bent spokes of a tubeless bicycle wheel. His hands shot out behind him as he tipped over, scrambling to regain his footing amid a sea of scrap metal—all of it sharp edges and tetanus. There was a flash of shadow. A dark shape bolting away from the house, deeper into the junked-up backyard. A twisted figure, hunched and lumbering on all fours.

Sasquatch! The word screamed through his head as he fell. He'd seen people hunt those things on TV. This was Oregon. Bigfoot territory. Except this thing wasn't hairy. It looked almost pale in the moonlight as it scaled the back fence, quick and fluid, contrary to the gracelessness in which it had shot away from the house. And then, just as quickly as Stevie had spotted it, it was gone.

It all happened within a span of two, maybe three, seconds. All the while, Stevie was trying not to break an ankle or snap a wrist. Darkness paired with distraction, he was left sitting on his ass, one leg jutting through the disembodied wheel of a ten-speed, the palms of his hands buried in tufts of white clover and dried-up dandelion stems. His heart was a butterfly trapped in a mason jar, beating fast enough to fill the sky with shooting stars. And the crash of the fender against an array of other detritus? Loud enough to wake the dead. Definitely loud enough to get The Tyrant out of his seat.

For half a second, Stevie's mind wheeled around the possibility that what he'd seen had been real. How else had the fender gotten pushed over? Something had been behind it, something had made it fall down. But, no. It couldn't be. He'd just imagined it, right? Like toads crawling out of the sink drain and snakes in the toilet; entire trees covered in green-winged bats instead of leaves.

The muscles in his legs twitched as he sat there, ready to spring into action, to lunge toward the fence. It could have still been out there, if it existed at all. It had ducked into the thicket of trees that turned into Deer Valley Woods. What if it was waiting to see if Stevie would follow? Or Stevie could have been having another freak-out, losing his—

"What the fucking hell was that?!" Out on the front porch, The Tyrant was pissed. Stevie struggled to get to his feet before he was spotted, tangled up in his stepdad's precious trash. He tried to shove the wheel past his ankle, but his sneaker was caught.

"What the shit do you think you're doing?" Too late to escape. Terry was already off the porch, giving his stepkid a scathing scowl. "What the fuck did I tell you about screwing around out here?"

Terry hadn't told Stevie much of anything. What he *had* done—having caught Stevie poking around the junk piles the summer before—was shove him into an old chest freezer and hold the lid shut. Stevie had wailed despite himself. He'd beaten his fist so hard against the inside of the lid, trying to get out, that the bones in his hands had ached for days. He didn't know how long The Tyrant had kept him captive in there—maybe a minute, probably less—but it had felt like hours. When Terry had finally thrown the lid open, Stevie crawled out of the decrepit unit like a solider out of a foxhole. Terrified. Deafened by his own frantic screams.

Terry would lock him in there again. This time, he'd stack an old engine block on top of the freezer and let Stevie die in there rather than letting him out. And when Stevie's mom would weep about her lost son, Terry would shrug and tell her it was for the better. *Probably ran off after his no-good pain-in-the-ass stupid fucking cousin.* But there Stevie would be, feet from his own bedroom window, rotting inside a kitchen appliance while his mother mourned.

"I—I—I thought I saw . . . I saw . . . seesaw something," Stevie explained, hoping to ply his stepfather with a lame excuse. "There was someone out here." Before the words ever left him, Stevie knew Terry wouldn't buy it. Whether there had been someone in the yard or not was, at this point, way beyond

The Tyrant's concern. He was a man who believed what he saw, and right now his disobedient little shit of a stepson was doing exactly what he'd clearly been told not to do.

"Get over here!" Terry's words snapped like the thick leather of a belt.

Stevie continued to struggle. He stood, hastily shoving the bike wheel down toward his foot. One of the broken spokes caught the bone of his ankle and left a jagged, bloody gash. Stevie bit his lip, kept himself from crying out, and tried to hurry, in order to keep his stepdad from becoming angrier than he already was. But his sneaker refused to come free.

"I'm coming, coming, coming . . ." He hated himself for the breathless, mindless echo that chased after his words like a tattered kite tail. It was times like these that he wished he were more like Jude. Furious. Defensive. Ready to rage at a moment's notice rather than ducking his head and murmuring *P-please* and *Th-th-thank you* and rhyming his way through an apology that the man he loathed didn't deserve. He wanted to spit in The Tyrant's face and tell him to go to hell. Sit and spin. *Kiss my ass.* Heck, if Jude had been in Stevie's shoes, he would have told the man and his idiotic mullet to fuck right off, regardless of the inevitable beating to follow. But Stevie didn't have those kinds of guts. Even Dunk avoided their stepdad when things got heated. It was easier that way. Safer, for sure.

The bike wheel finally came free of Stevie's foot. He shoved it away and floundered, nearly tripping over an old standing kitchen mixer that was missing more parts than it had left. His bloodied ankle hit the steel body of the mixer hard, sending a twinge of pain up his leg like a lightning bolt, straight up to his crotch. He wanted to stop, to cry out because it hurt so much, but he continued to hobble forward. When he finally reached the porch steps where his stepdad was waiting, Terry's blocky fingers seized his upper arm. He dug his nails into Stevie's biceps so hard, it felt like he was ready to rip muscle from bone. Stevie whimpered against the grip, but his show of weakness only seemed to incense The Tyrant more. Rather than letting him go, Terry marched him to the open front door of the house and shoved the upper half of Stevie's body into the jamb.

"You ruin that wheel?" Terry asked, as though the bent-up bike wheel had been in perfect condition before Stevie had stuck his leg through it and not something Terry had picked up off the side of the road.

"N-no. No. No, sir. No."

"Bull-fucking-shit." Terry pushed Stevie across the living room and toward the hall that fed into all the bedrooms. "I saw those bent spokes," he said. "What do you think, I'm blind, or just plain stupid?"

How about just stupid? Stevie wanted to ask, but his rebellious thought was derailed by Terry throwing open Stevie's bedroom door and thrusting him inside. Stevie lurched forward. The familiar jangle of The Tyrant's belt buckle rang like a funeral toll. Nausea did a full bloom in the pit of Stevie's stomach; a night flower efflorescing at high speed. He wanted to scream, to bolt out of the room. He wanted to set the house on fire. Set *Terry* on fire. Watch him burn while he danced around his scorched and smoldering body, howling at the moon.

Despite the thousands of fleeting thoughts he'd had about calling the police, or stopping into the precinct and showing them his bruised-up back, or just murdering his stepdad in his sleep, Stevie kneeled in front of his bed as if to pray.

"Wait," he whimpered. "I'm bleeding, I'm needing . . . uh, uh, a Band-Aid . . ." He glanced at his sock, mired with red from where his ankle seeped crimson, praying that this time The Tyrant would show some mercy. Perhaps today would be the day he sighed, shook his head, and abandoned Stevie in his room. But Terry continued to fumble with his belt, and Stevie pressed his face into his mattress, conceding, pushing his thoughts to Jude, to where he may have been, to not being sure how he would get through the hell that was his life without his best friend next to him.

He's taking pictures of a dumb old shark, he thought. *A shark in the park.*

Jude was at Universal Studios. He was having a good time. He'd come back. He had to be okay.

3

WEDNESDAY. DAY THREE. The thing returned.

It had come in the night, peered through Stevie's window, and watched him sleep with a pair of clouded, bulbous eyes. Its twisted fingers smeared blood down the glass—blood that wasn't there in the morning, but that Stevie was convinced had been there just the same. Jude had sent it, lonely out there somewhere, wanting nothing more than his best friend back.

Stevie woke up screaming.

Not that long ago, his mother would have played twenty questions, sure that talking it out would help her kid come to grips with whatever demons were grappling around inside his head. But that morning, she didn't ask about his bad dream and Stevie matched her silence. He didn't tell her about what he'd seen lurking amid Terry's junk the night before, and he certainly didn't mention how it had returned to haunt his sleep. But he didn't have to say a word to know she was more worried than usual. He could tell by the way she kept looking at him from the corner of her eye.

Ever since Stevie's dad had ditched them, Nicole Clark had worn an expression of perpetual dismay, and this morning her nerves practically rattled when she walked. She was likely thinking about how the nightmares were getting worse rather than better, probably scared of what would happen to Stevie if Jude never came home. And that was a legitimate fear, because today was officially beyond what the TV detectives referred to as that all-important forty-eight-hour window. That was precisely why *today*, Stevie would start looking for Jude, and there was nothing anyone could do to stop him.

After breakfast, he walked into town and found himself standing at the edge of the wood. Men in safety vests and hunting gear combed the trees. They looked ridiculous as they trekked across an open expanse of forest in a loose and crooked line, disorderly, as if hunting for a lost set of truck keys rather than a kid's body. Their heads were bowed. Their boots kicked at dead leaves and pine needles, as though somewhere in that open space they'd happen upon a boy so tiny, so well concealed, that even the dogs that accompanied them hadn't noticed the slightest bump in the dirt or the smell of human decay.

With his nerves steeled, Stevie stepped forward to approach the team. But his determination was suddenly weakened, watered down with all sorts of other stuff: guilt for lying to his mom about where he was going—*Gonna go pick up some gummy gummies at the general store*; grief that he had to be in those woods at all; a lurid, subdued excitement that he was about to participate in his first-ever official investigation; terror of what he might find once he really started to look. Because what if the worst came to pass? What if Jude really *was* gone and Stevie, having joined the search party, was the one who stumbled across his corpse? It was one thing to see an actor pretend to be dead on his dad's old *Unsolved Mysteries* episodes, but the possibility of a dead body in real life, let alone that of someone he knew so well . . . He wasn't sure he'd be okay after something like that. And if Stevie wasn't okay *now*, where would that leave him? In the mental hospital, probably; hell, he was almost already there. Tossing and turning at night. Recollecting Dunk's Max Larsen story. Replaying the time when Jude had gone scary with the malevolence Stevie had seen in his eyes.

It had been earlier that very summer, only a few days after school had let out. Jude had waited in Stevie's backyard, eyeballing Terry's shit piles when Stevie had come flying out of the house. He ran past his cousin in a frenzy, into the trees behind both their houses, until he hit the trail that led out to Cedar Creek. Jude followed, and when they were good and far enough into the copse, Stevie started to cry. He held his arms rigid against his sides. Hands balled, teeth clamped, eyes squeezed tight. The metallic zing of blood dribbled from his freshly split lip, snail-trailing down his chin. Jude struggled for something to say as Stevie wept, because Jude wasn't what you'd call a sensitive guy. Even after Uncle Scott died, Stevie hadn't seen Jude cry. He just seemed mad all the time, ready to rip apart the world.

Jude eventually opened his mouth to say something, like *What's the matter with you?* or *Your lip is bleeding*, or maybe even *Stop blubbering like a stupid baby*, but Stevie cut him off with a garbled scream of such fury it made his cousin lurch back a few steps.

"*I h-h-hate him!*" Stevie roared. "*I hate him! Hate, fate, elimi . . . limi . . . limi . . .*"—liminate.

Jude stood silent as Stevie wound down, taking rough boxer's swipes at tears and blood with the back of his hand. They hadn't talked about it, but Jude wasn't dumb. He knew why Stevie loathed his stepdad. Even Aunt Amanda hated him, and she liked practically everyone. Stevie had heard her crying in his mom's kitchen once, murmuring about how she didn't understand . . . couldn't comprehend *how my own big sister won't stand up to that monster, how you just sit there and take it, Nicki. For the boys, sure, but look what he's doing to your family.*

For the boys. Yeah, right. Maybe for the money, but for him and Dunk? No way.

"If that were *my* dad," Jude spoke after a moment of frazzled silence, "I'd slit that guy's throat from ear to ear, and I wouldn't even feel bad about it. You know, *eliminate* him."

Was that why Stevie had said the word, why it had tumbled out of him in a moment of involuntary clanging? Eliminate. As in murder. Eliminate. *Exterminate.* For Stevie, it was just a passing thought. Jude, though? He had a darkness to him, a kind of animus that Stevie didn't possess, no matter how much he wished it upon himself. Jude's kind of talk was for bad guys, for villains and highwaymen and jerks just *like* Terry Marks. But Stevie couldn't say that, not to his cousin. He'd be marked as a coward. A chicken. A kid who didn't have the balls to stand up for himself, let alone for anyone else.

And though he wouldn't admit to it in a million years, sometimes Jude scared him.

Like when he had waved that piece of nailed-up wood at the cat in the tree and had gotten busted for it. Or when, searching for plywood behind one of the Main Street shops, he had found a jagged piece of metal and had jokingly held it against Stevie's throat, like he was going to slash him up and leave him there to die. Or the time when, while they were both inside the fort, Jude had threatened to shove Stevie down the open square in the floorboards that served as a hatch, acting as if he was ready to push him straight out of the tree and fifteen feet down to an inevitable broken arm or leg, or worse.

What had been weird about those instances was that they had come out of nowhere. One minute, he and Jude were having a good time collecting scrap lumber or wandering around in the woods. The next, Jude had that look. Like he didn't want to live his life not knowing what it felt like to hurt someone. Like he didn't give a damn if he ended up in juvie if it meant being able to vent his rage. Like, how for an inkling of a moment, the devil himself had crawled right into him and was itching to get out.

It was times like those that made Stevie question who Jude really was, how well he knew him. Which was why, now, as he shuffled his way through the trees toward the bumbling search party, a queasy pit-of-the-guts feeling robbed him of his equilibrium. Doubt hit him all over again. What if Jude had been planning to run away all along, had kept it from Stevie all this time, scheming his escape from this stupid no-horse town with its dumb outdated movies and lame stores and nothing to do?

No, he thought. *No, that's not right.* Stevie may have been able to persuade himself that Jude had escaped if this were four or five years into the future. But Jude was a month shy of his thirteenth birthday. What kind of kids run away to live it up in a bigger and better place when they are twelve? *Hollywood kids—they smoke cigs when they're, like, eight. They go to cocktail parties and stuff.* Yeah, they'd talked about kids living as adults, discussed how cool it would be to do whatever the hell they wanted without any consequences, without stupid adults watching their every move. Jude had a pretty big ego and some pretty crazy ideas. In that same conversation, he had convinced himself he was suave enough to find a sugar mama to buy him video games, feed him junk food, and let him drink beer out of a can. Maybe even let him touch her boobs every now and again. *Her* bare *boobs*, he had specified. *With my* bare *hands.* That had cracked Stevie up big time. He had laughed so hard, Jude had actually gotten mad. But Jude had been joking about all that . . . right? He wasn't idiotic enough to think he could really make it out there on his own. Not yet, anyway.

The search team continued walking in their ambling, cockeyed way, regardless of the fact that, had there been a body out there, it would have taken all of two seconds to find it among a few downed branches and lone ferns. They lumbered forward, a couple of the guys randomly chuckling every so often. Someone pulled a flask out of their back pocket, took a swig, let out a belch, got a few laughs.

"Bring enough for everyone?" A guy in a trucker's cap had made the inquiry—the hat so neon orange it set Stevie's retinas aflame. Another round of snirks ensued. *Yep, just looking for a dead kid. Good times!*

If this was the only search party Deer Valley was able to scrounge up, Jude was royally screwed.

One of the men finally noticed Stevie looming on the outskirts. As soon as they made eye contact, Stevie's entire body went electric with dread. The guy was decked out in his hunting gear—camouflage accented by strips of reflective safety tape. Deer Valley wasn't one of those ironically named places like Ocean, Arizona, or Buckets-O-Rain, Nevada. It was, in fact, exactly what it implied. Most of Deer Valley's dads took their boys hunting every weekend once the season started up. Except for Terry Marks, and that was for the best. Stevie didn't like the idea of being around his stepdad while in the presence of a loaded gun. It made him imagine bad things, like Terry getting mad and blowing Stevie's head off. Or Stevie finally finding his courage and blasting a hole straight through his stepdad's middle—a perfectly round porthole, like on a ship, except meaty and through a dead man's chest. *Yo ho ho.*

"Hey. Kid." The man in camo regarded Stevie with an aggravated look—*What the hell are you doing here?*—then broke ranks to stalk toward him. Stevie recognized him almost immediately, having seen him at a couple of basketball games and wrestling matches; school stuff Stevie wasn't into but attended anyway, because anything was better than sitting around the house with The Tyrant only inches away. The guy was somebody's dad, probably the patriarch of one of the bullies who called Stevie names and gave him hell during lunch.

"Kid." The man again. "Hey." He snapped his fingers, his big working hands clicking with an odd, papery crackle. Stevie would never be able to snap like that—not his right hand, anyway. "You can't be here."

Never one to challenge authority, this time Stevie somehow managed to resist his urge to bolt. "I—I—I . . ." *Stop. Breathe.* "I want to help." He squeaked out the words, his mouth dry. Chest constricted. Suddenly sweaty, despite the lingering coolness of morning.

"Yeah, well . . . Hey, Marv!" The man motioned for one of the other guys to come over. Stevie watched Marv break the line—a guy even bigger than the bully dad who was regarding him. Marv didn't look the least bit amused.

Stevie pulled in a breath and steadied his nerves, then blurted a line he had practiced in his head during his trek from the house. "My name is Stevie Clark, Clark, Cl—" He winced. *Stop it.* "I'm Jude's cousin." Family, he had decided, trumped friendship. At least that was the case in the movies and TV shows, so that's where he was placing his bets. "Please, let me help." He bit his tongue, desperate to hold back the ticks and rhymes that were trying to leap from between his lips like a colony of jack jumper ants.

Bully Dad blinked at Stevie's request while Marv completed his approach. "What's this?" Marv asked, nodding to Stevie as though he were a yard sale toaster rather than a real boy.

"Stevie Clark," Bully Dad said. "The Brighton boy's cousin." He gave Marv a look, as though Jude couldn't have possibly had family. A wild kid like him? Everyone knew Jude was feral, raised by wolves.

"Awh, *Christ*, kid." Marv steadied his gaze on Stevie. "You can't be out here, you know that? This is an *investigation*." He annunciated the word—*in-ves-tuh-gay-shun*—sure that Stevie hadn't heard such an impressive bit of vocabulary in all his ten years. Twenty-five cents, fair and square. "A possible crime scene," he added, as if to hammer home the point.

"Where are your folks?" Bully Dad asked. Stevie stared at a Remington rifle patch crookedly sewn onto his jacket. Couldn't he have at least *tried* to place it straight?

"At the house," Stevie told them. "The house. I just . . . I want to help."

"Yeah, we got that," Marv said, "but you can't be out here. You want to help? Go home."

"Who are your folks?" asked Bully Dad. "Clark, huh? Are you Nicki's kid?"

"Isn't that Mandy's sister?" Marv asked.

"If I remember right," Bully Dad said with a shrug. "She wasn't in my class. Older by a year or two, I think."

"Amanda Brighton is my Aunt Mandy. She's my aunt." If he clarified exactly how he was related to Jude, they'd *have* to let him participate. But his conviction seemed to sour both their expressions even more.

"Goddamnit, okay, I'm callin' Terry."

Stevie suddenly felt sick. *Terry?* These guys knew his step-dad? Of course they did. They probably frequented The Antler, and The Tyrant had told them how worthless of a kid he thought Jude was. That's why their noble quest of finding a missing boy was lackadaisical. All because of Terry's stupid, worthless, no-good opinion. And now these guys were going to rat *Stevie* out?

41

Marv fished a cell phone out of his pants pocket.

"W-wait, wait, wait, wait!" The word came tumbling out of him, desperate, on repeat. "No, you can't . . . he, he, he, he . . ." *He'll kill me*, he wanted to say, but he got stuck, that single-syllable word making him sound like a robot trying to laugh.

"He doesn't know you're here, does he . . . ?" Marv sighed, squinted. "Kid, you're going to get yourself in a shit-ton of trouble."

"You can't *be* here," Bully Dad repeated while Marv messed with his phone. Stevie couldn't look away from that old flip design. It was the kind you couldn't even play games on; probably ancient, bought from the customer service desk at the Safeway on Main. Stevie coiled his fingers up tight, sure that at any moment he'd reach over and grab that cheapo phone out of Marv's hand, toss it to the ground, and stomp it beneath his sneakers as hard as he could. He'd demand they allow him to be there. How dare they try to run him off? Jude was Stevie's best friend. Who were *these* guys to him? They probably didn't care whether they found Jude or not. Heck, they probably hoped they *wouldn't*.

But all he could manage was "Please don't call Terry." *Scary extraordinary cemetery.* The plea came out as a dry whisper. Weak. Afraid. *Yellow like chicken shit*, Jude would have moaned. He wanted to beg some more, but those words—the rhyming and clanging—all of it was itching to get out, eager to make him look nuts, and nuts would buy him a one-way ticket back home for sure.

But Marv had already connected the call. Turning away from Stevie and Bully Dad, he murmured a "Hello, Missus

Clark?" beneath his breath. Stevie's body went rigid. He shot Bully Dad a desperate look, one that pleaded for him to intervene, to suggest to Marv that *Hey, it's not that big of a deal, just let the kid be on his way. You know as well as anyone that Terry is a sick dick prick.* But Bully Dad wasn't paying attention, and Marv didn't get a chance to explain the reason for his call. Rather, both men were distracted by a sudden yell from a good way down that crooked line of men.

"Hey!" It was the guy with the flask who had let out that lip-curling Homer Simpson belch. He was standing knee-deep in a big thatch of coastal wood fern—not big enough to hide a body, but definitely big enough to hold a clue. *"Hey!"* His yell was more adamant the second time, accentuated by a mélange of surprise and realization; the kind of sound Stevie made every time the toilet seemed like it was going to flush but backed up and overflowed, all because Terry was too busy to fix it, just like the stupid dishwasher. "I think I got something over here!"

The entire line buzzed with murmurs as soon as Flask made the claim. They broke formation, fanning out like disorganized geese, trudging quick and determined toward the man who had made a find. Bully Dad booked it back to his brethren. Marv snapped his phone shut and shot Stevie a stern glare, barking a demand.

"Don't move."

But before Marv could make his way over to the rest of the group, Flask held something up with the tip of a stick, something that, despite Stevie's resolve, forced a bleated whimper from his throat. Because he recognized it right away.

It was a hooded black sweatshirt. The faded white screen print on the back was one that Stevie knew by heart. It was an outline of a giant fist with white top and bottom rockers reading GRIP IT AND RIP IT. A BMXer design in the vein of a biker insignia. A young person's safer version of what you'd see on the back of a Hells Angels or Bandidos cut.

Jude's sweatshirt.

Which brought only one detail to light.

This was real.

June Brighton was really gone.

4

STEVIE SPRINTED OUT of the trees and bolted down Main Street so fast he nearly tripped over Mrs. Lovejoy's yappy Pekingese, its retractable leash pulled tight enough to be a trip wire. He leapt over it, lost his footing, and knocked into six-year-old Bobby Benton, who was on his way out of the general store with a cellophane bag of gummy worms in one hand, a Slim Jim in the other, and his big brother, Sam, bringing up the rear. Sam just so happened to be Jude's nemesis—a kid Stevie remembered vividly from years before. He was the kind of kid who smashed your lunch tray against your T-shirt and said, *Oh, gee, you should probably look where you're going next time.*

Bobby, on the other hand, was a cry-baby pip-squeak, and he proved it by eliciting a nerve-fraying whine as soon as his bag of worms hit the sidewalk. *"Heeeeey!"*

Stevie careened onto the street, partly because he wasn't in control of his own two feet, and partly because he wanted to get as far away as he could before Sam grabbed him by the back of the neck and showed him what was what. Who did Stevie think he was, knocking into his kid brother like that? And while Stevie stumbling into the road may have given Sam

45

the Jerk a wide berth, it nearly got Stevie creamed by a minivan. The van simultaneously slammed on its brakes and blared its horn while Sam yelled, "Sack, you creep!" Mrs. Lovejoy gathered her shivering dog against her heaving breast, as though witnessing a felony or something equally dramatic. *Hooligans, the lot of them.* Stevie was sure that, had Mrs. Lovejoy not been standing on that street corner, Sam would have replaced *creep* with a far more colorful insult.

Stevie continued to run—his legs pumping like twin pistons, his heart thudding inside his skull like the crashing cymbal of an offbeat marching band. Sam's antagonistic yell did something weird to Stevie's insides. It twisted up his guts, resonating more than it ever would have if Jude had been right beside him. If Jude never came back, Stevie would be nothing more than a punching bag for kids like Sam. He'd be the boy everyone loved to trip, to insult, to spit on because he was weird.

More than a block away from the scene of his near-death minivan experience and still running as hard as he could, Stevie came to the realization that part of why he couldn't catch his breath wasn't because he'd been sprinting for a solid two minutes straight; it was because he was bawling. He couldn't get the image of Jude's sweatshirt out of his head; how that guy, Flask, had held it out on the tip of a branch as though it had been crawling with maggots. Or maybe he had held it out that way because it had been covered in blood.

The mere idea of it brought him to a sudden standstill.

He stood on the sun-dappled sidewalk, staring down the pine-lined road that would take him home, and he imagined it:

black cotton soaked in something thick and viscous, something that should have been red but blended into the background the way the camouflage the search party was wearing blended into the shrubs and trees. He tried to picture Jude running away from something just as disguised as that search crew. A shadow thing, twisted and lumbering, yet somehow unspeakably fast. The thing Stevie had seen in the side yard; the one he'd dreamed about—or had he really seen it?—that had come to his window and watched him through a thin sheet of glass.

Stevie threw himself forward and, as if stuck in a perpetual stumble, ran at the street sign that would point him toward home. He cut across the intersection as abruptly as he had jumped into the road, and a guy sitting in his car at the stop sign yelled something out his open window. Something like *Watch where you're going* or *I bet your cousin is already dead*. Stevie hardly heard him as he continued his sprint.

He buzzed the trees that flanked the road, but hesitated when Aunt Mandy's house came clear. There were police cruisers parked out there; one by the curb, another blocking in Aunt Mandy's old Civic, as if to keep a missing boy's mother from bounding out of the house and trying to flee from her own growing horror.

Seeing those cruisers was a blow to the gut. Stevie gulped air, his sprint slowing as he continued his approach, ignoring the pang of nausea that squeezed his stomach tight, threatening to make him heave his breakfast all over the sidewalk for everyone to see.

And a lot of people *would* see. They were there in their

houses, standing at their front windows, the curtains rustling just enough to erase any doubt they were spying on what was transpiring down the street. And who could blame them? Jude's disappearance was the first big thing to happen in Deer Valley in years. The last time there was any real buzz in town was when a farmer had reported a couple of his cows being mutilated overnight. There was the usual talk of aliens. Stevie had been five or six, and all that summer he and Jude pretended to be little green men shooting imaginary ray guns at anything that moved. They tried to eat nothing but hamburgers, because honestly, why would aliens target cows unless it was for the delicious beef? Their plan didn't fly, though. Both Stevie's mom and Aunt Mandy continued to force-feed them stuff like boiled carrots and broccoli.

Beyond aliens, murmurs surfaced of satanic worship. It was, in fact, the first time Stevie had heard of a creature named Satan at all. This was care of Duncan, always quick to tell his baby brother a story that would make him squirm. But the Satan stuff was quickly squelched by Deer Valley police, and the blame for the farmer's livestock was placed on the predators that roamed the woods. Dead deer were a pretty common occurrence around these parts, and cougars weren't exactly the type to discriminate between species. A meal was a meal. Gruesome, but not nearly as cool as burger-loving spacemen.

Stevie hoped that Jude's story could be just as stupidly fantastic: aliens beaming him up into a crazy spacecraft, stuffing him into a human-sized pod, threatening to harvest his organs and dissect his brain if he couldn't eat a five-pound bacon double cheeseburger in ten minutes flat.

But there was the sweatshirt. The two cops outside Jude's house with their roof lights whirling in soundless sweeps of red and blue. And there was the squirming, wormy ball of dread ever-growing in Stevie's chest, filling him up so entirely that it was suddenly hard to breathe. His heart found a new home in his throat. Pins and needles bit at his hands and feet.

Finally reaching the front porch of his own house, he nearly tripped over the steps as he blindly lunged for the door, desperate to put walls and glass between himself and Aunt Mandy's place, if only to fend off the inevitable news.

Inside, the house was empty. Terry was at work, sitting on top of a bulldozer or backhoe loader hours outside of town. Dunk was either sleeping or out with Annie, and Stevie's mom was undoubtedly next door. But rather than panicking at the silence, he was thankful for the isolation. He didn't want to talk, didn't want to hear anything anyone had to say about what was going on. He knew the direction those conversations would take.

They found Jude's sweatshirt.

It doesn't look good.

He stumbled past the couch and coffee table and lumbered to his room, slamming his door behind him. He threw himself onto his bed and buried his face in his pillow. Considered screaming but didn't, because Jude wouldn't have. Screaming was for sissies and scared girls running from crazed, ax-wielding killers. Not for tough guys who built forts with hammers and nails.

He had to suck it up, keep his head on straight. He had to

figure out what the hell to do, *not* doom his best friend because of mindless hysterics.

He continued to lie there, trying to calm himself, making a genuine attempt to gather his wits and control the rhymes—*rude unvalued Jude, blued and discontinued*—that were spiraling through his head. He tried to will himself to stop being a baby and start acting like an adult. It took a while to gather his wits.

By the time he looked up from having shoved his face into his pillow, the light had turned soft and purple outside. There was the sound of shuffling out in the front room. For a moment, Stevie considered that he may have been alone with Terry, which was never a good thing. But his mother's stifled sobs assured him that The Tyrant had yet to return.

Weary, Stevie sat up, swatted at his hot and tear-swollen face, and eventually crept to his bedroom door. He cracked it open an inch, put an ear to the jamb, and echo-located his mother in the kitchen by the sound of plates scraping against the bottom of their stained porcelain sink. Her crying drew him out of his room and into the hall. Suddenly, all he wanted was to wrap his arms around her and tell her it was going to be okay, it would all work out. Jude was smart. He was strong. They couldn't give up hope. All bullshit, but sometimes lies felt better than the truth.

But he stalled when he finally saw her. With her back to him, Nicole Clark's reflection appeared pale and ghostly in the window above the sink. It was strange to see her so fragile. Stevie's mom was the one who kept things together. Aunt Amanda had always been the weaker of the two. When Uncle

Scott had died, Stevie's mom had stepped up and taken charge, arranging everything: the funeral, the flowers, the wake, the food. The most vivid memory he had of that awful day wasn't the dozens of sniffling mourners shuffling past the church pulpit to place a hand on Uncle Scott's closed casket lid. Nor the small tear in the bottom hem of Aunt Mandy's dress. It wasn't even the way Jude had sat in the front pew, uncomfortable in a too-small Goodwill suit, staring at his hands as if trying to summon the power of reanimation. Stevie's clearest memory was that of his mother, standing stoic and blank-faced in Aunt Amanda's kitchen, surrounded by a wailing wall of women, all of them blotting at their eyes with tissues and handkerchiefs. Some of them wore sad smiles. Others—like Aunt Mandy— wept openly while men scooped grocery-store spinach dip onto plastic plates and fussed with lukewarm cocktail shrimp. Stevie remembered that moment because, amid all of those crying ladies, his own mother looked like she was made of stone; a mom of marble holding a tray of cheese and crackers, ready to feed the anguished as soon as they caught their breaths.

And yet, in these last three days—after Jude had become a ghost—his mother had been different. Aunt Amanda had come over only once since then. She was otherwise locked away in the crumbling house next door. But that visit had been the only time Stevie's mom had seemed like her strong, unflappable self. She had put on a brave face, pulled her mouth into her best effort of a smile, and plied her sister with chocolate truffles and tea. Throughout all of those other endless hours, she wiped at her eyes and looked as though she had a stomachache. Her comfort started and stopped with Aunt Amanda. It was as if she'd forgotten that Jude was Stevie's best friend and that Stevie was just as afraid as anyone.

Then there were the cops. They hadn't bothered to ask him anything. There was the search team, yukking it up in the forest as though there wasn't a chance in hell of stumbling across a kid tucked against the trunk of a tree or drowned in a creek. There were the reporters, spreading lies of Jude's decampment, judging him not based on who he was, but on what strangers thought of him. There was Terry, who simply didn't give a damn that his step-nephew was missing. Hell, even Dunk didn't seem to care, going off to the movies to feel up his girlfriend while Jude was out there somewhere. Alone. Scared. If he could still be either of those things at all.

Stevie's mom continued to cry at the sink, but rather than stepping into the kitchen and giving her a hug, he backed into the hall. Suddenly, his need to be close to her was replaced by anger. Because nobody was doing anything. They were all just waiting for another funeral. All of them. Even him.

Wandering back to his room, he went over the facts in his mind. Jude understood Stevie's passion for investigation. Every time they didn't have school but it was too rainy to go outside, Stevie forced his cousin to sit with him and watch all the shows about cops and missing people. *CSI. Bones. NCIS.* As well as true crime stuff; shows that got actors to pretend they were the people who had disappeared or gotten killed, reenacting the crimes with fake blood and everything. Those were Jude's favorites.

But Stevie's heart belonged to *Unsolved Mysteries*. Once, during a particularly miserable winter break, they had marathoned old episodes his birth dad had recorded on VHS, videotapes he'd left behind when he had taken off. They were the few shreds of evidence Stevie had that Dennis Clark had actually existed. Funny, then, that most of Stevie's favorite episodes featured people who just up and disappeared.

Max Larsen had turned up dead, but he'd been six or seven years old. Definitely not as clever as Jude. Not nearly as smart or as tough. Could it have been all that impossible that Jude—suddenly reminded that Stevie was a crime show fanatic—had dropped his sweatshirt as a clue for Stevie to find? Was it that far-fetched to think?

"Oh man." The words left his throat in a whisper. "Oh *man*." That's what Jude had been doing. The sweatshirt was a goddamn *clue*.

Stevie's grief blinked off like a light, replaced by blinding inspiration. All at once, he was sure that Jude was relying on him to figure this whole thing out, just *sure* of it, and he was determined to not let his best friend down.

Abandoning his room, Stevie ran down the hall and skidded into the kitchen, startling his mom. She was drying the dishes, her eyes red-rimmed, fresh out of hope.

"Hi, sweetheart." Her greeting warbled with emotion. A second later, her face was twisting up as though she was about to bawl again, and he knew why. The cops had announced what the search party had found. What she didn't know was that Stevie had been there. He had watched those guys swarm around

Jude's sweatshirt like wasps around melting ice cream, greedy for a closer look at the talisman that spelled inevitable doom.

He looked away from his mother and to the shaft of sunlight at her feet. He didn't want to see her expression crack. Her helplessness put a bad taste in his mouth. Hesitating only for a moment, he finally got his legs to move, marched past her, and launched himself onto the counter before she could insist he stop. His feet banged against the crummy bottom cabinet beside the refrigerator, its paneling scratched up and hanging crooked on its hinges—yet another item on an endless honey-do list of household renovations Terry would never start, let alone complete.

"Stevie!" she yelled as he hefted himself up, the sound of her displeasure only making him scramble faster. Atop the counter, he rose to his feet, suddenly eight feet tall and towering over the kitchen. He slapped his hand against the top of the fridge. His palm hit the spiral binding of his little notebook, and the mechanical pencil his mother had confiscated rolled across the fridge's enamel top, then tumbled onto the kitchen floor. Stevie watched it bounce against the cracked linoleum before he jumped to the ground.

"Damn it!" The exclamation came out as more of a shout than he intended, but if there was a time for yelling, it was now. His mom fluttered her eyes, as though she'd never heard such foul language in all her life. Like anyone would have believed *that.* Terry swore like a Tourette's-riddled parrot. *Squawk! Fucking hell. Squawk! Your ass is fucking grass.* "N-now all the lead is gonna be b-busted up!"

"Stevie, honey . . ."

He spun away from her, both his notebook and pencil tight in his hands. He had to write down what he knew about Jude's disappearance before he forgot the details. Most times, it was the smallest facts that cracked a case wide open. He couldn't afford to lose a single bit of information. If his mom started blabbering, he was destined to forget something imperative . . . omit the one thing that could end up bringing Jude home.

But rather than being allowed to stomp out of the room, she caught him by the arm. "Hey, we need to talk . . ." Yes, about Stevie. About his issues. Not about Jude or the search party or the odds.

"I don't want to talk!" Another yell. This one more jarring than the last. He squeezed his eyes shut, shoving the rhymes to the back of his mind. He yanked his arm out of his mom's grasp, stared defiantly into her face. He could still see faint traces of her black eye from beneath her flesh-toned foundation. Nicole Clark reluctantly pulled her hand away from her youngest son, her expression straining between what looked like compassion and the need to be authoritative.

"Stevie . . ." She exhaled a sigh of surrender. "I understand you're upset, sweetheart, I really do." Except she didn't understand anything. She was nothing but an idiot. To her, Jude was just a kid. To Stevie, he was *everything*.

"Upset?" He backed away from her, nearly laughing at the suggestion. Maybe she was the one who was crazy. Perhaps Terry had finally knocked her so hard into the wall that her brain had come loose. "Don't you get it? He's my best friend!"

Before she could stall his exit with some harebrained comment, Stevie bolted out of the kitchen and back to his room. He'd had it with adults, the cops, that stupid search team that wasn't even looking, and the news, poisoning Deer Valley with their detrimental hopelessness. What was the point? Jude was surely already dead. Nobody wanted to believe that Jude could be alive, to let Stevie help, to give him a chance? Fine! He'd take a page out of his cousin's book of conduct instead. Because Jude never asked anyone for permission to do anything, which meant Stevie didn't have to, either.

"Fuck it," he murmured beneath his breath, and then slammed his bedroom door.

. . .

He spent the entire next day pounding the pavement, and while there was no doubt his mother knew exactly what he was up to, she didn't try to stop him. He went in and out of Deer Valley's main businesses, asking to speak with owners, interviewing shop regulars, asking whether or not they'd seen or heard anything suspicious around the time Jude had disappeared. And while he tried to ignore the grumbling, he couldn't go for more than half an hour without hearing someone mutter about how Nicki Clark was an irresponsible parent. Who in their right mind let a ten-year-old kid run around town, harassing people; especially after another kid—a *family* member—had gone missing?

Stevie did his best to ignore the whispers. He focused on his little notepad, which was quickly filling up with chicken scratches. He cornered Mrs. Lovejoy outside the hardware store while she picked through small containers of strawberries and herbs, her shopping cart full of gardening stuff. Her dog, the yappy Pekingese, shook and coughed inside the cart beside a bag of potting soil; nothing but a panting, snarly faced ball of fur.

"I don't know anything," she told him, not once looking away from the mint plant she was inspecting. Her voice wavered, but it was with old age rather than compassion. "You kids ask for it, running around that forest like a bunch of heathens. Not like my Lulu." She cooed at the dog as it sniveled and sneezed, clearly unhappy with how close Stevie was standing next to its master. "Now stop bothering people." Her tone turned sharp. "Get out of here, go."

Inside the general store across the street, Mr. Greenwood scratched at the psoriasis that crusted the top of his balding head. "Suspicious?" he asked. "Not that I can recall." But something dark and knowing was shadowing his ancient eyes. Mr. G. straightened his crooked back, and Stevie cringed when he heard a succession of *pop-pop-pop*s, like someone dragging a tiny mallet across the spine of a percussion frog. The store owner's knobby fingers slid across the counter's scratched glass top. "But I'd stay out of those woods if I were you," he said. "There's something out there, and I can tell you it's not a cougar or any of the nonsense the police keep trying to sell."

Stevie stared at Mr. Greenwood for a good five seconds, his notebook in one hand, his mechanical pencil with a chamber of broken lead in the other. And for four of those five beats, he was convinced that old Mr. G. was pulling his leg. Would he do that; especially when he knew that Jude was Stevie's family? But there wasn't a single glimmer of amusement in the corners of those wrinkled, crow's-footed eyes. The man was dead serious. And suddenly, all Stevie wanted to do was cry.

5

STEVIE WAS MORE scared for Jude than ever after interviewing Mr. G., spooked by what may have been out in those trees. And so, rather than going directly to the forest the way he had initially planned, his hunt for clues was stalled. He instead decided to retrace his steps from the Sunday Jude had disappeared, if only to give himself time to think about the old man's warning; to hopefully discount it as the ravings of a crank who probably didn't like kids.

He started at Cree Meadows Elementary, where he'd graduated from the fourth grade only months before . . . but just barely. Stevie loathed the kids who went there, and in turn, he hated going to school. But the Cree Meadows playground was pretty cool with its updated playground equipment. The grounds were chock-full of crawl tubes and spiral slides, tire swings and whirlwind seats. They even had a thing called a sky runner, which looked like a giant umbrella with its fabric removed. On Sunday, Stevie and Jude had run full-sprint at it, grabbed the bars, and had gone flying around and around like capeless superheroes. That had been only hours before Jude had vanished. Strange how life could turn on a dime.

All of that fancy equipment was tucked away, hidden from view by the school itself. The playground butted up against a chain-link fence, which had never brought Stevie any pause until now. Sure, it seemed innocent enough. Little kids were dumb. All it took was a few seconds for an overgrown toddler to waddle his way a little too far into the trees and—*bam*—Amber Alerts all over the place. But after what Mr. G. had suggested, Stevie couldn't help but wonder, was the fence there to keep kids in, or to keep something out?

He squinted at a couple of cats just shy of the chain-link, pulled his notebook out of his back pocket, and scribbled *fence behind school* onto the pad. He'd go back to the general store and ask Mr. Greenwood about it.

Jude and Stevie's next stop had been the backside of Main Street; specifically, the Dumpster behind the hardware store. Every now and again, the workers would toss busted-up wooden pallets out next to the bin. Those boards were perfect for the fort, as long as you could get the nails out without splitting the wood. Jude had become an expert at yanking them, like a dentist pulling rotten teeth from an old bum's mouth. He'd stashed a hammer he'd found in one of Terry's shit piles in a bush behind the store for that very job.

Another cat here. It skittered away as Stevie stepped up to the juniper bushes that lined the gravel delivery truck road. He counted a few shrubs out from a crumbly concrete pylon, then pushed aside the branches of plant number four. The hammer was tucked inside the boughs like a baby bird, just as Jude had left it.

A pang of disappointment speared Stevie's heart. Had the hammer not been there, it would have meant that Jude had come back to retrieve it. Either that, or he'd had the hammer with him during the ambush or whatever happened, which meant that Jude was out there, and he was armed. Stevie wanted the comfort of knowing that his cousin had at least a little protection when whatever had happened to him had occurred. Then again, it was a naive hope. If that *had* been the case, Jude would have swung that hammer without a second thought, lodging it in his assailant's skull. That image was punctuated by the sorrowful caterwaul of an unseen stray.

Stevie left the Stanley where it was and moved on to the Mr. Frosty down the street. There, a skinny dog circled an overflowing trash can. After an unsuccessful afternoon of searching for lumber, the boys had stopped in for soft-serve and sat on the curb to watch cars cruise by. Dunk zoomed by them in his Firebird. He hung his head out the window and yelled, "Hey, Nutsack!" while his best friend, Murph, cackled in the passenger's seat—a hyena hopped up on laughing gas.

"You know what?" Jude had said between licks of his cone, super casual. "I just figured it out. Dunk is kind of a dick."

Stevie drew his tongue across the back of his hand, lapping at a trail of chocolate that had cut across his skin. "Yeah?" he'd asked, taking a giant bite of ice cream that was melting faster than he could eat it. He'd lost track of how many times Jude had called him a whatever-sack, just like Dunk had seconds before, but he wasn't about to bring that up. Instead, he replied with: "Then I guess you're kinda a slo-mo, Joe."

Jude laughed, but he socked Stevie in the shoulder just the same. And that punch had hurt, maybe because Jude had hit him a little harder than usual, or it could have been that, just as Jude's knuckles had made contact with Stevie's shoulder, Stevie's brain turned into a solid block of ice. He nearly fell over yowling while Jude laughed just like Murph had—wild, crazy, totally unhinged.

Stevie would have done just about anything to be able to sit down on that curb with a cone right then—to not move on to where he and Jude had visited after their ice cream was done. *I'd stay out of those woods if I were you.* But Jude's sweatshirt left no doubt that the forest was the last place he had been.

There were a million ways to get to the fort from any one place on Main Street, but on Sunday, the boys had ducked into the trees directly behind the ice cream place and marched their way along a barely there route. To accurately retrace their steps, Stevie had to go that way, the *long* way. Jude's favorite way, especially after they had discovered that abandoned old house.

He'd never been afraid of the forest before. But now, standing at the gaping maw of what suddenly felt like a forbidden land, all he could do was coil his arms around himself and stare into the green-glowing gloom. The trees were thick, taller today than they'd been before. The ferns—sometimes dotting the landscape like tiny ships, sometimes growing in massive groups like continents rather than islands—appeared almost bladelike in the way their fronds fanned out from their roots. The moss, growing fuzzy and thick on rocks and tree trunks alike, gleamed like toxic slime. He could swear all of it was moving as though alive, undulating only when he wasn't looking right at it, hoping for him to trip over a root so it could slither over his body and swallow him up. The boundless bed of last year's leaves was a blanket beneath his feet. A dense counterpane of decay thick enough to suffocate. *A playmate lying prostrate. Too late.*

The path Stevie and Jude had taken was little more than a few inches of exposed ground stomped out by years of wandering kids, mostly high schoolers looking for a place to drink cheap booze. Any time Jude found an empty bottle hiding in a thatch of ivy or lying inside the hollow of a tree, he'd take it with him, as though it were treasure rather than trash. At Cedar Creek, he'd shatter them against the stream's smooth stones, booby-trapping the place. Not that anyone went out there—at least not that far. That part of the creek was so remote, Stevie liked to think that he and Jude were the only ones to have explored it since dinosaurs had roamed the earth. But now, the idea of such detachment wasn't so appealing. And the thought of it having only been them, not likely.

I'd stay out of those woody woods if I were a woodpecker, you.

He picked his way through the trees despite the pounding of his heart, heading in the direction of the fort, in the direction of what Jude called "the zombie house." He went slow, his caution born both of trepidation and a search for clues. If he gave in to his anxiety and rushed, he would overlook things that may be important. And so, rather than running, he took deliberately sluggish steps, his gaze sweeping the trail for anything suspicious. His ears zeroed in on the occasional whoosh of a car driving down Main. That road noise was a small comfort, a reminder that, despite his nerves, he wasn't as far from civilization as he felt. But the sound of cars faded fast, and less than five minutes into his walk, Stevie was surrounded by nothing but the knocking of a lone woodpecker on the trunk of a pine overhead. *Stay out.* An owl dolefully complaining of insomnia. *Go back.* A squirrel bounding up the trunk of a Douglas fir. *Stay away.* Tree branches shivering from the occasional breath of wind, reaching out for him to keep him in place. The quiet bubbling of booby-trapped Cedar Creek, threatening to drown him, to slash him up on Jude's stockpile of shattered glass.

"I wouldn't go in those woods if I were you," Stevie whispered to himself.

But he continued onward, even when the well-worn trail became nothing but a meandering line of stomped-down earth. Eventually, there were signs that this territory belonged to two lone boys. A splotch of spray paint marking a crooked *J* on the bark of a tree. *Jude. Jitters. Judgment day.* A stack of rocks Stevie had piled on top of a downed log like an ancient cairn. A pyre of fallen branches, collected to keep their tiny hiking trail clean of debris; extra building material if they needed it on the fly. The hike was at least two miles, probably more. They'd never been sure. Jude tried to convince Stevie to snag his mom's phone so they could measure it with GPS, but Stevie didn't have the guts. And then, when it seemed that civilization was as good as lost, their path converged with a narrow, unpaved road. *That* road. The one where the house stood, haunted and alone.

He'd mentioned the area to his mom only once. "I don't like that, Stevie," she had said. "That's too far from home."

She made him promise that he wouldn't go out there, but that creepy house was the stuff of dangerous adventure, and Jude was obsessed.

"What's your mom so scared of anyway?" he had asked. "Does she think we're gonna get hit by a phantom truck?" And it was true; nobody drove on that defunct logging road anymore. They could have laid down in the middle of it and made up some stupid chant: *Semitruck, semitruck, squish me dead!* "Maybe it's not the phantom trucks she's scared of," Jude had continued. "Maybe it's the undead living in that house."

Except Stevie hadn't mentioned that, knowing that his mom would only freak out if she knew it was there.

The house was a good distance from where the trail crossed the road, but it was impossible to miss. Its white-painted clapboards and mismatched chicken coop stood out like an inkblot against an all-green backdrop. It had taken the boys nearly a month to gather up the guts to go closer, but once they finally steeled their nerves, the house lived up to exactly what they had imagined. It was old, dilapidated, verdant with mold; the entire structure appearing to lean to the left. There was a detached garage along the side. The pitched roof sagged in the middle, and moss had gobbled up the shingles. The house itself was two stories tall, a small dormer window suggesting an attic—a window that Stevie couldn't help but picture a ghost standing behind, watching them as they approached. That attic window had a perfect view of the road. Poised upon a hill, the gentle slope showed off the ancient bricks of a basement wall half buried beneath the earth. Small rectangular windows, like something belonging to a medieval prison, dotted the exposed stone. They looked painted-over from the inside, as if to keep the curious at bay.

Stevie had crept through the trees behind Jude without so much as a word, because once Jude had gotten up *his* nerve, he was determined to get a good look. They stopped only a few yards shy of a fence, in such disrepair it had fallen half inward, some of it propped up by stones and pieces of wood. There was chicken wire strung up between the slats.

"Looks haunted," Jude murmured as they hovered just outside the broken fence. "All green and moldy and stuff? Let's check it out."

"No way, Jose!" Stevie caught Jude by the arm as soon as his best friend made like he was going to trespass, but all Jude did was laugh.

"You really *are* a chicken shit, you know that?"

"Better than being undead," Stevie said.

"I don't know." Jude shrugged his shoulders. "I think being a zombie would be pretty damn cool."

Now, all alone a few days later, the tips of Stevie's sneakers toed the edge of that road. *I'd stay out of those woods if I were you.* He swallowed the wad of spit that had collected at the back of his throat, gripping his field book tight in both hands.

"You didn't," Stevie whispered to himself. "You *didn't.*"

He forced his attention to the notebook in his hands, then scribbled *ghost house* onto the page. His eyes were, however, quick to dart back to the building in the distance, because something felt off.

His pulse quickened, keeping time with the staccato *knock-knock-knock*ing of a woodpecker nearby. For a second he was ready to forget the investigation, forget being the hero, forget everything and book it back the way he had come. Crossing the road meant closing the distance, and at that very moment, Stevie would rather have choked down a Cedar Creek broken-glass sandwich than set foot across that washboard dirt. But that idea—that stupid, *ridiculous* idea—kept him cemented where he stood.

Jude is in there. Where? There. I wouldn't go in . . .

Stevie didn't want to consider the possibility, but if Jude had run away, perhaps this—not the fort—was the first place he had thought to come. Did the police even know this house existed? Stevie guessed they probably did, but who would have checked?

If Jude was in there, it meant Stevie had to go inside to find him. He had to reject his own dread, walk up those crumbling front-porch steps, and knock on the door.

Except, that was insane. Jude was *not* in there. And Stevie was *not* going anywhere near that house. If he asked Dunk to come with him, or Mr. Greenwood about—

There. A shift of light.

Something darted just beyond his periphery.

He jerked his head sideways, expected to see nothing. Shadow people, nothing but dark lingering vapor as soon as he looked their way. His imagination was so overwrought it wouldn't let him sleep, sometimes wouldn't let him eat, often so vivid it made him scream. But when his gaze finally tumbled across the house's front facade—

Something moved on the porch. Hidden in the darkness. Crouched. Not disappearing.

Reflexively, Stevie did an about-face and ran.

Bolting down the path he'd come in on, he broke left toward town, leaping over ferns like an Olympic hurdler, slapping branches out of his way. He nearly stumbled as the earth sank in on itself, spongy with vines and moss, with waterlogged leaves. Hands sprouted from the sodden soil, grabbing at his ankles, slowing his sprint, desperate to pull him under with each clawing, hungry swipe. Stevie exhaled a yell. A warning on repeat inside his head: *Run, run, run.* Because whatever had been on that porch was giving chase. He could hear it, its gasping breaths mimicked by his own. The pounding of its hands and feet setting off earthquakes behind Stevie's back. It was going to kill him. Just like it had killed Jude.

When he bounded out of the woods just shy of the main strip, he was screaming. People who had been wandering along the street stopped to stare; some window-shopping, others running errands as they flitted in and out of the hardware store and Greenwood General, startled by the boy who had come blasting out of the forest like a wild child. A couple of girls sitting outside the Mr. Frosty gave each other a look, then laughed and continued eating strawberry sundaes. Outside Cuppa Joe's, Mrs. Tassel, Stevie's third-grade teacher, rose from where she was sitting with a man who must have been her husband. "Stevie?" Across the street, Stevie's schoolmate Colby Clay gave him a blank stare, then followed his dad into the deli, probably looking to grab some lunch before going fishing or doing father-son stuff fit for *The Andy Griffith Show*.

"Stevie, are you all right?"

All of these folks could have been interviewed. One of them may have had just the detail to shake this whole case loose. But Stevie had lost his goddamn notebook, and he had no intention of questioning anyone else. All he wanted to do was get home.

He nearly jumped when Mrs. Tassel's hand landed on his shoulder. "Stevie, what's wrong? What happened?"

He was still heaving from his run, probably looking crazy-eyed and completely deranged. Mrs. Tassel moved her hand, delicately plucking a small branch from the wild tuft of his hair.

"Why don't you come sit down?" she suggested. "Let's get you some water." Her fingers caught him by the shoulder once more. She was trying to steer him, gentle but deliberate; herd him the way The Tyrant did. Through the house. To his room. On his knees. His belt. *Whoosh.* Out of the loops. The buckle. *Jingle jangle.* Ready. Aim.

"No!" Stevie spun away from her.

"Stevie, what—"

"No!" he yelled. "It's coming!" Then he booked it down the road, swinging wide onto Sunset Avenue, dashing for the safety of his mother's porch, no doubt leaving Mrs. Tassel and the folks of Deer Valley shaking their heads. *Poor Stevie Clark,* they'd say. *Sad little bastard. Not a friend in the world.*

He barged into the house so fast that he nearly tripped over the front mat. Dunk was on the couch, still wearing yesterday's T-shirt and the boxer shorts he'd slept in. His brother squinted against the sudden blast of sunshine that cut through the room, shielded his eyes, and barked a gruff "Close the goddamn door!" before Stevie swung it shut behind him. It slammed hard, knocked one of his mom's flea market pictures off the wall, but he didn't bother picking it up. He threw himself headlong into the kitchen, where his mother had just pushed a casserole dish into the oven.

"Mom!"

She jumped at Stevie's sudden appearance, lost her grip on the oven's handle. The oven door rattled closed, making her wince at the bang. Nicki Clark fluttered her eyes at her son as she tugged oven mitts off her hands. But Stevie was frozen in the doorframe, his brain churning around the information he was about to present, wondering if there was any possible way to say what he needed to say without sounding completely insane.

"Stevie?" She arched a brow over one eye.

"I—I—I—I"—*Dammit!* He took a breath, tried to calm himself—"saw, saw, seesaw something." It was only when he spoke that he realized how out of breath he was, his words just barely eking out of him before he had to gulp for air. And yet, despite toeing the line of physical exhaustion, he couldn't help but notice the small ways in which his mom tensed at his words—or she could have just been reacting to the clear and present backslide of his mental state. This had happened before, after Stevie's dad left. After Uncle Scott died. She wrung the bright red oven mitts in her hands, as if trying to drain them of a color she no longer liked, one that seemed to forewarn of some dreadful thing that would come to pass.

"Something . . . ?"

His mind reeled at the memory of it—the way that shadow thing had moved, so quick despite its scoliosis hunch.

"Honey?" Casting the mitts aside, she took a forward step. It was enough to snap him out of it, pull him away from the abandoned road and back to the present. He shot her a desperate look that pleaded for her to listen before she assumed, to at least *try* to believe him before she wrote it all off as Stevie just being Stevie, nothing but a bag of nuts.

"At, th-th-the . . ." He clamped down his teeth, reached across his chest and pinched his arm hard. ". . . the house!" Finally spitting out the words.

"The house . . ." She shook her head, not following.

"The house! On that road."

Her expression took a turn. What had seconds ago been worry was now aggravation. Stevie's tongue was suddenly superglued to the roof of his mouth.

"The road." Her eyes narrowed ever so slightly. "You mean the road I specifically told you not to go near. *That* road?"

"I was retracing our footsteps—"

"Stop."

He swallowed. "From Sunday," he said. "I was following where we had gone, and when I got there, I—I—I . . ." He paused. Forced his tongue straight. ". . . to the road, I saw this . . . this thing, this *thing, this thing-a-ling lingering* . . ."

"Stephen. Aaron. Clark."

His full name made the hairs on his arms recoil. She only ever used it when he was in serious trouble, but she couldn't possibly punish him *now*. Not without listening to what he had to say. He had gone off to look for Jude, had seen something. What if it was Jude's abductor? Jude's killer?

"Mom!"

"Don't you 'Mom' me!" she snapped. "What's gotten into you lately? Have you lost—" She cut herself off, closed her eyes and took a steadying breath. *Lost your mind?* Sometimes he wished she'd just go on and say it. It wasn't like it was some big secret, but it seemed to him that she was convinced that if she didn't acknowledge his mental state, the problem would eventually go away. "Stevie . . ." She was more collected now, but just barely. The tension in her voice was masked, but her gaze was still severe. "What do you think would happen to this family if you went missing, too? Did you stop to think about that? Did you stop to think that there might be someone out there who wants to hurt more kids? That wants to hurt *you*?"

"But there *is* someone!" He flung that statement at her without hesitation, let it flop at her feet, dead and slimy like a rotting fish. "There's someone, two, three, four! We don't want it at the door!"

"Stop it." That hard edge was back. "I need you to stop *right now*."

He snapped his mouth shut.

Her cell phone rang.

"You *know* you're not supposed to be anywhere near that road," she said, moving across the kitchen to answer it. "I told you to stay away from there, and you purposefully defied me."

"It was a *thing*!"

"Quiet!" The word came out of her with such force that Stevie's breath hitched in his throat. He glared down at his sneakers, listening as she answered the call.

"Hello?" A pause. "This is she." Another pause. "I . . . I see." He could feel her eyes on him, roving across his skin like a bug. "Yes, he's home." A big fat bug. A cockroach three inches long. "No, it's fine." Crawling up his arm. "Yes, I can see how that would be . . . startling. I'm . . ." Up his neck. "I'm sorry, I'll . . . Yes . . . Yes, I will." Across his face. "Thank you for calling." Up his nose.

"Stevie."

He blinked.

"Do you want to guess who that was?"

Glancing at his mother's face, he furrowed his eyebrows at her question. " . . . No?"

"That was your old teacher Mrs. Tassel."

Oh. Great.

"Do you know why she was calling?"

Stevie hated this game. What was he, a psychic?

"No."

"Really." His mom scoffed. "You have *no* idea? You didn't just scare the bejesus out of half the town by screaming your head off near the coffee shop?"

Bejesus. He liked that word. He couldn't help the smile that crawled across his face.

"You think this is *funny*? How about this: You're grounded. Is *that* funny?" Two words that no kid ever liked to hear. *You're grounded.* Like two gunshots—bang *bang*. Summer, over. Freedom, gone.

Stevie gawked. Incredulous.

"One month," she said, unmoved. "Starting five minutes ago."

"A whole *month?*" Despite his pulse having slowed, his breaths were coming in heaves again. The backs of his eyes started to burn. His face felt hot. Every time it flushed like that, he imagined himself turning red like a cartoon character, smoke coming out of his ears. As a matter of fact, there was smoke coming out of the oven behind his mom, giant toxic purple plumes forming the shape of a pair of hands . . . hands that he hoped would wrap themselves around her throat. Wrap wrap wrap and squeeze. "That isn't fair!"

"Life isn't fair." She threw that typical grown-up response in his face, as though he hadn't heard it a million times.

"You don't *care!*" He bellowed the words. "You don't care that he's gone."

She turned away from him, as if wounded. But rather than taking it all back—*Forget the grounding, it was a mistake*—she said, "I've had enough of this," toward the kitchen window. "We should go away. Just until all of this is over . . ."

"Go away?" His heart flip-flopped inside his chest. Suddenly, that burning at the back of his eyes turned into stupid crybaby tears. "Maybe *you* should go away."

"This is too much," she said, so low Stevie doubted she meant for him to hear her. "We can't do anything to help, and it's just . . . it's just getting worse. It's making *you* worse."

Suddenly, Nicki Clark disappeared, replaced by a woman who looked just like her. A close replica, but with a hole where Stevie's mom's heart had once been. She was a hollow person who only acted concerned, pretending to be terrified of what may have happened to Jude, but she didn't give a damn. Run away. Forget everything. Let whatever was going to happen to Jude happen and cry out her guilt at her nephew's funeral. She'd console herself with the lie that she had done everything she could. But she'd done nothing. Not a single fucking thing.

"Y-you're a bad person," he cried. "You don't give a shit one bit!" Jude's words coming out of his mouth, unfiltered. "Y-you should go away. Because I hate you!" he roared. "You hear me? I hate you, you stupid jerk!"

His mother's face whipped back at him, replaced by nothing but a pair of basketball-sized eyes. He didn't stick around for any more of her reaction. Rather, he stomped out of the kitchen and down the hall, catching sight of Dunk for half a second on the way to his room. His older brother had overheard everything. Still on the couch, he had twisted halfway around to get a better view. When their eyes met, Dunk pulled up his eyebrows in an impressed sort of way, but Stevie wasn't in the mood.

"Shut up, ass-wipe," he growled beneath his breath, and slammed his bedroom door behind him.

6

STEVIE SPENT THE rest of the day inside. But that didn't mean he couldn't sneak out if he wanted. His own mother may have been a total jerk, but Aunt Mandy would definitely want to hear Stevie's story of how he'd been pursued by the shadow thing. She'd always been patient with him, even when he struggled with his vocal outbursts, with his jumbled thoughts. Perhaps she'd go with him into the forest—drive him down the washboard surface of that abandoned road and park just shy of that creepy house. They'd climb the rickety steps together, and she'd speak words of comfort as they knocked on the door. *It'll be okay. Don't be afraid. We'll find him, you and me.* And there, with their forces combined, their joint need for Jude's return would make him materialize. Like magic. Like the space-time travelers of *Star Trek*. *Beam me up*. Except they'd be beaming Jude down.

There was a chance Stevie'd get caught, end up being grounded for a year instead of a month. But it was a heck of a lot better than sitting there, thinking about worst-case scenarios.

He shot a look at the bedroom door. His mom hadn't checked up on him since dinner an hour earlier—an awkwardly silent meal. She was still freaked out about everything, but she hadn't mentioned their fight or the phone call she'd received to Terry, and Stevie was thanking his lucky stars for that. If she had breathed even a word, The Tyrant would have taken great pleasure in laying into him after a long day at work. Terry thought Stevie's issues were bullshit anyway. The clanging, the nightmares, the echolalia when Stevie got worked up; according to him, all of it was made-up, a desperate ploy for attention. He'd be damned if a shitty kid pulled the wool over his eyes. But Stevie's mom had kept quiet, and now The Tyrant was in the living room, sitting in his ugly recliner, hogging the TV and slurping at a can of beer. Stevie's mom milled around the kitchen, never more than a gruff "Babe" away.

It was unlikely that she'd come in to check on Stevie before bedtime, which meant he had about an hour for a jailbreak. If he kept an eye on the time, his mom would never know he was gone.

Yanking open his desk drawer, he pulled out a crummy old digital watch—banana yellow and gotten from a Burgerville kids' meal. He shoved it in the pocket of his shorts, then struggled with the window. The house was old, and the sills were swollen with the summer's humidity. It took some muscle and a couple of grunts, but he managed to push it open, just wide enough to sneak through. And yet, he hesitated despite his resolve, his guts churning from the possibility of being found out. If his mom was next door, going to Jude's place was the equivalent of a prison escapee running into the warden's open arms.

Except she isn't there, if I were you, he told himself. *She doesn't care, wouldn't go in there.* Perhaps Mom was just as glad as Terry that Jude was gone. If Jude didn't come back, there was the possibility that Stevie would straighten out. Magically become normal. *Poof.* Like Pinocchio turning into a real boy. Everyone knew Jude was nothing but a bad influence. After all, it was after Uncle Scott died that Jude had gotten super rebellious. It was easy to blame him for Stevie's state of mind taking a turn for the worst.

It was convenient to forget the trouble with Stevie had begun long before the accident, when he had been five or six. Back then, Jude had been happy, but Stevie's nightmares were already keeping everyone up. He'd scream into the night, watching things crawl out of the walls, staring at monsters as they peered through the crack between the closet door and the jamb. During the day, unless Jude was there to distract him, Stevie couldn't focus. His schoolwork suffered. His speech became unhinged, which amused his classmates but scared his teachers. Mrs. Tassel had been the only one who had truly tried to help.

Stevie's problems seemed to stem from nowhere, and Stevie's mom and dad began to fight more than they talked. Dennis Clark insisted they take him to a shrink, but Stevie's mom wouldn't hear of it. There was nothing wrong with her son. He was fine. It was just a phase. It would pass. Everything would be okay.

He spent evenings listening to their arguments while trying to fall asleep. It had been impossible *not* to. The walls were thin. Stevie's dad was screaming about doctors. His mom talked about pulling him out of school, keeping him at home, changing everything about the Clarks' lifestyle to accommodate whatever it was her son would need.

That's what had pushed Dad over the line. "You can't just ignore it!" he yelled. "People like this, they can get dangerous, Nick! You want him to grow up to be a psychopath? A school shooter? One of those crazy fucking kids who end up on the news?"

"That's exactly what I *don't* want!" she had roared back at him.

"Yeah? Well it's going to happen. He's going to go off like an atom bomb. And you know what'll happen then? The people we know—the *entire world*—will put the blame on *us*. The irresponsible dipshits who let their kid blow up a cafeteria. Who didn't know he was buying guns off the Internet. Just a couple of blind *assholes*. You want that? Fine. Be my fucking guest."

The next morning, Stevie awoke to his mother weeping on the couch. Half of the master bedroom's drawers had been emptied. His dad's car was gone. Stevie patted his mom on the back and tried to comfort her as she cried. He supposed his dad just really truly didn't want to be an asshole, and so he'd packed up his stuff and left. But Dennis Clark wasn't the only thing that evanesced. Talk about pulling Stevie out of school, giving him anything he needed, it all went away as well. Because it was hard for Nicole Clark to stick to her guns when she was spiraling into the dark corners of depression; when she, too, felt like she was losing her mind.

Stevie still had the regular nightmares, but these days his fear of The Tyrant had taught him to keep quiet. He saw shadow people every day. Sometimes, he was able to talk himself through his own episodes, ignore them altogether; like the haze that had slithered out of the oven behind his mother earlier that day; like the time when, standing in the shower, octopus tentacles had come up out of the drain and whipped around as if searching for his feet. Or when, as he bowed over his morning bowl of cereal, his Cheerios turned into tiny serpents eating their own tails, their eyes blankly staring up at him as they bobbed in a man-made lake of milk.

Like how he'd seen a weird creature bound over their back fence.

Except, there was that fallen-over fender.

There was the cut on his ankle, created by a broken bicycle spoke; a reminder that what he'd seen must have been real.

Double-knotting his shoelaces, Stevie rose from the floor and crept to his bedroom door. He pulled it open a quarter of an inch—just enough to peer through the crack—and strained to catch sight of his mother, or at least echolocate her milling around out there. But Terry had the habit of cranking the TV volume way too loud. Football announcers yelled over the constant drone of a frantic crowd. He couldn't hear anything above the cheering. He'd just have to risk it and hope for the best.

He quietly shut his door, skittered across his room, and crawled onto his bed toward the window, then shimmied beneath the pane like a squirming fish. It was a tight fit, but he made it. His feet hit the dirt, and he squatted, half hidden beside one of his mom's flowering bushes, peering through the pickets of the side yard toward Jude's house. If he was discovered, he'd plead his case: he just wanted to make sure that Aunt Mandy was okay. But if he was caught hiding in the begonia bush, it would be pretty obvious he was sneaking around.

That in mind, Stevie rose to his full four feet five inches and yanked a withering flower off a branch. Only two steps toward Jude's place and he was already backpedaling, his back thudding against the siding of the house. A police cruiser eased up to the curb, its whirly lights at rest. Stevie ducked back down as he watched a couple of cops get out of the car. They didn't speak to each other as they strolled past Aunt Amanda's front fence and up her steps, out of Stevie's line of sight.

He held his breath, straining to hear over Terry's stupid game—muffled but still audible through the open front windows. Aunt Mandy's doorbell ding-donged, soft murmurs drifting up into the almost-darkened sky. And then, the muffled beauty of the evening was shattered by a wail. A soul being torn from a body. Tragedy shaped into sound waves.

The cry was so all-encompassing that it seemed to blast in from every direction, as though an angel had stuck her head through a cloud and screamed down from the sky, her cry wrapping around the world like a choking veil. But it was a familiar voice, Aunt Mandy shouting as if those officers were fileting her still-beating heart.

Stevie's muscles spasmed, realization punching through his chest. He bounded upright, ready to leap across the junk-littered yard, but an inexplicable stillness overtook him; a sensation that left him unfeeling and numb. That scream should have thrown him into a tailspin of terror, but all he did was stand there, motionless, thinking, *Dead, dead, red bloodshed . . .*

He told himself to move, either toward Aunt Amanda's squalling or back through his window. But before he could get his feet to cooperate, he saw his aunt stumble down her porch steps and launch herself across the sidewalk. She was screaming Stevie's mother's name.

"Nicki!" Like a bird with a broken wing. "Nicki!" Over and over—a parrot on repeat, an echo chamber loop.

A bang sounded against the front of Stevie's house, out of view but hard enough to send a vibration through the building's wooden frame. Aunt Amanda's fists hit the front door with enough force to shake the walls.

"Mandy?" Stevie's mom through the open front-room window, alarmed.

Another scream, this one more panicked than the last. Stevie pictured his aunt collapsing into his mother's arms, fainting like ladies did in the soaps she loved so much, limp as his mom tried to keep her from hitting the deck beneath her feet.

"What the hell is going on?" The Tyrant.

"Mandy, what happened? *What is it?!*" Stevie's mom. Concentrated dread.

But even he knew the solution to this dark riddle.

They had found Jude.

Dead, dead, limbs outspread.

7

STEVIE WONDERED IF it was possible to stay in his room for the rest of his life. Maybe, if he willed himself deaf, he wouldn't have to hear the news he knew was coming. And perhaps, if he couldn't hear the words, reality—at least for Jude—would cease to exist. It was like the riddle his teacher had presented at school: If a tree falls in a forest and there's nobody around to hear it, does it make a sound? The answer was no. Because without ears, sound didn't exist. Without eyes, light was darkness. And without a body, there was no victim. Which is why, despite his aunt's woeful cries, Stevie refused to believe it. Not until he saw Jude in a coffin, a waxwork dressed up in a suit he'd have never worn in real life.

But when he finally crept out of his room, Aunt Mandy's weeping was amplified, fifty times louder than it had been a moment before. The house was a cavern of sorrow. All the furniture, the pictures on the walls, the TV, even Terry's La-Z-Boy, had been swallowed up by all-consuming grief.

Stevie shot a look toward Dunk's bedroom, but the door was closed. Duncan was a champion at avoiding the family in general. Toss a tragedy into the mix and he was the Invisible Man.

Stevie inched down the dimly lit hall, dragging his right hand along the wall, the texture giving him comfort; like reading Braille, its message reprised over and over again: *Today will be okay, okay, someday someone will say* . . .

"Oh God." Aunt Amanda's voice filtered into the hallway from the living room. "I don't understand! How is this happening? What have I done?" A fleshlike thud.

"Mandy, stop." Stevie's mom.

"What have I done for you to smite me this way?" Aunt Mandy's voice rising with each word, escalating toward a full-on scream. *Smite. Smit. Smote.* A word Stevie didn't often hear, one he knew belonged in a church. His mom didn't drag him there anymore, not like Aunt Mandy with Jude. She used to, but stopped when she and Stevie overheard some ladies talking, watching them shoot suspicious glances at the two of them after the service. "Maybe if he isn't getting better, she should pray a little harder," one of the ladies had murmured beneath her breath. "Maybe it's a problem of faith."

He peeked around the edge of the hall and into the living room just in time to catch another pounding thump. Aunt Mandy was sitting on the couch, Stevie's mom next to her. She was hitting her breastplate with a closed fist, as if trying to crack her chest open to pull out her own heart. Stevie's mom was attempting to stop her. Every time that fist came down, she struggled to keep it from making contact. But Nicole Clark was failing to make an impact with her sister. At that moment, Amanda Brighton was stronger than both Stevie's mom and

The Tyrant combined. What had once been quiet sorrow had now grown into a snarling, clawing beast.

"It's just a shirt, Mandy." Stevie's mom. "He just dropped it. It doesn't prove anything."

His aunt's face was swollen, as if she'd been stung by a thousand bees. The skin around her eyes was raw. And yet, the rest of her looked gaunt. Her arms skinny, jutting out of her sleeveless top like dry and leafless twigs. The thin, silky fabric of her shirt gave her shoulders a birdlike quality, nothing under there but a skeleton wrapped in skin. It reminded him of Egyptian mummies, of sickness and starvation. Had he passed her on the street, he wouldn't have recognized her. She had changed almost completely in the past few days, looking weak and forlorn.

Stevie's mom glanced away from her sister. A distant look was cemented upon her face, as though she were trying to will herself to a happier place—*This is all too much.* She could have been thinking about the lake house they had once borrowed from family friends. The cabin had been beautiful, way fancier than any place Stevie had ever stayed before. He spent the week cannonballing off a private pier while his mom read paperback thrillers, his dad burned hot dogs on the grill, and Dunk screwed around on his phone. That had been only months before Stevie's first episode . . . before everything had started to fall apart.

Regardless of where her mind was now, his mother's eyes settled upon her youngest son, and for a brief moment it was as if she were looking *through* him, as though Stevie, like Jude, had simply disappeared. It took a moment for something to click inside her head, but when it did, her eyes cleared. She opened her mouth to speak, but no sound came. Stevie was sure that, at that very moment, she had forgotten his name.

Aunt Mandy was the one to jog her memory. "Stevie." She sat up at attention, seemingly startled by the fact that there were still children in this world, kids who were alive and well while hers was possibly forever gone. Or maybe she was just upset that he was seeing her that way, haggard, overwrought. "Oh God . . . ," she whispered, covering her mouth with a hand and looking away.

"I s-saw the cops," Stevie told them. His eyes dared to wander in his stepfather's direction. Terry was still in his easy chair, staring blankly at the TV, which was now turned down so low it was practically muted. His expression was hard, almost confused, as though he'd forgotten the rules of the game. Or perhaps he simply didn't understand why Amanda Brighton had to have a goddamn emotional breakdown in his living room when she had a whole house to herself right next door.

The Tyrant didn't regard his stepson. Not even a glance.

Neither his mother nor his aunt said anything, so Stevie pressed on.

"I—I—I know something happened." He took a steadying breath. If there ever was a time for keeping his cool, this was it. Jude was relying on him.

"Nothing happened," his mom replied.

"Wh-what do you mean . . . ?" *Halloween. Murder scene.* Was she really going to deny it? Stevie had seen the police with his own two eyes. Was she going to insist that he had imagined them there?

"Stevie, just . . ." A breath escaped her in a huff of impatient frustration. "We'll talk about it later, okay?"

"Go to your room." Terry snapped out of his daze, always eager to boss someone around.

"But I want to know what happened . . ." Stevie had assumed Aunt Mandy had been made aware of the sweatshirt that morning, but it seemed that he was wrong. Or was there more? Despite their ineptitude, that bumbling search party could have actually found another clue.

"Hey, are you *deaf*?" The Tyrant's eyes were fixed on Stevie's face. "Your ears as bad as your fucking head?"

Head. Stevie mutely mouthed the word. *Instead.*

Both Stevie's mom and his aunt winced at the profanity that came spilling out of Terry's mouth, but neither said a word edgewise. For a second, Stevie was tempted to duck his head between his shoulders and go back to his room, to not make trouble or risk getting pummeled. But the look on Terry's face—the total lack of sympathy for Stevie or his mother or his poor Aunt Mandy—tied up Stevie's insides into a tight double knot.

"I can see j-just as good as I can hear, my dear," Stevie fired back. "I saw the cops and I wanna know, you know? I wanna know what they said, meathead."

"Stevie . . . !" His mother gave him a disbelieving stare. He threw it right back at her, astounded as well, because, while Jude's disappearance had clearly messed up Aunt Mandy, it was now abundantly clear that it had done something weird to his mom as well. She didn't understand *anything* anymore. He had to yell every word he said for her to hear him, and even that didn't guarantee a response.

And on top of it all, he'd just accidentally called Terry out. He was going to get pounded, for sure.

"Oh, I'll let you know what they fucking said . . ." The Tyrant rose out of his chair.

"Oh God." Aunt Mandy wept the words, suddenly caught in a domestic crossfire. "Just stop it," she demanded. "Nicki, tell him to *stop* it . . ."

"Stevie, stop it!" his mom yelled, oddly automatic, desperate to ply her sister into a calmer state.

"Stop it!" Stevie squawked an echo, his yell pointed at his stepdad.

But all it did was make Aunt Mandy cry out, "They found Jude's sweatshirt!" as Terry wrenched Stevie by the arm. She just about choked on the words as they tripped over her tonsils, stumbling out of her throat like a drunk down a crooked set of stairs. This stalled Terry's inevitable drag of his ten-year-old stepson down the hall toward his room.

Stevie's mom gave her son a worried look, but Aunt Amanda continued talking, needing to purge her system of the words, fraught with worry, tragedy, dismay.

"They found his sweatshirt," she said again, quieter this time. "I know he's dead. I'm so sorry, Stevie, but I know he's dead."

Dead. His lips worked around the word. *She said "dead."*

"Mandy, no." Stevie's mom. Stern. Edging toward angry. "It's just a shirt. It doesn't mean *anything*." But Stevie hardly heard her. He was too distracted by his aunt's hollow eyes, too disturbed by her sunken cheeks. Her mouth looked three times too big for her face—huge and warped, downturned like soft taffy. He pictured her opening her mouth as wide as she could, her entire face disappearing behind a grief-stricken maw, a scream stuck in there somewhere, Jude's fingers suddenly jutting out of the blackness of her throat as though she'd swallowed him, as if it had been *her* that had made him vanish all along.

"He's okay," Stevie's mom said, softly now. "He's okay, Mandy. He'll come home."

It was his mom's statement that jump-started his stalled-out heart. Those two cops who had sauntered up Aunt Amanda's walkway—they hadn't knocked on the door to announce that Jude was at the coroner's office. They hadn't found him. Jude was still out there somewhere.

"He's okay." He found himself repeating his mother's statement, yanking his arm out of Terry's blocky grasp. "He's okay. Okay, okay . . ." Terry's face twisted up—a rabid dog eager to bite—but Stevie moved away from him fast, and ducked toward the couch, both to comfort his aunt and to find safety in her and his mother's presence. The Tyrant would keep his distance. He, like Dunk, was afraid of the crushing despair that was wafting off Amanda Brighton, as though it was a communicable disease.

But Stevie never made it to the couch. He nearly jumped at his aunt's reaction to his echolalia—a guttural squall that turned into a screechy cry. "Then why doesn't somebody find him? *Why won't someone bring him home?!*"

Because the search party was a joke. The reporters were convinced Jude had run away. Deer Valley didn't give a damn. Suddenly, all Stevie wanted was to set the entire town on fire. He hated every single person who lived there, all the jerks who had ever given him or Jude a sideways glance because they weren't like the other kids.

Aunt Amanda continued her lamentation. Stevie's mother rubbed her back, speaking in soft tones. Terry remained where he was, staring at his stepkid like a hunter down the barrel of a gun, for once looking like he wasn't sure how to proceed.

"I'm gonna find him," Stevie told the room. "Aunt Mandy, I'm gonna find him."

He didn't know how he was going to do it, but it had to be done.

With Terry still silent, Stevie turned away from the living room and marched down the hall. Shutting his door behind him, he gulped against the lump that had formed in the back of his throat. He was keenly aware of just how badly he was gnashing his teeth—hard enough to grind rocks into sand—but he couldn't bring himself to relax his jaw, because he'd heard of cases like this before. Folks thought if a kid went missing, people would search for them until they were found, but that wasn't true. Especially not when the kid was a nuisance—a gadfly who irritated the entire police force. Not if the kid's family was nothing but a badly-off single mom in a crappy one-bar town.

He choked out a sob as he stared at the carpet, the spot where he and Jude had played Monopoly only a few weeks before. They played by what Jude called *Mob rules*. You were allowed to rob the bank if you landed on GO, and could mug your opponent if you owned a hotel. Mostly, it was a game of Jude stealing funny money while Stevie stomped a plastic Godzilla figure across the board hard enough to rattle tiny green houses. Hopped-up on sugar and caffeine, they had rolled around on Stevie's floor, cackling and throwing rainbow-colored bills at each other like a couple of whacked-out Donald Trumps. The moment burned into Stevie's memory like a forever-scar. A reflection of perfect friendship no matter how imperfect the both of them were.

But now Stevie's room was a hollow cave. Laughter was replaced by sobs.

He shoved himself away from his door and grabbed the Monopoly box off his bookshelf, boomeranged it at his window. The box opened up midflight. Money rained down onto the bed and carpet. And still, Jude wasn't there. Not to roll his eyes at Stevie's dramatics, and not to cackle at the mess.

• • •

Aunt Mandy's bawling eventually tapered off and, accompanied by Stevie's mom, she was led down the porch steps and shepherded back home. A few minutes later, there was a knock on Stevie's bedroom door. Stevie's mom stepped inside and, interrupting his harvesting of funny money on the carpet, took a seat on the edge of his bed. He crunched a few colorful bills in the palm of his hand, gave her a doleful look. But rather than asking him about his freak-out downtown, or scolding him for his *I hate you* blowup, or demanding he pinkie-swear that he'd never go anywhere near that old road in the woods again, she gave him a faint smile and nodded for him to follow her into the kitchen.

When Stevie stepped out of his room, the house was empty. Terry was gone—probably at The Antler with guys who should have been looking for Jude—and Dunk was AWOL. Stevie and his mom sat down at the kitchen table, where a shoe box of photographs sat in the center, those pictures reflective in the dull glow of his mother's cheap brass chandelier. Inside the box were photos of all kinds—his mother laughing as she crouched in her tiny backyard garden when Stevie's dad had still been around; Dunk looking embarrassed while posing with Annie in front of his car for homecoming. And then there were shots of Stevie, many of them with Jude at his elbow. A few featured them flopped on the couch, watching movies or sitting on the floor with game controllers in their hands. Another was of Jude laughing his ass off while Stevie stood in the center of the frame, half-wrapped in aluminum foil, his arms shoved elbow-deep into empty Pringles cans. Jude was smiling in all the pre-death memories. Only a few had been taken after Uncle Scott's accident. In those, Jude's grin was either strained or completely missing.

Stevie's mom stopped on a photo that had been taken only a month before. In it, Jude and Stevie were sitting at the very table he and his mother now occupied. With their arms looped around each other's shoulders, the boys mugged for the camera over heaping plates of his mom's "world-famous" spaghetti. The picture seemed fake; hard to remember, hard to *imagine* that, despite Jude's dad being gone and Terry being a monster, they both still managed to find something to smile about once in a while. Now their smiles struck him as obscene. Stevie frowned at the snapshot, refusing to touch it, afraid that Jude's image would leer forward and bite off the remaining fingers of his right hand with snapping teeth.

"Let's use this one," his mom suggested, sliding the photo in question away from the box.

"Use it for what?" The funeral? That photo: blown up to ten times its size, propped up on an easel behind Jude's coffin, everyone shuffling past it with heads bowed and hands clasped. Aunt Mandy standing behind a podium, wailing into the microphone as though singing a horrible mourning dirge. Everyone filling pews, plates of spaghetti in their laps, big white napkins shoved into their collars, tomato sauce slopping down their chins like blood.

"Posters," his mom said. *Posters?* "The ones we're going to put up around town tomorrow morning."

Stevie slowly turned his head to look at her. Neither one of them said a word for a long while. Eventually, he gave her a faint nod, wanting to leave it at that—a somber response for a kid with grown-up problems. But his heart clenched at the offering, at the thought of Jude's face being pasted up all over town: *Have you seen this boy?* This was it, the thing that would spur him into action. This was the answer he'd been looking for.

He threw his arms around his mother's neck, coiled them so tight it was a wonder she could breathe.

"Thanks," he murmured, trying not to cry. But the tears came regardless. Because he wasn't alone in this anymore. Someone other than him believed it was possible that Jude would still come home.

8

———

FIRST THING THE next morning, Stevie and his mom went to a local print shop and got fifty flyers made. They stapled Jude's face to electrical poles and asked shopkeepers to put the black-and-white printouts in their windows.

It had been the ideal time to bring up the monster, the chase, the house. But he didn't. He didn't go next door after he and his mother returned home, either, too afraid to upset his aunt with stories that would make her look at him as though he'd finally lost it.

But the promise he'd made to help find Jude burned bright in the forefront of his mind. Thanking his lucky stars that his mom seemed to have let go of the enforcement of his grounding—he had stuff to do that couldn't wait—Stevie made his way down the sidewalk, back in the direction of the general store, less than an hour after combing Main Street with flyers in hand.

He hadn't seen Mr. Greenwood when they'd come in earlier, and even if Mr. G. had been there, Stevie wouldn't have started a conversation with the old man while his mom was around. But they definitely needed to have a discussion, because if anyone was going to take that shadow figure seriously, it was one of Deer Valley's oldest residents, the one who had suggested there was something living out there in those trees.

Stevie stepped into the place feeling more nervous than he expected. Spilling to Mr. Greenwood hadn't seemed like that big of a deal moments before, but now that he was inside the store, bringing up the monster felt like a shot in the dark. There was a chance Mr. G. would shake his head and call Stevie's mom—*Come collect your Looney Tunes kid*—or bark him out of his shop. But it was either give this a try or never forgive himself for giving up.

He spotted the old man at the back of the store, hiding out in a corner that smelled heavily of fresh baked cookies and something malodorously floral. Mr. G. was wearing his standard uniform; a short-sleeved polo tucked into khaki pants, which were hiked up to his chin. Mr. Greenwood dipped his hands into a cardboard box and brought out two jarred candles, then slid them onto the shelf of an open armoire that served as a display case.

Stevie watched the man work for a while, lingering in the small greeting card section of the shop. He had tried to find Jude a birthday card here once, but all Mr. G. stocked was grandma stuff: kittens in baskets, still lifes of roses, cranes flying over calm lakes; cards that were blank on the inside flap, offering ample room for old ladies to get gushy about how proud they were of their grandkids. Stevie had considered buying Jude a kitten card just to be funny, but ended up getting one about blowing out candles with farts, courtesy of the Walmart on the outskirts of town.

He took a breath and, although hesitant, stepped out from beyond the card shelves and gift bag display. "M-Mr. Greenwood?" He kept his distance, not wanting to crowd the man or seem too needy or desperate. When Mr. G. glanced over his shoulder, Stevie tried to smile, but it felt awkward. Stupid. An idiot grinning at the scene of a crime.

"Mr. Clark." Mr. Greenwood's greeting caught Stevie off guard. He hadn't expected the old man to remember him, let alone know his name, but he supposed that was silly. Mr. G. knew everyone, always regarding his younger customers by their last names, using first names with the older folks, probably having known them all their lives.

"H-hi," Stevie stammered.

Mr. Greenwood regarded him with a knowing expression, then turned back to his candles, arranging them by color. Stevie's mom sometimes bought the red ones, which smelled like apples, which was okay. Aunt Mandy had always preferred the pink ones, but those smelled terrible, like someone had sprayed an entire bottle of perfume on a bouquet of flowers just before setting it aflame. The pink ones gave Stevie headaches, and the throbbing sometimes made weird things come out of the walls. A pink one had cost him the tips of two fingers after he had crammed his right hand down the garbage disposal. They hadn't been fingers anymore, but a clump of fat, squirming earthworms. Stevie's mom had been at the grocery store. Stevie and Jude had been getting a snack during a commercial break. Aunt Mandy called 911. The ambulance came. There was a surgery involved, but the tips were gone. It had been a complete disaster. At one point, Aunt Mandy had passed out from all the blood. *The smell,* he had explained. *Brain strain, itchy crawly migraine.* Ever since then, he hadn't seen a single jar candle in Jude's house, pink or not.

"Finding everything all right, Mr. Clark?" Mr. Greenwood asked.

"Um, yeah, yes . . . ," Stevie said, then added, "Just browsing." A very grown-up line, one he'd heard his mom use a million times.

"Well, if you need any help, you let me know."

Help. That word resonated within Stevie's chest like a gong. Mr. G. was wise enough to know Stevie wasn't shopping.

Stevie peered down at the tips of his sneakers, somehow unable to gather enough guts to speak. *Yes,* he wanted to say. *I need help.* But he just stood there, mute, glaring at the scuffed-up floor beneath his feet.

"Mr. Clark?"

Stevie looked up.

"Everything all right?"

"Yes," he said. "Yeah, yes, thanks, yup." *Just browsing,* he nearly echoed. That flowery smell was starting to make his brain squirm inside his skull. He looked down at his damaged right hand, making sure his remaining fingers were just that. *Guess I'll go eat worms . . .* When he saw that they were, he turned and started walking toward the door, as if having forgotten why he'd entered the store in the first place, suddenly wanting nothing more than to be in the vacuous safety of his own room.

But he stopped midflight. What, exactly, was he going to do when he got there? Stare out his window and cry about how helpless he felt? Wonder if he'd ever see his best friend again? And if the police *did* eventually find a body, if Jude really *was* dead, how would Stevie feel then, going through life knowing that he was one of the people who lost all hope? Would he be able to live with that?

Stevie turned to face Mr. Greenwood again. "S-sir?"

The old man flipped an empty cardboard box onto its top and pulled a box cutter from his back pocket. Stevie stared at the blade for a moment, sure that Mr. G. was going to wave it in his face. *Get outta here! No loitering!*

"Do you know anything about that house . . ." He hesitated, not knowing how to describe the structure other than bringing up the nameless road it was on. But before he could figure out how best to explain its location other than *in the woods*, he noticed Mr. Greenwood's expression shift from curious to stern.

"You've been to the house?" he asked.

Stevie opened his mouth, but no sound came. *Yes, no, yes.*

Mr. G. took a few shuffling forward steps, the box cutter still in his hand, ready to slash at anything that might come his way. Stevie's eyes widened when the old man reached out and snatched him by the arm, his bony fingers surprisingly strong. Something bad was happening. Something in Mr. Greenwood's pruney old brain had snapped. He'd lead Stevie off into the shadows of the back office where no one would hear from him again. Another missing kid. And, lo and behold, Jude's body had been there the entire time, stuffed beneath Mr. Greenwood's desk. *And I would have gotten away with it, too, if it hadn't been for you meddling kids!*

"Come with me," Mr. Greenwood said, and while his grip was steadfast, he waited for Stevie to move his feet. When Stevie did, Mr. G. directed him to a back door that opened onto the gravel delivery road that ran behind the store. Just a few doors down, Jude's hammer was hiding in a juniper bush.

Mr. G. stepped into the sun, released Stevie's arm, and squinted against the brightness of daylight. Glancing at the box cutter still in his hand, he retracted the blade and shoved the tool back into his pocket with a single gruff move—an old-timey gunslinger, smooth with his trusty weapon. "How many times have you been out to that place?" He scrutinized Stevie through the tiny slits that now made up his eyes.

"I . . ." Stevie shook his head. He wasn't really sure. The first time he and Jude had spotted it, they'd stayed away, having spooked themselves with stories of witches and killers—because those were the only types of people who lived in rotten, broken-down homes like that. But eventually, Jude wanted to see it again. He dragged Stevie along. They'd crept close, just shy of the broken fence and the blue chicken coop, the place teeming with cats—like someone had been feeding them, and that's why they stayed.

After that, Jude kept wanting to go back, as though something had crawled into his brain, beckoning him over and over again. They started taking the long way to their fort whether they had to or not, because the house was in that direction, and Jude insisted.

So, when Mr. Greenwood asked how many times he'd been there, Stevie's brain tripped over itself. Had it been five times? Six? Probably at least a dozen, if not more. But he was afraid to fess up to that. So, instead of telling the truth, he said, "M-maybe three times . . . ?" and left it at that. Any number beyond that felt flagrant, as though he and Jude had been courting disaster. *If you ask me, your friend got what he deserved.*

Mr. Greenwood looked less than convinced at Stevie's answer, but he didn't push it. He turned away, gravel popping beneath the gum soles of his brown loafers. He stood motionless as he listened to the birds, a whole cacophony of them singing a hundred songs at once. Stevie's gaze fixed onto Mr. G.'s knobby fingers. They hung gnarled and lumpy at his sides. Old twigs.

"And have you seen something out there?" Mr. Greenwood asked.

Stevie opened his mouth, though he wasn't sure whether it was to confess or to question—had *Mr. Greenwood* been to that house? Had *he* seen something? Was that why he was asking, to compare stories? But before Stevie could form the words, his attention shifted to subtle movement just along the forest edge. That's what Mr. Greenwood was looking at. Suddenly, Stevie was sure that the shadow figure had followed him into town. He imagined the thing creeping out from behind the trees, leering like a lipless, sharp-toothed vampire, sinking its fangs into Mr. Greenwood's neck. All the while, Stevie would watch, frozen, gulping air, trying to yell.

Something moved around in the underbrush. Yes, he was positive. The brambly branches of a wild blackberry bush shuddered. His heart *thud-umped* and he took an instinctive backward step, opened and closed his mouth, ready to yell. *It's here. It's here! Run, run, RUN!* But before he could stammer out a single syllable of warning, he found himself staring at a rough-looking tabby cat rather than at some unspeakable monster—one that his mother would have insisted only existed in his mind.

It didn't take a genius to see that this cat—like all the rest—was sick. Its fur was patchy, having completely fallen out in certain spots, leaving it looking bare and mangy, like it had fought a thousand battles and had somehow won. It paused upon seeing both Stevie and Mr. G., then stepped out of the shade to approach the store. Stevie hadn't noticed them before, but there were two small bowls beside the back door—one for water, the other for food.

"You can't hold on to them around here, you know," Mr. Greenwood said. He was watching the tabby, too, though his expression seemed strained as the orange cat paused to rub against his khaki-covered leg. "You've probably never had a cat before, have you?"

"No," Stevie said. "But Dunk— Um, I mean Duncan, Dunk, Duncan Donut, my brother, he did once, he did, yeah."

"Oh?"

"He had a dog when he was little, I think, maybe. I guess my dad, my dad . . ." Stevie looked away from the old man, focused his attention on the cat that was now casually lapping water. Every so often, he'd slip up and mention his dad as though the man was back at home, still very much a part of Stevie's life. Every time it happened, he felt like an idiot. Now was no different. His chest got tight. His face flushed hot. He cleared his throat and tried to shrug off the sensation. "He got it at the doghouse place. The pound." He couldn't help knitting his eyebrows together, not sure how they had gone from talking about that spooky old house to pets, to his ghost of a father. "I—I—I don't think he had it for very long," he added. "Dunk, I mean. Doughnut. Had the dog. I think it ran away, which isn't that surprising, I guess." *Tell him. Confess.*

"And why's that?" Mr. Greenwood asked.

"Have you *met* my brother?" Stevie asked, and nearly jumped when a loud guffaw burst from Mr. G.'s throat. After the initial shock, Stevie couldn't help but smile as well. Mr. Greenwood wasn't half bad. He smelled kind of funny, and all those liver spots were pretty gross, but something about him made Stevie feel comfortable. Relaxed his brain. Helped his thoughts come out smoother, the way they were supposed to.

The old man continued to chuckle to himself as he watched the tabby finish up its water and meander back toward the trees. It paused only once to scratch behind its ear, and by the time it reached the tree line, Mr. Greenwood looked somber again.

"You see that?" he asked, motioning to the retreating animal. "She always goes back. I've tried to keep her. I bought her a little cat bed and one of those scratching posts, thinking maybe that would do the trick; got her into an old carrier I had lying around by putting a can of tuna fish in the back of it. Took her home. Thought a warm place to sleep and plenty of food would fix her up. I even picked up one of those feather-duster-looking doodads. You know, the kind you shake with the bells attached?

She seemed to like it for a while. She even sat on the couch with me when I watched TV once or twice."

Stevie shifted his weight from foot to foot. It was a nice story, he guessed, but he didn't see what it had to do with anything. Then again, Mr. Greenwood *was* old, probably older than Stevie thought. Perhaps Mr. G. was just lonely and needed someone to talk to. That, or there was that old-timers' disease.

But there was something to the way Mr. Greenwood was telling his story that suggested dementia wasn't at play—that, somehow, the stray cat had far more to do with Jude than Stevie knew.

"So," Stevie said, "you take your cat to work?"

Mr. Greenwood smiled at the thought. "I wish that were the case, Mr. Clark. No matter what I do, that little missus doesn't want to stay put. Every time I open the door or crack a window, she's off to the races. I find her back here the next day, prowling. I feed her. Water her. Sometimes I lure her back into the crate, take her home again. But no matter how much she likes the food I have in my kitchen or the catnip I have next to the couch, she always leaves me behind."

"That's sad." Stevie spoke the words before thinking them through. It was only after he said them that he realized they could have been construed as unsympathetic and rude. But it *was* sad. He pictured Mr. G. trying everything to make that cat love him, happily sitting on his couch with the tabby on his lap, no matter how scraggly it looked. And the next day: gone. Kind of like Stevie's dad. Or Jude.

"Yes, it's sad." Mr. Greenwood gave the woods a thoughtful

nod. "But it's probably what happened to your brother's dog, too. As a matter of fact . . ." He turned to face Stevie once again, looking as though he'd made up his mind about something that hadn't been previously decided. "I'd like you to ask him about it."

"Ask Dunk . . . about his dog?" Stevie blinked.

"Find out what happened, and then come tell me the story. I'd like to hear it."

"But, but, but—"

Mr. Greenwood held up his hand. "Get the story, and I'll tell you what I know. A trade is a trade." He began to shuffle toward the back door, his brown loafers kicking up gravel dust, but he paused in passing and caught Stevie by the shoulder. "Until then, you stay *out* of those woods, Mr. Clark. And you stay far away from that house. You understand?"

Stevie nodded as eagerly as a bobblehead figure on a dashboard, startled by Mr. Greenwood's sudden shift in demeanor. The old man pulled his twisted hand away and continued onward. It was only when he'd nearly reached the door that something clicked in Stevie's brain.

"But, sir . . . ?"

Mr. G. paused, turned to look back.

"W-what about Jude?" Stevie's tone was softer now.

The mention of Jude's name caused Mr. Greenwood's face to elongate with a deep sort of sorrow. He frowned. "I'm sorry about your friend, Mr. Clark," he said. No declaration that everything would be okay. Just an apology, which hung heavy with the promise that things would never be the same, no matter how hard Stevie wished them to be.

9

S TEVIE WAS EAGER to ask Dunk about his dog, but his brother still wasn't home. Stevie used his mom's cell to send a text, but of course Dunk didn't reply.

At dinner, Stevie sat at the kitchen table, picking at cheesy bread that had gone dry, staring at Duncan's empty seat. His mom tried to make conversation with Terry—*Did you have a good day? How was work?*—but The Tyrant wasn't much of a talker. Kind of like Dunk, who could have at least called for two seconds to see what was up. Maybe Terry was finally on a rampage, chasing Stevie through the house with a butcher's knife. It wasn't impossible to imagine. By the time Dunk came home, both Stevie and their mother could have been slaughtered by their psychotic stepdad. But Dunk never worried about stuff like that.

Stevie stayed up long past his bedtime, reading comic books and eating mini chocolate bars while waiting for his brother's headlights to slash across the side yard. The idea of not talking to him until tomorrow made Stevie nervous. He had to get back to Mr. G. first thing in the morning. But by eleven P.M., Stevie was starting to fade. He packed a cherry Laffy Taffy between his cheek and gum and chewed, fighting off drowsiness; grabbed a nearly empty can of soda and threw his head back, tossing the last warm dregs to the back of his throat. Nothing helped. His plan of waiting for Dunk to arrive was doomed to fail.

He slid off his bed and walked over to his desk, pulled open his drawer and searched for his field book, only to remember it was lost, probably soaked through with mud and dew, completely ruined even if he somehow managed to find it again. He grabbed a sheet of loose-leaf paper instead, uncapped a Crayola marker, and carefully printed his note:

> *Dunk,*
> *I tryd to wait up but am real tired so I went to sleep.*
> *Wake me up when u get home ok I need to ask u somthing.*
> *ITS IMPORTANT.*
> *Ur brother Stevie*
> *P.S. Dont forget*

Folding the letter into fourths, he wrote *DUNK* on the front flap in all-capital letters, then quietly opened his bedroom door. The house had settled down for the night, though he could hear the low tones of the TV playing in the living room. Terry was still up, and if he caught sight of Stevie sneaking around, hellfire would rain down. Rather than walking, he crawled across the hallway and slid the note beneath Dunk's door.

Back in his room, Stevie retook his post at his window, folded his arms across the sill, and rested his chin on his forearms. He watched, waited, hoped for something to happen. But what jolted him awake wasn't the grumble of Dunk's old engine. It was a familiar clamor: Terry's stacks of junk being jostled by someone who didn't know where to step.

Stevie tensed up. His pulse thudded against his tonsils, accompanied by a nauseating rush of sugar-spiked adrenaline. All of that soda flooded the wrinkles of his brain. He squinted, tried to see into the darkness that shrouded the side yard without having to open his window, without needing to stick out his neck and possibly getting decapitated by swiping claws. But if it was the monster, now was his chance. If his suspicions were correct, that thing would lead him straight to Jude.

Clamping his teeth against the irregular palpitations of his heart, he pressed the palms of his hands to his windowpane, ready to shove it open. But Aunt Mandy's front-porch light brought him pause. Motion-activated, the sensitivity on that thing was turned up way too high. All it took was a tree bending in the wind or one of those strays wandering across the lawn, and the entire yard went as bright as Wrigley Field. Yet there was no breeze tonight, no cat or wandering dog he could immediately pinpoint. But there *was* something.

An impossible something.

A figure standing on Aunt Mandy's porch. Not hunched. Not hiding. Not a monster.

"Jude . . ." The name whispered past Stevie's lips. He was dreaming. Imagining it. Because how could it be? "Jude!" It came out as a yell, so loud that he started at his own voice. He leapt off his bed, tore open his door, barreled down the hallway and into the now dark and empty living room. *"JUDE!"* There was sound behind his mom's bedroom door, likely her shoving away the sheets and tumbling out of bed. Stevie was too busy flying around the couch to look behind him, to check whether or not The Tyrant was in hot pursuit.

His palms hit the front door with a hard slap. He struggled with the lock, the stupid dead bolt suddenly not wanting to turn. He'd never had trouble with it before, but the damn thing was determined to stay locked. The universe was plotting against him, trapping him inside. Intent on making Jude vanish again, disappear within the few seconds it would take Stevie to get to his cousin's front door from his own.

"Jude!"

"Stevie?" The sound of his mom's bare feet moving fast across the scuffed-up hardwood. "Honey, what's wrong? What's happ—"

Her question was cut off by the sound of Stevie's panting half-screams. The bolt finally gave, turning in his sweaty hands. He whipped open the door, flew across the porch. Stray bits of gravel bit into the pads of his feet as he rushed down the walkway, but he ignored the pain, Jude's name tumbling out of his throat like a bout of Tourettes, terror riding along the fringes of that single syllable.

Because he wouldn't be there.

He wouldn't be there.

Gone again. Just a figment. His imagination, hellbent on doing him in.

Stevie could hardly breathe as he charged up Aunt Mandy's broken footpath; tripped over the first porch step, his hands hitting the planks of the patio beside a pair of unmoving, muddied

All-Stars. He craned his neck, looked up at the boy who was looming above him now, scrambled up the last few steps and, without saying anything at all, threw his arms around his best friend's neck.

He was screaming, jumping and screaming. His mother yelling joyous harmonies as she ran toward Aunt Mandy's house. And in their overwhelming excitement, neither one of them stopped to notice that Jude wasn't moving.

He just stood there, rigid, while they celebrated.

Like a corpse brought back from the dead.

10

Nicki Clark disappeared into her sister's house. There was yelling inside. Aunt Mandy started screaming before she ever made it out the front door. When her bare feet hit the porch, it was as if she'd stepped on burning coals. She stopped short, caught herself against the jamb of the door, and let out a gut-wrenching sob. Her reaction was so odd, so completely baffling, that her boy may as well have been lying in a pine box with a note pinned to the top. *Here's your dead son*, it would have said. *Since you miss him so much.*

Aunt Mandy fell to her knees, her hands frantically searching Jude for broken bones or missing limbs, for some horrible injury that surely must have existed.

Jude was dirty; wild-looking, as though he'd slept in some hollowed-out divot of earth or the vacant space in a rotten log. His face and arms were smeared with swaths of grime; a feral boy covered in all things forest. But other than the filth and a few rough-looking scrapes, he looked completely fine.

"Thank God." Aunt Mandy was crying so hard she could barely speak. "Where have you been?!" When Jude didn't answer, she shook him by the shoulders, but her effort was short-lived. *Sometimes*, Stevie remembered her saying, *good news just needs to be good news. Sometimes, asking questions only dulls the shine.*

Stevie's mom called the police. They showed up a few minutes later. A news crew accompanied them, hungry for a sound bite for their morning broadcast. This would bring in ratings. By the time they arrived, Aunt Mandy had stopped weeping. Terry had hovered on the front porch, but stayed back at the house while everyone else moved inside Aunt Mandy's living room—tidy and sweet with doilies strewn about. She had a penchant for peach, pink, and cream. Jude lived in a house that featured armchairs upholstered in floral prints. He sometimes ate grilled cheese sandwiches off mismatched gold-trimmed plates. Stevie would have been happy to exist in that odd, Anglophile world himself, having decided days after Uncle Scott's accident that a dead dad would have been better than being abandoned by his own.

"Jude?" One of the two visiting officers stepped to the couch where Jude was sitting with his mom. "Can we ask you a few questions?"

"Oh, *no*." Aunt Amanda was quick to cut in. "No, not tonight. He's so tired. He needs to sleep."

Jude did look exhausted. Maybe that's why he hadn't said a word to anyone since he'd returned. Or he could have said nothing because he didn't want to sound nuts. Stevie had been too overwhelmed by Jude's return to think about the creature that had leapt the fence, about the warnings Mr. Greenwood had given; but now, with the shock wearing off, the memory of that man-thing was back. It was impossible to think that Jude hadn't seen it, unfeasible that he hadn't encountered such a creature after being out there so long. But Jude just stared off into the distance, spaced out, only moving to scratch at one of his arms. It looked like there was a rash there. Probably poison oak.

"We understand he's tired," said the cop. "But we need some answers. This is a matter of public safety. If this was just a stunt—"

"A *stunt*?" Aunt Mandy gave the officer a disgusted look, appalled at the suggestion. "You mean like running away? Like the stories you've been feeding the press?"

"Jude?" The cop ignored Aunt Mandy's animus. His partner continued to hang back, scribbling notes on a legal pad attached to a metal clipboard. Stevie had thought about getting one of those—it was more professional than a spiral-bound notebook—but it looked clunky and cumbersome. Not nearly as convenient as sticking a notepad in the back pocket of your pants. "You want to tell us what happened?" the officer asked. "How did you get out there? Did someone take you? How did you get back home? Did they let you go?"

"This is insane," Aunt Mandy hissed, her attention now turned to her sister, imploring her for help.

"We really should let him sleep," Stevie's mom told the cops, offering them a placating smile. "I'm sure the department has a million questions for everyone, especially for Jude, but those can be delayed until tomorrow morning, can't they?"

"No." The lead officer, humorless, insistent. "The report has to be filled out now. We've put a lot of resources into looking for him. A lot of people gave up a lot of their time . . ."

Stevie wanted to snort at that. *Yeah, right.* But he held his tongue, only looking back and forth from the cops to Aunt Mandy to Jude to his mother. These guys didn't know the first thing about his mom. When she wasn't under the influence of The Tyrant, she had a knack for sweet-talking people and getting her way. Once, they'd gotten pulled over on the highway by a motorcycle cop, one who had looked like he meant business. But by the time the whole thing was over, his mom had the officer joking around. She got off with a warning, like it was some sort of weird Jedi mind trick.

"I'll be happy to help Amanda answer whatever questions you have for your report," Stevie's mom said, "but Jude is a minor. Unless he's being arrested, you can interview him tomorrow, after he's gotten some sleep."

The cops exchanged a look, with the lead officer finally sighing and issuing a relenting nod. Stevie considered speaking up, but his mom beat him to the punch. She placed a hand on Stevie's shoulder and gave him a pointed glance. "Get on home," she told him.

"B-but . . ."

"Now." Unflinching refusal. "You can talk tomorrow," his mom assured him. "Go home."

Home was the last place Stevie wanted to go. Terry was there, still up, waiting for Stevie's mom to come back and give him the scoop. Now it would just be Stevie scooting through the front door, and maybe that would make Terry mad. Except, no . . . the cops were right there. He wouldn't dare do anything. This time, Stevie would scream his head off if he had to.

"See you tomorrow, Jude," Stevie murmured.

Jude remained motionless, as though not hearing Stevie's farewell. Possibly not knowing that he was surrounded by people at all. He just kept scratching, his eyes fixed on some invisible point.

"I missed you." Stevie all but whispered the confession, the emotional warble that had crept into his tone leaving him feeling embarrassed in front of all of those adults.

Jude held fast to his silence, and Aunt Mandy gave Stevie a faint smile. She was trying to look happy, but to Stevie she looked half insane. "He's missed you, too, Stevie. He's just really tired."

He wanted to protest. Jude wasn't just tired. There was something wrong. He could have at least looked Stevie's way to let him know everything was cool, to tell him not to worry—a secret glance, a wink or a faint nod. *I saw it, too.* But there was none of that reassurance.

"Stevie." His mom. "Good night."

"I didn't give up on you, Jude," he said. "Didn't give up, I didn't . . ." Then he crossed the room and stepped out onto Aunt Mandy's front porch.

It was only as he climbed the steps up to his own front door that a pang of guilt hit him head-on. He wasn't sure why he'd said that—to make his cousin feel better, to remind him that they had once been and still were closer than any two kids could ever be? But those things weren't altogether true, because as he had carefully printed Duncan's name on the note he'd slipped beneath his big brother's door, an ugly, awful feeling had crawled into the recess of Stevie's heart. It had been a sense of surrender. Something about asking for help from someone who wanted nothing to do with him had felt like the beginning of the end.

Stepping inside, Stevie held his breath and tried not to cry. Because he actually *had* given up. And at the very moment of Stevie's concession, Jude had returned, almost as if to say, *You're just like everyone else. I knew you wouldn't care.*

· · ·

Stevie should have been exhausted the next morning, but rather than rolling over and groaning for five more minutes of sleep, he was ready to run next door more than an hour before his mom had a chance to tap on his door. His anxiousness was only slightly derailed when he spotted Dunk's Firebird parked along the curb. He narrowed his eyes at his brother's pride and joy as he sauntered toward the sidewalk, tailing his mom. Naturally, his note had been ignored.

He wanted to be pissed, but he couldn't bring himself to care about Dunk's typical discourtesy. And why should he have? Jude had come home, which rendered Dunk down to exactly what he was: useless.

"Sweetie . . ." Stevie's mom paused her steps before they reached Aunt Mandy's place. She looked serious; her eyes narrowed, her lips pressed into a tight line. "I know you're excited to talk to Jude, but you have to be a little careful around him, okay?"

"Careful?" he asked. "About what?"

"About what you ask him. Sometimes, when bad things happen, people don't like talking about it. You know that."

"But isn't it important to talk about bad things?" Stevie asked. "Sad things? Mad things? The cops are gonna ask him, they're gonna ask anyway, they're gonna ask, *Hey, Jude, we're gonna ask . . .*"

"Okay," his mom conceded. "But the cops are trained for this sort of thing. Right? Just like the guys on all your shows."

Stevie frowned, on the verge of posing a question destined to get him in trouble: Why wasn't Aunt Mandy demanding answers? It seemed to him that Jude should have been tied to a chair by now, lights shining into his eyes, being interrogated like how they did it in the movies. *You're gonna talk, see? You're gonna tell us everything, or you ain't gonna be walking on your own two feets anytime soon, see?* But Aunt Mandy had pulled a similar move when Uncle Scott died. Stevie remembered his dad muttering about how crazy it was. *She won't let us see the report?* How stupid it was of Aunt Mandy to not sue the hell out of the trucking company that had hit him. *He could have been over his daily eight. Hell, he could have been high. There's a whole culture of drug use with those guys, Nick. They're doped up. This could have been a DUI.* But nothing swayed Aunt Mandy's resolve. She didn't want to know. Stevie supposed that, for some people, it was easier to make things like that disappear. Having answers meant knowing what you could have done to prevent those awful things from happening. Stevie, though . . . he had decided days before that, for him, knowing wasn't a choice.

"Fine, whatever," Stevie huffed. "B-but I can talk to him, right? About things before he left, right?"

"Just don't push it," his mom said, then stepped past him to ascend the steps. He rolled his eyes at her back, then followed her to the front door. But as they waited for his aunt to answer the bell, Stevie decided that his mother had a point. The last thing he wanted was to freak Jude out. Stevie had missed his cousin like crazy, was eager to get back to the fort, but he knew that returning to the way things used to be would take a little time.

But that *thing* . . .

If it was real, it had to be dealt with . . . or avoided, at the very least.

11

E VERYONE WENT DOWN to the police station except for Dunk. He remained at home, sleeping. And while Stevie had been excited to visit a real-life police headquarters, nearly everything about the visit left him disappointed. For one, there was no jail—at least not that he could see—and the lobby was empty. No criminals in handcuffs. No crazy people blabbering on about The Man or how they'd been framed. And despite the cops questioning Terry and Stevie's mom, they made Stevie sit in the waiting room rather than inviting him along.

Twenty minutes later, after his mom and Terry were done giving their statements, the trio moved to leave the precinct behind. The plan was to hop across the street and have some breakfast while waiting for Aunt Mandy and Jude to be released. But before they could step outside the building, Stevie's mom hesitated. Her hand, which seemed to rest on his shoulder in perpetuity these days, gave him a backward pull. A lady reporter stood beyond the plate glass. Her cameraman was casually leaning against a news van. He looked bored, as if they'd been there for a half hour at least.

"Parasites," Stevie's mom glowered. "How did they know we were here?"

"Press conference." The voice came from a woman sitting behind the receptionist's counter. She looked a lot like Velma from *Scooby-Doo*, if Velma had been a hundred years old. "Detective Ridgewell is due to make a statement about the case this morning."

Stevie stared at Old Velma, then looked back at his mom in search of answers. "Jude is gonna be on TV?"

"I guess so." Stevie's mom didn't look too excited about that. She frowned at Velma as though the receptionist had called the reporters herself. "He's just a little boy," she said, then pivoted on the soles of her flats and stepped out of the building, head high and defiant.

. . .

The Gooseberry Diner was just across the street. Terry worked on a plate of eggs and sausage while Stevie's mom sipped at a cup of coffee. Stevie couldn't resist ordering a pile of French toast covered in gooey strawberries and whipped cream. By the time Jude came out of the station with his mom—nearly an hour later—he was stuffed to the gills and hating himself for eating so much, that sugary toast lead-heavy in his gut.

He watched through the windows as the news crews—of which there were now three—swarmed Aunt Mandy and Jude. Ravenous for a sound bite, they shoved their mics into Jude's face as if he were some famous movie star. And while Stevie couldn't hear them, he imagined their questions were echoes of his own burning inquiries. *Where have you been? What happened? Can you tell us about who kidnapped you? What about the monster? How did you get away?*

Jude stood motionless on the station steps, but he eventually leaned in to the bouquet of mics and said something. Aunt Amanda offered the news crews a tense smile and followed up Jude's statement with a few words of her own.

"W-what're they saying?" Stevie asked.

"No way to tell," Stevie's mom murmured against the rim of her mug. "But the whole state of Oregon will know by tonight."

• • •

With everyone packed into Stevie's mom's 4Runner, two news vans tailed them as they drove home. Stevie was forced onto his own porch by The Tyrant's hamlike fist while Aunt Mandy vetted questions next door. Stevie's mom stood a few paces away from her little sister so as to not appear on camera. Jude, like Stevie, had been made to go inside, surely to the newspeople's chagrin. When they all finally left, both Aunt Mandy and Stevie's mom disappeared inside, and Stevie retreated to his room, anxiously awaiting his mother's return so that he could take her place. But it took Nicole Clark more than an hour and a half to come back home, and by the time he managed to escape his house, he was greeted with an apologetic smile and a shake of the head.

"Sorry, Stevie," Aunt Mandy said. "Jude's taking a nap."

A *nap?* Stevie stared at his aunt for a long while, convinced that she was pulling his leg. And yet, her smile didn't crack into laughter. She was serious. All of that waiting, all of that *need*, and Stevie wasn't going to get to see Jude after all.

"Since when does Jude take crappy naps like a sap?" he asked.

"He's really tired." Aunt Mandy was being patient, but there was tension at the corners of her mouth.

"Like a crappy sap. It's a trap!" Admiral Ackbar's famous line came spilling out of him—not supereffective, since Aunt Mandy had heard the boys use it on each other at least a million times.

"I don't think he wants to see anyone right now anyway, honey," she said. "He's not feeling very well. Jude missed you just as much as you missed him, sweetheart. But he needs a little time. It's nothing personal."

My ass, he wanted to say. Nothing personal? There couldn't have been anything in the world more personal. How could Jude choose a nap over seeing him?

"I'm sure as soon as he feels up to it, you'll be the first person he talks to."

No. Stevie shook his head, refusing to believe it. No, Jude wouldn't do this to him. Jude *knew* how much Stevie had worried. They had a gazillion things to discuss. But rather than pushing past his aunt, he just stood there, feeling angry and hurt and stupid—not like the last kid to be picked for kickball, but like the one who didn't get picked by his best friend. Utter humiliation.

"I'll tell him to go over to see you as soon as he's up to it, okay?"

But why isn't he up to it now, brown cow? he wanted to ask.

He's had all night to sleep. Is he sick? Was it a trick? But all Stevie managed was a defeated "Y-yeah, okay."

And then he shuffled home.

.   .   .

Jude never came over.

Stevie found himself sitting on the couch next to his mom while The Tyrant occupied his armchair, the three of them waiting for the local news. When the broadcast finally blinked onto the screen, there was Jude's face. A reporter's voice-over explained that *Tonight, the missing boy from Deer Valley has been found, safe and sound. That story and much more, coming up next.* The show segued into a Ford truck commercial—Terry's pickup, shiny and new, pulling a giant horse trailer behind it. Stevie glanced away from the muscled farmer enjoying his super-manly set of wheels and looked at his mom.

"What's it called when they turn bad guys into zombies?" he asked. "Y-you know, when they scramble their brains like eggs and bacon for breakfast?"

Stevie's mom gave him a look he knew all too well—a disturbed expression that was feigning amusement rather than the unease he was sure she so often felt.

"Bad guys?" she asked. "What kind of bad guys?"

"Like the bad ones they put in prison jail because they're bad and do things that are bad because they're bad because they do bad things because they're bad and do ba—"

"You mean *criminals*?" Terry cut in, clearly annoyed by his stepkid's inability to rein himself in.

"Yeah," Stevie said. "Criminals."

"A lobotomy?" Stevie's mom seemed unsure, despite knowing the answer.

He frowned at the word. That was it: a lobotomy. Maybe that's what had happened to Jude. Whoever had taken him had messed him up, stirred up his brains with a screwdriver through the eye, and now he'd rather sleep than hang out. What other explanation was there?

"Don't they do it with electricity?" Stevie asked. His mom shifted her weight beside him, clearly uncomfortable with the conversation. "They hook something up to your head and flip a switch, right? Kinda like the electric chair, except it doesn't kill you? It just, like, fries your brain like fries with a shake? Shake and bake?"

"Watch your words," Stevie's mom said, calm as ever, ignoring his line of inquiry. She got up and left for the kitchen without so much as an *I'll be right back*, and Stevie found himself turning his attention to the last person he'd ever expect to get an answer from. Terry Marks wasn't someone Stevie wanted to converse with, but he was a cruel son of a bitch. If anyone knew about fiendish ways to mess up a person, this was the guy.

"You're talking about electroshock therapy," Terry mumbled, as if bored with the discussion. "They don't do that anymore. Lobotomies, either."

"What do you mean?" Stevie asked. "They do it in hospitals, to crazy people. I've seen it on TV."

Terry grunted, offended by his stepson's ineptitude. "Crazy?" he scoffed. "Crazy is as crazy does, huh? I just *told you*, they don't, didn't I? That stuff is inhumane, outdated. Don't believe everything you see on the fucking tube."

Inhumane. Stevie almost laughed, but he knew to hold it in. He didn't feel like experiencing The Tyrant's own brand of inhumanity that night. Rather, he pressed his lips into a tight line and turned his attention back to the television. The truck was gone. There was a warehouse full of mattresses now; probably the same kind that Jude was lying on next door. A bulldog sat on one, like the fat and slobbery king of springs and memory foam. *Rosco says our mattresses are great; no bull!*

His mom was banging around in the kitchen. There was the soft sucking sound of the freezer being opened, the metallic ting of silverware against the counter, the clap of cabinet doors slamming shut because they were missing their felt bumpers. Stevie kept quiet through a fifteen-second Budweiser ad, wondering if he'd ever be like one of those guys—laughing and having a good time with a bunch of girls; partying on a beach next to a bonfire. Nah. At least not if he and Jude stuck together. Jude wasn't the type to party on beaches. If things kept going the way they were, he'd be the guy robbing those people's cars while they got drunk; and the fact that Stevie even considered something like that bothered the hell out of him. Because wasn't that what everyone else thought, too? Wasn't that why Deer Valley had only pretended to be interested in finding Jude instead of actually looking for him?

Stevie's mom returned to the living room just as the news logo reappeared. She was carrying mugs of Rocky Road ice cream, handing one of them off to Terry before retaking her seat. She was trying to make things better, but eating ice cream while watching Jude on the news felt indecent. Sure, it could have been seen as celebrating Jude's return, but a party seemed a little premature.

Stevie had eaten hardly more than three spoonfuls of his dessert before Jude's face flashed on the screen. There was the blond reporter lady he'd seen outside the police station, looking both serious and concerned. She yammered on about the details of Jude's case as she faced the camera head-on, retelling the story of how Jude had been missing only to appear out of nowhere on his front porch in the middle of the night. *Yeah, yeah, yeah.* Stevie knew all that stuff.

Finally, the story cut to Jude and Aunt Mandy stepping out of the police station. Jude looked dazed, like the cops had bonked him on the head with a frying pan. Aunt Mandy was all smiles in her polka-dot dress. Stevie could tell she was eager to soothe Deer Valley's frayed nerves. *Everything is fine now, thank you all for your concern.*

"How does it feel to finally be home?" the reporter asked.

Jude squinted at the camera, as if never having seen one before. He seemed to sway as he stood there. It was slight, but definitely there, as though he'd spent those lost days on the deck of a ship. Aunt Mandy could have been right; perhaps Jude was out of it because he was just *that* tired. But there was something about Jude's eyes, about the blankness of his face, that turned Stevie's stomach inside out.

"Can you tell us anything about what happened?" The reporter tried again, hoping that, if she put her words in the right order, her question would break Jude's silence. "Do you know who took you, where you were?"

She hit something—a nerve, a quick flash of memory. Something in Jude's face seemed to shift, as if a particular thought was finally squirreling its way out of his brain and into the muscles of his face. His mouth tensed. His eyebrows knit together. He scratched at his arm. Leaned into the microphone. And, with lowered eyes, said, "I don't remember."

Suddenly, Stevie could no longer feel the cold of his ice cream biting at his palms, making the missing tips of his fingers ache like ghosts. He gripped the mug tight as Aunt Amanda jumped in with a pensive smile.

"We just thank God that he's home," she said, saying *we* as though Jude's dad was celebrating in his casket, tossing confetti and whooping in victory while lying six feet beneath the ground. "We prayed, and our prayers were answered. We're just so happy Jude is home."

And Jude? He just kept staring into the camera with that dark, bottomless look.

Stevie couldn't watch anymore.

He shoved himself off the couch, all but dropping his cup of Rocky Road onto the coffee table as he ran for the hall.

"Stevie?" His mom, alarmed, but there was no time to respond.

He flew into the bathroom and crashed to his knees not a second before his dinner splashed orange and chunky against the toilet bowl. The bleach scent of bowl cleaner made him heave again. Bits of chewed-up lasagna bobbed up to the surface like tiny rafts in an ocean of puke. He sensed his mom appear behind him, hovering just inside the bathroom door.

"Oh, honey . . ." She crouched next to him, pushed his hair away from his forehead. "I'm sorry."

Another cramp seized his insides. He heaved again. The foamy contents of his stomach burned as it came up and out of his throat, but he was too distracted to care.

That wasn't Jude on the TV. It *looked* like him, but it wasn't his cousin at all. That blank stare—he'd seen it in the past. Blank, like just before Jude had threatened to push Stevie out of the fort, when he had held that piece of rusty metal to Stevie's throat. And there was Stevie's mom, apologizing, like she knew it was over. Stevie and Jude. Their friendship. The way things used to be, as though she knew Jude was different, too. Mr. G. had said the same thing. As though both of them were certain that it would never be the same; that the only good thing in Stevie's life had come to a cruel and sudden end.

Sorry about your friend.

PART TWO

PART TWO

12

————

ROSAMUND ALEKSANDER HAD always wanted a child, and yet it seemed that her wish was constantly denied. She had tried everything, from old wives' tales to homeopathic remedies. She prayed, confident that as long as she had faith, a little miracle would eventually make her whole. But it was hard to stay hopeful year after barren year; difficult to be optimistic when, after so many failures, even her husband, Ansel, seemed to have lost interest in the idea.

"Perhaps," he said, "we aren't meant to have children. What if it's supposed to be just you and me?"

Rosie wasn't willing to accept that. After all, Ansel spent most of his time at his office in Deer Valley. As the town physician, he was well liked, had plenty of opportunities to have a drink at the local bar, and turned down many an invitation to join families for dinner after helping a child beat strep throat or the flu. Ansel Aleksander was a face everyone knew, and a man like that had no lack of attention. He wasn't as desperate as Rosie was, and she doubted he could ever truly understand her need.

Unlike her husband, Rosie wasn't comfortable around strangers. She'd grown up shy and hated looking people in the eye. She refused to smile with her teeth, her father having recklessly teased her while growing up. *Gully mouth* had been a frequent insult. *Gap tooth* had made it in there once or twice as well. Rosie's mother would occasionally dress her up, sometimes in pretty store-bought skirts and blouses, other times in crafty homemade clothes. Meanwhile, Rosie's father would make his offhanded comments; had it not been for the asymmetry of his daughter's face, the girl wouldn't have looked half bad. *All that's missing is the paper bag.*

Rosie's mother assured her that her dad didn't mean it. *He loves you,* she'd say. *He means well.* But his thoughtless cruelty had crawled beneath Rosie's skin.

Ansel was nothing like Rosamund's father. He was kind, as humorous as he was peculiar with his shock of white-blond hair and a nose far too big for his face, and his broken English only added to his charm. Rosie had met him in the produce section of an Everett, Washington, grocery store. When a pyramid of oranges had collapsed around her feet, she'd been mortified, nearly having run out of the place without purchasing a single item on her mother's shopping list. It was Ansel who saved the day, grabbing three oranges off the ground and throwing them above his head, juggling as expertly as a runaway circus clown, diverting attention so that Rosie could compose herself, and so that *he* could catch her eye.

On their first date, which fell on Rosie's twenty-second birthday, he called her *älskling*, and tried to teach her a few phrases in Swedish. Rosie never did pick up the language—she found it horrendously difficult, regardless of how much Ansel spoke to her in his native tongue—but Ansel was nearly fluent in both English and romance. Rosie's parents considered the eleven-year age difference scandalous, but for once, Rosie couldn't have cared less. She was in love, and the two were married less than six months after they met. A week before their second anniversary, Ansel was hired on as a physician in Deer Valley, Oregon, and Rosie couldn't wait to get away. It was a promise of a fresh start, of life away from the hurtfulness she had come to know.

And yet, despite Ansel's love, Rosamund couldn't quite shake her lack of self-assurance. Her excitement over Deer Valley dwindled fast. She found herself uncomfortable in town, sure that people were staring at her when she walked down the street or gardened in the front yard, because her father had been right. She was ugly. An eyesore. A strange girl in a new town without a friend in the world.

Ansel's work hours grew longer, and so did Rosie's aversion to social interaction. She found herself contemplating which of the two was worse, the cruelty of her father or the loneliness she now felt. Ansel tried to make it right. He'd drag her into town for dinner each weekend and introduce her to the folks he knew. But it only made Rosie pull further into herself. That was when he made an executive decision: he and his wife would move three miles north, into the woods, where Rosie would feel more at ease; where she could push aside the haunting torment of her father's callousness and get some relief.

The land was cheap. The plot was situated alongside a busy logging road, but at least access to and from town was an easy drive. It took nearly a year for *Hus Aleksander* to be built, but when they finally moved in, Rosie was smitten by their new lifestyle. It was a little noisy by day, but after the trucks stopped running, the evening was a fairy tale. She adored how green it was outside each window, and loved sitting on her covered porch to watch the sunset, or to read and sew out there when it rained. She spent most of her time cooking and baking and gardening, and by their first summer, Rosie had a vegetable patch large enough to keep her out of the produce section for good. Which was convenient, because Ansel was busy with work and she refused to shop alone.

Less than a year later, the loneliness started to creep back into her bones, the isolation growing heavy. There was Sasha, a gorgeous gray and black California spangled cat that Ansel had given her as a birthday gift, but the cat did little in the way of company. While Sasha wandered the woods, Rosie floated from room to room, unsure of what to do with herself. She read book after book, but they left her feeling empty rather than inspired. She tried to write one herself—a love story about an ugly duckling and a charming prince—but decided that she didn't have the patience, let alone the talent. The idea of a baby bloomed within her as naturally as wildflowers along the base of a white picket fence. And then the desire spread, as invasive as a weed.

She couldn't wait to have a little Ansel to dote over while the baby's daddy was busy healing the sick, and Ansel wanted nothing more than for her to be happy. And so, after lots of trying, a few visits to a fertility specialist on Ansel's request—*Everything's in working order, as far as I can tell*—and lots of prayer, Rosie became pregnant. It took three years.

Rosie was over the moon. She danced through the rooms of the house while Ansel was away, sang herself through the days until he came back, took all-day walks in the forest and collected massive wildflower bouquets that she'd place in drinking glasses and mason jars. Every room burst with color, especially the one she had decided to turn into the baby's nursery. She painted the walls blue, small robins stenciled here and there in frothy white. Little Ansel would grow up a lover of nature like his momma, and just as intelligent as his dad.

And then, without rhyme or reason, everything changed.

While taking a walk along her usual route, and a trimester into her pregnancy, she doubled over in pain and screamed as white-hot agony speared her through the middle, her beloved solitude suddenly her worst enemy. She found herself on her hands and knees in the dirt and scrub, a freshly plucked bouquet spilled before her. She wept, screamed for Ansel despite his being miles away, eventually managed to stumble back home despite the pain. But by the time she arrived, the insides of her legs were smeared with blood. The baby, which Rosie gave birth to alone and in an empty tub, was stillborn. Hours later, Ansel discovered it against once-white porcelain. He found his wife in the closet, naked and weeping in the dark.

She was inconsolable.

As soon as Rosie was back on her feet, she raged through the rooms she had danced in just months before. Plucking up every bouquet she had so carefully arranged, she threw them against the walls—vases and all. Water-filled vessels exploded like bombs. Floors were left riddled with wilting stems and broken glass. Bloody footprints dotted the hardwood like mangled hopes. Ansel tried to comfort her, but when nothing worked, he threatened her with hospitalization, because she was hysterical, unable to calm down. He was worried that her pain was beyond grief, sure that it was closer to madness than anything resembling sorrow. Frightened and betrayed by Ansel's threat, Rosie's all-consuming mourning pushed her out of the house and away from her husband, away from Deer Valley and the forest she had come to love.

She snatched his keys off the foyer table, climbed into his car, and drove away.

Highway 101 unspooled southward before her. She didn't know where she was going, only that she was leaving behind the life that had forsaken her—a life that she had never truly deserved. She slept in the car and ate whatever sad sandwiches or stale pastries she could find at gas station convenience stores while listening to the Elton John CD she found in the glove compartment. She spent most of her time staring out toward the horizon of an endless ocean, hating herself when she couldn't muster the courage to do what she wanted to do. End the pain. End it all.

She got as far as Big Sur before the guilt of abandoning Ansel turned her inside out. They had only one car. Undoubtedly, Ansel was walking to work, sick with worry as to where Rosie could have gone. She had to go back.

She spotted a ramshackle sign reading HAPPY HOPE RETREAT and pulled off the winding highway to make a U-turn. Her maneuver sent her bouncing down a narrow, rutted road. There was a fruit stand along the path that led to the place, but it was empty and unmanned. A quarter of a mile later, she found herself rolling up to a stunning farmhouse. A rusty red pickup was parked along the side of the place. Its round headlights watched her as she pulled up to the sunny house, fully intending to do a three-point turn and go back from where she'd come. But she found herself stopping instead, drawn toward the house by some inexplicable pull. There was something about this place that felt right, as though her impromptu trip was for the sole reason for ending up in the very spot she found herself now. She pulled the emergency brake and slid out of her seat—just a few minutes for a break, and then she'd get back on the road.

She looked up at the windows of the well-kept farmhouse revival, its stark-white exterior blazing in the sun like a beacon, like its namesake: Happy Hope. It was beautiful, but it also reminded her of her own home, of Ansel. Before she had time to climb back into her vehicle, the farmhouse's front door swung open and an older gentleman stepped onto the low-pitched porch. He was stout, bearded, and held up a hand in greeting. Rosie mimicked his motion, using the other to shield her eyes from the sun.

"Come on up," he said. "Have a sit." No question of what she was doing there or how he could help her, just an invitation to join him in the cool afternoon shade. Rosie hesitated, but eventually left Ansel's Maxima behind. The man was plump, his skin having taken on a brown patina from spending too many days on a Harley—at least Rosie *assumed* that was his past, judging from the Grateful Dead T-shirt he'd paired with some threadbare jeans. Those baggy pants were rolled up above his ankles, leaving his bare feet to bask in the breeze coming off the Pacific. His bushy eyebrows matched the hair atop his head and hanging from his chin, which was so gray it looked silver in the shade.

"I'm so sorry," Rosie said. "I just . . . I pulled off the highway so I could turn around." She gave him a smile, then immediately looked away. She could sense him studying the contours of her face, more than likely thinking how peculiar she looked with those too-big eyes and that trench between her teeth.

"A change of heart?" he asked. "Those are the only type that come up here, I suppose. It's the sign that reels 'em in."

She nodded lightly, then glanced over her shoulder at Ansel's sedan. It wasn't the fanciest car. Most certainly not representative of what her husband could have afforded. But Ansel had always been both modest and thrifty. His only extravagant expense beyond *Hus Aleksander* had been a beautiful orange-colored Persian rug he'd bought her as a housewarming gift; and what had Rosie done to thank him for his devotion? Stolen his car and left him. Another punch of guilt.

"So, young lady, are you looking for some happiness, or have you come here seeking hope?"

Rosie looked back to the man, blinking at the rainbow-colored bears that danced across his shirt. The Deadhead had taken a seat in a high-back rocking chair, and the juxtaposition of that T-shirt with the quaint country charm of the house struck her as both funny and odd. He looked like a cross-country drifter, a guy who rode a motorcycle thousands of miles just to feel the wind blow through his now-snowy hair; a man who would be just as comfortable playing Santa Claus in the town Christmas parade as he would be knocking in someone's teeth at a local bar. An angel with a devil on his shoulder . . . or perhaps the other way around.

The man didn't seem to be bothered by her long stare. The corners of his eyes crinkled like parchment as he stared right back, slowly rocking in his chair like the pendulum of a metronome, waiting for a reply.

"I don't think hope is in season," Rosie finally answered. "The stand along the road looked fresh out."

The Deadhead gave her a chuckle. "Clever," he said. "I like you. What's your name?"

"Rosie."

"Are you a Roseanne or a Rosemary?" he asked.

"A Rosamund."

The guy quirked an eyebrow skyward. "Rosamund," he said. "You don't hear that one everyday. Nice and classic."

Rosie gave him a little nod, then self-consciously diverted her gaze.

"Well, it's nice to meet you, Rosie. The name's Nick. I run this old joint." He motioned with his hand to the house behind him. "But everyone calls me Ras."

"Ras?" She looked in his direction.

"As in Rasputin, on account of the beard." He gave his bristles a stroke and offered Rosie a wink. His eyes were bluer than any she'd ever seen.

"Well, your home is beautiful." She gave him a faint smile. "The sign said it's a retreat?"

"Just a place between a start and end point," Ras said. "I like to make it sound fancy, but it's just me, myself, and I out here. Sometimes a guest or two, unless it's June."

"What happens in June?"

"Closed," he said.

"All month?"

"Yes, ma'am. Most of it, at least." Ras flashed his teeth. They were surprisingly white. Straight as soldiers during morning count. "I summer in Redding, partake of the debauchery that they call the Redwood Run. Heard of it?"

She hadn't.

"Bike rally," Ras said. "Best in the country, if you ask me. Just me and a couple thousand of my closest pals."

Rosie gave herself a mental pat on the back. She was right—he *was* a biker, maybe an outlaw. Perhaps this place wasn't a retreat as much as it was a hideout. She cast another glance at the house, giving a couple of the windows a longer look.

"So, this place is like a bed-and-breakfast?" she asked, somehow doubtful that a guy like Ras could run a hotel on his own, no matter how small.

"Yeah, without the breakfast." Ras barked out a laugh, as though it was the best joke he'd told in a while. "I've had folks stay here for a night, and folks stay here for a month. Some people are on their way after a good night's rest, others choose to stay until they find what they're looking for."

"And what are they looking for?" Rosie canted her head, curious.

"Happiness and hope, mostly," Ras said matter-of-factly. "Just what it says I'm selling on the sign out front. I don't do false advertising, little miss. I'm not much for lawyering up." He winked.

"If it only were that easy," Rosie murmured to herself. If she could follow a couple of signs and end up with what she wanted, she would have led a gilded life.

"And how do you know it isn't?" Ras asked. Rosie looked back at him. He was no longer smiling. Rather, he wore a deadly serious expression—a man asking a question about God's honest truth.

She opened her mouth to reply, but she found herself stammering, debating whether telling a stranger about her problems was in her best interest. Despite his profession, Ansel was a fiercely private man. They had always kept to themselves—only she and him out in the forest, their secrets safely tucked away between them both. But there was something about Ras that was urging her to spill it, to confess why she'd driven so far west for so long just to turn around and head back home. She pursed her lips, looked back at Ansel's car. Ras continued to wait with unnerving patience for her reply.

"Well," she eventually said, "I assume you don't adopt out children, so . . ." Her words faded in volume. She swallowed, and forced a pained smile at the planks at her feet, feeling as though she'd revealed too much far too soon.

"I'm sorry," she said, suddenly overwhelmed by the urge to escape the situation. Ras's eyes were roving. She could feel him sizing her up, picking her apart, figuring her out. "I'm taking up your time. I should go." She clenched Ansel's keys in her right hand and made to turn away, but the old biker stopped her short.

"Well, what would *you* do?" he asked.

"Sorry?" Rosie gave Ras a sideways glance. She was feigning confusion, but she had an idea of what he meant.

"To make your hopes and dreams come true," he clarified—exactly what Rosie had thought he'd been getting at. "What would you give up to get what you want?"

She watched him for a long while, thrown off balance by the directness of his inquiry. It was a question she'd contemplated so many times, vacillating between giving up everything and nothing at all. Back when there was still hope, it hadn't felt as though sacrifice was necessary. Patience would remedy the situation, and in a way, it had. She'd waited for years and finally been given what she wanted, but it had been torn away. Hope, born dead in a bathtub. White porcelain left soiled with swaths of blood. And why? Had she angered God somehow? Had she done something so terrible in a past life that she was now the butt of some evenhanded joke?

No, that couldn't be. Rosie had grown up a good girl; she'd always been a pious woman. She had done her time in church pews and had prayed every night. At least, she had until her baby had been snatched away.

"Anything." The word passed over her lips, three syllables riding upon a shallow breath. *Anything.* Because without a child, Rosie wasn't sure she mattered. She wanted to be bigger than herself, wanted to give meaning to someone's life beyond her own.

"Why don't you stay for dinner?" Ras offered.

The invitation snapped Rosie out of her stupor. "Oh, no," she said. "No, really, I don't want to impose. I should be getting back." She had a good six hundred miles to drive. It had taken her nearly two days to get to the Happy Hope Retreat. She was sure, however, that if she hurried, she could be back in Deer Valley by morning. She'd arrive in time to make Ansel his breakfast—an apology for vanishing off the face of the earth.

"Well, sorry, Rosie, but you're on my turf now," Ras said. "It's going to be dark in a few hours, anyhow, and it's dangerous out there on the one-oh-one. You'll stay here, get some sleep, and be on your way first thing."

Sleeping in the car—even if it was for a few hours—wasn't the most appealing thought. Last night had left Rosie's back aching. Just thinking about another evening behind the wheel made her spine creak with a throbbing pain. And she *was* tired. Getting down here had been one thing; she'd been fueled by grief and anger and bitterness. How dare Ansel threaten her with hospitalization? As though she were some . . . some *lunatic*. Of *course* she was upset. Her baby was gone.

But those resentful, hateful thoughts had melted with every mile that rolled onto the odometer, and now, knowing that she had to explain why she'd left, would only make the journey that much more exhausting. A night at the Happy Hope sounded good, just what she needed to get her head on straight. Ras, though . . . While he seemed nice, he didn't particularly strike her as on the level. What if some of his biker buddies showed up? What if she found herself in a situation she couldn't handle? Strange people lurked on the upper West Coast. Like Ted Bundy. Or the Green River Killer. The police had yet to catch that one, and for all anyone knew, Ras may have been the culprit, keeping a low profile while living in Big Sur.

"I don't have any money," she explained, sure her lack of funds would be enough to have Ras waving a dismissive hand her way. She'd left home in a hurry, only had the cash that had already been stuffed into her wallet—she needed that for gas if she was going to get back, and it may not even be enough to fill the tank. Credit cards had never been Rosie's thing. She had a MasterCard in her name, but it was something she used only in emergencies. It was safely tucked away in the kitchen junk drawer. Useless to her now.

"Then you can help with dinner," Ras said. "We'll call it even."

Rosie's stomach flipped. He wasn't going to let her leave.

"Okay," she eventually agreed, nervous, but unable to shake the irony of it. Here she was, fearing for her life when, having climbed into Ansel's car days before, her only reason for driving to California had been to end up dead. "Okay," she repeated, giving Ras a smile. Because, just standing there, she *did* feel a little better. Perhaps hope wasn't out of season after all.

13

THE HAPPY HOPE RETREAT left Rosie feeling rested and optimistic. Ras had offered her a warm bed and a home-cooked meal, and while it seemed impossible that such simple kindness could do much for her resolve, it had somehow been enough to invigorate her faith in the future.

There was the nightmare, however; the way she had awoken in the dark, pinned to the mattress, hardly able to breathe, suffocated by her own misgivings. She hadn't been able to move her arms, her wrists immobilized by invisible weights. Sleep paralysis brought on by stress and anxiety, no doubt. Too much guilt. It would all be better soon.

Despite the nighttime incident, she awoke unusually refreshed, sure there was magic in that blazing white farmhouse; a revitalizing energy that had wormed its way into the very marrow of her bones. The idea of facing Ansel after what she'd done felt less daunting than it had yesterday. He'd still be upset, of course, and that fact alone had her searching the house for her now-absent host. Perhaps Ras could offer just a little bit more comfort before she hit the road, but she couldn't find him. He was probably out riding his motorcycle, or tending to the land in his rusty red truck. Regardless, she was confident she'd be able to handle Ansel on her own, sure she'd instill in him the same sense of sunniness that Ras's old place had ingrained in her. Onward and upward. For better or for worse. Happiness and hope. Everything would turn out fine.

. . .

When Ansel got home from work that evening, the house was neat as a pin. Rosie—having arrived hours earlier—set to making dinner and cleaning the mess she'd left. She heard the front door open and close from across the house, but Ansel didn't immediately appear in the kitchen's threshold. It took him more than a minute to show himself in the doorway. When he finally did, he was pale, as if he were seeing a ghost.

"Rosie?" He stared at her, as though trying to clear his vision. But he didn't yell. And he didn't begrudge her.

Over dinner, she told him about her trip—one that had begun as a desperate escape and ended with a newfound sense of understanding. He held her hand and gazed at his plate, not once bringing up the hurt he surely felt. When Rosie's story was done, he offered her a small smile. Nothing more, nothing less. Rosie looked away from him, still feeling terrible about the past few days. She thought about begging his forgiveness, but couldn't bring herself to swallow that much pride. They went to bed without a word.

And then there was the sadness. Neither had time enough to recover from the sudden loss of their unborn child, but Rosie vowed to limit her tears to the upstairs bathroom. If she needed to cry, she did it while soaking in the tub in which her baby had died. Whether or not Ansel wept for their child, Rosie didn't know. And because she couldn't soothe his pain any more than he could take away her own, they didn't talk about it. It was too raw. *Be happy, have hope,* she told herself. It would all work out as long as she remained cheerful—at least when Ansel was looking her way.

But Rosie's idealism was only able to stanch reality for so long. When Ansel failed to come home from work on time, she assumed he'd gotten stuck with an emergency patient; a case of whooping cough or a broken bone. One hour turned into two, and she began to worry. Ansel's dinner dried out in the oven as she paced the house like a sentry on patrol. She tried calling the office, but the line was already being forwarded to his messaging service. She paged him, but he had yet to respond. That was definitely unusual, seeing as how that beeper was fastened to his hip as securely as if it had been a pacemaker buried deep inside his chest.

At the three-hour mark, she was convinced this was his way of getting back at her for what she'd done. This time, it would be Ansel who would go missing for days without a word. Or maybe he was in town, drinking at the bar. With Rosie's disappearance, her fiercely private husband could have bent to the will of his emotions and mentioned it to a friend; said something without realizing he'd done so. And if he had? It meant all of Deer Valley knew about how she'd abandoned him. It meant they were whispering. *It's a wonder she's been able to keep a husband with a face like that. Poor dear can't even make a baby. Not fit to be more than an old maid.*

Four hours overdue now. Rosie envisioned calling the police. But while she vacillated on whether or not to report her husband as a possible missing person, her decision was made easy by the carnival whir of blue and red lights outside. She spun away from the phone that sat beside the couch—olive green to match the drapes—and watched a police cruiser pull up to her white picket fence. Two uniformed officers exited the car and stalked up her walkway.

Her first instinct was to hide, pretend she wasn't home. Hearing the police thump on her door, Rosie couldn't help but hope that, if she ignored them, bad news wouldn't exist. Schrödinger's cat was, after all, one of Ansel's favorite theories. *If patients don't want to hear the truth,* he'd once joked, *they shouldn't listen.*

And quantum theory wasn't the only thing keeping Rosie from rushing toward the door. She didn't want the officers to see her face twist up with ugly fear. She knew it was crazy to be self-conscious right then. Ansel was missing, and here she was, worried two strangers would find her impossible to look at. Had she really gotten this bad?

She forced herself to move toward the entryway. Sasha the cat appeared beside Rosie's feet, materializing from wherever he'd been napping to lend emotional support as she pulled open the door with a trembling hand. His pathos was, however, short-lived. He rubbed past his owner's leg and made a casual exit. Bad news wasn't in the cards for him this evening. He had better things to do.

Rosie watched Sasha slink away into the darkness before looking up at the police. They were both staring at her with twin expressions of pensive austerity.

"Missus Aleksander?" The officer's name tag read BATTEN. "Rosamund Aleksander?"

She only nodded, doubting she could speak even if she tried.

"There's been an accident." She clung to the doorjamb, her fingers gripping it tight enough to make her palm ache. "Ma'am, your husband . . ." Officer Batten hesitated, but the policeman behind him quickly stepped in to pick up the slack. This one's name tag read TRELAWNY.

"You understand that you live along a logging road. With the trucks coming and going, it's not meant for regular traffic . . ."

Rosie swallowed. Yes, those trucks. They screamed down the road so many times per day that she'd learned to block out the noise. It's how Ansel had gotten the land so cheap, buying it off a man selling his acreage to logging companies. He'd given Ansel a more than fair price for a small plot just big enough for a house. The owner had planned on building his own place in this very spot but had changed his mind, and at first Rosie couldn't fathom why someone would decide against building their forever home in such a gorgeous spot. But that had been a Sunday, and on weekends, those trucks didn't run.

"Missus Aleksander, maybe it would be better if you came with us," Trelawny suggested.

"Oh my God." Realization. "Is he hurt? Did he get an airlift?" If Ansel needed serious medical attention, they'd helicopter him in to Portland. And how was she supposed to get there without a car? Even if she *did* get there, how would she navigate a city so big? Who would feed Sasha while she was away? And what about Ansel's patients, his practice? What about her garden? Her tomatoes were just starting to come in.

"Missus Aleksander . . ." The officers were being patient. Ansel had more than likely treated them or their families in the past. Their fondness for Ansel was surely the only reason they weren't shaking her by the shoulders—a childless, wretched waif with zero social graces, unable to follow a simple conversation.

"I don't have a car," she explained. "What about the cat? He's in Portland, right? I don't know how to find him. I don't even know where to *start*."

"No, ma'am . . . he's not in Portland." Batten this time. Rosie gave him a blink. "But, I'm sorry . . ."

"I'll need a ride," she told them. If he wasn't in Portland, he was more than likely in McMinnville, thirty miles away. Leaving the house was the last thing she wanted to do, but there was no choice. They'd have to take her to wherever Ansel was, drop her off at the correct hospital.

"A ride, ma'am?"

"To the city," she said. "I just need to get my bag."

She left the officers on the porch, staring at each other.

.   .   .

They gave her a ride, but it was a short one. Officer Batten opened the back door of the cruiser, motioning with the sweep of his hand for her to exit. There was no signage on the outside of the brick building, but that was remedied as soon as the trio stepped through an unmarked door and into a cold, harshly lit hall. The fluorescents gave off an alien buzz overhead. Signs with various bits of information were posted every few yards. Then, a sign with a single word printed in big block letters above an arrow pointing left: CORONER.

It was only then that she understood. Only then that it started to come clear. And yet, she couldn't shake a thought. An awful, inappropriate thought.

At least I don't have to go into the city.

As far as she was concerned, she'd never leave Deer Valley again.

They reached a door. A room. The officers ushered her inside. There was a metal gurney, a sheet, a body beneath. A man in medical scrubs pulled the sheet away, exposing Ansel's face. Not a scratch on him. But she could tell the coroner's assistant was careful with just how far he folded it down, keeping most of Ansel hidden beneath linen that looked starch-stiff and paper-thin.

Rosie stared at her husband for what felt like forever. She considered reaching out to him, but couldn't bring herself to raise her fingers to his already graying skin. Somehow, despite the panic that had seized her at home, now she felt nothing but emptiness, as though her beating heart had been cut from her chest and replaced by a void that would never be filled.

She tried to cry, to scream, to collapse onto the floor and wail before blacking out with grief. That's what a good wife would have done. She searched for something appropriate to say, something sorrowful and soul-sick that would haunt Officers Batten and Trelawny and the man in medical scrubs for the rest of their lives. But all that came out of her was "Yes, that's him." Cold. Unfeeling. As though Rosie had seen Ansel die a million times.

Officer Batten drove her home, and while standing on the porch, he asked if there was anything she needed. Rosie didn't understand the question. She needed her husband. Was he able to raise him from the dead? She turned away and, despite the officer's kindness, closed the door in his face.

Alone in the living room, she stared into the quiet space that still smelled faintly of Ansel's cologne, her gaze pausing on all things remanent of him. His books. His medical magazines stacked on the side table next to the phone. His collection of CDs and DVDs, alphabetically filed on the bookshelf next to the TV. Old vinyl records he had inherited from his dad.

She took a few steps into the living room, paused, eventually continued on toward the couch. Taking a seat in her usual spot, she stared at the dark screen of the television. And then she quietly wept, wondering how in the world she'd ever live without him.

14

THERE WAS A FUNERAL.

Rosie wore a plain black dress—long-sleeved and ankle-length—with her hair pulled back in a braided chignon. She could have stepped straight out of colonial New England, which is what it felt like; Hester Prynne's inheritrix, a scarlet *W*, for widow, pinned to her breast. Standing stiff in the town's tiny cemetery, she kept her hands clasped and head bowed, sure that those who had come to bid their physician adieu were casting sideways stares, wondering why Ansel Aleksander had ever married a woman like her. There was, after all, no telling what part Rosamund had played in the good doctor's untimely demise. Because after a man like Ansel died, there was money involved. There was the practice, which now landed on Rosie's shoulders. The gossip would spread. *She killed him. It's certain.* Except that, when Ansel and Rosie had said their vows, neither of them had a dime to their names.

Rosie wasn't sure what those blathering prattlers expected her to do with the practice. Keep it? She was no doctor. What use was it to not let it go? It was clear, however, that they disapproved of her signing over the deed. Their eyes roved over her like horseflies. Incessant. Biting. Buzzing in a different direction as soon as she looked up.

She had no intention of buying a car, especially after the accident. She'd only ever driven a handful of times. The trip to Big Sur had been a record—one that she was perfectly happy to let stand for the remainder of her life. But regardless of whether she drove or walked, there were responsibilities attached to her newly widowed existence. There was grocery shopping to do. She still had the garden, of course, but without things like meat and cheese, she'd waste away to nothing. Ansel had been the one to swing by the market after work when they needed extra supplies. Now she'd have to do it herself, no matter how anxious it made her feel.

There was the post office box to check—no mailman came out to the house. There were the bills; yet another chore Ansel had performed without so much as a complaint. She'd have to start stocking up on cords of wood or start chopping her own for winter. All of these things were destined to become a source of Rosie's already formidable malcontent.

Part of her began to hope that, with how tragically Ansel had passed, someone would reach out to her, perhaps offer to be her friend. One of those circling funeral gnats could take pity on her, if only to have something to drone on about behind her back. But they only watched from a distance. Nobody made eye contact, let alone lent a helping hand.

She spent the next few weeks imagining herself moving to Big Sur, certain that Ras would let her live at his retreat until she got back on her feet. She'd cook, serve as the housekeeper, get that empty place up and running, maybe even turn it into Northern California's preeminent bed-and-breakfast. But without a car, getting down there would require a bus ticket out of town, and the Greyhound didn't run into Deer Valley. McMinnville was the closest place with a station. She supposed she could take a cab, but the idea of sitting in a car with a stranger, even for half an hour, was just too much. She'd rather be alone.

Except that, even in the loneliest of hours after Ansel's death, she had never truly been by herself.

The first time she missed her period—only weeks after the funeral—she dismissed it as grief-stricken stress. By the second month, she was spending hours bent over the toilet. *Food poisoning,* she assured herself. *The stomach flu. A terrible diet. I haven't been eating well since . . . since . . .*

But there were only so many lies she could tell herself. When reality became too obvious to ignore, all she could do was cry.

Considering all the times she and Ansel had tried, it was a fiendish joke that she should be pregnant now.

She cursed God, dared him to strike her down. She no longer wanted what she had been so desperate to have, because everything had changed. Even the road that ran alongside the house had started to go quiet, becoming less and less busy until there were only one or two trucks passing per day. It could have been due to the accident—the company pulling out of the area, scared off by the grave. Or the world truly was forsaking her. She had wanted to be alone, and so it would come to pass.

The stillness was hard to handle. Sadness was replaced by anger. She'd find herself standing naked in the mirror, disgusted by what she saw, revolted by the idea of a human being twisting around inside her like a worm. She did nothing to make the baby's survival any easier. She dug up a pack of stale cigarettes stashed years before—Ansel had reprimanded her for smoking while upset—and sucked down every last one until she was nicotine sick. She bought bottles of booze during weekly shopping trips. If she drank enough, there was a chance she'd miscarry. Hell, if anything, she'd at least be numb. She stood at the top of the stairs, trying to will herself to let her muscles go lax, to tumble one story down; that ought to take care of the malady, and as a bonus, she very well may break her own neck. But she couldn't gather up the courage. Instead, she went in and out of the blue-painted room, refusing to set up a stick of furniture in that nursery. If the child survived her negligence, it would be welcome to sleep on a blanket-covered floor. No crib. No comfort. She'd wash it in the kitchen sink like a stray, like something she'd found out in the woods. But treat it like a *real* child? Not without Ansel. Never.

She knew all these things were wrong. Wishing bad things on that baby after having spent so long desperately hoping it into existence was cruel. But she couldn't help but cross her fingers that this pregnancy would end like her last. Abrupt. Painful. If she was lucky, terminating in a double death.

And yet, there was a tiny seed of optimism refusing to wilt in the shadow of even her darkest thoughts. Ansel had been the most loving person she had known. He had saved her. God had taken him away, yes, but now God was giving her a gift in exchange for her grief. This baby was a godsend, not a curse. A second salvation. Wihout this child, all was lost.

But those women in town. Those vapid she-snakes. She wouldn't dare go into Deer Valley without hiding her condition. By her third trimester, baggy clothes would only do so much.

It was fear of public humiliation—*A pregnant widow, how positively tragic*—that pushed her to shove a handful of money into an envelope and walk herself to the only used car lot in town. She handed the salesman at Mel's Motors five thousand crumpled dollars and requested he put her in something reliable.

"Just something that works when I turn the key," she said. No specifics, just in and out as quickly as possible. The man—was it Mel himself?—had no office to speak of, so she was forced to stand in the lot with him, which was on Deer Valley's main strip. Little plastic flags whipped above her head in the wind. Cars drove by. People looked out their windows, staring at her. *Is that the Aleksander woman? How dare she show her ugly face around here. Buying a fancy car with her dead husband's money, no doubt.*

Maybe-Mel pointed her to a sedan with a giant $1,400 soaped onto the windshield.

"I don't want something for fourteen hundred," Rosie told him. "I want something for five thousand. Something dependable." The more money she spent, the longer the car would last, right? She wanted it to run forever, if it could.

"Right-O!" Maybe-Mel said, but despite his enthusiasm, he looked dubious in his lime-green polo shirt and bright red button—NO CREDIT CHECK!. After a moment of thought, he motioned for her to follow him across the lot. "Come on down. I'll show you the best goshdarn car I've got."

It was a four-door Ford. The dark blue paint appeared to be in relatively good shape, but overall it looked skimpier than Rosie had expected for five grand. A big $2,500 price tag stood out against the glass.

"This?" she asked. Was he purposefully ignoring her request? Or maybe he thought she was as stupid as she was unalluring? Perhaps he knew exactly who she was, and he wasn't about to make her buying experience easy. *Murderess!* She looked away from him and back to the car, mortified by how picky she was being. She should just choose something and get out of there . . .

"Yes, ma'am. And lookie here, its right in your price range."

"But I have five thousand . . . ," she reminded him, the envelope held fast in her hands.

"Oh, the price on the windshield isn't the total price of the car, ma'am," he explained, his smile as wide as a watermelon slice. "That's just how much you pay to get it off the lot, you see? We call that a *down payment.*" He enunciated those two words nice and slow for her—a highly educated man speaking to a losing-her-wits broad. "This one's got only *one* payment after the initial down, which is great. Three thousand bucks after the down brings you to fifty-five hundred total."

Rosamund frowned, certain that this man thought she was born yesterday. She had told him five thousand, tops, and here he was trying to squeeze her for more. *This town,* she thought. *If I could only get out of this town . . .*

"But, because you're demanding the best, and because I can tell you're a lady who knows her cars, I'm knocking five hundred off the price, no questions asked. You can take this baby for five thousand flat. I won't even charge you for taxes or plates." His smile somehow became even more triumphant, and he slapped the hood like a cowboy slapping the flank of a horse. Giddyup.

Rosamund hesitated for half a second, then handed him the cash. Something about Maybe-Mel made her think he was taking her for a ride, but she didn't exactly have much choice. She needed a car, and this whole ordeal was taking much longer than she had anticipated. Suddenly, the Ford looked fine, just fine. All she wanted was to crawl inside it and drive away.

One signature later, she nervously pulled the car to where the curb met the road. Rosie glanced into the rearview mirror just in time to catch Maybe-Mel tucking some of the cash into the back pocket of his crumpled khaki pants. She didn't like the way he had treated her—like she was an uneducated dimwit. And now he was pocketing her husband's hard-earned money for himself? She imagined throwing the car in reverse, confronting him—*Excuse me, but are you the owner of this establishment?* That fantasy vanished with the blaring of a horn.

A passing car squealed its brakes and Rosie bleated out a startled scream. She had drifted into the middle of Main Street, too distracted by the salesman in her rearview to notice she'd put herself in the path of oncoming traffic. Mortified, she stared at the man in a giant pickup a few feet from her front fender. He was yelling, gesticulating with his hands. She was no lip-reader, but his insults were a no-brainer. *Crazy bitch! Goddamn moron!* Shaken, she forced her attention forward and guided the car in the right direction, slowly driving away, snippets of Elton John singing beneath the crackling static of the radio. She tried to keep her tears at bay, but it was hard, because the last time she'd driven anything, it had been Ansel's car, and Elton had been on the radio then, too.

•　•　•

By the time she started showing, Rosie had grown accustomed to the thirty-mile drive into McMinnville. The trip had its benefits. McMinnville had better stores, and the cute downtown area was just small enough, with strangers distant enough, to keep her anxiety relatively in check. There was a pretty park in the middle of town, one that sported a jungle gym in the shape of a dragon that she imagined Little Ansel playing on when he was old enough. McMinnville could be the place where she would scatter her loneliness to the wind and finally find a friend—a shop-keeper, or a park regular, another new mother attentively watching her firstborn from the shade of Douglas firs. But despite these daydreams, Rosie rarely ventured off course. It was to the grocery store and back—never *ever* the grocery store in Deer Valley despite how much closer it was. Sometimes she'd stop to fuel up the car, but otherwise it was a straight shot onto the highway. The faster she got home, the quicker her nerves would abate.

The fact that nobody knew her made no difference in the end. She failed to schedule a doctor's visit, afraid that the nurse would ask about the baby's father, force her to rehash the painful story. And for what? It wasn't as if Rosie would be able to drive herself thirty-plus miles while in the throes of labor. A doctor could tell her whether the baby was healthy, but that didn't matter. If the baby was born sick, she'd take care of it. If it was born with no arms, she'd figure out how to deal with that, too.

Rosie didn't know a thing about being a mother, but one thing was certain. She was alone in this. Nobody would help her. To expect anything from anyone was a mistake.

She was in the kitchen when the first contraction struck. It doubled her over the counter and sent her crashing to her knees. She grasped the edge of the sink, squeezed her eyes shut, and thought of how happy Ansel would have been to be a father. It was the only thing that got her upstairs and into bed.

The pain lasted for what seemed like days, though she couldn't be sure how long it really was, too delirious to keep track of time. She didn't hold back the screams, feeling as though the devil himself was tearing her organs free, one artery at a time.

This was it, then. She was dying.

She rolled onto her front and pulled her knees beneath her, and with the mattress firmly in her grasp, she took a shuddering breath and exhaled a wail. And then she pushed until the world blurred. Pushed until flashes of memory brought Ras and his striking blue eyes into the forefront of her mind. Pushed until, finally, everything went black.

When she roused—minutes later? An hour? A day?—the pain was twice as bad. Her hand flew backward, touched the space between her legs, jerked away. There was something there, a bulbous bulge of bone. She shrieked, trying to purge herself of the thing that had grown inside her, every muscle contracting, her breaths coming in gasping, sobbing heaves. Something loosened. Slid. Liquid geysered down her thighs and, again, she reached back to feel. The baby's head was out, but the body was still firmly seated inside the womb. She rolled onto her back, spun herself around, pressed her bare feet against the headboard, and grabbed the intricately carved dowels of the bed frame with both hands. She pushed. Screamed. Her arms and legs trembled with effort, her entire body covered in sweat.

But . . . nothing.

The baby was stuck.

It would never come out.

She'd be forced to live out the rest of her life as the woman in perpetual labor—a gruesome pair of conjoined twins; one head where it should have been, another one—smaller, bloody—emerging from between her legs.

Oh God.

Panic.

Oh God, get it out!

She reached down, recoiled, reached down again and grabbed ahold of the baby's skull.

Get it out, get it out!

She began to pull, scream-weeping through the process, too pained to spend a single second worrying about whether or not she was hurting the child, too horrified by what was happening to her body to care if she was slowly beheading it with every tug. One final yank. Another spout of hot liquid. Rosie gave a concluding yell as she felt the child hit the bed.

She lay motionless, every muscle in her body quivering with exhaustion. Suddenly, all she wanted to do was sleep, but the silence of the room jarred her eyes open. The baby wasn't crying, and from what she could feel, it wasn't moving, either.

I've killed it, she thought, and for half a trembling heartbeat, she was glad. But the thought of Ansel's pain—his face, reliving the horror of another still-born child; the idea of the last remaining piece of him dying right there, next to her—had her scrambling to sit.

Oh no, oh please.

She stared down the length of her nightgown, her legs bare and blood-smeared. And there, lying atop sheets saturated in amniotic fluid and blood, was a baby unlike any she'd ever seen. Its head grossly oversized. Its limbs small and twisted, like fleshy tree branches that had coiled and zigzagged as they had grown. Pink. Unmoving. More than likely dead. The shock of what was in front of her rendered her motionless, transfixed by the child's chimplike hands and feet, by its twitching vestigial tail.

It stirred, as if waking from a nap rather than having been just born. Rosie pressed her wet, blood-slathered hands to her mouth when it moved. And then, just as she was sure it was going to leap up and snarl at her, it let out a cry. A *baby's* cry. Desperate for affection, for its mother's touch.

Rosie hesitated. Did she dare? She could leave it. Let it die.

She reached down, her fingers curling around the umbilical cord that kept the thing tethered to her body, readying herself to pull it free and run. But the moment her hand grazed that cable of flesh, she felt a tiny heartbeat radiate into her palm. It was a reminder of what this boy represented, no matter how deformed he may have been.

Rosie reached out to the crying child, brought him to her chest and held him close to her heart. And for the first time in her life she felt that she was needed, and that she would forever be justified in her solitude. She hadn't intended on telling anyone about the baby before, but now no one could *ever* know.

15

R OSIE CONSIDERED CALLING the baby Ansel, but something about naming the child after his father felt wrong. Otto seemed more appropriate; a rare name, just as he was a rare creature. It was a name familiar to Sweden—a callback to the child's long-lost father's beloved home. The moniker felt like a nickname, a funny alias to give a pet. And while Rosie knew that was a gruesome thing to consider, it made her feel more at ease about how utterly deformed the poor thing was.

Otto's ailments weren't his fault, of course; they were hers. She'd deal with the consequences of nine months of selfishness for the rest of her life. Or only for the rest of Otto's, because, really, how long could a child like this survive?

Sasha the cat was less compassionate about Otto's afflictions. The type to meander through rooms to be close to his owner, Sasha now stayed as far away from both Rosie and the baby as he could. Even when Rosie set out a dish of tuna for the moody feline, Sasha dared not approach. He skirted the kitchen wall as if considering the risk, ultimately deciding against it whenever Otto started to scream.

And Otto screamed often.

He yowled, it seemed, for the entirety of the first three months of his life; silent only when he slept, and even then a strange gurgle bubbled up from his throat. Had he been born normal and his mother not been crippled by her own social anxieties, he would have won himself an immediate trip to the pediatrician. Surely, that noise was a sign of some sort of blockage. He could have been dry-drowning, his insides just as twisted up as his odd-angled arms and legs. His eyes: those, too, were strange. Spaced impossibly far apart, the whites were actually the palest shade of blue, as though the color beyond the iris had bled like an ink drop blooming across the surface of milk.

But a doctor's visit was out of the question. It was hard enough putting little Otto in the car when Rosie had to go to the grocery store. She tried to quell her unease with jokes—Otto in the auto—but it only fanned the flames. Her volatility was merciless on shopping day.

She'd leave him in the car during her supermarket trips, the windows covered with towels, the windshield blocked by a sunshade so no one could see inside. When the weather was warm, she'd blast the air-conditioning for a steady five minutes, shivering in the driver's seat before making a run for the store. She'd shop the aisles as fast as she could, throwing things into her basket as though she were robbing the place, all the while praying for a checker who didn't try to make small talk—*How's your day going so far? Can I get someone to help you out with your things?*

Sometimes, if the trip was fast enough, the inside of the car would still be cool. But for the times she got stuck behind a maddening coupon clipper, the car would be warmer than it should have safely been. And while she was terrified that, one day, Otto would start screaming and a passerby would call the police, it had yet to happen. Strange as it was, for all the noise Otto made, he seemed to know that wailing while alone in the backseat would only bring bad things. And so, by some bizarre mother-son telesthesia, he remained complacent while she shopped for food.

She did everything she could to stop his screaming, getting up every few hours when the boy would start to fuss. When her even-temperedness began to dwindle, she imagined Ansel putting his arm around her shoulders and whispering in her ear: *You're the best mom in the world*. And maybe she was. Hell, she doubted that any of those Deer Valley gossips could handle the living nightmare that had become her life.

But things could have been worse. And so they were.

Sitting on the covered porch, the baby in her arms and a breast exposed, Otto greedily fed while she enjoyed the chirping of the birds; and then, as if to join in on their song, she let out an abrupt yelp. The birds spooked. Burst out of the trees and flapped away in alarm. Involuntarily jerking Otto away from herself, Rosie looked down at her son in surprise. And there, just above her nipple, was a tooth mark, red and angry.

"Ouch!" she said. "That hurt!" But rather than being angry, she prodded a finger inside Otto's mouth, feeling around for the offending assailant. She found it front and center—his first tooth. Despite that aching bite mark, she laughed. "Well, look at *that*. You're becoming a big boy, aren't you? Little snaggletooth," she cooed. "That's right. That's what you are."

She had tried, especially in the first few weeks, not to get attached. It was doubtful the boy would ever be able to walk, let alone sit up on his own. Convinced that the child was on a short timeline, she would take care of him until he died. And yet, despite her attempt at stolidness, she loved him. Despite his incessant wailing, she was Otto's one and only. His mom.

"All right, all right," she said to his grumbling. "But no biting. Be gentle." She moved him back to her breast and exhaled a sigh, leaning back in Ansel's old rocker. Ansel would have gotten a good laugh out of the kid chomping down on her boob. She chuckled to herself, imagining him in the bedroom, mimicking the move—his idea of being cute. And then she just about leapt out of her skin. Otto had clamped down again. This time, twice as hard.

The fulmination of four months of frustration ignited inside her like a flare. She jumped out of the chair, placed Otto on the floorboards a little more roughly than she intended, and doubled over in pain. With both hands pressed to her chest, a whine escaped her throat. She tried not to cry, but it was useless. It felt like fire, and now she was bleeding.

She took a few steps away from him, and Otto began to cry. Naked save for his bulky diaper, he writhed on his back. A slash of sun cut across his malformed rib cage, more convex than it should have been, like a dog's or a bird's. He screamed but she ignored him, his yowling so commonplace that she'd all but taught herself to block it out, just as she'd once blocked out the rumble of those awful trucks. Pulling her hands away from her wound, she winced. It was bad. Had Ansel been around, stitches would have been involved.

"Oh God," she whispered past her tears. Because what if it got infected; what if she ended up delirious with fever and couldn't do her job? Sure, she was upset with Otto now, but he was just a baby. Mothers got bitten by their teething children all the time.

She left him on the veranda—he would be fine on the floor, at least for a few minutes—and went straight for the bathroom to tend to her wound. Thankfully, the medicine cabinet was well stocked. She dabbed the wound with a hydrogen-peroxide-soaked cotton ball, then slathered a triple antibiotic across the gash, topping it off with a bandage that looked as ridiculous as it was uncomfortable. She supposed she'd have to stick to the left breast for a while. It would leave her lopsided, but she didn't exactly have another choice.

It was then, as she stood there in the bathroom, staring at her exposed chest and wiping at her tears, that Otto *really* raged. Rosie tensed as soon as she heard the pitch shift from his standard *Pay attention to me* screech to something more urgent. She hesitated for half a second, convinced she was about to overreact. So he was bawling his head off, what else was new? But there was something to his tone; it was less colicky, far more helpless than she'd ever heard.

She spun around, dashed out of the bathroom and across the house to the open front door. Her bare feet hit the porch planks, and she stopped short. Otto was exactly where she had left him, but there was something undeniably different about her son. There, across his chest like a beauty queen's sash, was a band of angry boils. Rosie's eyes went wide. There was no denying it had been the sun.

"Oh my God, Otto!" She snatched him up, but he only screamed that much louder. Those horrible pustules were rupturing beneath the palms of her hands. Even the slightest touch was making them split open and ooze. Rosie held him out and away from herself, her hands jammed beneath his crooked arms. Otto threw his big head back, rolling it atop his neck like a bowling ball on a weak little spring, and exploded into an agonized squall. Finally, Rosie caught a good glimpse of the tooth that had torn into her minutes before; almost gray in color, with a mother-of-pearl sheen.

And while he wailed, she couldn't help but wonder . . . just what was he? What had she brought into this world?

. . .

Otto was allergic to the sun. There was no rhyme, no reason. Like all of Otto's ailments, it simply was.

Rosie watched the yard for days, timing the shadows, plotting where she could keep her boy while she tended the garden. She brought out a rusty roll of chicken-wire fencing from the detached garage and created crude pens in the shade of the trees—different enclosures for different times of day. Otto spent his outdoor time behind a fence to keep him from shimmying his way into the light.

It made her feel awful, but there was no way around it. The boils that had bloomed across Otto's chest had left scars. Every time she changed his diaper or got him ready for bed, those calloused, discolored blemishes reminded her of how truly delicate a boy he was.

He was eight months old now—worming his way along the floor more than crawling, more independent than ever. Still breast-feeding despite her attempts to wean him; no matter what she put in front of him, he didn't like the taste. Pureed fruits and vegetables from the garden were promptly spit out, leaving his tiny gray teeth slathered with muck. Baby foods and formulas from the market were just as despised. She began to experiment with the stuff Ansel had rightfully called *garbage*—sugary applesauce and soft processed cheese, *anything* that might catch Otto's taste. The only thing she struck on was peanut butter, but there was only so much of that a kid could eat.

Both of Rosie's breasts were covered in bites. Only a week before, Otto had clamped down so fiercely that she'd cried herself to sleep. The gashes that were in the process of healing itched like day-old bee stings. She had never liked looking at herself in the mirror, but now she could hardly manage it, disgusted by the lesions. The skin around her nipples was ravaged and swollen.

Then there was the illness. Nausea and vertigo. The flu, but more intense. Her head throbbed like an exposed heart. Her nose was red and runny. Her throat felt like salt-gritted sandpaper, and the dark circles that Ansel's death had placed like badges of mourning beneath her eyes were now a ghastly shade of blue.

Weeks of feverish malady turned into months.

Each passing day had her skin growing more plasticine, as though this disease—whatever it was—was trying to transform her into a walking wax figure from Madame Tussauds. She was weak. The feedings were agony. Otto was a tiny vampire, draining her of what energy she had, of which she had almost none.

After a particularly brutal morning, Rosie found herself sitting in the driver's seat of her car, staring at a baby store while Otto fussed in the back, dirty diaper and all. Her desperation was as loud as her anxiety; her pain and failing health starting to match her social ineptitude. She tried to psych herself up. She'd just walk right in there and buy a breast pump, no big deal. If some nosy associate asked her about her baby, she'd smile politely and say it was a gift. If they brought up that she looked like hell, she'd toss some crumpled bills onto the counter and tell them to mind their own business. Pay and get gone. In and out. Nothing to it.

And yet, she simply sat there, wanting to go in, *needing* to, but the store looked so far away. As the minutes ticked by, the parking lot seemed to elongate before her very eyes.

She drove home empty-handed, weeping at her own weakness, not understanding why she felt so terrible or why she hadn't been able to accomplish such a simple task. That shit-stink of Otto's diaper. The crying, now little more than the soundtrack of her life. It had kept her rooted in her seat no matter how desperately she wanted to escape.

She continued to feed him.

He continued to bite.

Her blood mingled with the milk he consumed. And when the cocktail wasn't strong enough, he'd bite harder, and she'd press him to her and scream.

. . .

Otto learned to crawl a month before his first birthday. Rosie could hardly believe her eyes as she sat on the couch—gauze pressed to one breast, her free hand idly scratching at the other—when he glided across the living room floor. Otto's limbs had straightened out a little, but they were still oddly angled and awkward. Nearly a year, and he hadn't shown much interest in moving around on his own, so the crawl was a shock. But most surprising was how quickly he managed to get from one end of the room to the other. No hesitation. No pause or struggle. It was as if he'd been holding out on her, seeing whether or not she'd break, testing how long she'd last with him fused to her side.

He chased Sasha around the house. Rosie tried to stop him in the beginning, but for what may have been the first time, Otto looked like he was having fun. Had anyone heard his laughter from a distance, they'd have sworn the joyous, giggly sound had come from a normal child. She wanted him to be happy. His contentment would bring a bit of peace and quiet to the house. So she laid off asking him to give Sasha a break.

And Sasha *did* need a break, especially when another miracle blessed their house: Otto started to walk. Not on two legs; that would never be possible. His spine was too twisted; his legs little more than gnarled twigs. But crawling wasn't getting him to where he wanted to go fast enough. Eventually, he discovered that he was speedier when he rushed about on all fours, mimicking the pet he seemed to be obsessed with—a fascination that Rosie couldn't help but consider endearing. A boy and his cat.

She went so far as to corner Sasha, pluck him off his paws and present him to Otto so he could finally feel Sasha's soft speckled fur. But when she brought him close, Sasha thrashed and hissed, scratching Rosie's forearms so deeply she tossed the cat aside to spare Otto the attack.

"Jesus, Sasha!" Rosie yelled at her otherwise-beloved friend. Two long gashes decorated her right arm. One bisected her left like the slash of a NO ENTRY sign. His reaction left Rosie stunned, worried that the animal would lash out at Otto when she wasn't around.

Otto, however, thought the whole situation hilarious. He laughed until, despite the cuts on her arms, she couldn't help but smile as well.

The months rolled on. Otto grew more proficient in ambling about, but that seemed to be all he could manage to perfect. She tried to teach him how to eat his peanut butter with a spoon, but his hands were too mangled to grasp the utensil. She repeated her name, *Mama*, over and over, but he didn't make a peep. With Otto's newfound mobility, she did her best not to take him outside until well after dusk. The shades remained drawn to keep the rooms dim—the emerald that Rosie had loved so dearly now blotted out by tapestry during the day and by darkness at night.

If there was a level of solitude beyond the one Rosamund had been living in for the past year, she had reached it. Even the sun was deemed too intrusive, too optimistic for her private hell.

With Otto so kinetic, trips to the store were made that much more trying and complex. She could no longer leave him in the backseat when she went into town, certain that if she tried it, he'd either crawl into the front and blast the horn, or yank the towels away from the windows and broil himself to death. Instead, she left him in what she considered the relative safety of his room, but she returned to a nightmare. Having ripped the curtains away from the wall, Otto had spent more than an hour stuck inside a sun-drenched room. Rosie wept as she patted the open sores that dotted her son's face. He had never been beautiful, but now he was all the more monstrous; a leper exiled to live in the woods.

The next time groceries were needed, she put him in the basement just to be safe. She came home to Otto screaming so loudly she could hear him all the way from the detached garage. All the things that had been left down there—old furniture, boxes of clothes, kitchen bric-a-brac—had been scattered and torn apart, as though the child had traversed insanity while his mother shopped for Campbell's soup and saltines.

Those fits were how Otto found himself not in the cellar, but in his father's secret vault beneath the stairs.

The safe was small, which meant hurting himself while locked away would be more difficult. She emptied it, removing anything he could destroy out of spite or in a rage. It was reinforced per Ansel's specifications—a chamber large enough for all his files, fireproof just in case. And despite Rosie's penitence, silence was, at times, a much-needed respite. Otto could scream all he wanted in there, but nobody would hear him. Not even her.

She began to fantasize about escape. Pack a few of her things. Put *Hus Aleksander* in her rearview. Just a little trip, two unshackled weeks away from the house that had become a cell. A cabin out in the country. A trip to the Oregon coast. She'd even endure the drive to see Ras in Big Sur. If he took her in, perhaps she'd forget to come back. Otto would perish in that secret room while she was away. His body would decompose, but the smell would be contained. No one would discover him. She could have her life back. Hell, she could start a whole new one if she wanted, if she could live with the guilt.

Impossible.

And so, just as Otto had inexplicably kept her from getting out of the car to purchase a breast pump, he now kept her close to the house. He was still feeding, despite his age, gnawing rather than suckling. But she couldn't abandon him. This was her job.

A few weeks after Otto started "walking" on all fours, he finally cornered Sasha in the living room. Too tired to rise from the couch to separate the two, Rosie found herself caught up in her own ambivalence, too exhausted to care whether or not Sasha slashed his claws across Otto's gruesome, pockmarked face.

She watched from across the room, scratching at her wounds as Otto caught hold of Sasha's fur with one twisted, apelike hand. She didn't flinch when he sank his teeth into the back of Sasha's neck, didn't look away as Sasha thrashed and hissed and yowled in pain. All she did was sit there, massaging an oozing breast, thinking to herself that she should have seen this coming, willing Sasha to stop struggling. Because if anyone knew that struggling was useless, it was her.

But now, watching Otto attack the cat, something else was also finally made clear.

Rosie had birthed a demon, and for that she'd be forever bound.

16

ROSIE WASN'T SURE how Sasha survived the attack, but Otto didn't kill him. Whether the cat had clawed his way to freedom, or whether Otto had let him go, there was no way to tell. Every time she approached Sasha to check the awful wound that surely must have been festering beneath the softness of his fur, the cat darted away. And while Sasha continued to avoid Rosamund as if *she* had been his aggressor, he was now interacting with Otto as though the two were the best of friends. She couldn't understand it. Watching Otto pet Sasha's fur, the cat rubbing lovingly against the boy's crooked back, she felt stupid for the pang of jealousy that put a squeeze on her heart. But Otto needed a friend; and now, with Sasha to keep him company, he'd be a little less demanding of her.

For once, she was right.

Otto and Sasha took to disappearing into various rooms of the house, leaving her to cook or clean or read—pure heaven after the now nearly two years of ceaseless servitude she had endured. In the early evenings, after the sun set and it was safe for Otto to venture outside, both he and Sasha would prowl the yard. She didn't care what they were doing out there, as long as they weren't hurting each other and she was left alone.

The thick bramble of spiky blackberry bushes was what finally got her to go outside. She assumed Otto was gorging himself on the berries, but when neither he nor Sasha moved from where they sat after a few long minutes, Rosie dropped the scarf she was knitting—and thoroughly mucking up—onto the couch and moved down the porch steps to approach the pair.

"Otto . . . ? What're you two doing?" She knew he wouldn't reply, but there was something about sneaking up on him that made her uneasy, especially when he was crouched the way he was, bent at his typical slump, protecting some unseen treasure. Sasha sat a few feet away, his tail idly twitching, watching the child with what appeared to be curiosity. Or it could have been pride.

"That's a thorny bush," Rosie warned, eventually reaching out to place a hand on the toddler's back. It was then that Otto spun around, forcing a cry of surprise from his mother's throat. She pulled her hand away, her eyes wide with disgusted disbelief. Because there, in Otto's gnarled hands, was a field mouse—the kind Sasha had a habit of catching and dragging home. Otto wasn't eating blackberries. He was feasting on the mouse's small body instead. Horrified, Rosie took a few stricken, stumbling backward steps. She gaped at her boy as he chewed, trying to tear that small dead rodent apart with his teeth.

It took a second, but instinct finally overrode disgust. She lunged forward, grabbed Otto by his arm, and wrenched the half-eaten vermin away from his grasp. "Otto, no! No, that's *bad*!" She threw the mouse into the bushes, cried out when it left a smear of gore across her palm. "Oh God, that's revolting. Otto, *that's revolting*!"

She was about to dry-heave, but that, too, was stalled when Otto sprang for where the mouse had been tossed. He screamed when she yanked him back, thrashing against her as though she were leading him to the gallows—death for mouse murder; death for thoroughly grossing her out. But Rosie couldn't care less about Otto's protests. She was far too busy spinning worst-case scenarios inside her head.

"What if you get sick?" she yelled at him, then yanked on his arm again, trying to put an end to his fit. "What if that thing had a disease? What if it was full of worms?" Of course, Otto didn't understand. Sometimes she wondered if he ever would, if he had the capacity for language at all. He didn't babble. Not *Goo-goo* or *Gaga* or the *Mama* she had tried so hard to teach him; just high-pitched wailing whenever he was unhappy, which was almost all the time.

But Rosie understood the implications of her worries more than enough for them both, and the more she thought about it, the more her panic grew. Did mice have rabies? Parasites? Surely they had to be the carriers of something foul. And it wasn't just Otto's health she had to worry about. Its guts were smeared across her own hand. It had taken her months to feel better after her initial affliction. She *still* got vertigo when she stood up too fast. What if she got sick again? What if, this time, her illness lasted longer? What if she didn't recover at all?

Otto yowled as she dragged him up the porch steps and inside the house, probably a little too roughly, but she was too worried about possible pandemics to be gentle. "Stop it!" she demanded. "Stop it right now! This is serious, Otto!"

Otto knew it was serious. His mom had confiscated his mouse. And to add insult to injury, she had chucked it out of sight. All he wanted to do was go back out there and find it, and he made yet another attempt as soon as his mother let him go, scurrying for the door so much faster than he should have been able. But Rosie was prepared. She grabbed him by the seat of his ill-fitting pants—lumpy from the diaper he wore underneath, from the tail that was tucked inside—and pulled him back. He hissed at her the way Sasha had when she tried to introduce the cat to his now-best friend. Surprised by Otto's response, Rosie nearly let him go, but this time refused to relent.

"Oh no you don't." She seethed right back at him. "I'm your *mother*!" No matter what Otto looked like or what afflictions he had, she'd be damned before allowing him to show her such disrespect. She hadn't given up her life to be mistreated, especially by the likes of him.

Otto continued to thrash. His mangled hands reached for her, ready to shred her arms with fingernails he never let her cut. He snapped his teeth as if to bite, the sound of their gnashing pushing her over the edge. She clenched her own teeth and marched him to the door beneath the stairs, yanked it open. There, on the far wall in what looked to be an ordinary coat closet, was the door to Ansel's secret vault. It was camouflaged by damask wallpaper and dark shadows, nothing but a finger pull at the top edge, hardly visible unless you knew where to look.

She struggled for a moment, trying to keep Otto from tearing up her arm while she opened the concealed door. When she finally got it to swing open, she shoved Otto inside with a bit more force than she intended. The boy stumbled on his twisted legs and hit the inside wall.

She immediately felt terrible for being so harsh with him. He was just a baby. A *child*. But she slammed the door shut before he could get out. And then, after taking a moment to compose herself, she shuddered at the drying gore on her palm and rushed to the bathroom to scrub her hands.

Wiping her hands on her skirt, she made a beeline across the house to Ansel's study, untouched since his death. She thumbed through books she'd read the spines of a thousand times, searching for one in particular: *The Encyclopedia of Diseases*. It was an antique, outdated by at least fifty years, but that made no difference. Flipping through the pages in a rush, she found the section on rodents and gasped.

Meningitis.
Hemorrhagic fever.
Leptospirosis.
Plague.

She pressed her hands over her mouth, then jerked them away, rubbing her palms against her hips despite her fingers still smelling of soap. What would she do if . . . ? What if . . . ? "Oh no, please, no." Because despite the nightmare that had become her life, Rosie couldn't imagine losing her child. Not to something like this. Suddenly, she found herself reconsidering her stance on doctors, but Otto was as good as feral. They'd institutionalize him. They'd arrest her. She had let him grow wild. They'd call it abuse.

No, she couldn't. Diseases were a possibility, but Otto being taken away from her was a guarantee.

She had to risk it. Wait it out.

Sliding Ansel's medical text back into its rightful spot, Rosie exhaled a slow and deliberate breath—*Calm down*—then ventured back across the house to retrieve the boy. He'd been in Ansel's safe only a few minutes, but what she found in the foyer left her just as wide-eyed as the ailments she'd read about.

In her rush to get Otto into the house, she had left the front door wide open, an unconcerning detail, seeing as to how she frequently left it open on warmer days. The draft was refreshing, bringing in the scent of moist earth and pine. But today, Sasha had taken advantage of that open door, not to go in and out as he pleased but to make a special delivery instead. There, upon the door's threshold, was a neat little pile of dead mice, left like an offering to a Hindu god. A sickly-looking Sasha sat beside his alms, scratching behind an ear and staring at the door that kept his best friend captive. His tail flicked back and forth. Patient. Obedient. Loyal in a way that cats were never meant to be.

.   .   .

The next morning, Rosie pulled Otto to her for breakfast, but for the first time in his short life, he wasn't hungry. She went down to the basement—the best solution she could manage when it came to keeping her now mostly nocturnal child out of the sun—to change his sheets. That was when she discovered it: another rodent hidden in folds of linen, all but torn to shreds.

Sasha had brought him another gift, and Otto had devoured it, no longer hungry for his mother's milk.

17

THE MICE BECAME ROUTINE.

Rosie tried to keep Sasha from bringing them inside, and she tried to prevent Otto from hunting them when he was in the yard. But save for locking the cat outside and keeping Otto a prisoner indoors, her efforts accounted for little. There was always another one—its small gray body lying lifeless in a corner of a room or near the edge of the fence. She thought about separating boy and cat, but Sasha was looking weaker by the day, and Otto was, after all, happier with Sasha at his side. That, and it had been a week since Otto had ravaged the first mouse; the same amount of time that he hadn't fed from Rosie. It would take months for the wounds to heal, and there was no doubt there would be scars. But even after such a short amount of time, she was starting to feel more like herself again. Though the itching never quite relented, no matter how much Bactine she smeared onto her skin.

Otto seemed healthier, too. Stronger. Seven days, and he had hardly screamed. So she let him keep eating those foul things because, by God, she couldn't very well continue to let him feed from her. The mice had the potential to make him sick, even kill him. But what about Rosie's well-being? If she was too weak to take care of him, healthy or not, Otto would die.

It took less than a month for the first cat to appear, orange-striped with a black collar. Its tags glinted in the slow-setting sun as it prowled along the fence perimeter. Rosie assumed it was stalking Sasha. Perhaps he had come across the newcomer during one of his outings, or he could have ventured into Deer Valley with the sole intent of sparking a cat's interest. Sasha, the poor dear, wasting away, hardly ever eating his dinner anymore. Rosie swore he'd caught fleas, or had wandered into a patch of poison oak. His once-beautiful, spangled coat was nothing but a collection of bald spots. His back right leg was the worst—hairless, sallow skin hanging off the bone.

The visitor continued to linger near the fence, unsure of itself, as an anemic Sasha meandered through the front yard. Rosie watched from her regular perch on the porch. It seemed to her that Sasha was luring the thing, as if wanting to introduce this new visitor to Otto the Great.

The gate-crasher took its time as it crept closer, eventually confident enough to slither through the fence slats. Sasha continued to ply it with the promise of something unspoken: food, shelter, good company, perhaps all three. Otto, who was seated on the porch close to Rosie's feet, watched the animals from behind the rails of the balustrade like a boy at the zoo. It was only when the cats continued to move closer that Rosie heard a low rumble emitting from her son's throat—a dangerous, predatory growl.

Rosie stared at him. What she was hearing couldn't have been real. Was this an ambush set up by the two? Impossible. No matter how smart Sasha was, there was only so much intelligence a cat could possess. Maliciousness was a human trait. There was no such thing as one animal leading another to purposeful harm . . . was there?

Before she could answer her own question, Otto's muscles coiled up, tight as springs. He leapt off the front steps. The orange cat was quick to respond, but not fast enough to avoid Sasha's simultaneous lunge. The blind-sided cat yowled in surprise, reared back, and stumbled upon the grass. Sasha forced it onto its side and pinned it down among the weeds, but the visitor scrambled back to its feet in a flash. Sasha's diversion, however, was all it took for Otto to clear the distance between the porch and both felines.

Rosie jumped from Ansel's rocker and threw herself forward—an observer to an inevitable tragedy. Otto had the orange cat pinned to the ground before Rosie's hands hit the rail.

"Otto, *no!*" The words left her in an involuntary rush, but her plea came too late. By the time her voice reached his ears, he was sinking his teeth into the caller's throat. When he finally backed away, the cat lay limp among the dandelions, unmoving, almost certainly dead.

And Otto couldn't have looked more satisfied—like a child having its fill of cake and ice cream. Like a vampire with a stomach full of blood.

*   *   *

It was just the first of many.

Sasha became a pied piper, leading both strays and collared cats to their doom. Some managed to run away after being attacked; most, Rosie had to bury behind the house in shallow graves. Inexplicably, those that did escape returned looking worse for wear. She recognized them by the smears of blood dried onto their fur. And yet, despite their previous waylay, they came bearing gifts.

By the time Otto's second year lingered on the horizon, Rosie avoided the backyard like a spooked child skirting a haunted tomb. Dozens of carcasses were buried there. And it wasn't just cats. There were birds, squirrels, a fox. Otto didn't discriminate, and Rosamund was hardly surprised when, finally, she found a dog in the yard.

It was a small thing—one of those yappy Chihuahuas that women carried around in their arms; something Rosie assumed this particular canine had become accustomed to, judging by its pink rhinestone collar and heart-shaped tag. Fifi had more than likely been a good girl. Shaky and nervous, but loyal just the same. It was easy enough to put the story together. Fifi's owner had let her out before locking up for the night. Fifi had gone into the yard to do her business, as per the routine. Except that something lingered in the shadows beyond the garden's gate. Perhaps Otto had scoped out the dog, but Rosie doubted he had that much restraint. It had more than likely been nothing but bad luck on Fifi's part. The wrong place, the wrong time. Poor Fifi, vanished like a magic trick.

Rosie felt terrible for the animals Otto left behind, but this time was particularly hard. She sobbed as she removed Fifi's collar and dumped her body in the small hole she'd dug, reminded of her own childhood dog—a cocker spaniel named Trudy, found in a heap along the side of the road, having been hit by a car. Rosie had saved Trudy's collar then, and she saved Fifi's collar now. It was her way of paying tribute; an apology for not knowing how to stop all this, for not knowing how to keep Otto happy without allowing him to rage.

She covered Fifi with earth and stepped back inside the house, that glittering collar catching the hazy light of the living room lamp. It joined the others in a drawer of Ansel's rolltop desk—collars and tags of all sizes, many of them dappled with stains the color of rust.

After Fifi, she locked Otto up. But it only resulted in a night of screaming and banging so loud that Rosie could hear it upstairs. It broke her heart to think that they were both prisoners in the home Ansel had so lovingly built, a place he had hoped would bring their family comfort and peace. And despite her own revived heartache for poor Trudy, she had to remind herself that those cats, they were just animals. Fifi had been heartbreaking, but wasn't it even worse to take away a child's unrestraint?

And so she let him wander.

She let him hunt.

She buried the bodies.

And if, every now and again, the victim belonged to someone, well . . . that was something she'd have to get over. Because her child was more important than someone's rhinestone-adorned lapdog. She refused to lock up her son for the good of someone's wandering cat.

• • •

A year passed. Then two. All of Rosie's attempts to civilize her child were failures.

At five years old, Otto still didn't understand the mechanics of using a toilet. By six, baths became a thing of the past. She did her best, but for the most part she let him do what he liked. They began to lead separate lives—she, awake during the day; he, prowling the forest at night. She told herself it was better this way, natural; a boy and his mother, slowly growing apart. She convinced herself of these things while digging small, square holes in the backyard with calloused hands. It was little more than muscle memory now. She did the work with a blank mind.

Sasha's was the only marked grave in Rosie's potter's field, set back a way from the rest of the dead. She'd bought a small metal cross in McMinnville after he'd died. Flowers bloomed at the head of Sasha's plot. He had lived far longer than Rosie had ever expected, especially after looking so ill. After he passed, she had caught Otto sitting near Sasha's grave, gazing upon the cross as it glowed in the moonlight, illuminating her boy's asymmetrical face. It was the first time she had seen any humanity in him. And yet, she couldn't help but think that his torment was a result of something far different from her own. Rosie missed her cat because he had become the only living creature she'd known since before Ansel's death, because Sasha had been a friend. Otto missed him for his servitude. Life was harder without a slave.

After Sasha died, collars became more frequent. Otto quickly learned that it was easier to steal than to lure.

But even in her worst nightmares, she never believed Otto to be capable of what came next.

With eight-year-old Otto asleep—still having never spoken a word—Rosie stepped onto the front porch and breathed in the fresh morning air. It had rained nonstop for days and the sun was a welcome change. It lit up the dew-dappled leaves like diamonds—like poor Fifi's rhinestone collar, still tucked away in Ansel's desk after all these years. With the weather having trapped her inside for nearly a week and Otto in the basement, she couldn't resist a long-needed walk.

She dressed herself, threw on a pair of mud boots, and started out. As she moved into the woods, she again considered an attempt at independence. With Otto hunting the way he was, he was self-sufficient now. He'd never been interested in her company. She was little more than a digger of his graves. He would have been just as happy if she let him go. *With the wolves,* she thought, *is where he was always meant to be.*

But the fantasy was derailed by a blip of red.

There, just shy of the muddy trail, was a child's sneaker, crimson, with dirty laces that had once been white.

Her breath caught in her throat as she stared at that shoe, waiting for it to move on its own, to crawl into the underbrush and wipe itself from view. But it wasn't the sneaker that had her mind reeling. It was the fact that nobody ever ventured in this direction. The trails were overgrown, wretched for hiking. The three-mile span between the house and Deer Valley proper was distance enough for Rosie to feel comfortable in knowing that, by the time Otto was out and about, the town's children were inside their homes, not outside in the dark. And yet, here she was, facing a nightmare she hadn't once considered an actual possibility.

She pressed her hands over her heart, as if the touch of her palms could sequester her thudding pulse. Took a single backward step. Considered another escape. If she returned to the house now, she could pack up her things and go. She'd be hundreds of miles away by sunset. Otto would wake to an empty house. He'd have to face the consequences of his actions alone.

And yet, that very thought stopped her.

Otto.

Alone.

Abandoned.

Not understanding his crime because he didn't understand right from wrong.

"Whatever this is," she whispered to herself, "it isn't his fault."

It couldn't be, because fault could only be placed on those with reason. Guilt was reserved for those who could comprehend misdeeds.

Rosie forced herself forward, propelled by a single disturbing thought. The sun had risen two hours ago, which meant Otto had been home for at least three. That shoe had been lying just shy of the overgrown path all night. Whoever its owner may have been had been missing since the previous evening. People would come looking, and they'd come soon.

She snatched the waterlogged sneaker off the ground and scanned the area, frantic to find the body she knew had to be there somewhere. But there was nothing—at least not that she could see. The ground was a chaotic pastiche of ferns and downed trees, a coat of moss shining through in shades of neon chartreuse. Brambles of wild blackberries and snarls of ivy obstructed her view. She turned in a circle once, twice, three times, her gaze scanning the woods that suddenly appeared the same no matter which direction she looked. For half a second, she couldn't remember which way *she* had come. But, eventually regaining her bearings, she fell into a run.

Because Otto always brought the bodies home.

. . .

When she reached the house, the little sneaker was still clasped in her hand. It was evidence. Damning. It couldn't be found. But it was also proof of her worst suspicion. Deer Valley was too far for kids to wander near her home, but it wasn't distant enough for Otto not to visit in the night. The older Otto grew, the bolder he became. The owner of that shoe had been lured. Or dragged. A shudder quaked her from the inside out as she pictured the attack, pictured Otto, pictured the child . . .

No. Don't.

She pushed those images out of her mind, searched the front yard, but there was nothing for her to find. Because she was wrong. Otto had nothing to do with this. She was wrong. A family had gone hiking along the trail, regardless of its overgrown state. She was *wrong*. The owner of the red sneaker had been small, unable to push through the undergrowth. He'd lost it while riding on Ansel's shoulders, Rosie bringing up the rear with a picnic basket, the three of them singing a round of "Row, Row, Row Your Boat." A kick of the foot, or the snag of a branch. Lots of things could loosen an untied shoe. *Yes,* she told herself as she trudged through the yard and around the back of the house, those rain boots clomping with every step. *Otto would never. He wouldn't. He knows it's wrong.*

Yes. He knew it was wrong. Which was why he hadn't left the body in the front yard, but had dragged it to the back.

Rosie screamed when she saw it; the sound involuntary, clawing its way up and out of her throat. The body was nearly impossible to identify. But the sneaker's twin left no doubt. There had been no picnic. No singing. No hike. Stuck onto the end of a disembodied leg, the shoe winked in the sun like a red flag. Red for the unforgivable thing Otto had done; for the terrible acts Rosie had allowed him to commit; for the horrible, pulsating love she had for a child that was more monster than man.

If there was ever a time when thoughts of abandonment should have overtaken her devotion, it was now. Her mind yelled *RUN*. It screamed *DRIVE*. Drive as far away as she could before pulling over to sob. Drive to Big Sur. Find Ras. Ask for help. But even as she stood there—her mouth hanging open, her pulse hammering hard enough to ignite sparks behind her eyes—the urge was sequestered by a single, throbbing thought:

Protect him.

She wept as she picked body parts off the grass, her yellow gloves—retrieved from beneath the kitchen sink—shining crimson as she dropped that sneakered leg into an open grave. She stopped to vomit, her body expunging every bit of breakfast and bile until there was nothing left to purge. And still she continued to heave, as though God himself was trying to cleanse her of the responsibility she'd taken on as her own.

When she was too tired to cry, she found herself staring into the hole at her feet. This body, this *boy*, was not like the others. She couldn't bury him, not here. Dead dogs and cats could be whittled down to her being crazy; just a batty outlier with a soft spot for interring strays. But a child? If anyone found the bones . . .

Not here. *Not here.*

Her gaze shifted to the home Ansel had built, a home that had once been bright and sunny and perfect with its picket fence and big, clean windows. The place was starting to go green with mold and neglect. The wooden roof shingles were turning up at the edges, and the bottom porch steps had taken on a distinctive slump. And there, in the shade of a porch that needed a new coat of paint, was the nightmare that had become her life.

Otto sat crouched in the shadow of the awning, watching his mother stand among the dead. He lifted an arm—not his own, but a disembodied limb belonging to the dead boy at Rosie's feet—and brought it to his blood-smeared mouth, as if to remind her . . .

This is your life. Because I say so. Because you are mine.

PART THREE

PART THREE

18

J UDE STOOD IN his sunny backyard, the lawn nothing but a dry husk. His mom didn't run the sprinklers anymore, and the grass had turned yellow despite occasional rain. Standing in the far corner of the property and staring at the back fence, it was as if he was studying a particularly interesting knot in the weathered pine. At least that's the way it looked as Stevie approached.

"H-hey, Jude." Yeah, Stevie got the reference. Once upon a time, Uncle Scott followed up every greeting Stevie offered his best friend by singsonging lines from that famous tune. Don't bring him down. Don't make things bad.

Don't be afraid.

At first, Jude didn't move, as if he hadn't heard Stevie speak. It was only when Stevie closed the distance that Jude turned to face him, but he didn't smile, and he didn't give his cousin a *Hey* in return. He only scratched at the inside of his arm; the skin red and irritated, a rash on the cusp of needing medical attention.

"What's up?" Stevie asked, trying to play it cool. Maybe things would be okay if, like the adults, he pretended everything was fine. Jude shrugged at the question and chewed on his bottom lip, gnawing at a bit of chapped skin. Nothing was up.

Stevie frowned as his friend turned away, casting a glance at the fence that held Jude's rapt attention. He didn't see anything particularly interesting in that corner, just old and splintery planks of wood that needed paint. There was a hole in one of the boards where a knot had once been, one that had either been punched out or had shriveled up and fallen away on its own. But there wasn't much to see through that peephole other than a bunch of trees; nothing out there but forest and leaves.

"Hey," Stevie said. "Guess what. Guess what. Guess."

Jude narrowed his eyes at the fence, continuing to scratch just above the crook of his left elbow. That slow-growing blotch was making Stevie uncomfortable. It looked gross, nearing infection. Jude eventually gave Stevie a sidelong look—*What?*—but he didn't speak.

"I s-saw you on TV." Stevie hoped the possibility of fifteen minutes of fame would perk Jude up. "On TV," he repeated. "You were on the news last night, on TV when the news came on, and there you were, on the news like Wolf Blitzer." He cracked a grin. Wolf Blitzer. Neither of them knew who that guy was, but the name? Epic. "Wolf *Blitzer*." Stevie echoed the moniker once more. How cool would it be to go to school with a name like that? He bet Wolf never got a tray of mac and cheese smashed into *his* shirt during lunch.

Jude didn't smile. He said nothing.

"You looked like a real dumb dummy," Stevie said. "Like, a *huge* dumb dimwit smelly armpit idiot. I bet you're gonna be famous now. They're gonna put your name in lights, blink blink, casino flamingo pink with the neon like the Monopoly guy." He lifted his hands up, imagining the marquee above the ValleyPlex on Main. *"Jude: biggest armpit in town."*

"Oh yeah?" It was the first thing Jude had said to him—possibly said at all, other than the three words he'd muttered to the newslady the day before. And while Stevie knew he was running the risk of making Jude mad, it seemed to be paying off. There was a glimmer of a smirk at the corner of his cousin's mouth.

"Yeah," Stevie challenged, pushing just a little harder.

"And how's that gonna work, jerk?" Jude asked. "You're just gonna let me take that title from you? After you've been holding on to it since the day you were born . . . *Sack?*"

Stevie grinned at the smart-ass comment—*work, jerk*—suddenly overwhelmed with relief. Heck, that blank stare he had seen on TV was probably just Jude being camera shy or embarrassed or something.

Stevie closed the distance between them a little more. He wanted to stand close—arm to arm, if he was allowed; replace the fear that had settled into the corners of his heart with the comfort of proximity. He would have reached out and given Jude a hug if he wasn't so sure he'd get socked for it, but standing close was enough. It felt real, like something he hadn't been sure he'd ever get to experience again.

They stood in silence for a few seconds, both of them watching the planks of the fence like a pair of lunatics. But before Stevie could settle into things being good, being *right*, something in the air shifted and that comfort was replaced by a strange sort of weight. Jude was scratching again, and it was giving Stevie the creeps.

"Wanna go to the fort?" Stevie asked. Getting away from the house would do Jude some good. They still had work to do out there. Before Jude had vanished, he had been adamant—*That thing isn't gonna build itself, dude.* But now, with the question floating in the space between them, Jude didn't seem compelled by the idea.

"Not really," he murmured.

Not really? What the hell? Stevie looked away from the spot Jude was scratching and squinted at the ground. "Is it because of what happened? What happened? Where did you go, Jude? How come you didn't run away if you knew the way, because you did know the way, didn't you? You know because I know you know. I know you know." This was loaded, dangerous talk—his mom would ground him for the rest of his life if she only knew what he was saying. But nobody else was throwing down this type of inquest, at least not that Stevie could tell. Perhaps the cops had, but how was he supposed to know what Jude had told them? It wasn't as though Aunt Mandy was going to be like, *Oh, hey, Stevie, here's a transcript of Jude's interview with the police, since you're really into all that investigation stuff.*

Jude didn't reply, though Stevie could hear the soft rustle of his cousin's T-shirt: a disinterested rise and fall of his shoulders. *I'm not telling you anything.*

"If we go to the fort, it'll be okay if we *both* go," Stevie assured him. "Nothing's gonna get us out there, not if we stick together it won't. You don't have to be scared."

"*Scared?*" Jude snorted. He turned to face Stevie without warning, and for a second he looked rabid with offense. He pulled his right arm back, his hand coiled into a fist. "Why don't you get the fuck out of here?" he hissed. "Go. Leave me alone."

"But . . ." Stevie backed away as Jude stepped toward him. Was Jude abandoning their project, after all the work they'd put into it? After all the plans they had made to construct the coolest fort in all the Pacific Northwest? And was he really going to pummel him, right here in the backyard with both their moms home? Stevie's gaze shifted from his cousin to a stray in the corner of Aunt Mandy's yard—possibly the same one he'd seen a few nights back, hanging out in rectangles of window light. Jude noticed it, too. He leaned down, swept a rock up off the ground, launched it at the feline, and missed it by a good two feet. But the cat spooked anyway. It veered around the side of the house, out of sight.

"I—I—I don't want to go, Jude," Stevie said. "I can't do it by myself. It's *our* fort, remember? . . . *Remember?*"

That last part was a slipup, and he knew it as soon as the question crossed his lips. It was born of that blank stare, a result of that gentle, alarming sway. That terrifying look, nothing but emptiness behind Jude's eyes. Because Stevie had been right the first time. It hadn't been shyness or embarrassment or sleepiness, like Aunt Mandy had tried to suggest. There *had* been something wrong with Jude.

"Yeah, well, then don't do it by yourself." Jude's tone was sharp. "Hell, I don't give a shit."

"B-but Jude . . . dude . . . Jude . . . dude . . ." Stevie swallowed, then whispered, "Fortress of Solitude." *I'm screwed.*

"But nothing," Jude said, cutting him off. "I'm not building some stupid baby fort with some crazy Dr. Seuss, so forget about it, okay? Do it yourself, or get some of your dumb-ass friends to help." He turned away, back to the punched-out knot in the fence. There would be no ass-beating, at least not right now; not if Stevie watched his mouth from here on out.

The Dr. Seuss thing, though? That was low. Jude had made fun of Stevie's speech stuff before, but he'd never stooped to calling him names. And *dumb-ass friends?* Stevie didn't get it. He didn't *have* any friends. The Dr. Seuss thing was exactly why kids didn't want to hang out with him. That, and his missing fingers. Because you never knew if and when crazy could be contagious.

"I only have one dumb-ass friend," Stevie said under his breath, "a-and that's you, *Jew.*" Ass-kicking be damned, mean deserved mean back.

Jude scowled. "You call me a Jew one more time and I'm gonna mash your teeth straight into your brain, you get it?"

Stevie swallowed the spit that had gone sour in his mouth. He waited for Jude to recant his warning the way he always did. Sometimes, Jude's anger got the best of him, but after a few seconds he *always* remembered who Stevie was. Never in the history of their friendship had he left a browbeating hanging between them like a guillotine blade. But Jude continued to scowl, still scratching, his posture reminiscent of a bully ready to give a scrawny kid the whupping of his life.

And now that Stevie was looking at him, *really* looking, Jude appeared to be getting quite the sunburn, as though he'd been out in the yard for hours rather than minutes. His skin was starting to peel above the apples of his cheeks, which were chapped like his lips.

Stevie took a couple of steps away from his cousin. "Hey, I'm sorry, sorry, so—" he stammered, then cut himself off. "I didn't mean it." Jude ignored him as if to say, *Yeah, whatever*, while Stevie stood there, chewing his bottom lip, staring at clumps of dried-up grass, trying to keep his tongue from knotting itself around his brain. The stray was back, slowly high-stepping through the weeds, trying to be quiet as it kept to the side of the fence, as if not wanting to be spotted again.

"You're toast," Stevie said, turning his attention back to his cousin.

"What?" Jude barked out the word. Did Stevie just *threaten* him?

"N-no, I mean toaster strudel, Judel." Uncontrollable. "Burnt like toast, Jude. You should put on some block." *Rock in a sock. Coldcock. Ticktock.*

He hoped a change of subject would get them back on track, realign his thoughts, help him stop thinking about Jude busting him in his mouth. This was all part of the process, right? Jude had that post-dramatic soldier thing. Sometimes vets could hear gunfire in their bedrooms, so why couldn't Jude think he was still in the woods? That must have been why he was being so weird.

"I went to look for you," Stevie said. "I saw something swing like a spring, ding-a-ling. On the porch . . ." He paused, squeezed his eyes and fists tight. "Of that, of that house."

"What house?"

What house? Jude had only been obsessed with the place, and now he didn't remember it, either? "Along the road . . ." The cat crept closer.

"Oh." Jude glowered back at him, like *Yeah, of course I remember.* "So?" He was still scratching at that one spot on his arm, and while Stevie couldn't be sure, he swore his cousin looked even more sunburned than he had a few minutes before. The chapped bits on his cheeks were drying out and curling in on themselves the way scorched paper does. "So what did you see, genius?"

Stevie hesitated. Now may not be the best time to bring it up.

"H-hey, maybe we should go inside and hide inside?"

"Are you gonna tell me what you saw or *what?*" Impatience peppered Jude's tone.

"A shadow," Stevie said, except as soon as the word left him he was distressed by how benign the whole thing sounded. "I mean, I mean, no, I mean . . . It wasn't *just* a shadow, it was a thing. A creature . . ."

"A creature," Jude repeated.

Stevie's gaze darted to the opposite corner of the yard. *Another* cat? He squinted, wondering if there really was a pair of strays, or if he was just seeing double.

"Or maybe it was a person . . ." Stevie lifted a hand, pointed to cat number two, but Jude didn't seem to notice. "A missing person." The figure *could* have been human. A really weird, mangled one, but a human nonetheless.

"So you went into the woods and you saw a person," Jude summarized. "Big whoop." He crouched, grabbed another stone, let it fly. Cat number two scrambled. Cat number one froze, still undetected by the boy with the rocks.

Stevie couldn't seem to take his eyes off the spot on Jude's arm, wondering how much more scratching it would take before it started to tear open and bleed. Or how much longer Jude had to stay outside before his skin began to blister beneath the sun and he caught fire like a firework fuse on the Fourth of July.

"Didn't I tell you to get lost?" Jude asked. He kicked at a rock with the tip of his sneaker, as if to suggest that it had Stevie's name written all over it. The cats had gotten theirs; Stevie was next.

"Okay," Stevie said, reluctant but conceding. "Okay, okay." He had pushed too hard. He had to back off. "B-but can you come over later, maybe if you feel like?" he offered, still hopeful. "We've got Rocky Road, à la mode."

Again, Jude didn't bother with a reply, and while Stevie still had a million things he wanted to discuss, it was time to pack it in. He'd try again later. Or Jude could actually take him up on his offer and show up on his doorstep for ice cream and video games. Rather than Stevie pushing, Jude would hopefully come to terms with what had happened on his own.

Except, that didn't solve Stevie's problem: that thing was still out there. What if it came back? What if it really *was* human? The idea of it made his skin crawl. *Like something out of an old-timey freak show.* Except, no. Impossible. He just imagined that stuff, just like the snakes and spiders and worms. Because monsters weren't real . . . right? "Right," he whispered beneath his breath, then turned on the balls of his feet to go. With his head down, he shuffled toward Aunt Mandy's weedy side yard, kicking up dirt as he went. A third cat awaited him, blinking up at Stevie with its almond-shaped eyes.

"Hey, Sack," Jude said, the hard edge of his tone softened, if not altogether gone. Stevie stopped just shy of cornering the house when he spoke up. "We should go to the fort soon. Finish it up."

Stevie could only stare at the cat before him—dirty and injured, like it had been in a street fight. And while he wanted to be happy about Jude's offer, all that seized his heart was stammering fear. This time, it was his turn to be silent. He didn't respond, only walked a little faster toward his own house. Because something was wrong with Jude. Really really wrong.

. . .

When Stevie stepped back into his own home, it was quiet, empty. The TV was off because Terry was at work. Dunk was sleeping or screwing around on his computer, and his mom was somewhere—perhaps next door, or in the shower. He didn't know, and he didn't care.

The way Jude's mood had shifted from mute to amused to aggressive within the span of seconds had left Stevie dizzy, vulnerable, angry at Jude's inability to balance himself out. Stevie was supposed to be the weird one, unable to control his speech patterns, sure of evils that lurked in shadows that no one else could see.

Across the house, a spoon clanged against the inside of a bowl. Stevie blinked out of his daze and turned his attention to the kitchen where, for the past week, his mother seemed to be baking funeral casseroles on an everlasting loop. He sucked in a breath, pushed himself away from the front door, moved past Terry's ugly armchair, and slowly made his way to the heart of the house. But rather than finding his mom in her usual spot over the stove, there was his stupid older brother, eating cold breakfast cereal at half past noon, his phone glowing in his hand. Stevie loomed in the kitchen's threshold, wondering if he should ignore the oaf he called a sibling and just go to his room. But annoyance was scratching at the walls of his chest, offering up a wooly itch for a fight. Letting Dunk have it would make Stevie feel better, and feeling better sounded good. Because so far, he'd had a pretty shitty day.

But Dunk beat him to the punch. He looked up from his phone and smirked. "What's wrong with *you*?" A single brow arched high above his right eye, which made him look like a curious idiot; nothing but a waste-of-space high school kid who nobody would go looking for if *he* went missing; a guy nobody would cry about if *he* were eaten by whatever it was that was looming out there in that forest. Heck, Stevie bet even Annie would be relieved. *God, that stupid haircut!*

"Nothing." Stevie's response was clipped. On second

thought, fighting with Dunk wasn't worth the effort. He had bigger fish to fry. "Where's Mom?"

Dunk looked back to his phone. "Grocery store, probably. Picking up more shit for Aunt Mandy."

Stevie frowned at that. It seemed to him that Aunt Amanda should have been back to cooking her own stuff; seemed to him like everything in the Brighton house should have gone back to the way it had once been. But it hadn't. And for whatever reason, that thought made him want to rage.

"H-how come you didn't wake me up?" Stevie asked, but Duncan wasn't paying attention. Less than two seconds since he had spoken, and there he was, already absorbed in whatever game he was playing, or article he was reading, or whatever it was that he did on that thing in the first place. *Facebooking*, his mom liked to stay. *Stop Facebooking for just one second, would you please? There's life beyond that stuff. Real live people, Duncan . . .*

"*DUNK.*" Stupid punk.

Duncan glanced up, albeit with a nasty *What the hell do you want?* look.

"W-why didn't you wake me up?" he asked again, adamant. "I left you a note. It was in red marker right under your door. Did you read it?"

Dunk shoveled a spoonful of cereal into his mouth. His expression said it all: he hadn't woken Stevie up because he didn't give a shit. Stevie clenched his teeth as he watched his brother crunch a mouthful of Frosted Flakes. The seed of anger that was nestled into the center of his heart grew with every cowlike chew. Suddenly, all he wanted to do was rush his sibling and shove that bowl into Dunk's lap.

"J-Jude came home," Stevie told him, his eyes not once leaving his brother's face, waiting for some sort of reaction, some proof that his brother was a living, breathing human being. "Last night, all right?"

"So I huh-huh-heard," Dunk responded. "Cuh-cuh-congratulations to him on finding himself. Like an elf on a shelf. Now, if you don't muh-mind, I was enjoying alone time with myself."

Something tripped over itself in Stevie's chest. Dunk had made fun of him before, but all at once he found himself breathless, his bottom lip trembling as though his brother had said the most hurtful, infuriating thing he'd ever heard. He swallowed hard, looked down at his feet, tried to hold it together as best he could, all the while wondering why his urge to scream had suddenly morphed into the need to cry.

Memory of Jude's threat washed over him. His best friend's own hurtful insult: *Dr. Seuss*. The way he had stared blankly into the TV camera, swaying ever so slightly, like a reed in the wind. It pushed Stevie over the edge, and all at once, tears were stinging the backs of his eyes.

"What's *wrong* with you?" He couldn't keep his tone from wavering. "H-how can you not care that he was gone for so long? What if he hadn't come back and the things that happened . . . the things, that *thing* . . . they were awful when he was missing and now he's back but still gone even though he's back because of the bad stuff?" He paused mid tirade, gulped a breath. "What if he's got drama?"

Duncan snorted. "You mean *trauma*?"

"Trauma!" Yes. That's what Stevie meant, and Dunk knew it.

Dunk looked back to his phone, pretending that he was somewhere other than in the kitchen being asked such heavy questions, being scolded and yelled at by his delicate flower of a kid brother. But Dunk's lack of response only reminded Stevie of Jude's blank TV face. He narrowed his eyes, looked for something to throw. When he found nothing, he kicked the doorjamb instead.

"You suck," Stevie said, shoulders squared, unabashed. "Next thing you know, you're gonna be just like terrible Tyrant Terry. A no-good loser, a *snoozer*, that's what you are! A snoozer who doesn't care about anything except stupid basketball. And you're not even good, so you better go practice!"

That did the trick. Dunk snapped to attention. His face twisted as though he'd been genuinely insulted. He opened his mouth, ready to slam Stevie with some witty locker room comeback. *Fag. Moron. Dipshit.* But rather than giving him the chance, Stevie stomped out of the kitchen and moved down the hall to his room. Because no matter the situation, the last thing he wanted was for stupid Dunk to see him cry.

He slammed his door and crawled onto his bed. He shouldn't have said that basketball thing to Dunk. That hadn't been fair. He'd have to apologize, and the sooner he did it the better. But just as he gathered himself up to march back into the kitchen and deliver an embittered reparation, he paused at the sight of Jude—not in the backyard, where Stevie had left him, but now in the side yard between Stevie's house and his own. He was just standing there, facing Stevie's bedroom window, his hands resting atop the crooked fence that cut the two properties in half. That faraway look was back, like the lights were on but nobody was home. *Knock knock.* Stevie slowly pressed his hand against the glass of his window, offering his best friend a mute hello. Jude lifted his hand, too, but not to mimic Stevie's greeting. Rather than waving, he scratched at that spot on his left arm. His expression as vacant as a freshly cleaned chalkboard. As though Stevie were invisible. Just like the cats, that surrounded him now, but Jude didn't seem to notice—four of them in total, with one rubbing up against his leg.

19

THE NEXT MORNING, Stevie found his mother in the tiny laundry room just shy of the kitchen pantry. She was squeezed between the wall and the dryer like a fly between a window and a screen, tossing clothes into a plastic basket sitting on top of the washer.

"Mom?" Stevie shifted his weight from foot to foot as he stood in the doorway, watching his mom pile laundry into the bin while the back of her jeans polished the wall behind her clean.

"Hey, baby," she said. "What's up?"

"D-do you have time to talkity-talk?" He paused, whispered to himself, as if to check his words. "Tockity-tock . . ."

The question made her falter. She paused, her right hand held aloft, one of Dunk's basketball jerseys crumpled in her fist. "Talkity-talk?" she asked, her smile shifting to concern.

"Talk," Stevie corrected himself, looking down at his feet. What ten-year-old asked his mother to *talkity-talk*? Only him. "D-do you have time to talk for a minute," he asked again. "*Talk* for a minute."

"Sure, honey." He didn't need to look at her to know that

she was worried. He could hear the strain in her voice. Every time he slipped up, he imagined her replaying the yelling, his dad muttering about how Stevie would eventually lose it, how he'd end up going on a rampage. It was part of the reason why he wasn't able to meet his mother's gaze, afraid that what he was about to say would make him seem even crazier than his constant verbal ticks.

"It's about Jude," he finally said. "I really th-think there's something wrong with him, I think. I know, I think, I *know* it sounds weird, b-but . . ." His words tapered off. He gave her a wary glance, unsure of himself.

"Tell me what's wrong." She offered a reassuring nod. *Go on.*

"It's h-hard to explain," he said.

"Well, give it a shot."

He chewed on his bottom lip, trying to figure out how to put the words together so that they made sense. "He's just acting really weird . . . ," he said. "Not like himself. Like, yesterday I saw him in the backyard, in the back . . ."

"Well, *that's* good, right?" she asked. "At least he was out of his room. That's an improvement."

"Except that when I went over, when I went . . . I went over, red rover, he was looking at the fence. Just *staring* at it. The fence. Staring-contest staring. Like he didn't even know I was there," Stevie recalled. "I said *Hey, hey, hey, hey, hey*—"

"Okay, Stevie." She placed a steadying hand on his shoulder. "Take a second."

He paused. Squeezed his eyes shut. Gave his brain a minute to recalibrate.

"A-and he didn't hear me for a while, like he'd gone deaf or something."

"Maybe he was just zoned out," his mom offered. "Don't be so critical, sweetheart. You zone out all the time." Fair point, but zoning out in front of the TV was a heck of a lot different from what Jude had been doing—staring at the punched-out knot in the fence slat like he wanted to crawl through it and to the other side; like he knew something was out there, just beyond it. *Zoned out* wasn't strong enough a modifier. Jude hadn't just been zoned out. He'd been *gone*.

"Okay," Stevie said. "But then he got really *really* weird."

"Weird how?" Stevie's mom blindly jutted her arm into the dryer and felt around, searching for clothes she couldn't see. She wasn't able to fully open the door in those cramped quarters. Laundry day was a contortionist's act.

"L-like, *mean*. I was just joking around—"

She gave him a look.

"I was just saying, just playing, I *swear* . . ."

"I told you not to give him a hard time," she reminded.

"I wanted him to feel better, but he got so mad, so Mad Hatter with the cats that he threatened to punch my teeth in, throwing rocks and everything."

Stevie's mom stiffened. She knew just as well as anyone that Jude had a penchant for drama, but threats weren't something she was about to tolerate. And rock throwing? "That's unacceptable." Her words were clipped. She shoved a handful of clothes into the laundry basket and slammed the small metal door closed with a bang.

"That's unacceptable," Stevie whispered to himself.

"I'm going to talk to your aunt Mandy about that when I go over there."

Stevie frowned. He hadn't meant to get Jude into trouble, and yet there he was, ratting him out. "B-but, Mom . . ."

"No, Stevie," she said, giving him a stern look. "We aren't okay with that kind of thing."

"I *know* that . . ."

"I mean, I understand that he's got issues," she murmured.

"Mom . . ." He was getting impatient.

"But threatening *my* kid . . ."

"M-mom?" She wasn't listening again. Why he was surprised, he wasn't sure.

"I swear, if—"

"Mom!" Stevie hadn't meant to yell, but it had come out that way, regardless. She started, nearly dropping the basket she'd gathered off the top of the washer, and stared at him with wide eyes. "A second later he was fine, Frankenstein," he explained. Another pause. Another regroup. "He was *fine*, Mom, like he didn't even know he had said what he said, what he had said. And then I asked him if he wanted to go to the fort. I asked him, *You want to go to the fort?* And he acted like it was the dumbest idea he'd ever heard, like he'd never been to the fort before at all. So I left him alone to go home alone and, and, and, and when I . . . when I . . . when I started walking he said that maybe we should go work on the fort since we need to finish it before school gets back in." For half a second, he was distracted by the fact that he'd been able to say so much

all at once. He actually felt proud until he caught sight of his mother's face.

Her mouth was open, like she was ready to say something. She looked bewildered, disturbed. *Finally*, he thought, *an appropriate response.*

"I really think there's really something really wrong," he reiterated. "I think he n-needs to go to the doctor to make sure nothing happened to his brain." Like a lobotomy, or that electroshock stuff. "I thought about telling Aunt Mandy, but I don't want to scare her about the monster and maybe there isn't anything wrong, maybe *I'm* the one who's being weird, but that thing, that thing, that . . ." He bit his lip. *Crap.*

Silence.

Stevie and his mother stared at each other for a long while. Finally, she spoke.

"Stevie?" She slowly raised an eyebrow at him. He hated when she did that. It made him feel stupid and small. "The monster?"

He swallowed, not sure whether he should fess up and tell her about it, or whether he should pretend he didn't know what she was talking about.

No. Better not.

When Stevie held firm in his silence, she sighed. "Okay," she said. "I'll talk to your aunt about it."

"About w-what?" The monster? No, she couldn't . . .

"About Jude— Stevie, are you feeling okay?" Her gaze was unfaltering. She wanted a solid answer to ease her nerves, even if it was a lie. Reaching out, she pressed the back of her hand to his forehead. He took a step back, out of her reach.

"Sure, yeah, fine, great, thanks. J-just don't let Jude hear you, okay? Don't let him hear you." Jude wasn't big on relying on adults for anything. He thought adults were just as fake as the kids at school, and most of the time Stevie agreed. And yet there he was, asking his mom—the woman who had grounded him rather than listening to what he had to say—for help. He'd betrayed his friend by squealing, but he was desperate.

"I'll be quiet about it," she promised, then gave him a little smile of reassurance. "But I want you staying inside for the rest of the day, all right?"

"How come?"

"It's hot," she said. "Just watch some TV."

Stevie didn't completely trust his mom with the information he'd given her, but he took a step away from the laundry room door. He really did hope she didn't blab, because if Jude *did* overhear her, Stevie knew their friendship would be over.

·   ·   ·

Two hours and three episodes of *Unsolved Mysteries* later, Stevie found Jude standing on the welcome mat of his front porch. He was the last person Stevie had expected to see. But rather than questioning what his cousin was doing there, Stevie simply smiled at his peeling, lobster-red friend and offered his typical "Hey."

"Hey yourself," Jude replied.

"Jeez, doesn't that hurt?" Stevie asked, wincing at Jude's killer sunburn. The chapped bits of skin on Jude's cheeks were spreading like some sort of flesh-eating disease. The only time

Stevie had seen a burn that bad was on his dad. They had gone to Indian Beach, camped out, climbed rocks, built a bonfire and everything. The next thing Stevie knew, his dad was moving around like a robot in need of oil, hissing through his teeth and holding his arms out as though they were made of fire.

Jude, however, didn't seem to be bothered by his sizzled skin. He shrugged, as though the burn looked worse than it was—and it looked awful; like a boiled tomato shedding its casing.

"Wanna go to the fort?" Jude asked.

Stevie couldn't help it; he faltered. His heart felt as if it were swelling to ten times its size, crowding out every other organ with a concurrent sense of optimism and doubt. Jude could have been having a bad day yesterday; cranky, annoyed by all those cats. Perhaps Stevie had just caught him during an off moment and all Jude had needed was a whole lot of sleep. But now he was good to go. A-OK. Ready to rumble and feeling fine.

Unless it was a trick.

A warning voice whispered at the back of Stevie's mind, setting his teeth on edge with a nefarious purr. *Don't believe it. It's too good to be true.*

And yet, Stevie caught himself nodding. Yes, he wanted to go to the fort. Sure, he'd venture into the woods with a kid he was no longer sure he could trust. Why not? What could possibly go wrong?

He pleaded his case to his mother.

"I *can't* just tell him no." And in a way, that was true. Stevie's mom may have been worried about the stuttering and word salad, but Jude was the priority here, at least in Stevie's mind. If

Jude wanted to wander around in the forest, if that was some-thing that was going to help him get back to his old self, it was Stevie's duty as his best friend to comply.

"I don't know," she said, unsure, and right away Stevie knew he should have never said anything about Jude's threat. That's what she was thinking about—Jude punching Stevie's lights out, throwing rocks, stoning him to death. "I'd rather you two stay out in the yard where I can see you."

Stevie raised both eyebrows at her, then exhaled a little laugh like he was in on the joke. She was kidding, right? The yard? "The fort isn't in the yard, retard." She frowned and he blanched, immediately looking down to his feet. His mom didn't like that word. "Sorry," he said.

"I know the fort isn't in the yard." She tossed aside the dish towel she'd been holding. "But the woods . . ." He could see it in her eyes, in the way she was gripping the edge of the kitchen counter with one hand: she was scared that, out in the trees, the psycho childnapper who had snatched Jude would grab her kid, too. Or that Jude would turn on him, become the danger rather than the ally. But in that very instance, *No* was the wrong answer, no matter how much she wanted to refuse her son's request.

"Okay," she finally said, exhaling an unhappy sigh, giving in for the good of her nephew. Stevie spun on the heel of his sneakers, ready to bolt for the living room. "But I want you home by seven at the latest! The *latest*! Or I'm sending a search party!" And for that, Stevie was thankful. Because if Jude flipped his lid and finally shoved Stevie out of that tree house, it sure as heck would be hard to make it home for dinner on a pair of broken legs.

.   .   .

Stevie and Jude were halfway down Sunset Avenue a few minutes later, but the farther they walked, the more Stevie began to doubt that Jude wanted to go to the fort at all. He tried to make conversation, talking about stuff he knew Jude loved, like the Avengers and how to get their moms to buy them the BMX bikes they wanted so that they could ride the trails instead of walking them like dopes. These were topics that, a week before, Jude would have discussed and debated for hours. But today, he remained steadfast in what was becoming typical silence, as though he didn't know who the heck Iron Man or Captain America were, and he couldn't have cared less about dirt bikes or riding trails. That lack of interest made Stevie nervous, but again, it could have been that Jude simply didn't feel like talking. There had been plenty of times during their friendship when Stevie hadn't wanted to talk, either, especially when he couldn't keep his words straight.

But after a few minutes of trudging in heavy silence, with one of those strays tailing their every move, Stevie couldn't help himself. He breached the quiet. "Is everything okeydokey, smoky?"

"Sure," Jude said, his tone flat, affectless.

Had his mom been as quiet at Aunt Mandy's as she had promised to be? What if Jude had heard their moms talking and now he knew Stevie had ratted him out? Jude had no interest in going to the fort—he was just luring Stevie out into the middle of nowhere to beat the crap out of him for tattling.

Stevie's nerves flared up at the sight of their usual trail. Suddenly, he wasn't so sure he wanted to go into those woods after all. Because if it wasn't Jude kicking his ass, then it might be that hunchback thing crawling out of the bushes. And really, what would it care if there were two of them instead of one? Two boys meant more to eat.

"What's with you?" Jude asked, noticing Stevie's hesitation. "Pick up the pace."

"N-nothing. I'm just, just, just—"

"Scared?" Jude cut in. But rather than laying into Stevie for being a chicken, he looked up at the sky, as if bothered by the particular angle of the sun. Stevie wondered how it felt to be so seared and still be outside. Had that been him, he would be sitting in the kitchen with his head in the freezer and aloe vera gel dripping from every limb.

And then there was the fact that Jude was scratching again. It was that same spot on his left arm. Tiny dotlike scabs had formed where blood had broken the surface. Every now and again, Jude would catch one of those scabs with a fingernail and yank it off, and Stevie would have to look away with a wince.

"You know how you were on the news?" Stevie asked, searching for something else to talk about. "Did you tell that reporter lady you didn't remember anything just to get her off your back, Jack?" *Attack, hack, hacking, attacking* . . . He clenched his teeth against the words. No, *those* particular ones wouldn't be allowed to come out.

Silence.

Stevie glanced up from his feet only to realize he was being left behind. Jude had increased his pace, as if fleeing the conversation, continuing down the trail without him, that cat at his side.

"Were you going to the fort when, when . . ." Stevie jogged to catch up. "Did you see someone, two, three? Or maybe, or maybe not someone but some*thing* . . . like I did? Like me?"

"Like *you*?"

"Like an animal, I mean. A mean animal. An animal."

"Why can't you talk *normal* for once?" Jude continued to march. The cat ignored them, content in being part of the group.

"W-when you went missing," Stevie said, refusing to be deterred. "Do you really not remember?"

"Can we get out of the sun?"

Stevie nodded as he followed Jude a little ways down the path. They both tucked into a patch of shade, but Jude didn't stop to rest, and neither did the mangy-looking cat. They both moved from shadow to shadow, avoiding the sunshine like deep-ocean fish.

"Jude, I gotta tell you something." The way Jude was walking—so unfaltering, razor-focused and determined—Stevie couldn't tell whether his cousin was hearing him or not. He simply continued to walk ahead, his hands now shoved deep in his pockets as if to keep himself from bloodying his arms, his head down as though he were walking to the gallows. "Gotta tell you . . . Hey, can we stop on top for a minute? It's important."

Jude didn't slow. Didn't turn his head to regard him. Out ahead, a second stray surfaced from behind a fern. Those things were everywhere lately. Stevie hadn't ever seen them so active, or so eager to be near people.

"Jude, can't you wait? Don't you *get* it . . . ? I saw something!" Jude slowed.

"I went lookie-looing for you-ing, remember? I retraced our steps, thinking that maybe I'd find a clue, two, three, fo—" *Stop it. Stop it!* His fists came up, knocking hard against both temples. "I—I—I ended up at the road . . ."

Jude was still now. Frozen. Staring at the path, *glaring* at it, as if trying to ignite the leaves beneath the soles of his All-Stars with a single, deadly look. His intensity raised a red flag, but Stevie had said too much this time to let it go.

"There was something at the house . . . on the porch," he explained, carefully choosing his words, speaking them slowly so his tongue wouldn't betray him. "L-like an animal or, or, or something. I couldn't see it real well. It was in the shadows, like it was hiding." Like Jude was now hiding from the sun.

"So, it was probably scared of you," Jude concluded. "Who the hell wouldn't be?"

But the explanation only triggered a sudden shaking of Stevie's head. "No, it wasn't scared. *I* was scared. I turned to run, and I heard it behind me, chasing, chasing like, like, like . . ." Like it wanted to kill him. Except, had that actually happened? What if he had just been afraid? How was he supposed to pick apart his imagination from what had really occurred?

"Like how you shoved your hand down the sink?" Jude

asked. "Or how you thought Dunk was playing basketball with a severed head that one time? Or how you were sure Mr. Frosty had switched our ice cream for cold mashed potatoes that may have been poisoned? Like *that*?"

Stevie stared at his cousin, speechless.

"There's something wrong with your head, Sack. You know that, right? You see things that don't exist. You say things, *do* things, that don't make sense. It was just another freak-out," Jude said. "Like all the rest."

"No! I saw it again after that!" Stevie swore. "In the side yard beneath my window."

"You mean where your fucktard of a stepdad stores all his crap?"

"It was there, Jude! It was crouched down. Hunched, you know? It was hairless, pale, like, like, like Dr. Evil's creepy cat, Mr. Bigglesworth. You know Mr. Bigglesworth?"

"Of course I know Mr. fucking Bigglesworth," Jude snapped. "Why are you asking such stupid goddamn questions?"

"Was that what it was? That it was, that—?" Stevie clamped his mouth shut, waited a beat.

"What?"

"Is that what took you?"

Rather than answering, Jude turned and started to walk away.

"Jude!" Stevie stood rooted to the ground, staring at his best friend's back, a cat flanking him on each side. Was this how it was going to be, every question answered with a cold shoulder?

"*What?!*" Jude abruptly turned around, his eyes narrowed,

just like when Stevie had visited with him in his backyard. "You expect me to buy your crazy fucking story? That you're seeing fucking monsters?"

Stevie was taken aback by Jude's aggravation. "I'm just worried . . . s-scared that—"

"That what? Godzilla is going to crawl out of the woods and get you? You made it up inside your head, dude." He thudded a finger hard against his own skull. "Nothing but the same old crap. This is why your dad left, Sack. He couldn't handle it."

A wad of tears clogged up the back of Stevie's throat. First it had been the Dr. Seuss insult. Now he was responsible for his father running away. *You should be relieved,* Stevie thought. *He's being a dick. He's back to his old self again.* But there was something about Jude's rage, about how the angrier he became the harder he scratched at that spot on his arm.

"M-my mom said that asking you about what happened would m-make you mad," Stevie warbled. "But don't you get it?" He gave his friend an imploring look—a friend who, at that very moment, was more interested in kicking at a rock jutting out of the path than listening to what Stevie had to say. "Remember that Max kid? That Max kid? What he did, that kid, Max?" They'd heard the story a billion times.

"Yeah, I remember the Max kid," Jude said, a little less angry now, possibly feeling bad for bringing up Stevie's dad the way he had. "But nobody knows what happened to him, and what happened to him didn't happen to *me*. I'm not some stupid baby who got lost in the trees."

"B-but what if you just got lucky?" Stevie blinked at the audacity of his own question. *What if you were minutes from being torn to pieces like Max had been?* It wasn't the prettiest picture to stick in Jude's already post-traumatic head, but Jude didn't seem to be phased by the insensitivity. He just stood there, scratching at his arm. The cats continued to hover, but were starting to lose interest.

"Sorry," Stevie told him. "Sorry, Jude, I'm sorry, so sorry. I'm really glad you're home. Really, really glad." He didn't want Jude to get the wrong idea. If he hadn't come back, Stevie didn't know what he would have done. His mom was right—he needed to drop it. Aunt Mandy could have been right, too. Sometimes it was better to simply be happy that something had righted itself rather than questioning why it had occurred.

"You've gotten real weird, Sack," Jude said. "Worse than ever. Like someone twisted *you* up."

Stevie tried to come up with a reply, but Jude didn't feel like waiting. Rather, he turned down the path and continued in the direction of their fort, still scratching.

Pleading could work. "The Tyrant won't be back from work for a long, long time. Wanna watch *Unsolved Mysteries*? Maybe we can get my mom to drive us to the Y." Nothing. "Dunk can take us to a movie." He was willing to try anything, no matter how slim the chances, just to walk in the opposite direction. "W-we went to see *Jurassic World* and there were velociraptors. It was good. I'll watch it again if you wanna go see it, you wanna? I've got some money saved that I've been saving in my room that we can get it if we go back, Jude. Let's just go back."

Jude wasn't listening. He was still walking forward, cats at his side, taking the path that would lead them into the glowing green shade far from town.

And yet, despite all his good sense, Stevie continued to follow.

Because he had to.

There was something out there. Something bad. He was *sure* of it. And he loved Jude too much to let him go alone.

20

R OSIE SPENT THE DAY staring at that red sneaker, eventually tucking it into the drawer with all the collars she'd collected throughout the years. And thank goodness for that, because just that evening, a police cruiser pulled up to the house, lighting up the woods like a carnival with a swivel of red and blue. She stood at the front window, her mouth dry, her mind reeling, because how did they know? She had taken all the precautions, had spent the entire day making sure she'd done everything to cover Otto's tracks. The only way they could prove the dead boy had been there was to swab the backyard for DNA, and even then she wasn't sure they'd find anything. It had started to rain again. The lawn was soaked so thoroughly that there were pools among the pitted grass.

And yet, there they were: two police officers in rain slickers, sliding out of their car, dragging their feet along crumbling paving stones, their guns holstered upon their hips. One held a clipboard. The other spoke something into a walkie-talkie attached to his shoulder. Would they interrogate her first, or would they slap the cuffs on her wrists, no questions asked? Because that was the only reason for their being out there. The shoe. The body. *Somehow*, despite her efforts, they knew.

The doorbell chimed. The house constricted, shrinking in on itself like the White Rabbit's Wonderland cottage. Rosie clutched the window curtains, willing the cops to go away.

The doorbell rang again, and a whimper escaped her throat. She could hear them talking, muffled on the opposite side of the door, probably deciding which one would draw his weapon, which one would tackle her to the ground.

A stern knock now. Authoritative. *We know you're in there.* If she didn't answer, she was only giving them probable cause.

"Coming!" She tried to singsong the word to suggest nonchalance. After all, she had nothing to hide. Pulling open the door, she gave the officers a cheerful smile. "May I help you?"

The cops—Myers and Sanderson, according to their name tags—gave her a pair of tight-lipped smiles. This was strictly business. If they caught an eyeful of her son, there would be condemnation above all else. And after first-degree murder, they'd throw in a charge of child neglect.

"Missus Aleksander?" Officer Myers looked down to his clipboard, making sure he got the name right. *Like he hasn't been staring at that thing the entire drive over here,* she thought. More than likely, he simply didn't want to look at her pallid skin, her washed-out face, her widely spaced eyes.

"Yes, that's me," she said.

"Ma'am, we're looking for a boy . . ." Myers handed her a small picture. Glossy. Smeared with fingerprints. The edges were bent, as though it had been pulled out of a back pocket one too many times. The child she'd discovered in the backyard had been mangled, and in a way she had been relieved. Had she been able to see what he had looked like in life, she would have broken beneath the weight of her own culpability. But now, there he was, back from the dead, staring up at her from the rectangular confines of a school photograph.

"Maxwell Larsen," Myers said. "Six years old."

"Oh no." Two involuntary words. *Six?* Too young.

"He's gone missing from Deer Valley just up the road," Myers continued. "His folks think he may have headed into the woods. He had a dog with him. We thought that maybe he'd wandered this way."

A beautiful little boy. Blond hair cut in a typical bowl. Blue eyes. A shy smile that suggested both bashfulness and mischief. He wore a black turtleneck beneath a vest striped that looked homemade by either Mom or Grandma, specifically for picture day. Maxwell Larsen. The child Rosie wished Otto had been. The son that should have been hers. The son that she deserved.

"Ma'am?"

She felt her face flush. A tremor rippled just beneath her skin. She handed Officer Myers the photo, unable to look at it any longer, not sure how a stranger's child was able to so thoroughly reflect her dead husband's gaze.

"You haven't seen him, then?" Myers asked, taking the snapshot back. A few steps behind him, his comrade, Officer Sanderson, was scoping out the place, looking for a body, a trail of blood, a satanic symbol scrawled onto a wall.

"I'm sorry." She couldn't look either of them in the eye. "I don't get visitors up here. It's much too far. The trails aren't maintained."

The cops waited, possibly for a confession.

She looked up just for a moment, just in time to see Myers's attention flick past her shoulder. He was looking inside the house just like his buddy, trying to see if she was making up stories, hiding the Larsen boy in there somewhere. Perhaps she had him lounging in a cauldron while it simmered over a fire—little boy stew, what witches eat.

"He may have been out this way, but without him knocking on the door . . ." She shrugged. *Sorry.* The forest was endless. He could have gone anywhere. "Would you like to come inside?" She took a backward step and swung the front door wider; a bold move. But despite her sudden bout of courage—or was it stupidity?—her heart was pounding hard enough to make her feel faint.

"You live alone, Miss Aleksander?" Officer Myers asked.

"Yes. For eight years now. My husband passed away a while ago. Dr. Ansel," she said. "You may have known him."

Officer Myers didn't, but Sanderson perked at the name. "I think I remember him," he said from behind his colleague. "He was my little sister's physician. Real sorry to hear about what happened, ma'am. A little late, but my condolences just the same."

"Thank you." Rosie gave Sanderson a faint smile. Myers, who looked as though he'd been considering taking her up on the invitation of a tour, appeared satisfied with the exchange.

"No need to go inside," he said. "But we'd appreciate you keeping an eye out." He popped open his aluminum clipboard, fished out a business card, and handed it over. "If you see anything, give us a call."

Rosie took the card. "I don't have a working phone at the moment, but I'll certainly drive in."

"There'll be a search party," Sanderson said. "If you hear dogs barking or people yelling out here, that's what it is. No need to be alarmed."

"I see." She looked down at the card. A search party would be problematic. "Just during the day?"

"Not much to see at night," Myers chimed in.

"And . . . for how long?" she asked. "Not that I mind, it's just . . . I have a cat. Sasha." Poor, dead Sasha. "He doesn't much care for dogs." Rosie gave them a conciliatory smile. "I'd rather keep him indoors if they're going to be close by. He spooks easily." Surely, they could understand her concern.

"Just *one* cat?" Meyers asked. "There are a couple under your porch."

"Oh." Rosie waved a hand, as if to shoo the idea away. "Strays. I don't know how they find me." *A couple.* If it hadn't been raining and they hadn't gone to hide, there would be half a dozen at least.

"The search should last a week," Sanderson said. "More than likely two, though there's no telling exactly where they'll be looking. They'll start at sunup and be done around six or seven in the evening, if that helps."

"It does," Rosie said. "May I join the search?" She had no intention of looking for the child she knew would never be found, but it seemed like something a guilty party would never suggest. Just as a killer wouldn't invite a police officer inside the house, especially with the body hidden only a handful of steps left of the door.

"Absolutely," Sanderson said. "They're meeting at five thirty tomorrow morning, Trinity Church parking lot. From what I gather, that'll be their regular spot. Everyone willing and able is encouraged to come. They'll have doughnuts, I think." He flashed her a smile that made him look half his age.

"Doughnuts?" She feigned interest. "Well, in that case I'll certainly try to make it." Then gave him a wink. "Thank you, officers."

"Thank *you*." Sanderson seemed nice; a good man just doing his job, an overgrown kid in uniform. Rosamund almost felt bad lying to him. "And if you're having trouble with those strays, don't hesitate to call the nonemergency line. We'll dispatch a unit."

"Good luck with your search," she told them. "May God help that little boy return home safely." *Oh, you're a piece of work,* she thought to herself. *A real actress. Next up, the Academy Awards.*

"Have a good night, ma'am," Myers said.

"Night, Mrs. Aleksander," Sanderson bid farewell. "Hope to see you there."

Rosie watched them descend the stairs, step into the rain, climb into their cruiser, and slowly roll away. She stared out at the logging road—once busy, now hardly ever used—and waited for the car to disappear, imagining those officers mulling over their visit. Sanderson was probably reminiscing about Ansel and how much his little sister seemed to have liked him; fantasizing about free jelly-filled pastries, the kind that Ansel loved best. Myers had seemed more suspicious. Rosie glanced over her shoulder, curious as to what it was that he had found so interesting inside her house. It was only then, as if seeing the place for the first time, that she realized just how much of a wreck it was.

What had once been a bright and happy home was now a tangle of furniture and misplaced objects. The couches, which had once sat next to each other at a perfect right angle, were strewn about, as though she had started rearranging them only to grow bored with the task. The same went for the side tables and lamps. Her beloved Persian rug—once the jewel of the living room with its vibrant orange color and intricate design—was now nothing but a faded, tattered tapestry pushed halfway across the room, so far from the randomly placed couches that it appeared as if Rosie had simply unrolled it and let it lie, skewed angle and all. There were no sharp corners to anything, no interior design. It was hard to keep a house looking like something out of a magazine when the child who lived in it belonged in a zoo.

But an unkempt house was none of Officer Myers's business. She had made a point to bring up Ansel's death, which, in her opinion, permanently excused her from worrying about feng shui for the rest of her natural life. If Officer Myers wanted a case against her, he'd have to report her to *Better Homes and Gardens* for judgment; the honorable Martha Stewart presiding.

And while seeing the house with a fresh pair of eyes was disconcerting—because really, how *did* it get so out of sorts without her noticing?—she had bigger problems. Satisfied that the police weren't going to return—at least not that evening—she made sure the front curtains were securely drawn, double-checked the front-door lock, and moved toward the staircase. She pulled the door built beneath it open, pushed a few old coats aside, and accessed the second, nearly invisible entryway along the back wall. When she opened it, Otto rushed past her and into the house like a dog in urgent need of being let out.

She gaped at the small room she'd left him in. The trash bags and their unspeakable contents were torn open. Shredded black plastic decorated the room like morbid party streamers at a murder scene. Rosie winced away from the horror of it. She'd be scrubbing up Otto's ungodliness first thing in the morning—and possibly cleaning it over and over for weeks if she couldn't get rid of the body, at least until Max Larsen's search party threw in the towel. But there wasn't time to dawdle. Spinning around to look behind her, Otto was out of sight, but his bloody prints trailed from beneath the stairs and into the kitchen. She found him struggling with the back-porch door, his gnarled hands smearing blood up and down the white wood trim as he pawed at the lock.

A black thought slithered across the wrinkles of her brain.

A terrible, awful, seductively tempting thought.

If she kept Otto locked up for long enough, there would be no body to bury.

If she let her son do what came naturally, there would be nothing but bones picked clean.

21

THE BOYS ARRIVED at the fort empty-handed—something Jude would have found exasperatingly unproductive only a week before. But as they both stood there, staring up at their nearly completed structure, Jude seemed just fine with it now. And for the first time that summer, their once-masterful hideout struck Stevie as cheap and crummy, a sorry attempt at a tree house if there ever was one. The whole thing looked more cockeyed than before, not a single straight board to the place. And despite the hundreds of salvaged nails they'd used to secure it to the tree, he was positive that even the most sapless summer storm would knock it off its perch. Strange, seeing as how he'd considered it man's greatest achievement just days ago. But now, an undeniable pang of disappointment began to unspool inside his chest.

Jude was still scratching, and Stevie was compelled to grab his hands and hold them still, but he was sure he'd get popped in the mouth if he tried. That, and Jude's arms were peeling—something Stevie hadn't noticed until just then, or perhaps he hadn't noticed because it was new.

Jude made a move for the fort, caught one of the ladder

boards they had nailed to the trunk, and began to climb. Half-way up, he shot Stevie an expectant look, but Stevie didn't move. There was a good twenty feet between them now, and unlike yesterday, when Stevie had craved closeness, today he wasn't the least bit interested in closing the gap.

"Are you coming or what?" Jude asked.

No, Stevie didn't think he was. He wanted to be out here with Jude, hoped it would help his cousin come around. But Jude had threatened to push Stevie out of that citadel before, and that was when he had been normal. Who knew what he'd end up doing if Stevie followed him up now?

"Um, I don't think so, no."

"What the hell do you mean you *don't think so*?" Jude glowered from his perch. "What was the point of us coming out here, then?"

The point had been to rekindle the thing that they had lost; to right the wrongs that had displaced the past.

"I thought you just wanted to see it again." Maybe, just maybe, despite its dilapidated construction and splintery boards, the fort would remind Jude of how things between them had once been. There had been magic in that tree house. Each crooked nail told the story of their unshakable bond.

But if that fort ever had magic, it appeared to be gone. Roosted a good six feet overhead, Jude pushed away from the ladder nailed to that tree and took a flying leap down to the forest floor. He looked frustrated, angry, but Stevie was too mesmerized by the grace of his cousin's vault to pay Jude's annoyance much mind. Had Stevie tried that same jump, he would have twisted an ankle, possibly even broken his leg. But Jude? He'd sprung to the ground with the confidence of one of those loitering strays, and he'd landed just as elegantly, too.

"Why would I just want to see it again?" Jude glared up at the tree house with a clear sense of disdain. "It's a piece of shit. I bet this tree is so embarrassed to have that thing in its branches, it'll be dead by next summer."

That was it, then. The only question left now was whether it had been Stevie's fear or Jude's disappearance that had opened their eyes to the harshness of their crooked, weatherworn reality. Or had it been both, and now neither Jude nor Stevie could see the good around them?

"I told my mom I'd be home soon. Balloon. Name that tune." He needed to back out of this whole thing, to turn tail and book it back into town. But Jude wasn't buying it.

"Uh-huh," Jude said, his face sour with aggravation, his fingernails clawing at his skin. "I can name that tune in one note. That tune is 'Bullshit,' performed by Stevie Chickenshit Clark."

"Serious," Stevie insisted. "She didn't even want me"—a pause, a correction—"us, *us* to c-come out here. She's scared."

"Scared of what?"

"I guess of just, like, just, like, just, like, someone taking us again."

Jude shifted his weight, crossed his arms over his chest. "You mean someone taking *me* again," he said. "You can't be taken again if you haven't been taken before, dumbass."

"Dumbass," Stevie echoed quietly. "Dumbass, dumbshit."

"Who're you calling a dumbshit, Shitsack?"

"N-no-nobody . . ." Stevie held up his hands. It was as if Jude *wanted* to fight, something inside scratch-scratch-scratching at the part of him that yearned for violence.

"Whatever," Jude said flatly. "Seems pretty weird for your mom to worry about what happens to you out here when she doesn't give a shit about what happens to you at home."

Stevie's mouth went dry. His chest clenched. Now he was going after Stevie's *mom*? But Jude looked beyond giving a damn. If Stevie's feelings were hurt, it's because he was a pansy. Not Jude's problem. Maybe Terry could fix Stevie's gutless condition with a few hefty swings of his belt.

"You know what I think?" Jude asked. "I think you can't even stand up to your own old man, step- or not. You don't have the guts to tell The Tyrant to fuck off. So, whatever you think you saw at that house? There isn't a chance in hell you've got the balls to go after it. Not that it was even real . . ."

Stevie stared at the person he felt he knew best in life, and hardly recognized him. He looked down at his feet a moment later, unable to meet Jude's gaze. Sure, there were shades of Jude there—the cant of his head, certain turns of phrase—but otherwise it was some other boy. Some kid Stevie would have never been close with because he was cutthroat and mean.

"Well, what do you say? Let's go check it out. Do you got a pair, or what?" Jude asked.

Stevie didn't know what it was about the situation that made him pivot from near-tears to anger so fast. But now, rather than crying, he imagined himself charging forward, knocking Jude over and pummeling him with his fists. He pictured spit and blood flying from Jude's mouth, his own hands aching each time his knuckles gnashed against Jude's teeth. That's what Jude needed—not patience and understanding, but a severe ass-kicking. It could have been just the ticket to helping the real Jude resurface. Or that could have been Terry talking and, like Dunk, Stevie was slowly turning into a carbon copy of their bastard stepdad. *There isn't much a good beating can't fix.*

"Yeah." Stevie nearly spit out the word. "I've got a pair to spare."

"Then I guess we're taking a hike," Jude said. "Right?" He waited for Stevie to respond—probably expecting him to back down, but Stevie wasn't going to do that. Not this time.

"S-sure," he said. *"Whatever."*

Jude snorted, amused by Stevie's gumption. He rolled his eyes, then glared—not at Stevie, but at the spot on his arm that appeared to be bothering him more and more.

"What's wrong with your arm?" Stevie asked, trying to change the subject, hoping like hell that Jude didn't actually go through with dragging him out to that old house.

"Nothing," Jude said in a *Mind your own business* sort of way. Except, if that was a bug bite he was scratching, Stevie could only envision the insect. Pinchers like needle-nose pliers. One of those Ancient Egyptian scarab beetles, as big as your hand and mean as hell. Except this one would be man-sized, hunched and naked beneath its hard and glossy exoskeleton. Stevie's eyes flicked away from Jude and to cats hiding in the ferns. He could only see one of them, but it looked heinous.

He could swear it was grinning, like a nasty Cheshire cat. And the trees: the branches were teeming with those scarabs, hissing and snapping their pincher mouths, ready to strike. Stevie's fingers drifted to the inside of his arm, mimicking Jude's actions, scratching at a phantom itch.

"We should really get some of that itchy cream from my bathroom," he said, tearing his attention away from the beetles overhead. "And you sh-shouldn't scratch like that. It's gonna get infected."

"Maybe *you're* gonna get infected," Jude fired back, but he didn't bother to look Stevie's way. He was too focused on the crook of his arm. Giving up on mere scratching, he pressed his mouth against the affected area and began to nip at his skin, like a dog biting at fleas. Stevie grimaced. It looked as though Jude was about ready to eat his own flesh. But now Stevie was scratching, too.

Maybe you're *gonna get infected.* Infected by the brain worms that were going to leap from the cats and burrow into his skull through his ear. Infected by all the bugs and biting spiders that were waiting to Geronimo out of the trees and onto his head. His hand flew from his arm to his hair, scratching, then slapped at the back of his neck, sure he'd just felt an arachnid skitter down into his shirt. He spun around, grabbed his T-shirt by its hem, shook it.

"Spider!" he yelped. "Hider spider!" He started to jerk his shirt up over his head, but stopped short when he noticed how wide Jude's eyes had become. "W-what?" he asked, distracted by the sudden flash of fear in his cousin's eyes. "Jude, *what?!*" He pirouetted, looked behind him, certain he was about to come face-to-face with that creature thing. It had snuck up on them while Stevie had been doing the buggy cha-cha; while the duo had fought rather than paying attention to their surroundings.

But there was nothing there.

"Jude?"

Jude's eyes remained wide, silver dollars stuck to his half-hidden face. It was only when he jerked his arm away from his mouth that Stevie saw the blood.

"Holy crap!" Stevie gasped. "What did you do?!"

It wasn't a ton of blood, but it was way more than there should have been. And on Jude's arm, teeth marks. Stevie could see them from ten feet away.

Jude tried to play it cool, but Stevie could tell he was scared. He kept giving that laceration the side eye, as though waiting for a colony of mites and their unhatched eggs to come pouring out of the wound.

"Jude, we gotta go home!" Stevie insisted. "You're bleeding all over the place, all over your face, all over and under and on to the next!" A trail of crimson was making a fast track for Jude's wrist. Stevie was about to turn in the direction they had come, ready to lead the trek back home, and fast. But Jude breezed past him, walking too quickly to be casual.

"Jude, wait!" Stevie rushed after him.

"Shut up!" Jude barked, but he didn't slow.

"Does it hurt?" Of course it did. It had to. Jude had gnawed a hole right into his goddamn arm.

But Jude only repeated "Shut up" and continued to walk.

Less than a minute later, he was scratching again . . . this time at a different spot.

•   •   •

Stevie kept replaying it in his head, but no matter how he tried to explain the incident away, one thing was clear: Jude hadn't realized what he was doing until he had chewed a tear into his flesh.

"Oh my God, Jude." Aunt Mandy looked as beside herself as Stevie felt. "Sweetheart, what happened?"

"Nothing," Jude said, full of angst, just a bunch of mumbled syllables, another Duncan in the works. "It's just a scrape." But it was a gash, one bad enough to require soap and water, possibly stitches, judging by the way it had bled.

Stevie and his mom stood just outside the open bathroom door while Aunt Mandy washed Jude's arm. And Jude? He just stared into the sink as though not remembering doing what he had done.

"He had a scratch," Stevie whispered, waiting for Aunt Mandy to recoil at the teeth marks her cleanup job would inevitably reveal. "Maybe it's bugs. Maggots. Beetles. The Beatles. 'Hey Jude.' He kept scratching and scratching and biting and *biting*."

"Biting?" Stevie's mom raised an eyebrow. Surely he was making it up. She shot a glance at her sister and nephew, as if trying to decide where her loyalty laid, which only made Stevie wonder what the heck was wrong with her. Did she really think he'd make something like this up?

"It was so weird, Mom. The grossest thing *ever*." He kept his voice down, not wanting either Jude or Aunt Mandy to hear. "I thought, I thought, thought he was gonna gobble chew his whole entire arm off."

"It doesn't even hurt," Jude said coolly. "I just scraped it climbing down from the fort. It's no big deal."

"You did not! Why are you lying?" Stevie was stunned by his own outburst. If he wanted to wreck their friendship, he was on the right track. But this—the fact that Jude had injured himself—it seemed important, something that would possibly convince Aunt Mandy to take him to the hospital. Stevie didn't have much room to talk, especially after the garbage disposal incident, but he knew: autocannibalism wasn't what normal kids tended to do.

"Why are you such a *nutsack*?" Jude asked.

"Boys." Aunt Mandy.

"It's, it's, it's . . ." If he said it, there'd be no turning back.

"Stevie." His mom.

". . . because of the monster." He spit it out. "The thing!" There. Now Jude *couldn't* lie. The adults were in on it. Now things *had* to get fixed.

"It's because you're a whack job," Jude said.

"Jude." Aunt Mandy again.

"Well, look at him!" Jude retorted.

"A *monster*, Mom." Stevie gave his mother an imploring look, ignoring Jude's jab. "Monster, mom. Monster mom. My mom is a momster mom—"

"Stevie . . ." His mother's hand landed in its usual spot on his shoulder. She gave it a squeeze. *Take a second. Regroup your thoughts.*

Aunt Amanda gingerly patted Jude's arm with a washcloth. Stevie looked over at her, waited for her to recoil from the sight of Jude's teeth marks, to stare wide-eyed and openmouthed in horror at the wound he had left behind. Those impressions would bring about another demand for answers. What had they been doing out in the woods? Where had Jude gone while he had been missing? What the hell had happened? *No more silence,* she'd yell, shaking Jude by his shoulders. *Talk, goddamnit! I need to know what's going on!* But instead, she only turned off the faucet.

"Well, it definitely looked worse than it is. Just a scratch," she said, relieved. "Lots of blood for a little nothing. Just a scrape, like he said."

Stevie opened his mouth, ready to protest. No, that was impossible. He'd seen the bite marks on Jude's arm with his own eyes. Pulling away from his mother's touch, he moved to the sink and peered down at the crook of Jude's arm. But it was true. The gash was now nothing more than a faint scrape, as though a branch had caught him during his leaping descent; as though he'd never stuck his mouth to that part of his arm at all. It had all been in Stevie's head.

"But I saw it," Stevie said softly. "I saw . . ." He looked up to catch his mother's reflection in the mirror. Her disbelief was replaced not only with worry, but also with distress. And not fear for Jude, either, but fear for *him*.

Only then did he notice Jude staring into the mirror as well, his gaze fixed on Stevie's confusion, on his disbelief. Their eyes met, and Jude gave Stevie a ghost of a smile. Stevie knew it well. Like a kid smirking after telling a particularly dirty joke; the same smile Jude always wore when he knew he was getting away with something bad.

. . .

That night, Stevie kept seeing Jude chewing on his arm in his dreams, and each replay just got worse: Jude jumping down from the tree-house ladder, scratching at his arm, and finally raising the crook of his elbow to his mouth. Jude, jumping from the tippy-top branches of the tallest tree. Scratching harder, tearing at the chapped skin on his arms. Taking bigger bites, giant hunks of flesh separating from bone. Tendons snapping. Gore dripping down his chin. There was, however, one constant in every intensified version of that nightmare: the fort. There, up inside, was the crouching demon thing, watching Stevie's face twist up in horror as Jude consumed himself; its wicked smile a grim reminder of what was coming to get them, waiting out there in the dark.

He couldn't sleep. Closing his eyes while simultaneously trying to keep his imagination in check was a form of brain gymnastics that Stevie hadn't trained for. And those teeth marks, the fact that they had vanished as though they'd never existed? It was only making things worse. Stevie knew what he saw. He had watched Jude bite down. Except, hadn't his shirt been half over his head when he'd first noticed the blood? What if, when Jude had climbed the tree, he had . . .

No, you know what you saw him do.

After Jude's wound had vanished like invisible ink and Stevie's mom had dragged Stevie home, she kept her eye on him the way someone keeps their attention rapt on a puppy about to pee on the carpet. Hawk eyes, always peeking around corners, forever on high alert. She was waiting for him to start pounding the crap out of couch pillows because there were bugs inside, waiting for him to give a repeat performance of the garbage disposal trick. Maybe this time he'd lose his whole hand.

It would be tomorrow or the day after, but eventually Aunt Mandy would tell Stevie not to come over anymore. Jude would tell her to do it. *That nutsack is creeping me out.* That's all it would take for Jude to start wandering into the forest alone. Meanwhile, Stevie would be trapped inside the house. An animal in a cage. A butterfly in a bell jar. A bedbug behind a mattress spring.

Stevie kicked his sheets off his legs. "Get offa offa offa me, awful me," he murmured at his blanket, suddenly sure it was teeming with ticks. His feet hit the rug in front of his bed—just another place nasty things could hide. His toes curled at the thought, and he jumped sideways onto the bare planks of the floor, ready to march across the room and flip on the light, get those roaches to scatter back into the walls from which they had come. But he froze instead. Because there, in the house next door, was Jude, silhouetted by the pale and bubbling glow of his fish tank. Standing at his window, he was staring out the glass and into Stevie's room.

Both boys stared across the side yard at each other, and all Stevie could think was *That's not Jude he isn't he himself anymore.*

He was glad that there was a physical barrier between them. Not like that afternoon, together in the woods, Stevie wondering if Jude would turn on him, if either of them would ever make it home again.

And yet, as soon as Stevie felt that relief—*Thank God I'm here and he's not here but over there where it's not here, I don't want to be there where he is*—that comfort was speared through by self-reproach. Because no matter who the boy across the way was now, he *used* to be Stevie's best friend. And if Jude couldn't count on Stevie to not give up on him, who did he have left?

Stevie swallowed his trepidation and pulled his window open, ready to have a whispered conversation across the yard; something they'd done a million times before. Unable to sleep himself, it could have been that Jude was finally ready to talk.

But rather than opening his own window, Jude slowly canted his head to the side—an animal with its curiosity piqued. And while Stevie couldn't see his expression through the darkness, Jude's stillness made it clear.

The doppelgänger was laughing at him.

A sharp-toothed bogeyman, grinning from ear to ear.

22

J UDE HAD HIT Stevie in earnest for the first time the day his dad had died.

The two had gotten into punching wars a million times in the past, all of them friendly slug-bug games. But that day, Stevie asked why Aunt Mandy was crying so much, why Jude was acting so weird, why everyone was looking like they'd seen a ghost, and Jude laid into his arm with a newfound sense of ferocity. Stevie wasn't yet eight, and nobody had told him about what had happened to Uncle Scott. Being a pain in the ass came naturally, involuntarily; something Jude couldn't handle that afternoon.

Stevie ended up running home in tears, his arm throbbing beneath the thin veil of his Oregon Ducks T-shirt sleeve. Hours later, when his mom made it home from next door, he heard the news. "He's dead" was all his mother could muster. "Your uncle Scott is dead." Not gone. Not passed away. *Dead.* She stepped into the master bedroom and shut the door behind her while Stevie sat alone on the couch, whispering "Dead, dead, dead" for God only knew how long.

Stevie had spent the last two years watching Jude's anger

grow in much the way one observes a tumor enlarge: little by little, year after year, slow enough to not be obvious, but eventually impossible to ignore. It would have been easy to write Jude off as nothing but a bully, but Stevie knew better. Jude had been happy once. It was true that he had always had his share of behavioral problems—issues with authority, getting in trouble at school—but that had been small stuff. Back then, Jude had been a regular kid. Now he was broken; no longer himself.

And maybe it had been the stress of Stevie losing his uncle, or the fact that he had to witness his aunt and best friend struggle with their emotions, relentlessly suppressing their grief . . . but after the funeral, the night terrors got worse. The verbal ticks became unmanageable. His mom pulled him out of school for a few weeks when he was unable to keep his outbursts under control. The principal gently suggested a visit to a counselor. Stevie's mom had looked scared, then, but by the time they crossed the school parking lot and climbed into the car, she was pissed off. "A counselor," she scoffed. "Of *course* he's having problems. His uncle just died. He's just a boy. He's just . . ." She looked over to the passenger seat, Stevie struggling with his safety belt. And then she sighed and gave his arm a squeeze. "It's going to be fine, sweetheart. I promise. Everything is going to be okay."

Except things just kept getting worse.

And now, standing on Aunt Mandy's front porch with a Monopoly box pressed against his chest, Stevie gave his aunt his own lying, optimistic smile, despite the tremor at the pit of his guts. She eyed the board game the way a wary housewife would inspect a traveling salesman's briefcase: with equal parts dubiety and interest. *Behold, Tupperware in a variety of pleasing colors! Watch in wonder as our latest vacuum sucks your carpet clean in ten minutes flat!* "Hi, Stevie . . . ," she said, a little more forlorn than he would have liked. "I wasn't expecting you."

"I th-thought maybe Jude and I could play a game with Jude if it's okay," he said. "He's got that bad burn that's bad, so it's probably better to stay inside and hide inside from the sun." Such feigned thoughtfulness. It made him feel like a phony. He'd just brought that Monopoly game over to get his foot in the door because, just like his mother, Aunt Mandy seemed reluctant to let the boys hang out ever since Jude had come home. And to be honest, Stevie wasn't sure he really *wanted* to go inside. It was his duty, yes, but soldiers didn't exactly clamor into battle. This was simply something he had to do for his friend.

"Well, that's very sweet," she said. *But?* He was waiting for it. *Jude is resting.*

"He said he missed playing, Miss Mandy. We were talking about it yesterday, so I thought, hey, maybe it would be fun out of the sun since he's so red he's peeling."

Aunt Mandy's expression opened up—like a gloomy room made sunny when a window curtain was pulled aside. "He did?"

He didn't.

"Uh-huh." Stevie nodded, a little too enthusiastic. "Yep, yes, yessir, yep."

If a genie had come down and granted Stevie three wishes, they would have been as follows: Stop talking the way he was talking, because it made him feel like a blubbering idiot; win the lottery so he and Jude could go to Star Wars Land and live there for at least a year—longer if they could manage it—and become an adult so he would have the guts to ask his aunt all the questions that were scratching at the interior of his skull. Like: Had Jude said anything about what happened to him while he had been gone? Did she know he had been standing at his bedroom window in the middle of the night, just staring across the yard into Stevie's room like some sort of creeper? And wasn't she worried that Jude was shedding his skin like a just-boiled shrimp; didn't she know about sun cancer and melon nomas? He considered mentioning the wound on Jude's arm, telling her that it had been so much worse before they finally reached home. But no. She'd just get upset all over again and tell him to scram.

Standing in the doorway, Aunt Mandy looked dazed despite her smile, as though she'd just been roused from a dreamlike state. For a moment, Stevie wasn't sure she saw him there anymore. "So, um . . . can I, can I come in now maybe?" he asked, giving the Monopoly box a little shake.

"Oh, sorry honey, sure . . ." She stepped aside. "I guess I'm pretty tired this morning."

"Maybe you should take a snappy nap," he suggested, stepping inside.

Aunt Amanda's expression glazed over again, as though the idea of a nap was the most luxurious suggestion she'd ever heard. "That *does* sound nice," she mused to herself. "Okay." Sighing, she touched the top of Stevie's head with her hand, as if to thank him for the recommendation. "How are you feeling today?"

"Fine," Stevie said. "Good, great, thanks, yeah."

"You sure?" she asked. "You were pretty upset yesterday." When he'd gone on about monsters nobody believed existed. When the gash on Jude's arm had somehow magically healed itself, but not all the way. When his mom had ushered him home.

"Yeah, I'm okay today."

"All right." She gave him a wary smile. "If you boys need anything, come wake me. I'll be right in my room."

Stevie watched her drift into her bedroom and softly shut the door behind her. As soon as that door closed, he was suddenly nervous. If Jude told him to go home, that was one thing. But if Stevie knocked on his cousin's door only to have some leering loup-garou yank it open, if he was jerked forward by the front of his shirt with a claw and taken hostage . . .

"Don't be a stupid Chicken Little," he whispered. "That's not gonna happen. Not gonna happen." Not with Aunt Mandy in her room and his mom next door, Dunk sleeping away the hot afternoon, and the mailman making his rounds. All of Deer Valley was awake. Everyone knew bad stuff didn't happen in the middle of the day, especially not on one as clear and sunny as this.

Narrowing his eyes, he forced himself to step across Aunt Mandy's rose-filigreed rug and around her doily-covered coffee table. He moved into the hall and, not giving himself time to think or an opportunity to back out, knocked on Jude's door. And then he waited, clutching that game box to his chest like a cardboard shield.

It took a while, but Jude eventually opened up.

Stevie found himself staring, his mouth slack. If Aunt Mandy had appeared tired, Jude looked absolutely fried. Stevie shrunk back at the sight of the bags beneath Jude's eyes. No, not bags; big overstuffed *suitcases*, steamer trunks plump and dark from lack of sleep. Jude's nose was red, as though he'd spent the entire night and all of that morning rubbing it raw with sandpaper. And his mouth . . . Stevie tried not to wince as Jude slid his tongue across his bottom lip, so chapped it was cracked in the middle. "Jeez, Jude." The words escaped him before he could stop himself. "You look . . ." Like what? A plague victim? A zombie off *The Walking Dead*? Stevie used to think the undead were awesome, but not anymore. Not after this. ". . . really, really, really sick."

"And you're really, really, really stupid," Jude croaked. "What's with the game?" He lifted his hand to take a broad swipe at his nose. As far as Stevie was concerned, Jude shouldn't have been home sleeping off whatever it was that he'd caught; he shouldn't have been standing at his window at night or staring at the back fence with strays scrambling around his feet. He should have been in an ICU, hooked up to machines to make sure he didn't keel over and die.

"I th-thought we could play, if you wanna," Stevie suggested, unable to look Jude in the eyes. "Mob rules." When Jude didn't reply, Stevie forced himself to look upward, waiting to see his cousin's eyes glaze over, for him to ask what the hell Mob rules were anyway. He'd cant his head sideways the way he had last night, his chapped mouth curling up into a terrifying smile. If *that* happened, Stevie wasn't sure what he would do. Run home, probably. Tell his mom Jude was an alien parading around in his cousin's skin. It was like that whole thing with the cows and the farmer. What if aliens really *did* exist? Maybe he wasn't Jude because he wasn't Jude.

". . . maybe he wasn't . . . ," Stevie whispered. "He wasn't because he wasn't . . . Isn't because he—"

"Mob rules," Jude said, snapping Stevie out of his loop. "What the hell other rules would we use, the idiot ones that came with the game?"

Stevie breathed a small sigh. His arms relaxed around the box, if only a little. Jude remembered. That was good.

Jude retreated into his room, and Stevie followed. Though he made sure to leave the door open behind him, just in case. But less than two seconds later, he was met with a command. "Close the door."

"Uh . . ." Stevie glanced over his shoulder to the door behind him, as if not having realized he had left it open. He didn't want to close it. Not with how weird Jude was being. Not with the way he looked. "Y-your mom said to leave it open, she said. Leave it open."

"So *what?* Close the stupid door, Sack."

Stevie swallowed and did as he was told, allowing his gaze to roam the walls, hesitating to go farther inside. He'd always thought Jude's room was the coolest; a perfect reflection of what his cousin considered the most important things in life. His walls were covered in BMX pics and superhero posters. Batman was his favorite—the Dark Knight era, not that weird rubber-nipple stuff from way back whenever. Iron Man was second on that list, not so much for the armor as for how impressive of a smart-ass Tony Stark could be. Jude liked the guys who didn't fit in. Clark Kent? Just a wuss in a cape.

Jude took a seat on his mattress, the bed frame creaking beneath him, and stared at the perpetually glowing fish tank against the far wall. Inside: Jude's goldfish, Cheeto; a bubbling skull wearing a pirate hat; a tiny empty bottle of Grey Goose vodka they had found along their walking path. Jude had put it in the tank as a joke. *It's like Cedar Creek now,* he had said. *Totally booby-trapped.*

"Did you really come here to play that dumb game?" Jude asked.

"We don't have to if you don't want to. I just thought it would be fun, son. Sun." *Sunburn.* Every time he caught a glimpse of his cousin's sizzled face, a shiver skittered up his arms and to the top of his head, nesting in his hair like a wolf spider waiting to bite.

"Yeah, well, your idea of fun isn't so fun, Sack." Jude grabbed one of his BMX magazines off his bedside table and flipped to a dog-eared page. A moment later, he was scratching at the bandage stuck to the crook of his elbow. Stevie bet Aunt Mandy's church would be pretty excited to hear about *that* modern-day miracle. Supernatural healing. Strange metamorphosis.

Still hugging the Monopoly box to his chest, he swallowed, his throat feeling particularly parched. He watched Jude's tongue roll across chapped lips like a dry slug dragging itself across a cracked and dusty badland, then frowned down at the game box. Monopoly didn't appear to be in the cards. "You wanna go to the backyard and dig through Terry's crap?" he asked. "The jerk's at work, so it's safe." Jude liked snooping through The Tyrant's worthless treasures. It's how they had found the hammer, which they'd used to build their once-esteemed fort. And today, Stevie would like snooping around, too, because being closed up in Jude's room was suddenly making him claustrophobic. Every time Jude licked his lips, Stevie's guts clenched up. The inside of Aunt Mandy's house felt awfully hot, as though the air conditioner hadn't been run for a while. Jude, however, didn't seem to notice the spike in temperature. He just shrugged at the suggestion of Terry's shit pile and flipped a magazine page.

"Um, hey." Stevie glanced up from his hands, spurred on by a question. "W-what, what were you doing last night at night?"

"Huh?" Jude raised an eyebrow, not getting it.

"I woke up because . . ." Of nightmares, but he wasn't about to bring that up. His eyes flicked back to the Band-Aid stuck to the inside of Jude's arm. It was way too small, totally pointless. The redness had crept beyond the bandage's edge, though he supposed even a larger one wouldn't do the trick. Jude didn't need a Band-Aid—he needed a straitjacket. "You were standing at the window there, just standing . . . statue standing like a museum thing with the Cheetos glowing in your head." He looked away from Jude's irritated arm and nodded to the window just shy of his cousin's left shoulder. "I waved, but you just stood there, frozen, like Mr. Frosty. Staring, staring, stair ring a round the—"

"Um, no?" Jude gave Stevie a dubious look.

"Yuh-huh." This wasn't Aunt Mandy, it wasn't his mom. Stevie wasn't going to let Jude lie to him, not when he knew what he'd seen. "You were. I waved, Jude, but you didn't see."

"You imagined it," Jude concluded, unimpressed. "You were probably sleepwalking. Dreaming or something. Another freak-out."

"No, Jude, I—"

"Anyway, I don't feel like playing, Mob rules or not," Jude said, changing the subject entirely. "Let's do something else."

Stevie chewed on his bottom lip as he slid the Monopoly box onto Jude's desk chair. Fine. They'd do something else. He'd talked himself into coming over here, and no matter how hard Jude was to look at right then, Stevie refused to bail.

Jude got off his bed and pulled open his door. "Where's my mom?"

"Taking a nap, she said."

"You sure?"

Stevie lifted his shoulders up to his ears. How was *he* supposed to know? "I'm n-not a psychic."

Jude shot Stevie a smile, one that looked positively lecherous; like a serpent had crawled into the body of a boy. "Yeah, not a *psychic*," he said. "Anyway, let's go." Dashing across the room with light feet—not acting sick despite how terrible he looked—he grabbed his sneakers off the floor and, still barefoot, rushed down the hall toward the kitchen.

Stevie was left blinking into Aunt Mandy's silent house. Were they going to pick through The Tyrant's junk after all? He had no choice but to follow. When he finally got moving, he found Jude outside on the back steps. He was cramming his feet into his worn-out sneakers, double-knotting the laces in big, sloppy loops.

"Where are we going?" Stevie asked. Jude didn't answer. He simply got up, crossed the yard, and scrambled up the back fence, dropping to the opposite side without so much as a glance in Stevie's direction. If Stevie didn't hurry, he'd lose him in the trees.

And yet, despite the growing distance between them, he found himself standing motionless in Jude's backyard, suddenly needing to pee worse than ever, pretty sure he wouldn't make it over that fence without wetting himself. He was scared, but this time it wasn't for his own safety. Seeing Jude retreat into the forest, a memory came flooding back; one that he wasn't sure was actually real. Jude lumbering into the woods more than a week ago, wearing the black sweatshirt the cops had found. Jude pausing, turning, his eyes nothing but black. Grinning with jagged, broken teeth. Something dark oozing from between his lips. Oil, or squid ink. Dead blood. *Scratching* at that arm.

He shot a look back through Aunt Mandy's kitchen, considered running inside and throwing open her bedroom door. *Jude's running away!* Yes, running away like all the Deer Valley folks had said. Running away *again*, because they had been right all along. Something bad had happened to his cousin, something beyond whatever had occurred in the woods. A screw was loose. Jude's mind was gone.

Which is why, rather than turning him in for flying the coop, Stevie found himself yelling "Jude, wait!" instead.

He dashed across the dead grass, tried to scale the fence. His shorts snagging on the jagged and splintering wood. So did the skin of his knees. They burned like fire, already bleeding by the time his feet hit the ground on the other side. By then, Jude was a good distance away, but still close enough for Stevie to notice him clawing at the Band-Aid stuck to his arm. If he had wanted, he could have been down the trail and out of sight, but Jude was waiting. He was trying to act like he wasn't, but Stevie knew his cousin was stalling, letting Stevie catch up.

He hesitated, glanced over his shoulder, this time toward his own home. Then fell into a run away from safety, away from Aunt Mandy and his mom. Stevie had already given the adults their chance to help, and they hadn't. Now it was up to him.

23

THE BOYS ENDED up on the gravel delivery road behind the shops of Main Street, but Jude ignored the wooden pallets stacked against the back of the hardware store. And yet, Stevie couldn't help but feel optimistic. After all, Jude hadn't snapped at him for the moment, and they were here, their usual fort supply spot. This time, they'd drag a bunch of stuff into the forest with them, like they always did. Because things were getting back to normal. Soon, everything would be okay.

But rather than approaching the pallets stacked against one of the shop's back walls, Jude remained in the shade of the trees, near the row of shrubs. When he stuck his arm inside the fourth juniper, well past his elbow, Stevie's positive attitude was replaced by a sour taste in his mouth. The thought of the hammer hidden there made him tense, but being scared was stupid, right? Jude didn't want to hurt him. Not a chance.

You're being a dumb no-fun son of a gun, he told himself. They couldn't work on the fort without supplies, and they couldn't use the supplies without the hammer. *That's* why Jude was retrieving it from the bush. Except, Jude didn't seem the least bit interested in those pallets. When he began to retreat into the trees rather than approach the back of the hardware store, Stevie finally found his voice.

"Hey, what about the wood? It's good. Would be good to transport to the fort."

"Don't need it," Jude said.

"What do you mean?"

"I mean we *don't need it*. Now, are you coming or what?" Jude gave Stevie an irritated look. Stevie was right, he *was* being a no-fun son of a gun. But he found himself scanning the forest's perimeter anyway, only pausing when it fell onto Mr. Greenwood's cat. The tabby was sitting in the shade of a tree, watching them as it lazily scratched behind an ear. *Mangy*, his mom would have said. He couldn't imagine why Mr. G. would ever want that thing inside his house. At best, it had fleas. At worst, it was creepy enough to suck Mr. G.'s breath right out of his chest while he slept.

"I'm coming." Stevie moved his feet despite the thudding of his heart. "Coming," he whispered, as if to punctuate each step. "Coming, coming." The repetition was comforting. It took his mind off the things he didn't want to consider, kept him from hearing his pulse whooshing in his ears.

Mr. Greenwood's cat tailed them, keeping its distance, shaking sword ferns like isolated earthquakes; the world's worst ninja. When it was out in the open, it froze stiff as soon as Stevie gave it a look, shocked that it could be seen at all. *I'm invisible!* Or maybe it was surprised by how gross Jude looked, clawing at an already scratched-up arm, chewing the skin off his chapped bottom lip, wielding the old Stanley hammer in a fist covered in peeling skin.

And what made it worse was that they weren't going to-ward the fort, but in the direction of that defunct logging road and the house that sat alongside it, the very place Stevie had sworn—both to his mother and to himself—that he'd never, ever go near again.

But he swallowed his objections and reminded himself of his goal. This was about helping his cousin get back to his old self again, about making sure he didn't wander into the woods alone. Because, unlike Stevie, it seemed that Jude really didn't know what danger lurked just shy of town.

Except that . . . what if he *did*?

The realization dawned on him less than two minutes from that washboard road. Jude had retrieved the hammer with zero intent on pounding any nails, so why did he need it? Protection. It was a weapon.

Stevie's heart tripped over itself.

Jude needed armament because what Stevie had seen had been *real*. That thing . . . it had taken Jude hostage, and now Jude was determined to get his revenge. He was going to smash that shadow thing's head in, and he was going to let Stevie watch.

"Jude?" This was crazy. "Hey, *Jude*?"

"What?" Jude kept moving, determined. He didn't look back. Stevie watched that old Stanley bob in his hand with each step, as though his cousin were testing its heft, weighing his options, considering his plan of attack.

"Jude, can you stop, m-maybe stop, okay? Stop walking so we can talk, talking . . ." Stevie slowed his steps despite Jude's refusal to do the same. "Hey, come on, come on, come *on* . . . I know where we're going and I don't wanna go there. Stop going where we're going because I don't wanna go, okay?" All at once, he felt better for making the admission. Ten was way too young to die.

Jude stopped. Looked over his shoulder. The rawness of his nose, those chapped and tattered lips, the bags beneath his eyes—all of it made Stevie shrink back. When their eyes met, he could swear Jude's gaze looked weird. More vibrant somehow. Like a movie villain's eyes.

"Just come on," Jude said. No insult of how Stevie was being a stupid baby. No suggestion that he was a no-good momma's boy chicken-shit loser. "You said yourself, remember? As long as we're together . . ."

"The hammer . . . ," Stevie said. "What do you need that for?"

"For hammering. Now come *on*."

"What do you need it for?" Stevie repeated. He watched Jude's grip tighten around the Stanley, his patience wearing thin.

"For hammering your head if you don't stop asking so many stupid questions. Now are you coming or what?"

"And wh-why are you so damn mean?" Was Jude even *aware* of the threats that were coming out of his mouth? "Why's it always gotta be that if you don't like what I say, you're gonna rock 'em sock me in the face or knock 'em sock out my teeth or bust in my stupid head or cut off my arm or break my leg or pop out my eyes or—" Stop. "Pull out my hair or—" *Stop*. "Or . . . or . . . or *something*?"

Jude stared at Stevie for a long while, as if not understanding the question.

"I thought we were friends," Stevie told him. "*Best* friends. But ever since you came back you don't like me anymore. Something happened while you were gone. You changed. Stranged. Every time I ask you, will you answer? Every time. Can you answer? No. You just act like I'm some sort of, sort of, sort of friggin' *idiot*. And you look like crap, Jude. You look like *zombie* crap. M-maybe wherever you were, they did something to your brain, like those old-timey doctors where they aren't supposed to do that anymore but they still do because they're old and spiders are there, and nobody knows where, and the hospital is covered in webs, and maybe it's on the same road, the scary road where that house is, and there's a big chain. Maybe they did something to your brain and you don't even know it, Jude. You don't even know it. But *I* know it." Stevie hadn't expected to say so much or to be so earnest, but it poured out of him like water overtaking a levee, regardless of the verbal ticks that dotted his soliloquy.

Jude just stared. Stevie couldn't tell if he was processing his monologue, or if he was zoning out again.

Try again, he told himself. *Ask him one more, two more, three more times.*

"W-what's the hammer for, Jude?"

Jude glanced down at the Stanley in his right hand, his fingers tightening around the rubberized grip.

"You used to tell me everything, remember?"

Still focused on the tool in his hand, Jude didn't move, didn't speak. He only stood there, thinking. He could have been trying to remember those times—how excited they had been when they had installed that rickety fort ladder and climbed into the tree for the first time; how much fun they had walking in the freezing-cold creek with their sneakers on; how, during the summers, the whole house smelled like Doritos because it was almost all they ate while playing hours of Xbox—as long as Terry wasn't home to chase them off; or how they used to cut the crap out of the corners of their mouths on those Otter Pops Aunt Mandy bought, but they kept eating them because they were so dang good.

Mr. G.'s cat continued to watch them through fern fronds, as though it wanted to hear Jude's answer as much as Stevie did.

Stevie swallowed. Waiting. Hoping. His fingers were crossed that Jude wouldn't come back at him with another caveat. *Yeah, I remember. Remember telling you I was gonna hammer your head if . . .*

"She's down there," Jude said.

Stevie blinked. "What?"

"Down there . . . ," Jude murmured, a bit clearer this time.

"Who?" Stevie asked.

"The lady," Jude said.

"What lady?" His pulse was banging so hard against his ears he felt light-headed, disoriented, like he should crouch down and wait for the vertigo to pass or risk toppling over like a drunk guy tumbling out of a bar.

That was when he saw it, when he *truly* saw the change that had taken over his friend. Rather than softening at the memories of their friendship the way he had hoped, Jude's face twisted into a scowl. His shoulders slouched forward, as though the backbreaking tension coiled within them was finally too much to bear. Jude stared back at Stevie with a look that could only be born of nightmares. His brittle mouth pulled up at the corners; lips cracking, beads of blood springing up between seams of dead skin.

Stevie watched all of this happen, and he felt something within his own reality snap like a rubber band. The ground beneath his feet sloped like a carnival tilt-house floor. The spiders came crawling out of the trees, ready to pour down on his head. The ferns shivered, as if preparing their bladelike fronds for attack. The pines seemed to creek as they leaned in, blocking out the dappling sun, leaving both boys in a chasm of darkness that smelled of moist earth and decay.

Jude exhaled a hiss through his teeth, the sight of which made Stevie's heart pound like the bass drum in the annual Olympia High School Thanksgiving Day parade. Because Jude's teeth were glistening like the inside of an oyster shell, as though he'd used his back molars to grind pearls into dust.

But his eyes were the worst. The color of his irises hadn't changed, but the sclera wasn't white anymore. The whites of his eyes were icebergs; the palest shade of blue.

"W-what lady?" Stevie whispered those fear-choked words, simultaneously terrified to know the answer and to not know what Jude meant. His mind floundered for purchase, looking for a handhold, for some semblance of reality to keep from completely losing touch.

It's just a fusion illusion, it screamed. *Find something real to feel. Wake up, up and away. Run away. Far away.*

But the longer Stevie fought to regain his footing, the more awful Jude appeared.

Until, finally, his smile was a leering grin—identical to what Stevie had seen in his dream—and his answer rolled out of him in a sinister purr.

"Mother," he snarled.

And with that single word, a trail of warmth bloomed down the inside of Stevie's leg.

24

THE SEARCH PARTY wandered the woods for longer than two weeks, and in that time, Maxwell Larsen's remains underwent a significant change. Now when Rosie opened the door to the secret room beneath the stairs, the smell was overwhelming—the type of stink that crawled up your throat and stuck there for days. She covered her mouth and nose with the crook of her elbow, but quickly graduated to a kitchen towel, which she had wetted down and sprayed with old perfume. Still, the stench made her eyes burn. Otto, however, wasn't bothered by it. He seemed peaceful. Content.

She told herself to be thankful; the steel-lined box of a room had walls thick enough to block out most of the stench, at least when the door was closed. But every evening, after the sun set and the search party packed up and left, the door remained open. Otto wandered the house, unbathed, sometimes rolling around on the rug, rubbing the stink onto the corners of furniture while she slept.

Mornings had her dry-heaving as she stumbled into the kitchen. While Otto slept, she tried to air the place out, tearing down the curtains and throwing the rugs out onto the porch. If the police returned, she'd blame it on spring-cleaning. If they noted the smell, she'd hold the strays at fault. The officers had seen them hiding beneath her porch. Perhaps one had found its way inside the walls of the house and died. They'd seen the state of her home. They would buy it, one hundred percent.

She started to reconsider her refusal to bury the body. If she had disposed of it when she'd found it, she wouldn't be assaulted with the rankness every day. But the risks circled overhead like vultures. Just because the cops hadn't come back to ask more questions didn't mean they wouldn't eventually call on her again. She didn't want to keep them from exploring the property, didn't want to give them any reason to suspect her. And so she left the windows open despite the rain. Every rug and bit of upholstery was sprayed down with Lysol. Scented candles burned all day. If the police rang her bell again, she'd invite them in. Only guilty people asked the authorities to keep away from certain spots, and if Rosamund Aleksander was guilty of anything, it was of loving her son the way any mother loved her child.

She started picking up the newspaper when she went out for groceries, which she did far more frequently, if only to keep on top of the news. Nearly every day there was a new update about Maxwell Larsen, headlines that shouted: "SEARCH FOR DEER VALLEY BOY YIELDS NO RESULTS." There were interviews with friends and family, but she refused to read them. She felt horrible enough as it was. The police statements became grimmer by the week. No leads. No suspects. No sign of Max anywhere.

After three long weeks of waiting, deliverance was emblazoned across the front page of the *McMinnville Gazette*: "SEARCH FOR MISSING BOY MOVES EAST." Overwhelmed by relief, she bought herself a bouquet of grocery store daisies and a king-sized jar of Jif for her boy. She watched Otto scoop globs of peanut butter into his mouth with his twisted hands as she sat on the couch, and as he greedily sucked at his goo-smeared fingers, she was struck by a thought that curdled her blood: she was rewarding him. They had gotten away with murder, and now they were reveling in their success.

She had to lock him in the basement to clean out the room beneath the stairs. He screamed and thrashed against the door for hours, but his wails didn't bother her as much as before. It was safer now with the search party gone, and the constant rain dampened the noise. Rosie only hoped the police wouldn't catch her on her hands and knees, scrubbing bloodstains out of the floor with a tangle of steel wool. She had come too far for that to happen. This had to end today.

She loaded the garbage bag into the trunk of her car without any idea of where she would dispose of it; somewhere remote and out of the way, like the Happy Hope. She imagined enduring the long drive down the coast, pulling into the retreat's long and unpaved drive after dark. She'd bury the body behind Ras's oceanside home. And if Max was ever found, the old biker would be blamed. She was certain the man was no stranger to the criminal lifestyle. A perfect stool pigeon, if there ever was one.

But that drive was brutal, and with endless forest around her own home, it was overkill. She was being paranoid. And so she started the car and began to drive northwest toward the coast, up toward Washington State, in the opposite direction it was reported that the search party had moved.

After thirty miles, she pulled onto an abandoned road tucked into a thick tangle of trees—a good a spot as any. Parked just far enough away from the quiet highway as to not be noticed, she pulled the bag out of the trunk and spilled its contents onto the ground, scattering the remains in a way that would suggest an animal attack. The blood-smeared bag made its way back into the car. She'd get rid of it at a random rest stop trash can along the way.

And footprints? There were none to leave. The ground was covered with a thick blanket of wild grass, moss, downed branches, and leaves. Rosamund was no expert in forensics, but she'd wager that tracks would be hard, if not altogether impossible, to detect. The police had complained about the rain in the *Yamhill Valley News-Register* throughout the weeks. Dogs weren't picking up Maxwell's scent. There was just too much water. Whatever clues may have been out in the woods near Deer Valley had now been washed away. The search party's setback was Rosamund's boon. And as she pulled away from Max Larsen's final resting place, she was confident that, like the rain, this too would pass.

●   ●   ●

She tried to push the feelings of responsibility for what had happened to Max Larsen to the back of her mind, but the last thing she wanted was for it to happen again. Once was a mistake. Twice would most certainly get them caught.

It took her a couple of weeks of driving by to find the nerve, but she finally pulled into an old stock and feed place outside of McMinnville and parked next to a barn—quintessential with its peeling red paint and rusty tractor parked out front. The next day, the man she'd spoken with showed up in an old pickup to fix her dilapidated fence. He set the pickets straight and ran chicken wire between them. When he asked why she hadn't hired someone from Deer Valley to do the job—*it's a hell of a lot closer, probably cheaper, too*—Rosie simply smiled and asked him if he'd like something to drink.

The man built a henhouse and feeder, which he painted a bright, jewel-toned blue. The color reminded Rosie of the ocean, the way it looked from atop the California cliffs. That azure, so vivid against a sea of green, gave her hope that her idea would satiate Otto's appetite enough to keep him away from town, at least until she could figure out how to keep him out of Deer Valley for good.

The guy returned with Rosie's chickens a few days later, half a dozen set free in the yard. They ran and clucked and ate seed from between blades of grass, growing comfortable with their new surroundings as the sun began to set.

Otto discovered them at dusk.

His eyes widened with wonder before he burst into the yard to give chase, the chickens flapping their wings in panicked surprise, white and brown feathers fluttering up into the sky and onto the ground like pillow-case down. He tore the first chicken's head off with his teeth and gazed up at Rosie almost adoringly as he chewed. She had to look away as the bird's body continued to twitch in his hands.

He killed another the next day, but seemed gentler with it, as though conducting an experiment of just how much he could hurt it before the thing stopped fighting and died.

His third victim managed to last an entire day before succumbing to what Rosie assumed was some sort of hidden trauma. Each chicken—or what remained of it—was tossed into an open pit in the backyard in the morning, after Otto had gone to sleep.

She arranged another shipment of six birds within a week. When the same man arrived with her order, he looked more suspicious than she liked. "I left the gate open," she told him with a bashful laugh. "I'm not used to shutting it behind me." The man spent ten minutes trying to sell her on a spring-loaded gate hinge, meticulously detailing all the benefits of such an upgrade. All she had to do was give him a call and—*whammo bammo*—no open gate, no lost chickens, no problem. When he finally left, she made a mental note to call another place next time. He was too pushy for her taste. A bit too *I know best*.

Otto continued his reign of terror, but the chickens stopped pass-ing away. Instead, their feathers began to fall out, leaving bald spots of pale flesh exposed to the sun. Their wings drooped, and they seemed to waddle as they walked, their beady eyes squinting against the bright day-light. But rather than running from Otto when he charged into the yard, they clamored toward him. Rosie watched these fascinating exchanges from inside the house; Otto sitting on the grass, surrounded by cats, dogs, chickens, and the occasional wild-eyed squirrel. It was a clash of two fairy tales: Quasimodo meets Snow White.

Rosie hadn't been able to figure it out at first. Why had those strays started appearing around the house? But now it was becoming clear, and the reason was far more sinister than she had originally thought. It had happened to Sasha, too. The cat had been terrified of Otto until he had been attacked. It was only then, contrary to all logic, that Sasha took a liking to the boy who moved around on all fours.

Watching the animals crowd around her son day in and day out, like rats scrambling toward the last bit of cheese, Rosie started to understand that she had been right; little Maxwell Larsen *had* been a mistake. But the chickens had helped Otto learn. Fenced off and captive, they were the perfect subjects for experimentation. If he was too rough and killed them, they were gone forever. But if he fed from them and let them live, he could eat more than once. It meant less hunting for him, and less cleanup for her.

And hadn't that been what Otto had done with her, too; feeding from his mother's breast despite the pain it had caused her? He had been too small to kill her with his constant need—that's why he had screamed for the first year of his life. Hunger. Terrible, inexplicable, insatiable hunger. As soon as Sasha had been turned on to the Church of the Child, he had done what Rosamund couldn't; the cat had supplied Otto with constant food, disregarding its own well-being.

The death didn't altogether stop, however. Some of the weaker animals were put out of their misery, others simply lay down and expired. When Otto fell into one of his moods, he left a trail of slain in his wake, and the dogs were his favorite to maim. It could have been their loyalty to their original owners—their desire to return home—that fueled Otto's aversion to the breed.

Rosie's makeshift graveyard continued to fill up. She began to recognize the felled. There was a white cat with a black spot in the shape of a heart on its side. She had nicknamed him Valentine. For weeks, Valentine sat on the front porch step as though he'd lived with Rosie all his life . . . until one morning his body was left for her just shy of his stoop. Then there had been a dog—curly-haired, brown, with a black leather collar. Just a pup, he had appeared outside the fence a few times. Noodle had gone home one too many times for Otto's taste. His collar was tucked away in Ansel's rolltop desk.

Even poor Sasha—long dead—had eventually weakened to whatever affliction Otto had begifted him. Rosie had explained away his failing health; old age, that was all. But now it was clear to her: Otto's subservients were on a limited timeline. Was that chronology based on how subordinate each animal was, by how many offerings they gave, or how hungry Otto happened to be that day? That unanswerable question was enough to rouse a familiar itch beneath Rosie's old scars. If it was only a matter of time before each of Otto's slaves was put down, it was only a matter of time before . . .

No, she thought. *I'm his mother. I protect him. He would never.*

And what if children began to materialize from the woods? What if, unlike Max Larsen, they weren't torn apart but brought home instead?

Rosie pushed the gruesome images out of her mind. She told herself it was impossible.

And for years, she believed it. The potential of it would worm its way into her brain every so often, but it was *impossible*. No. It wouldn't happen. It couldn't. Not ever.

Time marched on. She got older, more numb, at times toeing complete ambivalence, but the routine stayed the same. The house became more run-down with every passing winter, and by Otto's twelfth birthday, there was a hole in the roof of the detached garage and the car had started to rust. The picket fence she had repaired was bent by wind, eroded by moist earth, and shoved over by her son's ever-growing bone-heavy bulk. And if Ansel could have only known how Rosie had spent the money he had squirreled away, he would have writhed in his grave. Writhed, or maybe laughed the way she did when she thought of it now. Chickens. All his education, his long hours, his hard work . . . for *chickens*. Hundreds, from wherever she could get them. And the funniest part? Throughout those years, she hadn't roasted a single one.

With no income of her own, the money ran short. The chickens stopped being delivered but Otto didn't seem to mind. The strays had never ceased to loiter around the property, and Rosie didn't care. As long as it wasn't another Max Larsen. No, Max had been a mistake. Otto wouldn't dare.

Until he did.

Stepping into the basement and finding her now-adult son stooped over something she couldn't make out, she moved across the floor while Otto gave her a glare. Two and a half decades together, and he'd never shown her affection. Today was no different. He snorted over his shoulder as she approached, warning her to stay away.

Because there, in the corner of the basement, was her worst nightmare.

There, in the underbelly of her home, was another child. And this time, Otto had let him live.

25

MOTHER.

A word that brought comfort to most had, instead, flipped some aggressive switch in Jude's brain.

He took a step toward Stevie, his route along the forested road forgotten. Reaching out, he grabbed Stevie by the arm—a sign that Stevie was going to accompany Jude to that house whether he wanted to or not.

"H-hey, what . . . ?" Stevie took his own backward step, the look on Jude's face churning his guts into a sickly green froth. He tried to yank his arm away.

I'm gonna smash your teeth in, s'gonna be a lot of pain.

The words were Jude's, but his crooked mouth—skewed by a newly acquired tick—remained unmoving.

Gonna bash in your brains in and run 'em down the drain.

Stevie hardly felt the urine that ran down the inside of his right leg turn cold against his skin, didn't hear the sleeve of his T-shirt tear at the seams as he turned away. He was too busy bolting toward home, listening to Jude's stomping footfalls behind him. "Sack!"

Hey, Suh-Suh-Suh-Sack attack, there's no turning back!

Stevie's lungs ignited like cylinder bursts as he pushed himself to run faster. He wanted to turn around, to crane his neck
to make sure that what he *thought* was happening was rooted in
truth. But if he paused, if he stumbled, Jude would be on him.

"Sack!"

*Time for payback, cracker jack! G-g-gonna give your skull a nice
big whack!*

Stevie veered left, sure there was no way he'd be able to
sustain this sort of pace. But if he tried hard enough, he could
make it back into town. There were people on Main Street.
Murder was unlikely on the front steps of Mr. Greenwood's
general store.

But why was this happening? Why was Jude coming after
him?

"Jude-not-Jude," he said, his breath rasping in his throat, his
arms pumping like twin pistons at his sides. "Jude-not-Jude."

If he'd have known he was going to die so young, he would
have pointed an accusing finger at Terry the Tyrant. Death by
killer stepdad. Never by his once-best friend.

"Jude-not-J—"

The toe of his sneaker caught on a tree root. Stevie flew
forward, his arm out in front of him, a cry whipping free of
his throat, the loop of his manic thoughts derailed. He skidded
onto his hands and knees, sure that the next few seconds would
be his last. Dirt jammed up beneath his fingernails. Leaves
crunched beneath the heels of his hands. The ground bit at his
already skinned flesh, a fresh sting of pain igniting like dry kin-
dling across his knees.

The sun beat down on his back as he breathed hard, staring at the ground beneath him, waiting for a shadow to throw his own into relief. *Jude-not-Jude.*

He heard quick footfalls. The snapping of twigs. Jerking his head to the side, he squinted against the sunlight in time to catch sight of his cousin. Except, rather than Jude lunging for him with those cracked lips and hollowed-out eyes, he stopped, grinned, actually *winked* as if to say *Balls, what balls?* and dashed in the direction of that awful, moss-eaten house— empty-handed, because the hammer was gone—as though the pursuit was nothing more than a game of tag.

What?

The dust Stevie had kicked up in his fall settled around him like a fistful of stars.

What the hell was happening? Was he seeing things again?

No, impossible. He was sure this time. Except . . . his brain could have misfired for half a second, confusing his best friend's face with the countenance of that creature thing; like when his hand had turned to worms—so real that he'd lost half of two fingers trying to shake the illusion. It wasn't a stretch to think, with how terrified he was, that he'd imagined it all. Because Jude was his friend. His *best* friend.

He would never, ever, not ever in a million billion gazillion—

There was a shift in the woods. A rustle. Stevie's heart sputtered to a hitching stop. His eyes darted in the opposite direction of town, where Jude had run.

It's only Jude, dude. He's just hiding behind a tree, see?

But the harder Stevie strained to find him, the more a figure became overt. Tucked away in the shadows of trees and overgrowth, it was hunched and naked. A face—lipless and burn-scarred—watched him from around a lodgepole pine. Not running after Jude. Not careening toward Stevie. Simply observing. A voyeur, watching an abandoned boy grapple with things that couldn't have possibly been real.

. . .

Stevie ran toward town.

Bursting onto Main Street, he left Deer Valley's residents wide-eyed two days in a row. Mrs. Lovejoy croaked something at him as he blasted by her, probably akin to Stevie finally having gone off the rails. *Call the police!*

And perhaps he *had* gone insane. That must have been why the only person Stevie wanted to see in the whole world just then was his stupid brother, Dunk.

Leaping up the porch steps, Stevie came flying into the house and crashed against Duncan's door. He didn't bother knocking, just burst in like a home invader.

Dunk jumped at the sudden intrusion. "What the fuck . . . ? Get out of my room, dipshit!" Sitting on an old beanbag chair so tattered it looked like a piece of rotting fruit, he snapped his laptop shut and readjusted it across his lap.

Stevie couldn't speak, at least not yet. He was too busy gulping in air like a marooned fish, his eyes fixed on the menagerie of stickers Dunk had slapped onto his computer's lid. There were sports teams—the Trail Blazers and Seahawks—athletic logos like the Nike swoosh; even a few skateboard company logos despite Dunk never having set foot on a board in his life. Stevie recognized those from Jude's magazines.

Jude. His attention veered back to his brother's pissed-off face. *Jude is gotta be Jude, is not-a-be . . .*

"I . . ." He gasped, trying to suck in enough air to form a coherent sentence. "I—I—I n-need your, your, your . . ."

"Nuh-nuh-need my what?" Dunk glared at him, as if daring his kid brother to make some sort of ridiculous request. Stevie needing something from Duncan? Fat fucking chance he'd get it. "Wait." He sniffed the air. "Is that . . . Did you *piss* yourself?"

". . . help . . ." The word just about squeaked out of him. "Please . . . help . . ." A breathless plea. If Dunk had ever felt bad for being such a douche, this was his chance to make up for it. Stevie waited, afraid that all he'd get was a demand to vacate the denlike confines of a room that stunk of corn chips and farts. But to his surprise, his brother actually looked a little concerned.

"Help with what?" Duncan asked. "Is it King Fuckface?" Dunk narrowed his eyes, as if imagining their stepfather chasing Stevie through Deer Valley Woods with an ax, finally having had enough of family life, ready to submit to his true calling: psycho killer.

Stevie shook his head. "J-Jude."

"The *Jewd*?" Dunk looked dubious. "What, did he miss his bar mitzvah? What is it, boy? Is the Jewd stuck in a well?"

"No, he, he . . ." He what, turned into a monster in front of Stevie's eyes? Chased him with full intent to bash his head in, only to give him a wink and a nod and run back into the forest?

What the heck was he supposed to say to get Dunk to listen, to keep him from kicking Stevie out of his room?

Stevie's eyes went wide. *Mr. Greenwood.* That was it! He needed to go back and see Mr. Greenwood. That old man was quite possibly the only person who would help him.

"C-can I ask you something?" The question came out staggered and wheezy, interrupted by huffs of air.

"You just did, nutsack."

"I—I—I mean . . . something else." Stevie heaved.

Duncan raised a single shoulder in ambivalence. "It's a free country, dude. As long as you don't hyperventilate, 'cause you're not getting another ambulance ride. And don't, don't, don't do that fucking repetition shit." As though Stevie could control it.

"Did you, you"—Stevie paused, slowed down, held it together—"have a dog, once?" Stevie's breaths started to even out. "W-when you were little? Before I was born?"

"Yeah . . . why?" Dunk looked suspicious, almost as if Stevie had something to do with whatever had happened to that canine; it didn't matter that Stevie hadn't existed yet.

"What . . . was its name?"

"Noodle." Dunk rolled his eyes.

"What hap-happened to him?" Stevie asked. "Did he run away?"

"Yeah, like a million goddamn times. Dad kept reinforcing the fence in the backyard, but somehow the stupid idiot kept getting out. I told Dad that he was jumping *over* the fence, not just digging under it, but he swore on a stack of Bibles that the fence was too damn high. But I saw that little fucker jump over that thing with my own two eyes. He just got a running start and—*bam!*" Dunk slapped his palm against the top of his laptop. "Right over. And it's, like, what, am I just seeing things? I'm not the one who's fucking crazy, man." Dunk gave his kid brother a look. *You, on the other hand . . .*

But Stevie was hardly paying attention to Duncan's judgy stare, because rather than picturing a dog scrambling over the back fence, he was picturing that *thing*. It had leapt up and over quick as anything, and just the next day, Jude had pulled the same trick.

"Why didn't you just t-tie him up?"

Duncan's smirk shifted into a sneer. "I did, moron. But I had to let him loose when the little shit nearly choked himself to death. He wanted to get away so bad that he just kept pulling at the rope until I couldn't hack it anymore, like he'd rather have killed himself than be my dog. So *fuck* that guy . . ."

Stevie frowned. "Pulling at the rope," he whispered to himself. It sounded awful; bad enough to explain why, despite his pleas for a pet, his begging had always been met with a resounding *No*. It's why Jude had a lame fish as a pet; why the only dogs anyone saw around Deer Valley were off leash and roaming the woods rather than in yards, chewing on rawhide bones and lounging in the sun.

"So, one day," Dunk continued, looking strangely forlorn now, "after hours of hearing Noodle choking himself out in the back, I couldn't deal. I walked out there and untied him. He didn't even stop to look at me. No *Hey, thanks for keeping me from murdering myself.* No *Fuck you, dude, you're the worst dog owner ever.* He didn't even bother to piss on my shoe or drop a steaming pile in front of my face. He just took off, leapt over that fence like a goddamn gazelle."

"A-a-and he didn't come back?" *Pulling and pulling and pulling.*

"Nope." Dunk shrugged again, as if to say he couldn't have cared less, but Stevie could tell he was still hurt by Noodle's departure. It must have been hard to care for something that didn't seem to care back. Kind of like Mr. Greenwood trying to take care of that rag-and-bones cat; like trying to be someone's friend when they didn't seem to want to be yours.

"He wasn't always like that," Dunk said. "We got him at a pet adoption place outside of town. A pound or whatever. When we brought Noodle home, he was cool, but after that first time he got out . . . I guess he just really liked living in the goddamn woods."

Stevie chewed on the pad of his thumb. He couldn't decide whether to keep his mouth shut or spill everything in a rush of possible delusion. He wanted to tell Dunk everything. How he'd been chased. How that monster thing had been screwing around in Terry's crap. How he knew he had weird stuff going on in his head, but this wasn't that, this wasn't this wasn't that, he was *sure.*

"That old, old house," Stevie said. "The old abandoned one out on that road, out there on that road, all alone. D-do you know that house out there?"

Dunk was staring at the top of his computer, probably still mulling over the memory of his long-lost dog. Stevie waited for him to acknowledge his question. It took a second, but Dunk finally looked up again. He didn't reply, but he knew the place. The way Duncan was looking at him assured Stevie that his brother had been out there with Murph more than a few times. He'd probably driven Annie out there, too; stuck his hand up her skirt and latched on to her neck like a sucker fish, Annie staring at that farmhouse through a dirty, bug-smeared windshield. Some wicked dark thing that she hadn't seen staring right back.

"Jude is out there," Stevie said, a chill crawling down his spine as soon as he made the confession. "He loves it. Loves it." Because while Jude's affinity for that place had always made Stevie uncomfortable, his cousin's fascination hadn't ever seemed as menacing as it did now.

Duncan furrowed his eyebrows at the statement. "What, you mean like he *walks* out there?"

"It isn't that far. You cut through the forest."

"That's probably why Mom is all pissed off at you, huh?" Dunk asked. "You told her you were going out there?"

"What's the big deal?" Stevie asked. "It's just an abandoned place, r-right?"

Duncan laughed to himself, as though Stevie had just said the dumbest thing he'd ever heard.

"What?" Stevie asked.

"No, nothing," Dunk said. "Just that you're more clueless than I thought."

"Why?"

"Because you're nuts, that's why."

"No, *why?* Why the house?"

"What?"

"The house!" Stevie yelled it. "Jude goes there and he loves it and he's there and why the house, why the house in the woods house, why that, Dunk, *why?*"

Duncan sighed and opened the lid of his laptop again. "Because that place isn't fuckin' abandoned, dumbass."

"But it looks—"

"Yeah, yeah, it *looks* . . . But people have seen her."

Stevie swallowed.

"You know," Dunk said. "The creepy old lady?"

Stevie's face flushed hot. The stench of his brother's room suddenly hit him head-on, threatening to double him over right there, only a few feet from Duncan's bed.

"Dude, if the Jewd goes out there like you say he does, he's seen her for sure."

Yes, Jude had seen her. *Mother.* He had hissed it, and grinned wide, his mouth nothing but a cavern of graying teeth.

26

THERE WAS A cop talking to Mrs. Lovejoy just shy of Main—
Stevie considered approaching, but stopped when he
watched the old woman lift her hand and point an accusing
finger Stevie's way. *There he is!* Stevie kept his distance, running
as fast as he could until he reached Mr. Greenwood's shop. He
had to stop along the side of the store for a few seconds before
going in, a wad of chewed-up breakfast waffle threatening to
make an encore appearance.

Pulling the crummy banana-yellow watch from the pocket
of his shorts, he glanced at the time. It was already past eleven.
Stevie had scarfed down an Eggo and gone over to Aunt Mandy's with the Monopoly game around nine. Lunch was at
twelve. That's when his mom would knock on his door, push it
open without waiting to be let in, and discover an empty room.
She'd go to Aunt Mandy's and learn that he wasn't there, either.
Noon was when Stevie would change from a real boy into toast.

And what about Jude? He'd run back toward that house.
Someone had to go find him before he vanished again. It's why
Stevie had wanted to bolt toward the cop, to scream about how
Jude had gone off again, how they had to send the search party

to grab him before it was too late. But old batty Lovejoy had screwed that up, and now . . . now there was no telling what was going to happen. He had to talk to Greenwood. He had to figure this out fast.

Luckily, Mr. Greenwood was behind the counter. Unluckily, he was helping someone sort through coupons, a stack of them as thick as the Deer Valley phone book—which wasn't that thick, but still. Stevie shuffled to the side of the front counter, staring at the old-timey glass jars of candy just beyond the counter's perimeter. He bounced impatiently from foot to foot, hoping Mr. Greenwood would not only notice him but also realize he was in a hurry. Except, his back-and-forth jig wasn't working. Mr. Greenwood didn't look Stevie's way.

Frustrated, he searched for another way to garner attention. He reached into his pocket, felt around that broken watch, and brought out two quarters, which he slapped onto the glass countertop. Paying customers were a priority, and Mr. Greenwood was more likely to give him the time of day if he saw those coins. As Terry liked to say, *Money talks, bullshit walks.* Today, Stevie really hoped bullshit wasn't part of the deal.

It took a minute—one that seemed to last an hour—for Mr. G. to ring up the lady who was vegetating at the register. Stevie kept pulling out his watch and peering at the digital readout. There wouldn't be enough time to relay Dunk's story about Noodle, let alone hear Greenwood's response. And how was he supposed to get home in time to not get into trouble *and* go after Jude? This wasn't going to work. He had to turn back. He'd beg his mom to listen, or ask Dunk to drive him out to that house. Hell, he didn't know, but he had to figure it out.

Clenching his teeth in defeat, Stevie placed his hand over the two quarters and began to slide them back toward the counter's edge. It was then, as if sensing that he was about to lose a cool fifty cents, that Mr. Greenwood stepped over to where Stevie stood and gave him a curious look.

"Mr. Clark," he said.

Stevie blinked up at the old man, surprised to see him there after being sure he was being overlooked. For once, Terry was right. Money *did* talk.

"Oh," Stevie said. "H-hi."

"Hi," Greenwood echoed back. He hovered behind the counter, seeming both patient and irritated all at once. Patient because here was Stevie Clark, best friend of Jude the Once-Missing. Irritated because here was Stevie Clark, a local kid with half a buck, about to waste his time figuring out which piece of candy he wanted when Mr. G. had better things to do, like stock shelves, or eat egg salad sandwiches, or drink his bottle of grape soda. Old people stuff.

"Um . . ." Stevie slid the two quarters back to the center of the counter. "J-just some chicken feet, please." *Chicken feet?* Jude was probably missing again, and all he could do was ask for some gummies? But it seemed weird to just say, *Hey, remember how you asked me about my brother's dog?*

Mr. G. slid the coins into the palm of one craggy hand and turned away, grabbed a small cellophane bag off a shelf, and moved over to the glass container filled with red and yellow candy shaped like disembodied talons. He doled out a few ounces and sealed the bag up with a twisty tie, then turned back to face Stevie, placed the bag of candy between them, and raised an eyebrow in inquiry.

"That all?"

"Um, yes, thanks." Stevie immediately hated himself for his answer. *Chicken feet?* He imagined Jude smirking. *More like chicken shit. Got a pair, my ass.* And then he'd wink. And smile. And run into the woods.

"Really?" Mr. Greenwood leaned in, as if to smell the lie on Stevie's breath. Stevie sniffed out something, too; onions, or maybe garlic. "You must really be fiending for candy, running all the way over here the way you just did."

"What?" Stevie squinted. "How did you . . ."

"You came in panting like a dog, hovering like a fly, and checking the time on that watch of yours like a man living out his last day. Did you talk to your brother?"

Stevie's eyes widened at the old man's observations. He could probably learn a thing or two from Mr. G., stuff that could help him with his future in detective work. But there wasn't time for that *CSI* stuff now. He was on a mission.

"Yes," he said.

"Took you long enough," Mr. G. said. "Why'd you wait so long?"

"Becau-cause . . ." Stevie stammered, not able to remember why he hadn't talked to Duncan right away. His thoughts tripped over themselves before the reason came stumbling back.

"I tried. But Dunk wasn't home, and then he ignored me even though I left a note, he ignored me. And then Jude came back and I forgot because he came back so I forgot." *A happy ending. Case closed.*

"That's right," Mr. Greenwood said, as if suddenly recalling something himself. "Mr. Brighton, the missing boy who miraculously reappeared on his front doorstep. Saw that on the news. Big story. Mr. Brighton's made us famous. Everyone's heard of Deer Valley now."

But he's gone again. Stevie wanted to scream it, wanted to reach across that crummy old counter, grab Mr. G. by the front of his polo shirt, and beg him for help. But instead, he simply stammered, "I—I—I guess . . ." His watch was itchy in his pocket. He could feel the seconds ticking away against his thigh.

"So?" Mr. Greenwood asked.

"So?" he echoed Mr. G.'s question to himself. "So?" Glancing down to the candy in front of him, he was pretty sure Mr. G. had given him more than two quarters' worth. "So?" Finally realizing what the old man was asking, Stevie cleared his throat. "So . . . Dunk had a dog named Noodle," he said.

"And what happened to Noodle?" Mr. Greenwood asked, apparently realizing that unless he propelled the conversation forward, there would be no conversation to be had. Stevie was too distracted to focus. His brain was tripping over a million thoughts at once.

"He ran away," Stevie said, looking up from the bag of candy. "He kept jumping over the fence." *Jude ran away. Over the fence. He's gone again.*

"And where did Noodle run off to?" Mr. G. suddenly looked stern, as if everything hung in the balance of Stevie's next response.

The cabin. The house.

"The forest?" Stevie formed it as a question, unsure as to why.

"Like my cat," the old man assessed.

Stevie squinted at the abstract reflections in the counter's glass. He didn't see what that sickly cat had to do with anything. Cats and dogs weren't anything alike, and they certainly weren't anything like Jude.

"Mr. Clark," Mr. Greenwood said. "Do you know why there's no veterinary office in town?"

"Huh?"

"There's no veterinary office in town," Mr. G. repeated, as if to hammer the point home. "I'd like you to take a guess as to why that is."

A riddle? Stevie hated those more than he hated math. The gunk inside his brain made both riddles and arithmetic problems almost impossible to solve. As if jump-started by his loathing for puzzles, a realization occured: time was running out. How long had he been standing there? Jude was *gone*, and here he was, clutching a bag of candy, and—

"Mr. Clark?"

"I—I—I d-don't know," Stevie said, having half forgotten what the heck they were talking about, groping for the busted watch in his pocket. He had three minutes before he'd have to start booking it back to the house.

"Gotta run?"

"Yeah," Stevie said. But he couldn't leave. Not before Mr. G.

told him the answer to the stupid riddle. "Why? How come there's no vet?"

Mr. Greenwood's expression morphed into something akin to sad amusement. He looked a little disgusted, too, as though Stevie's unwillingness to figure it out for himself made him dumber than the average bear. But the old man leaned in rather than stepping away, and he murmured across the counter so that only Stevie could hear. It didn't seem to matter that Mr. G.'s customer had left minutes before, or that they were alone together in the store.

"Because there aren't any pets in Deer Valley, Mr. Clark. None beyond a few gerbils and Mrs. Lovejoy's little dog. And Mrs. Lovejoy has that ball of fur attached to her hip. She never lets it out of her sight, which is the only reason it's still around."

What was he talking about? What about the cat out behind his shop? What about Sam Benton's ferret, which Jude and Sam had nearly gotten into a fistfight over after Jude had called it a weasel? What about Jude's fish, Cheeto? Or Kermit the hermit crab, which Jude and Stevie had painted green—which was probably why the dumb crab had died, but that was beside the point. What about all the strays?

Mr. Greenwood seemed to take notice of Stevie's aggravation. He leaned away to give him space, as though crowding him wasn't giving Stevie's puny brain enough room to expand. But suddenly, all Stevie wanted to do was yell. He had run all the way out here, Jude was back at that creepy house, there was a monster on the loose, and he was probably going to get grounded for the rest of his life. And all Mr. G. had managed to do was confuse him. He wasn't a sad and lonely man the way Stevie initially thought. He was a riddling kid-hater, and Stevie just so happened to be a convenient target for his loathing.

Stevie's eyes darted to the cellophane bag of gummy candy. All at once he was convinced that, no, Mr. Greenwood hadn't given him more than fifty cents' worth. He was almost positive that the man had given him less, and *on purpose*.

"They go to the woods," Greenwood said. "And like your brother's dog, most of them get there by running away."

Logic told Stevie to be patient; just stand there and nod and wait for Greenwood to reveal what it all meant. But something about the way Mr. G. was dancing around the subject was infuriating. He knew Stevie was in a hurry, and yet there he was, stretching out time, daring Stevie to stay longer. *How much is the answer worth to you? Two weeks? Two months? Two whole lifetimes in the hole, whole, hole?*

Stevie peered at his bag of candy. He didn't have time for this. Mr. Greenwood had nothing to offer. He was useless, just like the search team. Just like his mother. Like Aunt Mandy and her blind belief that Jude just needed to sleep it off despite looking like a scurvied pirate. *Because they can't see it. You have to save him because you're the only one who can see it. You know the truth and no one else does, because, because, because* . . .

Either Stevie figured out on his own what was wrong with Jude, or Jude was done for. Vanished but still there. Invisible but real, like that shadow, that creature that Stevie was *sure* Jude had seen, too.

He turned away from the counter, mad enough not to

bother with niceties. His lack of a good-bye would speak volumes: he was pissed, and he didn't appreciate Mr. G. wasting his time. Hopefully, it would make Mr. Greenwood feel bad about stringing Stevie along. *Thanks for nothing, you old fart.*

But as soon as Stevie turned, that cellophane crinkling in his palm, the store owner spoke again, his tone trying for reassurance. "The answer to the question isn't always obvious, Mr. Clark. The shortest distance between two points is a straight line, but sometimes a straight line isn't the quickest way."

More crappy riddles.

Stevie marched toward the door, not looking back.

"Remember Max Larsen?"

Stevie froze, his hand on the door. The hair on his arms stood on end. He turned, expectantly holding his breath.

"Something they don't mention because it seems arbitrary," Mr. Greenwood said, "is *why* Max had gone into the forest that day."

Stevie's mouth went dry. "Why?" he asked. What if Max had built a fort, just like Stevie and Jude had? In the very same tree, and that tree was haunted or something? And by building *their* fort there, Stevie and Jude had roused some shadow beast that was now determined to eat their brains right out of their skulls? Maybe there was a lady ghost in the woods, vexed by some mysterious event nobody quite understood, vengeful enough to steal kids.

"He was taking his dog for a walk," Mr. Greenwood said. "A new puppy. The puppy was acting out, digging under the fence, trying to escape."

Stevie stared hard at the old man.

"Max's dog *did* get out, Mr. Clark. It was the first or second day he had it. Max and his mom came in here with flyers. Max was crying his eyes out. He was a small boy. A lot younger than you."

Stevie's fingers squeezed. Cellophane crinkled in his grip.

"The dog showed up on the front step after a few days. A miracle," Mr. Greenwood recalled. "Max was so happy. He brought him over to my house to show old Pop-Pop how good of a dog Sammy was. But Sammy wouldn't eat, and he wouldn't sleep. He came back with fleas, and he kept trying to escape the yard no matter how much attention Max gave him. So Max's mom told Max to take Sammy for a walk, hoping that some exercise would do the pup some good. And that was the last we saw of them, Mr. Clark."

Until two weeks later, when the cops found the body. At least that's how the story went.

"The police never did find the party responsible for what happened to Maxi; fat lot of good they do around here," said Mr. G. "But the dog . . . same as the cat, the one that lives behind the store . . ."

Was that the answer? The stupid cat? That would have possibly made sense if Jude had been walking his dog the way the Larsen kid had. It would have had a semblance of meaning if Jude even *owned* a dog, but he didn't. No. Greenwood was just screwing with him.

Bullshit walks.

"I g-gotta go," Stevie murmured, having had enough. He wasn't going to figure out the riddle, not at this rate.

He pushed his way through the screen door and let it slap closed behind him, shoved his hand into the pocket of his shorts and drew out his watch, then squinted at the readout that was almost impossible to see against the glare of the sun. His heart flipped when he finally managed to make out the numbers.

Five minutes till noon—an impossible feat, but he ran anyway.

With the bag of gummies swinging back and forth in a pendulum whip, he cut across unfenced yards to save on time, flying down the street as fast as his sneakers would take him. Mr. Greenwood—*Pop-Pop?*—was a kook, obsessed with that cat that lived behind the building, pushed to the outer limit of his sanity by that feline's rejection. Yeah, it was a mean thing; that cat should have been grateful that someone gave half a damn about it at all. Without Mr. G. leaving food and water behind the back-alley door, the dumb animal wouldn't have been more than a walking skeleton. But he didn't see why Mr. G. had to bring *him* into it. Cats were just like that: distant, independent, generally total jerks.

But what about Noodle? Dunk's dog skittered into his thoughts as he leapt over some kid's abandoned tricycle. He considered his own brother's heartbreak as he charged toward Sunset Avenue, his breaths coming in quick, locomotive gasps. Dogs weren't like cats. Some of them ran away, but for the most part dogs got attached to their owners. It was weird that Noodle would have been so dead-set on running off; strange that, if Dunk's story was accurate, Noodle had almost strangled himself in an attempt to escape the yard. Stevie had only ever seen dogs act that way when there was something to chase—a rabbit or a squirrel or a kid on a bike. And he supposed that could have been the explanation if it had happened once or twice, but from what Dunk had said, it was a constant thing . . . at least after the first time Noodle had escaped.

That's what Mr. Greenwood had said happened to Max Larsen's dog, too. It had gotten out, gone missing long enough for Max and his mom to put up posters all over town. And then he just reappeared out of nowhere.

The weight of that thought hit him head-on as he veered onto Sunset. It was heavy enough to slow him down, as though the concrete had gone soft and sticky beneath his feet.

Sammy had come back, but had refused to stay. Noodle had done the same thing. Mr. Greenwood's cat rebuffed the old man's hospitality despite actually *liking* Mr. G. And Deer Valley didn't have a vet, because nobody could seem to keep their animals from running off. Their pets would vanish, then reappear—unharmed yet completely different—never staying, always running back into the trees.

Into the woods, just like Jude.

. . .

Stevie shoved open his unlocked bedroom window, crawled through, and landed with a bounce on top of his bed. He gasped for air as the cellophane bag of gummies crinkled beneath his weight. The busted watch dug hard into his leg as he writhed atop his sheets, trying to steady his breathing, to keep his heart from exploding inside the cavern of his chest. Eventually, the burning in his lungs dwindled to a smolder. He sat up, shoved himself off the bed, and careened toward his door.

He didn't knock, just pulled open Duncan's door and stepped inside for the second time that day. Dunk was in the same spot Stevie had left him—half sunk into that ugly old beanbag, his laptop lighting up his face with an electric-blue glow. It didn't matter how sunny it was outside; the sheets he'd thrown over the already existing curtains kept the room dark, 24/7.

Duncan's attention shifted from screen to his kid brother, surprise deviating to leering anger in two seconds flat. "What the *fuck*? What are you doing in here again, you little shit?"

"I'm—" Stevie started, but he wasn't allowed to finish.

"You think you can just come in here any time you want? Get the fuck out!"

"B-b-but Dunk, I gotta, gotta—"

"Gotta get the fuck *out*. Before I break you in half, you turd!"

Stevie took a couple of backward steps, ready to flee. But he stopped before turning to go. No, he couldn't.

"Dunk, I'm sorry, okay? But I *gotta* talk and you gotta listen! Okay?"

Duncan pulled a hand down his face, as if trying to tear the skin off his skull, then slammed his laptop closed. His eyes were still blazing, but he relented. "This better be good, Sack, or I swear to God . . ."

"That house," Stevie said. "The one house along that road with the house—"

"I know what house you're talking about, moron."

"It's where Jude was," he said. "I *know* it was! We were a

few minutes away and he said there was a lady, remember? The mother lady, because it's not abandoned?"

Dunk exhaled a frustrated breath and fell back, Styrofoam beads crunching beneath the force of his head hitting the bag's cracked-vinyl upholstery.

"Before he came back home, I went there to find him. I thought that he had gone there and maybe the cops hadn't checked—"

"Why wouldn't they have checked?" Dunk interrupted. "You think watching all those stupid-ass shows makes you smarter than the police?"

Stevie stood there, his train of thought derailed.

"This isn't *Mysterious Mysteries*, dude," Dunk said. "Of *course* they checked. The cops knocked on every door within a fifteen-mile radius. They checked out that house, too."

"Th-then why didn't they find him?"

"Because *he wasn't there.*" Dunk was growing more irritated by the second. He rolled his eyes and opened his laptop again. Conversation over. "Besides, the Jewd is *back*. Who gives a shit? Get out," he said. "I'm busy."

"Then how would he know about the lady?" Stevie asked. Dunk may have been getting agitated, but Stevie couldn't help getting angry, too. Didn't Duncan understand that this was a big deal? "Dunk."

"Oh my God . . ." Duncan was seething, apparently at the end of his rope. "If you don't get out of my room in the next three seconds, I'm going to take my morning dump on top of your face."

"Dunk, *stop it!*" It exploded out of him as a yell. Dunk's eyes went wide, not having expected his kid brother to get so riled up. Stevie, on the other hand, suddenly wanted to cry, though he couldn't tell exactly what was pushing him toward that emotional edge. Duncan's relentless threats, the name-calling, the obviousness of his big brother's disdain, the fact that Dunk didn't seem to care about *anything?*

All Stevie wanted was for someone to hear him out, to forget about his stuttering and word salad and *listen.* All Dunk had to do was sit there and shut up for a second so that Stevie could try to get the words out right.

"Jesus Christ," Duncan said beneath his breath. "You're going to cry now? Fine, *what?*"

But Stevie wasn't sure he wanted to tell him anymore. Because *screw him.* Why should he tell Dunk anything if he didn't care? Except, who else did he have to tell? His mom had already proved that she wasn't interested in his stories. He couldn't go to Aunt Mandy. That was crossing some sort of line. Besides, she'd been there when Stevie had mentioned the monster; she'd been there when he told her and his mother both about how Jude had taken a bite out of his own arm. She hadn't believed him, either. Who else was left? Terry? The cops? If he told the police, they'd show back up at Aunt Mandy's place to ask questions. If they went into the forest to look for Jude and found him, they'd drag him back to the station, and then Jude would be in trouble and *really* hate Stevie's guts.

"I saw something," Stevie said, forcing it out before he could waste more time reconsidering.

"Saw something," Dunk repeated, his tone flat, uninterested. "Like one of your crazy fucking delusions, I bet."

"At that house," Stevie clarified. "W-when I went there by myself to the house. I went there, Dunk. All by myself."

Dunk didn't respond. He just sat there, not moving.

"It was . . . a thing. On the porch."

"On the porch," Dunk echoed.

"A *creature* thing . . . on the porch."

"A creature?" Stevie could hear it; his brother's interest was finally piqued.

"It was sitting in the shadows, so it was hard to see because it was, it was because, it was behind the shadows, sitting on the porch in the shadows on the porch of that house in the woods on the porch. It was hiding, I think, but I could see a little bit, and it was all curled up and mangled, *mangled*! Mangle-dangled like how the ape monkey apes sit at the zoo."

"Like a mangled ape," Dunk said, as if considering something, then continued. "A mangled, retarded monkey, and it was hanging out on the porch of a spooky old house." A beat of silence. "A ghost monkey." His voice cracked with amusement. "And you're sure you didn't take the crazy train to nutso town. Okay, buddy, whatever."

"It *wasn't* a monkey," Stevie insisted.

"A baboon, then. One of those red-assed ones."

Stevie ignored him. "You know how I asked about Noodle?" As soon as he name-dropped Dunk's dog, Duncan's expression lost all signs of humor. Another invisible line. Another subject that simply shouldn't have been breached. "I asked because Mr. Greenwood—"

"The old general store guy?"

"Yeah! He told me to, and I didn't see what that had to do with anything, but there's this cat—his fur is pretty much naked—it lives behind the store and Mr. G. feeds it even though it's a jerk. He tried to adopt it . . . but it keeps running away, just like Sammy did."

Duncan stared at Stevie for minute, as if dazed by his monologue.

"I mean, Noodle," Stevie murmured to himself.

"Coincidence," Dunk said. "Animals are dumb."

"Except that there's no vet in town. Did you know that? There's no pet vet, Dunk, because the pets keep running their legs off," Stevie said. "Unless they're in cages, I guess. That's probably why everyone has fish. Or weasels. Because something is out there."

"Out where?"

"In the woods, where Jude is!"

"Jesus, you're making my head hurt, you know that?"

"Noodle ran away with Mr. Greenwood's cat. There's no vet because there are no pets to vet, a-a-and Max . . . the dead Max? You remember the dead Max who died, that Max kid? Pop-Pop said Max had a Noodle dog, Dunk. He had a Noodle, too, except it was Sammy. He went into the woods to walk him and the Sammy dog ran, and Max was chopped up. Max," he whispered the name. "Max got the ax. Jude is screwed . . ."

Dunk peered at his kid brother through the dim haze of his

bedroom. "So, the monkey thing on the porch of the spooky house was Max Larsen's dog, and it had magically turned into an ape? Or did it turn into the old geezer's cat?"

Dunk was just messing with him now, but flying off the handle was just going to get the door slammed in Stevie's face. "Maybe that monkey thing has something to do with it, even though it wasn't a monkey. It was a *creature*. Maybe that thing had something to do with Jude disappearing, too."

"Except, reality check: Jude is back."

"But he's gone again, Dunk. He's gone again and not the same. There's something wrong. He's different. You've gotta see him. He looks like a sicko alien hamburger cow-killer. Why would he go out there again if he got stuck? Why is he going in the dark when there are monsters hiding there? Why?"

Dunk didn't reply. Too much to think about, or possibly Stevie was too excited to be coherent. His brain was too messy. He was speaking in tongues.

Dunk suggested: "Well, maybe if you're so goddamn interested in whatever's in the woods, you should wait until Jude goes out there by himself. Follow him, like in your stupid crime shows."

"I can't."

"Why not?"

"Because I told you, he's gone!"

"What the hell are you talking about?" Dunk furrowed his eyebrows. "He's probably wanking it next door."

"He's in the woods," Stevie insisted. "Back in the woods, he went back."

"Since when?"

"Like an hour ago." Was that how long it had been?

"He's next door, you idiot. I saw him out the kitchen window a few minutes ago. Go see for yourself. And if you're so worried about what he's doing out there, follow him and leave me out of it, huh? Now get lost."

Stevie couldn't help himself. He ran across the hall and back into his room to look out his window toward Jude's house. And there, just as Duncan had said, was Jude. In his room. Staring out the window, as if waiting for Stevie to come looking for him. Waiting, like the purveyor of some nasty prank.

"So, I still don't get it." Stevie jumped at his brother's voice, veered around, saw Dunk standing in his open bedroom door. "If there really is something living out there—if you *weren't* just hallucinating the hell out of your pea-sized brain, and you're even remotely close to being right and that thing, whatever it is, has been out there since that Larsen kid got shredded—why wouldn't the cops have figured it out? Why wasn't the body at the house? And why would Noodle *want* to go back into the forest? I mean, maybe he was just a stupid dog that didn't know any better. But if there was something dangerous out there, the last thing an animal would do is run *toward* it, you know?"

Stevie *didn't* know. That was the whole reason he had to follow Jude and find out for himself. He swallowed hard and turned back toward his open window, listening to his brother try to work it out for himself, surprised that Dunk was actually taking something seriously for once. Hope lit up like a sparkler at the forefront of his mind: What if Duncan was interested enough to go into the forest with him? Was Dunk deciding to act like a big brother and ease Stevie's anxieties by being there for him for once?

"Probably because you *were* hallucinating," Dunk said beneath his breath. "Noodle may have been dumb, but you're certifiable."

And just as quick as it had come on, Stevie's optimism vanished. Duncan turned away, stepped back into his room, and shut his door.

Stevie stared at the wood grain from across the hall, willing Dunk to change his mind and come back out. But he didn't.

And when he turned to his window again, Jude was looking at him with a hint of satisfaction at Stevie's disappointment. *Don't kid yourself,* the look said. *This is your nightmare. Ain't nobody going to help you figure this out, Sack. You're on your own.*

27

ROSAMUND PACED THE floor, her hands over her mouth, choking back dispirited sobs. She had been so stupid. She had convinced herself that Otto knew better, that he'd never repeat with another child what he'd done to Max Larsen so many years ago. But oh, silly optimism. Happiness. *Hope.* She had grabbed on to those ridiculous notions, had convinced herself that her child was more than an animal; that, behind his blank eyes, there was at least *some* understanding, and most important, at least a little love.

But the boy in the basement was her answer.

Otto didn't understand a good goddamn thing.

Rosie stopped her back-and-forth pacing, her legs weighed down by the heavy heart that had sunk to her feet. Perhaps all these years she'd given Otto the benefit of the doubt not for his best interest but for her own. She had grasped for something, *anything*, if only to protect herself from the knowledge that she had spawned a demon. But that's exactly what Otto was. Her first baby, gone. Ansel, gone. Then the Larsen boy. But this was too much. Too cruel. Just as God had felled Otto's stillborn sibling, he should have smote Otto before he ever had a chance to live. If only there was someone she could talk to, if she wasn't so alone . . .

The retreat.

Ras's easy smile flashed like a photograph across the backs of her eyes; the both of them sitting at the table, him listening while she rambled on about things she should have never revealed. He had listened and sympathetically placed his hand on top of hers, offering quiet support the way only an old friend could. *What would you give up to get what you want?*

Anything.

But what she had given up was everything instead.

Rosie took in the living room around her, the randomly placed furniture, a room she hardly recognized as her own. Her gaze fell upon the fireplace mantel. A wood-framed photograph of Ansel stared back at her. A doctor. A man who had promised to help people, never to harm. Now there was a strange boy in the basement who needed help, and with Ansel gone, it was up to Rosie to live up to the task.

But Otto was keeping his prize close, protecting him with a ferocity she hadn't seen before. He refused to come up from the basement, even after dark, coddling his newfound companion in a grotesquely maternal way. Rosie wondered if she had ever looked that way after Otto had been born—a mother, crazed and pining over a misshapen child. A woman who allowed that baby, that *thing*, to gnaw on her to the point of mangled flesh. She still stared at her own reflection every morning, wishing away those jagged, ugly scars. But they were forever, a tattooed reminder that Otto was nothing more than a snarling, growling devil, threatening her with hisses and snaps of his teeth.

No, this couldn't happen again. She had to get to the boy.

She steeled her nerves, marched across the kitchen to the basement door, and carefully descended the wooden staircase, hoping to intervene. But Otto was quick to shoo her away with a curled-lip snarl. She attempted to make eye contact with the child in the corner before taking her leave, just a quick glance to assure him that she'd be back, but the kid didn't see her. He was either dazed or in shock. His chest rose and fell, nothing but shallow breaths. There was no telling how long he'd live if she couldn't bargain for his release.

Rosie snuck downstairs throughout the following day, but Otto did not sleep. She tried to think of what she'd say to the police when they appeared at her door, but they didn't come. An oversight. They could have forgotten that she existed out here at all. Or maybe there was something about this particular boy that had them taking their time. In any case, why the authorities hadn't yet visited was beyond her concern. She couldn't afford more blood on her hands; and she refused to be destroyed by someone else's misdeeds. That, however, didn't keep her from fantasizing about escape.

On the second night of the boy's captivity, she again considered leaving it all behind. Perhaps the lack of police was a sign, a second chance for the opportunity she had let pass her by so long ago. Except, that, too, wouldn't work. Had she done it just after she had found Max Larsen, Otto would have died for sure. He had been just a child himself. But now Otto's vulnerability was long behind him. If she left, he'd run wild, become impatient. He'd inevitably end up in town. No. She wouldn't have a hand in that.

She devised a plan. It wasn't sure to work, but it was the best she could do.

Early the next morning, she climbed into her rusty car—the fan belt screeching like a gutted banshee—and drove ten miles per hour under the speed limit all the way to McMinnville, terrified of being pulled over. The car was in terrible shape. It coughed and sputtered, and the tires were bald. If she was stopped for so much as a broken taillight, she was positive it would blow the case wide open. Surely they'd recognized the guilt that was written all over her face.

The man at the feed store looked at her as if she was crazy.

"Five chickens?" he asked. "You want five chickens in the back of your *car*?" But after some hemming and hawing, he eventually managed to shove a wire crate into the backseat.

She nearly talked herself out of the whole thing as she drove home, those chickens—a delicacy Otto hadn't had in years—clucking and flapping and filling her car with dander and down. It was a gruesome plan, one that would make her feel that much more terrible, but she couldn't think of any other way to lure Otto upstairs.

After stopping at a gas station for a fill-up and seeing the daily newspaper displayed on its stand just shy of the register, she knew it had to be done. The boy who was trapped in her basement stared out at her from the front page. Jude Brighton. Twelve years old. History repeating itself. Rosie's second chance to make things right.

Back home, she struggled with the cage, but it was wedged in tight. Unable to maneuver it out of the backseat, she was forced to reach in and drag each chicken out by its feet. They flailed like demons possessed as she ran from the car to the front yard, lobbing them over the shoddy fence she hoped would keep them confined. It was as far as she got that afternoon.

On the morning of the fourth day, she went out into the yard. She spent hours in the unforgiving sun, chasing those birds, finally managing to grab the first two hours into the ordeal. The heat and exertion had dwindled her patience down to zero, and yet she hesitated before shoving the chicken neck-first onto the tree stump she used to split wood. Her bottom lip trembled as she lifted the ax and readied the blade. But her sympathy was extinguished when the chicken, falling into a panicked flurry of squawks, caught her thumb in its beak. Rosie screamed and, in a sudden flare of rage, dropped the ax and wrung its neck with her bare hands instead. She screamed again when she chopped off its head. But at least it wasn't flailing around anymore. At least there was that.

The trail of blood started in the room beneath the stairs, stretched into the hall, and dribbled into the foyer like a Jackson Pollock painting. With the police yet to pay her a visit, this was a dangerous move. They could come at any moment, and if they did, they'd see blood smeared across the floor. Blood that could easily belong to a child. They'd get a search warrant. They'd go downstairs. They'd discover Otto and his new-found pet. Rosie would find herself standing on the threshold of a very unhappy ending.

But if she didn't do something to get Otto upstairs, nobody would ever see Jude Brighton again. So she held that decapitated chicken upside down by its scaly talons and covered the hall in a crooked stream of gore.

One by one, all five chickens had their heads removed. Rosie wept and gagged through the whole ordeal.

When the sky finally blushed from sunset to dusk, she pushed aside her untouched cup of tea, leaned away from the kitchen table she had occupied for three hours, not moving, and reached down to the foot of her chair. Her fingers disappeared into a bloom of red-speckled feathers at her feet. She stepped across the kitchen, pulled open the basement door, and crept down the wooden staircase, taking her time as she moved, allowing blood to drizzle down each riser.

Finally reaching the ground floor, she spoke gently, as if sweet-talking a baby. "Otto, darling," she cooed.

Otto swung his head around, looking away from the boy, who sat in the same place as before. He snarled despite the softness of his mother's voice. Like a teenager with his privacy impeded, he showed her his teeth. *Get out. Can't you see I'm busy?* She ignored his sneer and lifted the chicken up for him to see.

"I brought you something," she said. "Come on, sweetheart. It's time to eat."

For a moment, he didn't respond, and Rosie was struck with a terrible thought: he wasn't hungry. He'd probably been feeding for days, drinking the blood of a child who was toeing the line of death. Except that, now that she got a good look at Jude—at least as well as she could in the dimness of that cellar—he looked . . . better, more alert, as though he were in the process of recuperating from whatever terrible thing Otto had done.

But as predicted, Otto couldn't resist the scent of a fresh kill. That was, after all, the way of the glutton. Rosamund dropped the chicken onto the cement floor, where a pool of its blood had formed at her feet. "Come on," she said. "Come have a bite."

Otto hesitated for a moment. He looked back at his captive, but he couldn't resist. He fell onto the chicken next to his mother's feet, and Rosie skittered backward, up two basement steps, as feathers flew. This time her eyes caught Jude's, and she gave him a faint nod to say that she'd be back as soon as she could. At least, if all went according to plan.

Otto was quick to finish his snack. Dropping the tattered creature onto the floor, he peered past Rosie at the trail of blood that led up the stairs, and for once she was thankful for his paltry intellect. This strategy was slapdash, simple, not likely to work on anyone who had the slightest amount of foresight. But Otto didn't seem to notice how obviously he was being lured, too interested in the metallic scent that went up the steps and into the rooms he hadn't visited in nearly a week.

It was against her better judgment to leave Jude behind, but she followed Otto regardless. Part of her wanted to grab the child and shove him out a basement window. But those blacked-out windows were nailed shut. They had been for years. All for Otto's protection. Now to her misfortune.

There was a chance, of course, that she was underestimating her offspring. Otto may have known *exactly* what she was doing. He could have been playing dumb, biding his time, planning his own ambush. There was also the danger that, with enough time to think about what was occurring, he might have some flash of realization, a blink of higher intelligence. If Otto actually witnessed Rosie trying to save Jude, there was no doubt he'd come to understand the double cross. Otto had to be restrained. If he wasn't, neither Jude nor Rosie stood a chance.

She found him lingering by the kitchen table, her cold cup of Earl Grey exactly where she'd left it. She'd placed a second bird just shy of the basement door. It was now pressed to Otto's mouth, and as he ate, his eyes flicked up to watch her approach. The blue hue that had always tinged the whites of his eyes had become more prominent over the years. His corneas flashed silver and were reflective, even in the dimmest light. She'd grown accustomed to the feeling of being watched, but now, with her nerves frayed and her pulse hammering in the hollow of her throat, those eyes were more unsettling than ever before.

Again, she was hit with a wave of self-loathing. She remembered the way her pelvis had creaked against the girth of that oversized head; recalled how she had prayed for death. All those animals, the cemetery behind the house. Collars stuffed into a desk drawer. A red sneaker. Otto, tearing into the fur of a small gray mouse.

She jumped at the thud of bird number two hitting the floor.

Otto sniffed at the ground, his nose inches from the planks, his tongue lapping at the trail of blood. He skittered across the length of the kitchen, pausing next to dead fowl number three just beyond the kitchen's threshold. Lifting it up to his mouth, he began to eat, but it was with less zeal than before. He was gorging himself, filling up. Dread swelled within Rosie's throat, because what if he went back to the basement after this one? What if she couldn't get Jude out of the house and the police arrived—*Have you seen this child?*—only to see the mess she had made? It had been so much easier with Max Larsen, so much simpler when there had only been a body and no living child to save.

The mere idea of such a convenience put a terrible thought in her mind. If she let Otto kill the kid, she could wait it out again, throw the body in the trunk, drive him out to the same spot she'd dumped the Larsen boy. She'd done it before, why should it be any more difficult now?

How can you even think that way? She exhaled a soft cry into the palm of her hand, appalled by her own callousness. She was sick. Had spent too many years alone. Otto may have been the one wearing the deformities, but her ideations had become as twisted as his limbs. She had been a good person once. Before she had been a mother. *The* mother. Before Otto had tainted her mind.

"Of the devil," she whispered to herself, watching as Otto casually worked on his special treat. "You aren't mine. You can't be."

It was then that understanding dawned, so overwhelming that she took a backward step. Her head felt helium light. Her stomach somersaulted inside her guts. The Happy Hope. It had made her feel better, but the sadness of her miscarriage had lingered. Grief had held her captive the night she had spent at Ras's farmhouse in Big Sur. It had weighed down her limbs to the point of incapacitation, had kept her pressed to the mattress. Sleep paralysis; that's what it had been.

But thinking back now, she could swear that Ansel had his accident before that lingering sadness had disappeared. She had been despondent. Ansel had kept his carnal desires in check. He gave her space, kept to his side of the bed. And then, the accident . . . and yet, somehow . . .

Her eyes darted to her son. *Her son?*

Her mind flashed back to Big Sur.

Otto was making his way down the hall to the bird she'd left near Ansel's secret vault. Her heartbeat cymbal-crashed as she watched him move on all fours—a terrible, less-than-human thing. She'd felt detached from him plenty of times before, but now the sensation was all-encompassing, the disconnect twisting her maternal instinct into a giant question mark that could be answered by no one. Except for Rasputin. Maybe him . . .

She swallowed against the suffocating revulsion that was filling up her chest. Because, Otto, what *was* he? Why hadn't she been able to move that night so long ago?

Sweet, thoughtful, patient Ras offering her cups of tea; dinner he had assured her she would help him prepare, but had refused her assistance in the end. Then there was the nightmare. The fact that she hadn't been able to find him before she left.

No, that couldn't be right. Ras had been so kind, so thoughtful. And yet, his eyes . . . those striking blue eyes, as bright as anything she'd ever seen. As supernaturally vivid as . . .

"You aren't mine," she whispered again. And just as those words left her throat, Otto's head snapped around. He bore his teeth, his mouth and chin slicked with blood. For a moment she was sure that, for the first time in his life, he had understood her; certain that he knew what she was putting together, aware that any moment now he'd be found out.

She stepped away from the hissing creature before her, lifted her hands to tell him to calm down. But rather than relax, Otto coiled up his odd-angled limbs. His muscles tensed, ready to spring up and pin her to the ground and, finally, after all this time, tear out her throat.

"Otto," she said, trying to keep her voice even. "Calm down." She'd never seen him so furious, so vicious. It was as if all their years together meant nothing. He didn't recognize her as his mother, and perhaps it's because she wasn't. Maybe she was just a host.

As a young girl, her father had taught her: never turn your back on an animal that means to attack. But she gave in to her fear and veered around, overwhelmed by her need to get away. If she could just make it to a room with a door, she'd lock herself inside and wait until morning. He'd have to go back to the basement to escape the sun. Jude would still be down there, but at least she'd be alive, able to come up with another plan.

But as she turned to escape, she stopped short at what she saw. There, not more than a few paces behind her, was the boy she intended to save, pressed so flush against the hallway wall that he may as well have been a picture frame. Otto hadn't been sneering at her but at the child—a kid she had hoped would stay put until she had Otto safely locked away beneath the stairs. But who could have blamed him for trying to escape?

Except that now Jude was in more danger than ever. Otto was impulsive, and for all of that lacking intellect, he offended easily. He knew that Jude was trying to get away, and for that the child would be put in his place.

Rosie turned her back to Jude as she continued to take reversing steps, closing the distance between herself and Otto's latest obsession. If Otto lunged, he'd have to go through her before getting to the kid, and she hoped that he wouldn't want to hurt her. Perhaps he really *did* love her. But she was still afraid.

"Otto," she said, her voice trembling, her hands groping behind her, searching for Jude. "Go to your room!"

But Otto wasn't in the mood to take orders, not when his most favorite thing was hidden behind her back. He leapt forward and shoved Rosie into the hallway wall, jamming Jude against it in turn. Rosie let out a yelp, reached out and grabbed Otto's hunched shoulders before throwing forward all her weight, partly to fend off Otto, but primarily to let Jude wriggle away and find someplace safe. Jude, however, didn't move.

Otto snapped his teeth. He hissed and clawed at her arms as she shoved him back. Saliva hung from his blackened teeth like glistening spider's silk. She could hardly look away from those blue-tinged eyes. They looked positively murderous now, holding no loyalty. To Otto, Rosamund was no longer his mother. She was the enemy, keeping him from what was rightfully his.

"Jude . . ." The name escaped her before she realized she was saying it. "Run away!" The whole point of this confounded plan was to set Jude free, and she'd be damned if she ended up dead with nothing to show for it. But when she shot a look back toward the hallway wall, Jude was gone. His absence was a relief, albeit a temporary one. She looked back to Otto, who was still fighting her with all his might, and gave him another backward shove. With Jude out of the picture, it all came down to how long she could suppress the savage before her. If she let him burst out of the house and give chase, he'd catch the boy in no time flat.

"He's gone!" she yelled. "I told you, never again!"

But Otto wasn't making a move for the front door, which didn't make sense . . . at least not until she caught movement from the corner of her eye. Jude hadn't left. Rather, he'd disappeared somewhere into the house to seek out a weapon. And now he came at them both, swinging a rolling pin like a Louisville Slugger. For a second, Rosie wasn't sure who he was aiming to hit, but she chalked that up to Jude's poor sense of balance, his weakness and delirium. Nearly a week abducted, anyone would have come unhinged.

Jude reeled back and brought the rolling pin down hard against Otto's shoulder and, in turn, Rosie's hand. She yelled out in pain, but rather than letting Otto go, she used her son's momentary bewilderment to fuel her strength. Bearing down, she clamped her teeth and gave him one final push. Otto stumbled backward, his already poor balance further compromised as one twisted foot slid out from beneath him, slipping on a streak of blood decorating the floor. He went flailing backward into Ansel's hidden room.

Otto roared in outrage as his back hit the reinforced wall. He came at her again as she struggled to get the door closed, but all his effort afforded him was a set of fingers gnashed against the jamb. That howl of anger suddenly turned into yowling yelps of pain. His fingers retreated into the room with a jerk, leaving skin and blood upon the frame.

Rosie slammed the door closed. She stood with her palms flush against it for a long moment, trying to steady her breathing, realizing the scope of what she'd just achieved.

Maybe she'd never let him out and this was it—this was the end. Her gulping breaths morphed into a dumbfounded laugh. *It's over.* Feeling empowered after all these years, she had saved Jude. She had saved *herself.*

Putting the secret door to her back, she stared at the boy before her. Jude was still holding that rolling pin high over his head. The kid was in shock, ready to swing. "Jude . . ." She continued to struggle with her own raspy breaths. "You're safe now. It's time to go home." As soon as he made it back, he'd tell the police everything. She could only hope that he'd tell them she had saved him, that she had nothing to do with the ambush, with the captivity he had endured.

But rather than bursting into relieved tears or bolting out of the house—two reactions that would have made perfect sense—Jude continued to stare at her, his expression strikingly blank. He took a forward step, as if ready to shatter that pin into a thousand pieces against the door behind her, wanting his captor dead. But there was no way Rosie was letting him in there, no matter how justified his rage. "It's okay." She caught the rolling pin in her grasp and slowly pulled it from his hands. "Let's get you home."

Jude still said nothing. He only stared at her like *she* was the bad guy. And again, she could understand. Because without her, Otto wouldn't have existed at all.

28

STEVIE WAS GOING out of his mind. He felt like, at any second, his restlessness would have him crawling out of his skin. The day dragged on. He spent most of it with his nose pressed against his window glass, staring at Aunt Mandy's place, his nerves sizzling with edgy eagerness. Because he knew, as soon as the sky shifted from blue to gold-trimmed gray, Jude would make his move. And when he did, there'd be no turning back.

He'd spent the day trying to stay patient. He reread a quarter of the first Harry Potter book, ate half a bag of Oreos, downed five Mountain Dews, and—to his horror—had fallen asleep with his chin on the sill . . . twice. Thankfully, Jude was still next door. Stevie could see the shifting shadows inside Jude's room, creeping beneath the ever-growing brightness of the aquarium's glow.

Just a week ago, Stevie would have marched himself across the yard and demanded to know why his cousin had run back to that house on his own, why he had abandoned him in the woods like that. After hours of contemplation, Stevie was almost certain he'd imagined everything beyond Jude's strange retreat: the way his face pulled into that horrible chapped-lip smile; the shouting he'd heard behind him, more than likely coming from inside his own head rather than from his once-best friend. But still, Stevie remained fixed to his mattress rather than knocking on Aunt Mandy's door. Because Jude *had* run in the opposite direction of Sunset Avenue. Stevie had booked it toward town. He hadn't stopped, not even for a second. So how was it that Jude had beat him home?

Because he's faster now. The thought curdled as soon as it surfaced. *So much faster.* Jude had always been quick, an expert at climbing fences—better than Stevie could ever hope to be. But the way he had leapt down from the fort, arms outspread like flightless wings, feet hitting the dirt without the crippling shock wave familiar to long-distance jumps; the sunburn and peeling skin; the bite that had healed itself in the time it had taken them to march home. All of it was proof that Jude had changed. *Physiologically* changed. That fact kept Stevie rooted to his bed, only leaving his room to choke down a few bites of Crock-Pot chicken. But he wasn't hungry after all the soda and cookies, and his mother didn't seem to mind. Terry was in a mood, grumbling about some "dickhead shit-stain asshole shift manager" who had cut his hours "because he doesn't like my attitude. *My attitude.* Motherfu—"

The Tyrant was too busy hissing through his teeth to notice Stevie excuse himself from the table. Stevie's mom gave him a faint smile and a nod. *Good night, sweetie.*

"I ought to track that son of a bitch down," Terry threatened. "Teach that pompous little prick a lesson."

Stevie ducked into his room and quietly shut the door, hoping Terry wouldn't hear the latch click. Sometimes, that's all it took to set him off. Tonight, he wouldn't need much more.

By the time the sky started to bruise, Stevie was sick with nerves. And yet, Jude remained in his room, as if not planning on leaving at all.

Stevie's mom peeked her head in a few minutes before bedtime. "What are you doing in here?" she asked. "You aren't in your pj's yet? Have you taken a bath?"

"Yeah," he said. "This morning, I did."

"You took a bath *this morning*." His mom didn't look even close to convinced.

"No," he said. "A shower, not a bath, a shower in the morning glory, gory . . ." His eyes shifted back to his window. "Ghost story," he whispered. That could have been what had happened to Jude. What if he really *was* dead? A zombie, just like he'd wanted.

Stevie's mom gave him a suspicious look when his attention drifted back to her. "I swear," he said. He didn't like lying, but he was coming to realize that the older you got, the more you had to do it.

"Well, it's bedtime." She surprised him by dropping the subject. "Shut it down." Mom speak for *Close the curtains, turn off the lights, get into bed.*

"I just want to finish this chapter." He lifted his Harry Potter book up from the sheets for her to see. She nodded and left the room, but she'd be back. Stevie shot a look toward Jude's room again. Leaving the window meant the possibility of missing his cousin's escape. But Stevie's mom *always* checked on him twice, like he was a baby or something, so he abandoned his novel, darted across the room to his closet, and replaced his T-shirt with a pj top. He kept his pants and shoes on—risky, but necessary if he intended to sneak out in a hurry. And that was another thing: if he needed to leave fast, he wouldn't have time to grab supplies. Hesitating for only a moment, he searched his room, then grabbed a mini flashlight off his desk and jammed it into the back pocket of his shorts. Jumping back onto his bed, he shoved his fully clothed legs beneath the sheets and stuck his nose against the window once more, all the while straining to hear his mother's footsteps over the muffled cheers of Terry's football game.

When the doorknob began to turn, he threw himself backward and reflexively drew the sheets up to his chin. The flashlight dug into his butt cheek, and he winced. His mom paused as soon as she stepped into the room, as if sensing that something was up. "What's wrong?"

"Huh?" *Wrong?* What was she talking about? There wasn't anything wrong.

"You made a face," she said. She watched him from the doorway, then scrutinized the open closet door and the T-shirt he'd left on the floor. Stevie's heart thudded once. For a moment, he was sure that her mom telepathy was in full effect—her witchy way that made hiding anything impossible.

"My stomach hurts." He threw it out there, hoping it would be enough to make her lose the scent.

"Really? You hardly ate any dinner."

"Because my stomach hurts," he said.

"Yeah?" She stepped across the room to sweep his T-shirt off the floor, then tossed it into the plastic laundry basket inside the closet. "Maybe it's all that Mountain Dew," she suggested, nudging the little trash can next to his desk with her foot. "We've talked about that before, haven't we?"

Stevie squeezed his eyes shut. He really didn't need this right now.

"And what's with the light?"

The light? At first he thought she meant the flashlight in his pocket, the one making his right butt cheek go numb. *How could she possibly know?* Until he blinked up at the fixture overhead—a frosted-glass dome with two lightbulbs and a couple of dead moths inside. He'd left the stupid thing on. If she made him get up to turn it off, he'd be forced to reveal his shorts and sneakers and then he'd *really* be in trouble. The mere thought of running off while his mother slept and The Tyrant stared dead-eyed at the TV made his pulse beat a little faster. Kids who did that sort of stuff were the types of kids who ended up on investigation shows. Kids who chased their crazed cousins into dark forests ended up hacked to bits.

"I forgot," he said.

"Forgot." He hated how skeptical she sounded. "Like how you forgot to put your T-shirt in the hamper?" If she looked in that laundry basket for his shorts, it was all over. But it was way too late for laundry, and the light in the closet *was* off. To Stevie's relief, she slid the accordion door closed and scanned his room—always looking for something to nag at him about. At his desk, she grabbed the container of Oreos and continued to scrutinize the empty soda cans in his trash bin. "No sugar tomorrow," she told him. "You're way over your limit."

"Okay," he agreed, probably a little too quickly than he should have.

"And I want you to clean this desk. Half of this stuff is probably nothing but trash and food wrappers. You're going to bring in ants again. We don't have the money for another visit from the exterminator."

"Okay, okay, *okay.*" The ants had been in Dunk's room, too, but Stevie got the blame. Leave a slice of pizza on the floor just once and you'll never hear the end of it.

The Oreo bag crinkled in her hands. She leaned down and grabbed his trash bin, taking a painfully long amount of time to vacate the room. He wanted to yell at her to hurry up and go. Jude could be halfway to the fort by now. *You gotta get out, get out, gotta get outta here, you!* But all he did was clench his teeth and wait.

"I know you've had a hard past few days," she said.

Oh God, he thought. *Not now.* "I'm just tired," he told her. "And I don't feel good." *So get out. Go!* "Just tired, fired . . . is . . . is Terry getting fired?" A masterful change of subject. He watched his mom blink at the inquiry.

"What? No, of course not." Except she didn't look so sure about that. As a matter of fact, she looked pretty worried, probably nervous that she'd be the sole breadwinner on whatever money she made answering phones at Duncan's school. No money for an exterminator, indeed.

"It's just all the stress," she said softly, as if reassuring herself that everything would work itself out. "Everyone has been stressed. Even Terry. The whole thing with Jude has been—" She cut herself off. *Go ahead,* Stevie thought, *just say it.* But she didn't, because words like *crazy* and *insane* were taboo when you had Stevie for a kid. She hovered in the doorway, then nodded as if deciding on something—yes, everything would be fine. She was sure of it. "Don't worry about Terry's job, sweetheart," she said. "I love you."

"Love you, too, Mom," he told her. And he did, he really did. He just wished she'd be a little more like how she'd been before his and Dunk's dad had taken off, before The Tyrant had moved in and blown up their lives.

It was only when she hit the light switch and closed the door that he breathed again, a rush of air bursting from his lungs as he scrambled to sit up in bed. He kicked away his sheets—a risky maneuver. There was a chance she'd turn right back around and open the door again. *One more thing,* she'd say, only to stare at him as he kneeled beside his window in his sneakers and shorts. But it felt like he'd been lying there for an hour—way longer than Jude needed in order to leave Stevie in the dust.

But Stevie startled at the sight of his cousin as soon as his hands hit the sill. Just like the night before, Jude was standing at his own window, staring ahead, his silhouette blotting out the bright blue of Cheeto's aquarium light. It looked as though he had watched the entire exchange with Stevie's mom the way Stevie had seen Aunt Mandy deliver Jude's lunch hours before. But the more Stevie squinted to see through the dark, the more he came to realize that Jude wasn't staring into Stevie's room. No, he was staring at something just outside of it, beneath the window, hiding in the nooks and crannies of Terry's junk.

Stevie smashed his nose flat against the glass, trying to spot what it was that held Jude so thoroughly transfixed, but he knew what it was without needing to see it. Struggling to swallow the wad of phlegm that had collected at the back of his throat, he couldn't help but make the conclusion.

That thing was there. It had to be. Whether Jude was seeing it for the first time or the fifteenth, what was important was that *he was seeing it.* And if that creature had been the thing that was responsible for Jude vanishing the way he had, it was here to take him back again. And that was something Stevie couldn't allow to happen, no matter how much he suddenly wanted to puke.

He braced himself, thought of all the superheroes he wished he could be, and shoved open his window before sticking his head out into the night. As soon as his windowpane slid upward, there was commotion in the side yard. A cat bolted from out of the shadows and toward the front yard, leaving Stevie breathless and blinking. Had that been Mr. Greenwood's tabby? He didn't have time to wonder. The sound of Jude's window sliding open stole his attention.

Jude leapt out of his room, pausing not to look in Stevie's direction, but to where the cat had come from. *Something's there somewhere.* Stevie opened his mouth, ready to call out to his cousin. *Go back inside and hide!* But before he could find his voice, Jude was at his own back fence. He paused, as if waiting for something—for Stevie to clamber out his window and follow?—then climbed the planks, launching himself over the top edge like some sort of amateur crime fighter.

This is really real. Those words screamed like a tsunami siren inside his head. Every nerve in his body buzzed with refusal to believe his eyes. He must have lost it; finally, really, truly lost it. Jude was going back to that house. *No way, no how, no no . . .* He was going to get himself killed.

Stevie forced himself to move. He squirmed out his bedroom window before he had a chance to reconsider, and he *would* reconsider, because this was nuts. Completely insane.

Running across the yard, he launched himself at the fence, caught the top edge, and struggled to pull himself up. Splinters bit into his hands, burying themselves into the flesh of his palms. He fought against his own weight at the very top, then tipped slow-motion over to the opposite side with the grace of a newborn colt. His sneakers hit the ground hard, the shock wave of the impact traveling up his calves and pooling into an agonizing ache behind his kneecaps. He winced, the pain dulled by a darkness so far-reaching it made his throat close up; an allergic reaction to a newfound fear of the dark.

The moon was out, so the trees glowed a little, but the forest was thick and the clouds were rolling in fast. He was supposed to stay undercover, but there was no way. It was too dark. He was way too scared. Thank God he'd shoved that mini Maglite into his pocket. Pulling it out, he twisted it on and pointed it in the direction Jude had gone. *Gone, gone forever, gone.*

The beam wasn't more than a pinpoint of light upon an

endless swath of black. He swept it back and forth along the path, pushing himself to walk fast, partly because he didn't want Jude to get away, but mostly because he was too scared to go slow. Jude had always been the braver of the two, not seeming to care about getting into trouble or getting hurt. Ever since his dad died, it seemed that he'd been daring God to kill him, and God had nearly taken him up on that challenge.

Stevie, on the other hand, was far less spontaneous. He was the one who always prepared for the worst, thought better of things, and backed out of stuff. His faintheartedness kept Jude's feet on the ground. But this time was different. This time, Stevie refused to be a coward. And maybe Jude would be happy to see him. *Hey, thanks,* he'd say. *I forgot to bring my stupid flashlight.* Because Jude never remembered things like that. He'd realize just how dumb of an idea this whole thing was, and together they'd turn back and run toward home.

At least that's what Stevie liked to think, but it was something only an idiot would believe.

In the dark, the trail looked like a whole other forest—someplace different and far away. Stevie didn't recognize any of the usual markers: the big tree whose roots grew across the trail like Mr. Greenwood's craggy old fingers; the giant boulder so covered in moss that ferns had started to grow from the top of it like crazy green hair. He wished he could see those things, if only to reassure himself that he was going the right way, but instinct pushed him forward. "It's the only path," he whispered. "The only path is this path is the only path is this one. This is the right one because it's the only one so it's gotta be." If he kept going, he'd be able to hear the babble of Cedar Creek. Once he reached its bank, it would only be a few minutes to the house he had hoped to never see again.

He almost yelled when something hit his shoulder. The beam of his Maglite danced crazily across the tops of the trees, then settled on whatever had landed on his arm. An insect sitting there, huge and grinning at him with a full set of human teeth. Jude's hand, the flesh torn away by too many bites. The shadow creature, leering and naked, hunched over on all fours like a Chernobyl baby. Stevie had watched a documentary about that place, and it had been chock-full of grotesque photos; pictures of kids who looked normal on top but had the legs of elephants on the bottom; infants whose faces looked like they had been split in half and then fused back together; kids born without arms, with fins for feet. And then there were the ones with massive heads, so big they looked like helium balloons.

But rather than finding a mangled, radioactive hand or a glowing, snarling spider beside his ear, Stevie saw nothing but a round wet spot. A moment later, another one bloomed beside it. He looked up, pointed his flashlight at the sky. Lazy raindrops cut across the beam in sporadic silver streaks. This mission was complicated enough as it was. The last thing he needed was a storm to top it off.

He jogged despite hardly being able to see the path beneath his feet. There was a fork coming up. One direction would take him to the fort, the other would lead him to a place he didn't want to think about. There was a sharp swerve in the trail and, after rushing around it, Stevie all but yelped, his heart giving him an inside-out sucker punch. There, sitting in the center of that unkempt route, was Mr. Greenwood's scruffy old cat, scratching at its tattered fur; Jude's ambassador, waiting for Stevie to catch up so that he could be led in the right direction. Its eyes gleamed in the flashlight beam like a pair of shiny tacks. Offended by the brightness, it began to move, not in the direction of the fort, but in the direction Stevie desperately didn't want to go.

He trailed the cat despite the clanging inside his head. *Turn back, heart attack, clack-a-lack, on death's fast track* . . . The feline lead him down that almost nonexistent path, the old farmhouse coming up just around the bend. And what if neither his mom nor Aunt Mandy were disturbed by Jude's appearance because they simply couldn't see the change? What if Stevie had magical vision, a third eye, some sort of psychic sight? Perhaps that's why he saw things differently—the shadow people, the maggots in his cereal, spiders stuffed inside his pillowcase that his mother insisted weren't there. It could have been that all the stuff that seemed real to him but invisible to others had been preparing him for his ultimate purpose: *this* purpose. Saving his best friend.

He braced himself for the appearance of that scary house, imagined it glowing ghostly in the moonlight that, tonight, was fading fast. What would he do if that shadow thing was on the porch again? Sweeping the flashlight beam back and forth across the path, he searched for a downed branch big enough to serve as a makeshift club. If that thing rushed him, he'd need protection. But when his torch light found Jude's back, Stevie reversed his trajectory in a quick backward scramble.

There, not more than twenty feet away, was his cousin, unmoving. Jude didn't turn. There was no *About damn time* smirk as a hide-and-seek consolation prize. Stevie's light outlined the slope of Jude's shoulders, hunched in a way that made Stevie's skin prickle beneath his rain-dampened sleep shirt. Jude's right shoulder was higher than his left, as though a crick in his neck had paralyzed him from the ears down. Except he wasn't incapacitated. That shoulder was twitching; a quick spasm of a muscle every other second, resembling a sobbing shudder . . . or a silent, quaking laugh.

Stevie's mouth was suddenly full of glue—tacky and bitter, threatening to cement his top and bottom teeth together if he continued to clench them as hard as he was. He imagined stepping around to his cousin's front, pictured a pair of glazed-over eyes upon an expressionless face. Or he'd see that seed of rage that was becoming more commonplace, the stuff that gave birth to Jude's manic anger, his threats.

And then there was the shiny thing that glinted in Jude's hand. Stevie pointed the flashlight at it to identify what it was, his stomach pitching like a Tilt-O-Whirl when he finally recognized Aunt Mandy's meat tenderizer—the kind that looked like a metal mallet with big diamond-shaped teeth; the kind of tool torturers used on their victims; a weapon that could inflict mass damage with a few good hits.

Stevie didn't want to believe that Jude would ever truly mean him any harm, but logic and the sour churn of his stomach advised him to put as much distance between himself and Jude as he could, and fast.

Hey Jude, he's not anymore, he thought. *He's something else, something dangerous, no good, very bad, dark.*

As if reading Stevie's thoughts, Jude became unstuck. He slowly turned his head, gave Stevie a look, spoke—"So, do you have a pair or what?"—and started to move down the path again, heading toward the house along the abandoned road. Stevie watched him for a moment, unnerved by the lumbering gait that seemed to have taken over his typical walk. It was a subtle thing, one that nobody but he and possibly Aunt Mandy would have noticed—except, no. If she hadn't noticed Jude's creepy plague-face, why would she ever take note of such a small and subtle difference? Stevie, however, was quick to pick up on it. It almost looked as if Jude had rolled both ankles during his nighttime hike, each step now hindered by obvious pain.

The butterflies in Stevie's stomach flailed, drowning in the acid of his belly, but he followed anyway, not daring to take his eyes off that meat tenderizer for more than a few seconds at a time. It was easy to focus on, catching the light of Stevie's flashlight. Better to fixate on Jude's weapon than on that stiff, ambling zombie walk.

Mr. Greenwood's cat was now heading the trio, and Stevie told himself he should have been happy. Animals could sense danger, just like Dunk had said. It's why birds disappeared before storms, why forest animals fled areas before earthquakes. If there was real danger where they were heading, Mr. G.'s cat wouldn't have been so eager to get there, no matter how weird and sickly it was. At least, Stevie hoped not, because that hope was the only thing keeping him from running away.

When the trail crossed the old road and the house came into view, Stevie's anxiety clanged like the bell at the top of a strongman High Striker game. Something about seeing that house in the dark made him want to vomit. The difference in energy was palpable; like watching a scary movie in the middle of the day versus watching it on a stormy night, alone, with a Ouija board at his feet and a grinning demon in Terry's chair.

That house, while thoroughly terrifying in the daylight, was nothing short of evil-looking in the dark. Everything about it was wrong, from the way the roofline sagged to how the moonlight reflected off its dirty windows and peeling paint. And the covered porch, the place where that thing had lurked, was now so enveloped in shadow it was darker than the night that surrounded it. Anyone, or anything, could have been standing there, licking its chops as it watched two hapless, approaching boys. Or maybe it was just one boy . . . and Jude, the something else. The Jude-not-Jude. The whatever-it-is. The not-who-he-was.

Stevie shined the light onto the house to make it less frightening. That flash of light garnered a sudden pause in Jude's movements, as though he'd been spooked by the glint of the beam reflecting silver off the windows. Stevie pointed the light down at the road again, nervous that his cousin was going to whip around and charge. But a half second later he was so distracted that he forgot his fear, because there, half hidden in some brambles, was the handle of Jude's old hammer.

The last time they had come here, Jude had sneered at Stevie like some starved, snapping beast—or had he? Stevie didn't know anymore. Regardless, he had run, but what he had been sure of was that a chase had turned into an unexplainable game of tag. Jude must have dropped the hammer during that relay, which was why, this time around, he had been forced to settle on that mean-looking mallet. And now, there was good ol' Stanley lying in wait, as if offering a warning. *You'll need me.* Stevie bit his bottom lip and glanced over to his cousin, who continued to walk toward that house. Before he could argue the fact that he didn't need a weapon—that this whole thing wasn't that big a deal because Mr. Greenwood's cat was there and he wouldn't have been, not if there had been any *real* danger around—he swept the hammer off the ground. Only then did he realize that his hands were shaking. Tremors at age ten. Like the last two leaves of a tree on the final day of fall.

Jude was halfway to the house when Stevie fell into step again. He nearly tripped over a root as he rushed to catch up. Jude moved past the broken picket gate, past the dilapidated chicken coop, and stalked across the front yard. Stevie's steps hitched like a windup toy at the end of its wound spring when Jude paused and looked over his shoulder, his eyes meeting Stevie's wide half-dollars. *Come on.* A faint smile quirked at the corners of Jude's paper-dry lips. *This is gonna be fun.* And then he turned back toward the house and made a beeline for the front door.

No, Stevie thought. *He's not just going to just walk in there just like that, is he going to? No way* . . .

His fingers squeezed the rubberized grip of the hammer in his left hand, still holding the small Maglite in his right. He paused at the base of the porch steps when Jude seemed to hesitate beside the front door. Stevie considered finally speaking up. *Please, Jude, think this through.* But before he could suggest a retreat, Jude shoved the door open and stepped inside. Mr. Greenwood's cat followed him in.

"Oh no . . ." Stevie could hardly breathe, let alone move his feet. "Oh no, no, no . . ." That open door. The darkness inside. But this is what he had wanted, wasn't it? Somewhere inside those shadows lay the answer that he sought. *What's happened to Jude? How do I get him back?*

He forced himself up the steps, his anxiety causing him to stumble over the last one. He floundered his way into the foyer, gawked at the house's interior. There was furniture strewn everywhere, as though there had been a fight. Spiderwebs clung to the corners of the rooms. And there was blood. Lots and lots of blood smeared across the floor.

"Holy shit," he whispered, the curse tumbling out of him without so much as a second thought. "Oh man . . ." He looked up from the floorboards, searched for his friend. "Oh shit, oh man." They weren't supposed to be in there. It was too dangerous.

But Jude was gone. Stevie was alone, his nerves left to buzz with electric terror. If he was going to run away from this place, it meant leaving Jude behind.

"I won't. I won't. Can't. Won't. Can't. *Won't.*" Using that mantra of refusal to propel himself forward, he followed the rust-colored ribbon—a trail that would inevitably lead him to something he was sure he didn't want to see. *The devil demon, schemin', dreamin' about boys like us, like us, like us.*

It led him through a kitchen.

An open basement door.

"Jude . . . ?" A whisper, nothing more.

He stepped over the threshold, paused on the wooden landing that creaked beneath his weight. The only light down there was the pale moonlit square that shone in from the door behind him, but it faded fast, eaten away by the shadows that lingered beyond the third and fourth steps. Stevie swept the darkness with the trembling beam of his flashlight, left to right, that back-and-forth motion keeping time with the rabbitlike quiver of his heart.

Something skittered across the shaft of light.

The sway of the beam stopped dead with Stevie's pulse.

It paused upon a leg.

A lady's leg.

A foot. An ankle. The curve of the calf. A ratty Birkenstock laying not too far away, knocked free, as if lost in a fall.

Don't be a chicken . . .

He moved the light up the appendage. Would the woman be lying facedown in a pool of her own blood, her eyes open, staring at him, imploring as to why someone hadn't come sooner to help? Was *this* the lady Jude had been talking about, the one he'd come back for with that meat tenderizer in tow?

He inched the light upward, his dread amped up to eleven. Because she wasn't dead. It was all an act. If this was "mother," she was a kidnapper. But as his flashlight beam trailed up that leg, it became clear: there would be no sudden upward bound. The pillar of light stopped just above the woman's knee, which was where the leg stopped, too. There was a heap of something a few feet away. Bloody. Tattered. The leg, though. It wasn't attached.

A yell punched out of Stevie's throat. He scrambled backward, lost his footing, his butt hitting the stairs hard. His Maglite jostled free of his damaged right hand. He lurched to grab it, but it was too late. The stubs of his pointer and middle fingers just grazed the aluminum body before it bounced down the stairs, lighting up the entire basement like a disco ball. The beam hit the ceiling, the walls, the floor, over and over, as it went flying off the side of the staircase to the cement floor ten feet below. It landed with a metallic clang, continued to roll, the ray crawling along the base of the far wall. Crawling until it stopped.

Stopped and shone upon the back of a naked, knobby spine. A fleshy tail. A huddled thing.

Stevie sucked in air to yell again, his fingers of his good hand instinctively tightening their grip around the hammer he had found outside. If the thing came at him, he'd embed that hammer right in the creature's giant skull. But Jude . . . *Where's Jude, Jude, Jude, JUDE?!* Jude had a mallet. He would come at this guy, too. They'd both get away.

The flashlight kept rolling, and when it came to a stop, the scream that had scurried up his throat was stunned into silence. Because there, just shy of where the hunched monster-man was crouched, was Stevie's best friend. The silver sheen of the meat tenderizer marred with blood. His hands smeared with dark.

Stevie's eyes jumped to the heap between Jude and the

beast. *It's the lady. The lady, mother, mom.* And yet, rather than Jude using his weapon on the monster, he sat beside it like a docile dog. And then, as if Stevie's once-best friend couldn't have been more terrifying, Jude spoke.

"He's here."

The twisted-up man-thing snapped its giant head around.

It sneered, its teeth black and glistening with gore. A cord was looped around its neck. Had Jude put it there? Was this thing some sort of pet? Was that why Jude kept returning to the woods, to this house? Was he taking care of this monster the way someone takes care of a pet? Stevie wasn't going to stick around to find out.

He scrambled away, shoved his hands against the step, rushed to his feet.

Something moved fast across the concrete floor behind him. There was a thump against the bottom riser. Stevie was sure he was about to be lifted off the ground and thrown backward. Any second, he'd join the boy that used to be Jude against that far basement wall. And yet, somehow, he found himself bursting into the kitchen, that trusty Stanley glued to his palm.

The blood trail . . . *Thank God for the blood trailing out the door, to the porch, into the woods, the trees, the trail through the trees, tree, flee, run, go* . . . Had it not been there, Stevie wouldn't have known which direction to take. But that macabre path kept him on track, pointing him out the open front door.

There was clawing behind him—long nails skittering across a slick surface. Stevie didn't know how he had outrun this thing before. But something assured him his luck had run out. If he tried to outrun it and barreled headlong into the trees again, it would catch him. Something about the darkness beyond the front door gave promise that *this* time, he wouldn't make it. He had to stop and fight.

Against all reason, he veered around and exhaled a scream as soon as his sneakers hit the warped planks of the porch. He swung Jude's hammer in a wide, blind arc, slashing at the air.

The freak came barreling through the house on all fours despite Stevie's continued swinging. Stevie increased his grip, his fingers aching against the handle of his weapon. And as soon as that snarling Mephistopheles was within range, he reeled back and slammed the hammer into its bony, sharp-angled shoulder.

The savage roared in pain. Stevie fell backward, startled not by the yowl, but by how manlike it was. He couldn't bring himself to look at the creature for long, but what he *did* see of it suggested that it must have been a man. Its hands and feet were apelike, but definitely closer to human than animal. Its ears looked normal in shape, but were puffed up and ill-defined; the cauliflower ears of a boxer who had taken way too many punches in the ring. It was a living picture of the Chernobyl disaster, but Stevie didn't let his sympathy for those radiated kids keep him from swinging the hammer again. He smacked the man-thing hard against the side of its skull. It roared again, faltered backward, shook its head as though trying to throw off the bite of the hit. It snorted and pawed at its face with a jumble of crooked fingers, trying to recover. Stevie readied himself to run, but before he could blast through the forest to find help, to finally tell someone, *anyone*, he found himself frozen in place.

Because there, in the doorway, was Jude. His hands holding that meat tenderizer tight. And what struck Stevie wasn't the fact that Jude had come up from the basement, possibly to help kill this creature dead, but that Jude was staring at *him* rather than the writhing monster between them.

Jude was looking right at Stevie.

And he was enraged.

29

R OSIE WATCHED JUDE disappear into the night, attempting to tamp the tension by telling herself that, come what may, the police would understand that she had been the boy's savior, not his assailant. Once the police came, she'd lead the authorities to Ansel's secret vault and show them what Jude's fate would have been had it not been for her. They'd take Otto away, releasing her of the burden she had endured for so long. She'd end up in the local paper, maybe even on the national news: the woman who had cared for an affront to humanity, because a mother's love is stronger than any other force; the woman who had turned her back on that love to save the life of a stranger. A saint hidden away, exiled by her own devotion.

Except, that was the trouble. She had continued to care for Otto after Maxwell Larsen's death, as though a little boy's life had never been cut short. There was a chance she could convince the police that she hadn't known about the Larsen boy. The body had been found far from the house. A story of Otto having gone missing for a few days would be easy to pass off.

But they'd find the pet collars. The graveyard out back. She'd created a catacomb of bones—bodies on top of bodies. Feigning innocence would be a hard sell.

Oh, they'd come all right. And yes, they'd take Otto away. But she was no hero. A clean soul didn't birth something so horrendous. A woman of God didn't raise the devil as her own.

Less than two minutes after Jude disappeared into the forest, panic set in. Rosie's confidence that everything would be all right vanished as quickly as the boy had. It was time. One last drive out to Big Sur to see the lush greenery and smell the salty air, then leap to the rocks below. Or she'd cut out all of that romantic nonsense, stick her head in the oven, and call it a day.

But there was that voice again. That nagging, maternal itch despite all that had occured.

You can't leave him.

But she hated him for what he'd done.

You're his mother.

He was the only thing she could truly claim in this life. Otto may not have been perfect, but Ansel would have loved him regardless. And she loved Ansel more than anything. She missed him every day.

"I can't," she whispered. *Can't leave him.* But she couldn't wait for the police to come, either. There was another option, but the mere idea of it made her tense. Rather than running away from her life, she'd take Otto with her. She'd get him in the car somehow, drive until just an hour before sunrise, rent a room at a roadside motel where she'd draw the curtains tight, then drive after dark until they reached the place that had been calling her back all these years. If Ras still lived at the Happy Hope, he'd accept them as he had accepted her so long ago. If he rejected them, Rosie would turn a blind eye one final time. Otto would take care of the problem. She'd replace the retreat's guidepost with a NO TRESPASSING sign, let the road grow over so thick it would be impossible to get through. They'd get no visitors, no prying eyes. Otto would hunt wildlife. He'd have his freedom. And she'd have the peace of mind of not being discovered. It was the only way to save them both.

"Yes," she whispered. "Yes, that's a good idea." She didn't want to think about what would happen if Ras refused. No, he wouldn't. She had confidence that he'd take them in. She was just trying to save her boy. *His* boy—a reality she'd have to make peace with later. But right now, she didn't have the time.

Turning away from the front window, she hustled up the stairs to pack a small bag; just a few things to tide her over. Anything else they needed could be bought once they reached the California coast.

She threw a hastily packed suitcase into the trunk of the car. It was heavier than she had expected, lined with the remainder of the money Ansel had refused to keep in the bank. There wasn't a whole lot left after all these years, but it was more than enough to start a new, simple life. Or at least enough to continue the old one in a new place.

She struggled with the wire crate that was still jammed into the backseat, finally got it to come loose and tossed it aside. Rushing back into the house, she stopped next to the stairs and opened the first door—the one that revealed an innocent-looking coat closet with a few old parkas hung up for show. But she hesitated. Unlatching the recessed door would release Otto from his prison. He was difficult as it was, but when he was angry, he lost all control.

Turning her back on the door to Ansel's secret room, she rushed to the kitchen. The chickens were dead, but there was a defrosted steak in the fridge. It had gone gray with spoilage, forgotten after she had discovered Jude in the basement nearly a week before, but Otto wasn't picky when it came to meat. And so she grabbed the glass dish the steak was sitting in, lifted the slab out of its juices with her bare hand, and rushed back to the hall.

"Otto," she said in a singsongy voice. "I have something for you . . ." She knocked lightly, realizing only then that if she couldn't hear him, he couldn't hear her, either. She steadied her nerves as she reached for the finger pull. There was a good chance he'd push past her and try to sprint after Jude, but the boy had a decent head start. Both the kitchen and front doors were locked. Otto couldn't open them. In all his years, he'd never been able to turn doorknobs with those twisted appendages he had for hands. But that didn't alleviate her worry. Sometimes he upended furniture when he was irate, and this was all a matter of timing. If he flew into a rage and didn't calm down fast, the police would show up. All would be lost.

Rosie glanced over her shoulder at the clock hanging on the living room wall. She'd give him half an hour. But that meant she couldn't hold off any longer. Pulling open the door, she expected him to come charging out of there like a bull into the ring. But there was nothing. No movement. Not a sound.

"Otto?" She leaned in just enough to peek inside that dark prison. It had been nearly twenty years since Maxwell Larsen's remains had been shut up in those confines, and yet the room never did smell quite the same since. There was an ever-lingering tinge of sweetness in the air, like something long-spoiled.

She swallowed, suddenly overwhelmed by the ever-constricting hands of inevitable catastrophe. If, by some miracle, she managed to get Otto into the car, she was guaranteeing herself a continued life of enslavement. If he refused, she would have to abandon him or kill them both. It didn't matter how it played out. In the end, she was damned either way.

No, she wasn't thinking straight. The promise of the police's arrival was muddling her reasoning. If she could just get out of that house, then she could figure out what to do.

"Otto, darling . . ." Leaning into the carious scent of that safe, she could just barely spot the outline of Otto's slumped shoulders. "We have to go." She extended her arm to show him the dripping, sallow steak clutched in her hand. *Toro!* The coldness of it was making her joints ache. Otto remained still.

She stepped farther inside, shaking the steak in front of her; a soundless Pavlovian dinner bell. "Aren't you hungry?" Of course he wasn't. Not after he'd gorged on all that fowl.

Not even a shift of weight.

"What you did wasn't right, Otto. That boy . . . He's gone home, and the police will be here soon. If we don't leave . . ." She was speaking as though he could understand her, explaining an escape plan to an infant mind. She supposed the talking was to soothe her own nerves, but the fact that Otto wasn't moving was as disquieting as it was unacceptable. She didn't have time for this.

Rosie stepped away from the shaft of light that shone in from the foyer and breeched the darkness. There had once been a light in Ansel's beneath-stairs room, but the bulb had burned out long ago. "I'm serious," she said, taking a sterner tone. "Get up."

Nothing.

"Otto, I'm your mother . . ." That word—*mother*—there was a possibility it would spur movement. Or perhaps it was just a reminder to herself.

It's your job to protect him.

Still nothing.

"This is ridiculous." Stepping even farther into the shadows, she lifted her free hand and pointed away from the vault, then gave him a stern and clipped command she was certain he knew. "Out!"

Otto jumped, scrambled onto four legs, and rushed past her, leaving Rosie stunned and empty-handed. The steak fell to the ground with a sloppy *plop* next to her sandaled feet. She spun around only to spot him at the front door, just as she had feared. He was pawing at the doorknob, frantic to escape.

"No!" She was yelling now, her nerves frayed, her patience gone. If she had any hope of getting him to the car, she needed something to keep him tethered—a leash. Otto was strong, but if she leaned into it and used all her weight, she was sure she could keep him from running away.

She marched across the living room and stopped at Ansel's old roll-top. Pulling open a drawer, she picked through its gruesome contents, knowing that at least a couple of the animals had arrived not just with a collar but with a lead. She snatched up the longest one, the kind that looked like a bungee cord with a loop on one side and a metal clip on the other. All the collars in that drawer were far too small to fit around Otto's neck, but if she looped the multicolored cord through the handle, she could slip the noose around his head like a lasso. The more he'd pull, the tighter it would get, and that was good, because the key to success was submission. It was about time Otto learned who was boss.

"We're going on a trip," she said, sliding the silver clip through the handhold of the leash. "To the ocean. You're going to love it." Well, *she* would love it. She was starting to care less and less what Otto would think.

He was still pawing at the doorknob, and his throaty whine ignited a long-sleeping resentment inside her, catching fire as quickly as a dynamite fuse. It was his obstinance that did it. She was about to be in a world of trouble, all because of something *he* had done. And couldn't he listen for *once*? Rosie clenched her teeth as she approached him with steady-paced steps. She'd spent her life making up excuses for him. *He doesn't know any better*, or *He's just a child*. But this time she'd had it. He'd either get his ass in the car or she was through.

By the time Otto's head snapped up to look her way, she'd thrown that bungeelike cord over his head and cinched it around his neck. For half a second, Rosie reveled in her victory. Could it really have been that easy? She could have been leading him around like this all this time? But her celebration was cut short when he scurried again. He jerked the cord hard enough to burn the skin of her palms. She let out a startled yelp and let go, her hands set ablaze. Otto bucked and hissed and threw himself against walls and furniture, pawing at the sides of his head in a panic, unable to free himself from his restraint; an untamed horse being saddled for the first time.

"It's okay," she told him, trying to keep her tone steady despite her irritation. "Calm down." She approached him again, but as soon as he saw her coming he put more distance between them. He was afraid and angry, not about to let her get close.

"Otto, please," she said, clutching her wounded hands to her chest like a nun praying for clemency. "We need to go. Just do this one thing, okay? Calm down and we'll go on a trip."

Every step she took forward made him increase the distance between them by two stumbling shuffles. Any second now, the night would be lit up by a swirl of red and blue lights. Before she knew it, she wasn't approaching him with even strides, but chasing him the way one would go after a mischievous puppy. They circled the dining table—unused since Ansel's death—Rosie pulling chairs into the room, setting up a makeshift obstacle course to slow Otto down. By the time she managed to shoo him into the kitchen, she was livid, half-tripping over her clumsy sandals as she pursued him down the hall.

"Come back here!" she screamed. "I should leave you! I should go on my own and let you die!" And had it not been for the risk, there was a possibility that she would have done just that. But the idea of Otto clawing his way out of the house stopped her from turning her back on this whole confounded plan; the thought of him doing to Jude what he had done to Max Larsen, of doing to a dozen children what Max Larsen had suffered decades before . . . the pain it must have caused his family, his mother, losing her perfect little boy; a boy that Rosie would have killed to have. Otto had murdered Maxwell Larsen almost as if to say, *Too bad, Mommy. You're stuck with me instead.*

They replayed their chase, this time around the kitchen table, Rosie whipping the chairs away the same as she had in the dining room, tossing them aside. All the while, Otto continued to struggle with the cord around his neck, but he was only tightening his bonds, amplifying his own hysteria.

"I'll take it off!" she yelled. "Just get in the goddamn car!" When

Otto paused to fight with the leash, Rosie bounded forward and stomped on the cord, but all it did was make him jerk away. The cord went taut. It snapped him forward while Rosie's foot skated out. She caught herself on the table while Otto's eyes went wide with a newfound sense of disbelief, unable to comprehend why she, his mother, would go to such extremes to scare him. He was toeing terrified madness, and so, despite knowing he'd more than likely tear the damn thing out of her hands again, she snatched the leash off the floor and looped it tight around her wrist.

"Calm down," she demanded. She was past trying to soothe him. Like a woman dealing with a full-blown temper tantrum in the middle of the cereal aisle, Rosie meant business. Enough of this acting out. "We're leaving."

But her authority did little to ease Otto's confusion, so he did what any other creature would have done: he retreated to his safe place. Rosie's right arm jerked forward with such force her shoulder all but pulled free of its socket. Tethered to him now, she was helpless as he dragged her away from the table and toward the basement steps. He was moving too fast. She couldn't regain her footing. Her sandals had no grip on the slick, blood-slathered hardwood. She let out a yell.

"Otto, stop!"

He leapt down the first few risers toward the darkness he considered a haven, and Rosie was dragged behind him. After the second step, her left Birkenstock twisted around her foot, her ankle torquing beneath her weight.

Otto cleared the staircase by the time his mother hit the basement floor. Her shoulder crashed against the cement first. Her temple followed. The world went black, but came into blurry focus fast. Managing to roll onto her stomach, she wheezed as the cord bit into her wrist. The pain was a shroud, enfolding every limb. Her head. Her ribs. Her arms. Both legs. There was no pinpointing her agony's source.

She couldn't tell whether it was the darkness, or whether her vision really was blurred, but she was sure that her ears were ringing like twin bells, trilling so loud she could hardly hear herself as she moaned his name. Her maternal thoughts flooded back: he hadn't meant to hurt her. He was scared. It was her own fault, roping herself to him the way she had.

Suddenly, she was thankful that the police would be there soon. She'd probably go to prison. Depending on her injuries, there was a possibility she'd never walk again. But at least she'd be alive. She didn't want to die in the basement, didn't want Otto to witness her last breath. Yes, he had made her life difficult. She'd spent his lifetime wondering what it would have been like without him, yearning for release. And yet, this wasn't the way she had wanted it.

Because it's never the way you want it, she thought. *The universe doesn't care.*

What Rosie had gotten for the past quarter of a century had been nothing short of cruel. And so, when Otto approached her as she laid prostrate on the cold basement floor, she was hardly surprised to see hatred rather than compassion flash across his twisted face. She turned her eyes upward to stare at those blackened teeth and gums, his blue-tinged eyes reflecting the shaft of light that came down the steps and into the darkness from the kitchen above. But he wasn't looking into his dying mother's face. He was staring at her hand, her wrist, the cord that was looped around it. Rosie tried to free it, but the pain that came with her attempt to move was too intense. She moaned again, and Otto snorted at the sound. It was a noise he was used to hearing after killing so many. Rather than being moved by his own mother's suffering, it ignited his savagery instead.

Leaning down, he glared at the rope around Rosie's wrist. Sniffed it. Bared his teeth.

Rosie shut her eyes tight and whispered, "I deserve it."

And then she felt it.

The anguish of the end.

There, in the darkness of the basement, Otto began to free himself of his mother's bond. And as she wailed in pain, a single thought pushed past the agony:

He will be free. Without me, he will be free.

30

STEVIE COULD HEAR Jude hot on his heels the entire way home. With the hammer still firmly in his hand, he tossed it over the back fence, then launched himself at the wood planks, struggling to scramble over as fast as he could. Fingers clamped around his ankle. He yelped and kicked, trying to throw off Jude's grasp. Flinging himself forward, inertia negotiated his release, and he flew headfirst onto the ground. His hip landed on the hammer, and a zing of pain bloomed outward from the point of impact. It veined through his body, traveling down his arms and legs as fast as a hairline crack on a lake of ice. As he writhed there, a whimper slithered from his throat, but he wasn't afforded more than a few moments to recover. Jude leapt over the fence after him, his Converse sneakers landing hard next to Stevie's head. Stevie exhaled a cry, scuttling backward to put distance between them. Jude crouched there, gargoylesque, staring down at his cousin, his face pulled into a mask of wrath. His hands, pressed flush to the ground. His right one landed directly on top of the hammer Stevie had dropped.

"J-Jude, d-d-d-don't . . ." Stevie's plea came out as little more than a stuttering squeak. Puny. Weak. The vocalization of a kid who was raising an arm up to shield himself from oncoming malice. A cowering kid—the same one who ducked his head and waited to be pummeled by an angry stepfather. Except that now, the punishment would be doled out by the one person Stevie thought he could trust.

Jude's rage shifted toward a scoff. *Chicken shit. Always were, always will be.* When his chapped and cracking lips curled, Stevie could see a flash of spotty gray gums. Jude leaned in, close enough for Stevie to get a whiff of him—something sweet but rank, like raw hamburger that had gone bad; something dead and rotting, because there were bits of *Mother* on Jude's hands.

"That lady," Stevie whispered past his fear. "What happened to that lady?" Jude's leer curled up at the corners, as if satisfied with the sudden flash of memory. Stevie struggled to swallow against the lump in his throat, his eyes darting from Jude's twisted face to the hammer beneath his hand. He was waiting for it to happen, waiting for his once-best friend to grab that weapon, raise his arm, and club him across his skull. But Jude snatched up Stevie's hands instead, the lady's blood sticky between both their palms. Stevie jerked his hands away only to feel something hard—like a pebble or a piece of seashell—scrape across his skin. He looked down, gaped at the long strands of hair that now clung to his fingers, nearly screamed when he realized what that small red-tinged shard against his palm must have been. Bone.

Not knowing where to look or what to do, he turned desperate eyes back toward Jude. Jude was no longer snarling. In the time it took Stevie to realize what was smeared on his hands, Jude's expression had gone from monstrous to a reflection that made Stevie's heart ache. It was his old friend. *Hey . . .*

"Jude?"

Stevie watched his lost friend come up from the depths of darkness like a diver breaking the water's dark surface. Jude's baleful expression was shot through with self-realization and dismay. He was staring at his gored hands, straightening from his stooped position, and for a second—standing tall, with his face full of confused trepidation—Stevie was sure that Jude was back. Finally remembering. Finally pushing through whatever evil had been holding him down.

"Jude . . . ," Stevie whispered the name, drawing his friend's attention down to where he sat on the ground. "Jude, are you . . . ?" *Are you you?* On the verge of tears, he was almost certain he was about to bawl out of fear and sadness, out of relief and disgust. The stress of the past few days rushed over him all at once, leaving him nauseated, nearly heaving. Because, of course, Jude wasn't okay. *Nobody* was okay. They were covered in a dead woman's blood. There were bits of bone stuck against Stevie's palm. That creature thing was still out there. Stevie hadn't killed it, that was for sure.

"What . . ." Jude's voice, tumultuous, bewildered. "What was that? What *was* that?"

Stevie shook his head, not understanding what Jude meant. What was the monster, the lady, the past nightmarish few days? Jude shot a look over his shoulder toward the back fence, as if dreading that man-thing's return. A second later, he was giving

Stevie an urgent glance. He, too, was coming unglued. "Go tell your mom," he said. "Go tell her, quick."

Stevie opened his mouth, ready to insist that she'd never listen; about to ask what made Jude think adults would help when he didn't trust them, when he never had.

"S-she won't believe," Stevie stammered.

"Yes she will."

"Aunt Mandy," Stevie said. If any of the parents would take notice, it would be her. "*Your* mom."

Jude shook his head. No, he wanted Stevie to go home.

"I want to come with you." Stevie started to get to his feet, to insist with action rather than words. But Jude was quick, pivoting away and hopping the short side fence.

"Go!" he yelled, and ran across his yard to his back door. He took the hammer with him, just in case that thing came back.

Stevie sat unmoving for a moment, as stunned now as he'd been when he'd found his cousin standing on the front porch days before. Was it possible that it could all be over; had seeing that thing up close knocked something loose inside Jude's head, forcing him back into his old self? All at once, Stevie found himself jumping to his feet. A spark of pain flared out from his hip, but he paid no attention as he limped toward his bedroom window. Jude had run off to warn his mom. Stevie had to do the same.

Squeezing beneath the pane, he left a bloody handprint on the sill. He careened down the hall. Rainwater flew from his clothes, wet drops blooming on the carpet beside the master bedroom door. Stevie barged into his mother's room, hit the lights, a gruesome handprint left in his wake. Both his mom and Terry immediately shielded their eyes against the glare. His mom sat up stick-straight, shocked into alertness. The Tyrant spoke first.

"What the fucking *hell*?"

"Mom!" Stevie weep-yelled into the room. He'd been too terrified to cry, but now that he was standing there, catching his breath, the hysterics were kicking in. What the hell had just happened? What had he seen? *What was on his hands?* "Th-there's a m-m-monster thing that took Jude is back and I went and it was there and I saw it, I saw it, I saw it, I saw—"

"*What?*" Stevie's mom went stiff. Every muscle in her body seemed to go stony with alarm. "Stevie, slow down. What are you talking about? Where's Jude? Oh my God, what is that, Stevie? *What is that?*" She threw the sheets aside, ready to race into the rain, to knock on Aunt Mandy's door. Surely Jude couldn't be missing again. But rather than rushing out of the house in nothing but her nightgown, she grabbed Stevie by the shoulders, her eyes wide as she stared at his dirty palms. Her hands retreated just as fast, the contact revealing the drenched state of his clothes, as if just as shocked by the wetness of his T-shirt as she was by the blood that crawled up past his wrists. "Why are you . . . what is . . ."

"I f-f-f-f-followed him to the blood. There's blood on the floor and the door, so much more underground, and he was just sitting there, and the lady . . . was eating . . ." Stevie was weeping full-on now, sure he'd never get that awful image out of his head. "N-no, not eating. Not eating," he cried. "*Eaten.* I knew he'd sneak out, I knew it. And that lady, mother, she was hurt, call 911—"

"What—a lady?" She didn't understand. "You hurt a lady?"

"You've got to be kidding me. Nicole . . ." Terry. "I've fucking *had it*. I'm calling the cops."

Stevie's eyes darted to the bed. To The Tyrant.

"What? The cops? Why? Terry, don't . . ." Stevie's mom gave Terry a wide-eyed stare, a look that implored him to hold off.

"Call the cops," Stevie whispered, echoing his stepdad to soothe himself as much as to encourage Terry to go through with his threat. "Call the cops." Because the lady needed help. Jude needed help. They were all in danger. That thing he'd clobbered with the hammer would be angry. It would come out of those woods tonight. It would kill them all.

"This has gone way too fucking far," Terry insisted. "Look at him. He's out of his goddamn mind. If he hurt someone . . ."

Stevie couldn't stop crying. It was true then, he *was* the reason his father had left. And now it was Terry's turn.

"No, I didn't, I didn't! You can't just leave! You can't do it again!" Stevie stammered through his sobs. He hated The Tyrant, but he didn't want to be responsible for his mother's misery. Terry had to go, but not because of something Stevie had done. "I'm not t-trying at lying!" He shot his mom a beseeching look. She had to believe him. Wasn't it some sort of maternal code? But the panic on his mother's face had shifted into something different. Something darker. It wasn't worry. It was suspicion. "I swear. I saw, saw, saw, saw—" But it didn't matter what he said. Doubt had done a slow crawl across her face, blotting out all signs of faith in his claim; of faith in him. "He's been going since he's come back, going back, going coming back and forth, and I wanted to see . . ." He stopped, tried to calm himself, tried to gather his thoughts. "See w-what he . . . what he . . . what he . . ." His bawling was growing more frantic by the second, but the words wouldn't stop trickling past his lips. "Was doing," he wept.

Terry started to climb out of bed, preparing to snatch his charging cell phone off the nightstand and dial the police.

"Oh God . . ." His mom whispered the words to herself, her hand pressing to her mouth.

"It's gone too far," Terry said, shoving the sheets away.

"*What?*" She spun around to face her second husband. "No!" Her arms flew out, her hands dancing across his chest, trying to keep him in bed. "No, just give him a minute," she implored. "He just needs to calm down, you know how he gets."

"Give him a minute? Give him a minute for *what*? He's done. This whole goddamn thing is done. You want him to hurt himself . . . or anyone else, if he hasn't already?" Terry's feet hit the ground.

Stevie didn't look at them. He couldn't. He was too busy trying to get it together, the words coming in a deluge of rhyme. "Mother," he whispered. "Blood brother." Was that why Jude had grabbed his hands, was that why he'd smeared that lady's blood across his skin, to eternally connect them somehow?

"Let him calm down!" Stevie's mom insisted. She was crying now, too. "Let him explain!"

But The Tyrant's footfalls were hard, impatient. His block

of a hand fell onto Stevie's shoulder, his fingers squeezing the bones beneath Stevie's skin hard enough to make them creak.

"Ow!" Stevie wailed, not caring how big of a baby it made him.

"Just *give him a minute*!" Stevie's mom raised her voice. "Goddamnit, Terry, can't you see he's sick?!"

Stevie started at his mother's yell, and so did Terry. That viselike grip dropped away from his shoulder, and while Stevie didn't look up at either of them, he could tell Terry was looking at his wife like he'd just been slapped in the face.

"He's sick," she repeated, softer now. "He's *been* sick. It's just getting worse. I don't know what to do."

Stevie swallowed, a fresh bout of dismay worming its way into his sinus cavity. Yes, his brain was broken, but that didn't mean what he'd seen wasn't real.

"Stevie . . ." His mother's voice was abruptly calm, like a woman talking a crazy person off a ledge. "Sweetheart, baby, I need you to focus. Tell me what happened, okay?"

But how could he calm down? A lady was dead, torn up like how they said Max Larsen had been. And the thing that had done it was still out there . . . Wasn't it? He looked down at the blood on his hands, the stringy hair that clung to his mangled fingers. It was why Jude had caught him by the hands in the first place. He knew they wouldn't listen, so he gave Stevie proof.

"Take a breath," his mom advised, her coolheadedness so thin a veil he could hear the hysteria behind each and every syllable that left her. "Whose blood is this?"

"Th-th-the lady's." Stevie wept the words. "The basement. Mother." He held his hands up to his mom's face. *Look, look, look! "Mother!"*

"Jesus Christ," Terry muttered. "I'm calling—"

"Stevie!" Mom again, no longer levelheaded. "Calm down, okay?" Yelling. Trying to push her son's gore-smeared hands out of her face. "Calm down. *Explain it to me!*" But before Stevie could gather enough breath to try to describe what had happened for what felt like the hundred-thousandth time, his words were stalled by a guttural wail.

Aunt Mandy.

She was screaming the way she had when the cops had shown up, when they had told her about the sweatshirt, about how Jude was probably dead.

Stevie's eyes bugged at the sound.

"It's back!" He tore away from his mom's grip. "I gotta get him! Gotta get him! Gotta go get him before he goes invisible again!"

He tore into the hall, his mom nipping at his heels, yelling a panicky "Stevie, *Stevie, STEVIE, WAIT!*" But Stevie wasn't going to. Not this time.

He flew through the living room, his bloodied palms slapping against the front door as he fumbled with the dead bolt.

"What the—" Dunk. Muffled. In the hallway somewhere. "What's . . . Is that Aunt Amanda?"

"Who's it fucking sound like?" Terry actually sounded freaked-out for once. "Hello? *Hello?* I need officers down here . . ."

"What's going on?" Dunk, losing his composure. "Sack, what the . . ."

"Mandy?!" Stevie's mom. Torn between her concern for Stevie and her fear as to why her sister was shrieking in horror, she reached over Stevie's shoulder, threw the dead bolt herself, and pulled open the door, releasing him onto the front porch. Stevie leapt down the stairs and into the rain, howling Jude's name as he sprinted for Aunt Mandy's place. His mom followed as fast as she could, cycling from one panicky name to another: *Stevie, Mandy, Jude.*

His mom was bolting for the front door, but Stevie knew better. He ran for the back of the house, sure the kitchen door would be open. Jude had gone in that way, and it was probably how the man-thing had gotten inside.

He could hear his mother yelling over Aunt Mandy's screams. "Call the police! Duncan, call the police!"

Clamoring up the back steps, Stevie was just about to grab for the knob of the back door when it flew open of its own accord, and he was left gawking at what he saw. There was blood on Aunt Mandy's pajamas. A thick swatch of the stuff was smeared across her left temple, half-hidden behind snarled blond loops.

"Aunt Mandy?"

She exhaled a cry, yanked backward like a yo-yo at the end of its string, staggering into an upturned kitchen that was usually neat as a pin. She hit the ground, her legs kicking out in search of purchase, her bare feet shoving the small kitchen rug across the floor. Stevie couldn't look away from her face—wide-eyed and twisted up in horror, exactly the way he'd pictured it inside his head. Except, there was no monster. Above her, his fingers tangled in her hair, was Jude, the Stanley gripped tight in his free hand.

Jude paused, standing in the space between the table and the back kitchen door. He stared at the interloper—at Stevie's O of a mouth and his giant owl eyes. Aunt Mandy wept, and with teeth that looked blacker than Stevie remembered, Jude canted his head at Stevie and snarled.

"Stevie . . . !" Aunt Mandy reached out a frantic hand. *Help, help, help me, please!* But she was given a fierce backward tug. Somehow, that leer became all the more malicious. As if it would be that easy for her to get away . . . as if things could possibly go back to normal now.

"Jude, what are, are, are, are . . ." Stevie's brain got stuck on the word, struggling to muscle past it. ". . . areyoudoing?" He managed to spit out the inquiry, hoping that somehow such a simple question would bring Jude back around. But Jude hadn't been himself for a while now. It seemed that he'd come back, but maybe not. It could have been a trick, a way to get Stevie to go right while Jude had gone left, leaving him to attack his mother while Stevie fought through his stuttering ticks.

The person who stood in front of Stevie now—his fist full of Aunt Mandy's hair—was the same person who had chased him through the trees. The Not-Jude, eyes little more than bruised hollows, glinting cold blue from the depths of those darkened pits; skin as thin as a rice-paper wrapper, peeling away from the apples of his cheeks in flesh-toned curls. That putrid basement smell filled Aunt Mandy's kitchen with the scent of warm garbage. And Jude's lips . . . they were no longer chapped as much as they were gone, corroded away to reveal those gruesome teeth, like a gaping hole in his head. In the short time Stevie had spent in his mother's bedroom, screaming at her in an attempt to make her understand, something terrible had taken hold of Jude for good. As though evil had been patiently waiting, finally allowed to crawl beneath his skin and breathe.

Aunt Mandy reached for Stevie again, stretching her fingers outward, trying to catch hold of salvation. Jude didn't like that. He'd told her no once before, and now she was defying him out of spite. He gave her another backward jerk, reeled up, and brought the Stanley down against her outstretched wrist. The sound of Aunt Mandy's agonized howl shot Stevie through with a frightened rage so all-encompassing, he felt like screaming right along with her, screaming loud enough to rupture his own ears.

"Let her go!" His voice wavered, but he was determined to stand his ground. Finally, he'd take the advice Jude had given him time and time again: *Don't be a chicken shit. Grow some balls.*

He clenched his hands into fists while Jude's fingers remained ensnared in Aunt Mandy's hair. "Stevie . . . just run," she wept. "Just run away." But Stevie didn't move. Not until Jude gave his mother's hair another unsparing pull. It was then—with Jude's attention at half-mast—that he sucked in a breath and charged.

He rammed his shoulder into his cousin's chest the way he'd seen football players do it a bazillion times during Terry's games. Jude stumbled backward, but he didn't fall. His reflexes were too quick. He grabbed Stevie by the front of his rain-soaked shirt, spun him around, and launched him toward the nearest wall.

Stevie flew forward, crashed into the kitchen counter, the cutlery inside the silverware drawer rattling with the impact. Glasses shuddered inside the overhead cabinet. Spice bottles shook from atop the stove's back ledge, tumbling onto the steel top, crashing and rolling across the kitchen floor. He grabbed one, lobbed it at Jude's head as hard as he could. *Stevie Clark, quarterback, gonna let it fly, here it goes!* It zinged just past Jude's ear, glass and brown powder exploding against the wall. The kitchen filled with the scent of cinnamon, tamping the raw, metallic fetor of death.

Jude spun around, glanced at the starburst of cinnamon against Aunt Mandy's peach-colored wall, and for half a second he looked as if he was about to laugh the way he used to—a little manic, a lot amused, totally enamored by the chaos unfolding before him. But he only readjusted his grip on his mother's hair and dragged her across the hardwood toward the door, far more interested in getting Aunt Mandy out of the house than wrestling Stevie to the floor.

His escape was blocked when Stevie's mom came flying around the side of the house. She was yelling "Mandy? *Mandy!*" and coming in too fast to keep herself from bolting up the back steps. At the last second, she caught herself on the jamb, her eyes wide with fright. Jude hesitated, caught off guard by this new visitor, debating whether to plow through

Stevie's mom or drag Aunt Mandy clear across the house and out the front door.

If Stevie had learned anything from all of those cop shows, it was to use any distraction to his advantage. Jude's momentary stall had Stevie twisting where he stood. He yanked open the drawer behind him and grabbed the first thing that fell into his hand: a giant two-pronged grilling fork, the kind he and Jude used for roasting marshmallows over the stove's gas burner on cold winter days. He didn't give himself time to think, knowing that if he hesitated, he wouldn't go through with the deed. *Chicken.* Like yanking off a Band-Aid or jumping off a high dive, he launched forward without considering the consequences. *Well, do you got a pair or what?*

Aunt Mandy continued to yowl. Stevie's mom screamed. Terry appeared behind her shoulder, looking bewildered as a low and threatening growl slithered from deep within Jude's throat.

Stevie ran for his once-best friend, pulled his arm back for added leverage, and buried the fork deep between Jude's shoulder blades. "Jude-not-Jude!" he wailed. "Not Jude, not Jude!"

Jude gave a high-pitched, doglike whine—a howl tinged with frenzy and pain. Aunt Mandy and Stevie's mom joined in the chorus as the hammer tumbled from Jude's left hand, thumping to the ground. His right hand tore from the tangle of Aunt Mandy's hair, taking a fistful of blond with it. He fell into a frantic high-step, both arms desperately trying to catch hold of whatever had stung him, his movements made all the more gruesome by hysterical dismay. He spun like a top, reaching so far backward he verged on dislocating his arms. Knocking into the table, he sent kitchen chairs flying, kicked fallen spice containers across the floor like tiny missiles, stumbled when his feet snared on the upturned rug. His right shoulder rolled out of its socket with an audible pop—a contortionist putting on an impromptu in-house show. Stevie had to think fast. In a second, possibly two, Jude would reach that giant fork, yank it out of his back, magically heal himself, and embed that utensil right through Stevie's heart.

Stevie crashed to his knees, his hands slapping the floor. If he could just get to that hammer, he could scare Jude off, chase him out the door and into the darkness, where he was sure the hunched creature-thing was awaiting his return. Because that was why Jude was so desperate to take Aunt Mandy with him, wasn't it? She was a sacrifice; another meal. Or had the dead lady in the basement been an accident? Jude had called her "Mother." Maybe he'd done so because the lady had been *that thing's* mom, and now that she was dead, a replacement was due.

He rushed across the floor on hands and knees while Jude danced above him—the devil jigging to a phantom fiddle. Stevie's blood-smeared palm hit the Stanley's rubber grip. He rolled back on his heels, ready to bound up and save the day. But his ascent was stalled when, looking up, he found Jude standing over him with a pitiless glare. His left arm was suddenly seized, his free hand yanked forward. Jude opened his mouth wide and crammed Stevie's good hand past those darkening teeth. And then he bit down.

The pain was a firework, a replay of the InSinkErator—a

burst of white hot sparks exploding inside his brain. He tried to scream, gasped for air, instinctively jerked his hand away from Jude's lipless mouth. That was a bad idea. With Jude's teeth ferociously clamped against his fingers, Stevie's pain was intensified tenfold by attempted retreat. The moms screamed as Jude gnashed his teeth harder, blood oozing down his chin. Stevie heard someone yelling *Terry, Terry!* as he searched for breath, unable to look away from his best friend's face, from those terrible shadows beneath his eyes, from the snarl that now struck him as a nightmarish smirk. *Finally,* it said, *we're having some fun in the sun, son.*

Stevie's inability to holler was supplanted by another cry. "Terry, stop them!"

A cacophony of voices. Indiscernible. All of them at a fevered pitch, punctuated by a masculine yell. Terry pushed through the women, spitting out open-ended questions that were speckled by swears. "The fuck . . . ?" If Terry said anything beyond that, Stevie didn't hear it. Something kicked on inside his brain, and suddenly his own inability to speak was replaced by shrieks. Another frantic yank away from Jude's mouth was enough to expose a flash of bare bone. Jude was gloving the pointer and middle finger of Stevie's left hand, as if gifting him a set of digits that would match his right. He gnashed harder, as if trying to take them off completely. Stevie continued to scream, the world starting to darken around the edges. A photographic vignette. He'd black out soon. Hit the ground. Wake up to a room full of blood. His mother dead. Aunt Mandy abducted. Terry, gone. Dunk . . . Dunk . . .

"Holy shit!" Dunk squealed somewhere within the confines of the kitchen, sounding completely unlike himself.

"Get the fuck offa my kid!" Terry's voice boomed in Stevie's ears. The world's edges momentarily brightened, overexposed, hyperreal. "Get the fuck off you fucking *freak*!" Even at the height of calamity, the irony wasn't lost on Stevie. The Tyrant to the rescue. Who would have thought?

But if anyone hated Terry more than him, it was Jude, and he was reminded of that fact when Jude's eyes snapped away from his screaming face. It zeroed in on the hulking man just beyond Stevie's shoulder. Before Stevie knew what was happening, his hand was free. He staggered backward, falling into someone—his mom? Aunt Mandy?—then crashed to the ground. For what felt like a century, he could do nothing but stare at the exposed bones of his hand. If there was a doctor out there who could save his fingers, his mother certainly wouldn't be able to afford it. He would lose them, just like the others. His fingers were gone. *Wee, wee, wee,* all the way to the hospital incinerator.

Duncan crashed to his knees in front of Stevie, his eyes wide and disbelieving. "Holy shit, Stevie, are you—" He was cut off, his attention snapped sideways along with Stevie's own. Above them, Terry reeled back and slammed his fist into the side of Jude's face.

Jude shook it off as though the impact were nothing, then lunged, jaws gaping wide—far wider than his mouth should have been able to open—catching Terry off guard. Stevie watched his big bad stepfather lumber backward, arms against his chest, as though protecting his hands from the fate that Stevie's fingers had suffered. But, as strange as it was, Jude backed off. The Tyrant meant nothing. He wasn't what Jude had come for.

Jude pivoted on the balls of his feet and darted across the room, straight for Stevie and Dunk. Stevie cried out, tried to crabwalk away. Dunk shifted his weight, as if to shield his little brother from whatever was to come. He grabbed for Jude's arm, but came up empty-handed. Jude lunged for his mother, still determined to steal her away, his eyes wild, his mouth smeared with Stevie's blood. It was then that Stevie did the only thing he could think to do. He lifted his right hand, his fingers still wrapped around that hammer's handle, took a half second to search Jude's face for signs of his once-best friend, and when he didn't find what he was looking for, he swung.

Jude fell back.

Stevie swung again.

"Don't touch her!" he screamed. Swung a third time. "Don't touch her, don't you dare, you don't!"

Aunt Mandy. "Stevie, stop!"

"You aren't my friend, not my friend, not anymore, no!"

"Stevie!" His mother.

"Holy shit!" Dunk, grabbing his arm.

But Stevie swung again.

The sound was a wet thud, like porcelain caving in on itself.

Again. And again. Until the hammer, blood-slick, slipped from his hands.

"Oh my God." He couldn't tell if it was his mom or Aunt Mandy anymore. The voices were running together. The walls were trembling. Any moment now, they would crack wide open and spill a deluge of blood across the kitchen floor. "Oh my *God*!" There was too much screaming behind him, too much commotion.

"Call the—"

"Jude? *Jude?!*"

"I am! I did!"

Not-Jude lay on Aunt Mandy's kitchen floor, Aunt Amanda huddled over the body the same way the beast had loomed over the dead lady in the basement. Dunk kept Stevie back, his raspy breaths reverberating in Stevie's ears.

Jude's old Stanley was left abandoned in the soft tissue and splintered bone of his skull.

"Jude." The name eked out of Stevie's throat in a breathless, nearly inaudible whisper. "It wasn't him."

". . . Stevie?" Dunk, pale-faced and terrified.

"It's gonna come back," Stevie murmured to his brother. The monster was still alive out there somewhere. "We gotta find it." His legs were wobbly with adrenaline. His left hand, an open spigot of blood. "Jude." He looked back toward the body. "Hey, Jude," he said, and then began to cry.

Epilogue

————

I T DIDN'T TAKE long for Laurie Lewis to hear the stories from her classmates. Urban legends, the kind of stuff you recited around campfires and on Halloween; tales that warned children to stay close to home, to listen to their parents, to not venture too far because you never knew what may be hiding in the forest.

But Laurie was hardly a child, and the stories? She loved them. Perfect fodder for her horror blog, which, admittedly, had become more of an obsession than a hobby after the move. She hadn't wanted to uproot herself in her sophomore year of high school, but rare was the day when anyone listened to the wishes of a fifteen-year-old girl, especially when her legal guardians were her grandparents and Grandpa Jim wanted nothing more than to "retire in goddamn paradise." Paradise, as it turned out, was a small town with a two-screen movie house and not a damn thing else to do. Except, of course, wander the woods.

Within the first few weeks of Laurie living in Deer Valley, she typed up an exposé on the death of six-year-old Maxwell Larsen. It was complete with quotes from newspaper articles—

dug up at the local library—and photos of all the locations mentioned in the police reports—care of her grandfather's Buick Skylark and Laurie paying for gas. Grandpa Jim had begrudgingly pulled onto the shoulder of the highway when Laurie pointed to the spot where the Larsen boy's body had been found. When she hopped back into the car, he couldn't help but grumble, not understanding her fascination with such morbid, awful stuff. Grandma Marcy was more understanding. She simply smiled and gave Grandpa Jim a pat on the knee, and then—with Laurie's phone full of murder scene photographs—they proceeded to Cannon Beach, where they had a picnic and fed the seagulls bits of sourdough bread.

When Laurie reached the end of her Maxwell Larsen investigation, she moved on to another case. The murder of Jude Brighton was as bizarre as it was tragic. Bludgeoned to death by his disturbed younger cousin, Jude had died in his own home, in front of his mother, who was cradling him when the police had arrived. Ten-year-old Stephen Aaron Clark was rumored to have been an undiagnosed schizophrenic, but his age made the pronouncement difficult to swallow. Of all the articles Laurie could find online, it seemed that schizophrenia in children was almost unheard of. But whaling on a family member with the claw end of a hammer? Surely there was something wrong with his mind.

Regardless of whether or not the analysis of Stevie's mental state was correct, he was relegated to a facility somewhere out in Tillamook, a place Grandpa Jim outright refused to take her, despite the possibility of an interview. "Sometimes," he'd said, "bad things happen to writers when they go one-on-one with the crazies." Like Grandma Marcy's favorite true-crime writer, who had nearly met a grisly fate at the hands of a cult devotee, getting a little too personal with his subject matter. That had happened just a hundred miles north of Deer Valley, in Washington State. "Too close for comfort," said Grandpa Jim. So, instead of arguing, Laurie wrote to Stevie about the three-year-old crime instead.

In his rambling letters, Stevie spoke of a monster living in the woods; a grotesque and hunched, pale-skinned creature with an enormous head and a vestigial tail. That monster had "possessed" Jude, taken over his cousin somehow, and it was still out there. But nobody believed him. Maybe, he said, if Laurie could prove it, she could be the key to Stevie's freedom. And when he got out, he'd return to Deer Valley, where the both of them would finally kill the thing that had murdered his best friend. There was no mention of Stevie's entire family bearing witness to the crime he had unquestionably committed. No hint of regret for what he had done. No suggestion that he remembered doing it at all.

They were the meandering thoughts of a twisted mind. Stevie's stories didn't match up with any of the Deer Valley police reports. Jude's mother never claimed that she'd been attacked by her son, and maybe that could be chalked up to denial. But the dead woman that Stevie insisted had been the caretaker of the beast, at least according to the reports filed, didn't exist. No body had been discovered, and no dismemberment of a random, outlying woman had been announced. When Laurie explained this in her own correspondence, Stevie's reply was exactly what she had expected: either the police had covered it up, or the monster had taken care of things itself. *Ask Mr. Greenwood*, he'd written. *He knows*. But Greenwood had packed up and moved weeks after Stevie had gone off the rails. The general store had been boarded up, and was now a motorcycle shop with a bike in the window and a few hostel rooms upstairs. The guy who owned the place called it The Redwood. He didn't know Mr. Greenwood, or anything about Stevie Clark.

Coincidentally, the shop owner had also purchased the deed to the old place Stevie said was where the monster lived.

Armed with the vague directions Stevie had relayed, she started at what had once been the Clark residence—now a shell of an empty house with a FOR SALE sign out front—and began to walk. She followed the overgrown trail into the woods, snapping photos both for her blog and her Instagram. After about three miles of nothing but ferns, trees, and moss, she came across an abandoned dirt road. A house was poised alongside its washboard surface, winking at her from a distance, just as Stevie had described.

She didn't hesitate to step over the fallen picket fence and climb up the porch stairs to cup her hands against a grimy window. It was empty but clean, as though someone had swept up the cobwebs in the hopes of living there. A few buckets of paint were stacked beside the front door. A rusty red pickup rambled up the road before she had a chance to retreat, and the guy from The Redwood sidled out of the truck—not angry, just smiling, so she wasn't completely busted for trespassing.

He was carrying a few Walmart shopping bags, probably full of renovation supplies.

"It's a damn wreck, don't you think?" the man asked, looking up at the place as if seeing it for the first time. "Not sure why I bought it . . . but I couldn't resist. It's got good bones."

She almost asked him whether he was scared to live there, only to reconsider. Scared of what? A nonexistent monster? "It's . . . pretty," she said. "Just needs a fresh coat of paint."

"Oh, I think it needs a bit more than that." The white-haired man turned his attention back to the house, crossed his arms over a faded Grateful Dead shirt, and laughed. "But that's fine by me. I've got the time. Much better place for a retreat than above the shop, though, don't you think?"

Laurie nodded, then idly stepped off the porch.

"Going already?" he asked.

Yeah, going already. The sky was growing gray overhead. Another rainstorm was rolling in off the Pacific. That, and she had ton of photos to sort through and edit.

Back at home, she scrolled through the shots and thumbed through the letters Stevie had sent, almost disappointed that she hadn't seen the blood-covered floor or some proof of the dead woman he'd described. Stevie Clark may have been nuts, but he told a damn good story.

As she sat there, sifting through photos on an obsessive loop, she stopped on one in particular. It was a simple shot—nothing but trees, a single trunk in the foreground, gently bending to the right. And there, in the fuzzy out-of-focus distance, was a shadow. Was that someone crouching, or just a half-hidden fern? "It's the monster." She chuckled, offering her golden retriever, Joey, a half smile from her desk. But it *had* been pretty out there, and that house deserved some professional shots with her SLR. The owner had seemed nice enough. She was sure he'd let her take a few more photos before he got to his renovations. She'd put a lot of time into this article, and a picture of that creepy house—just after sunset—would be the perfect finishing touch.

That, and Joey had been restless these past few days. He'd even gotten out of the yard a few times. "We'll go tomorrow," she told him. "Just before sundown, so the pictures will be nice and spooky." Some exercise would do them good, and there was nothing better than a long walk in the woods.

ACKNOWLEDGMENTS

To my team of friends and comrades—Ed Schlesinger, David Hale Smith, the folks at Gallery Books and Inkwell Management—thank you all for your effort, encouragement, and tireless dedication to the creation of this book and my ever-expanding oeuvre. Don't go soft on me, Ed. I *will* write that romance novel, and it will haunt you forever.

To my husband, Will, thanks for not freaking out when I confessed that I no longer want to be a soggy Upper Left vampire; I now want to be a Deep South backwoods murderess disguised as a mint-julep-sipping southern belle. I do declare!

To my dog, Sulley, thanks for taking me on walks every morning, buddy. I'd never get out of the house and talk to strange old neighborhood ladies if it wasn't for you. Me and you, our long conversations. I mean, I'd go crazy without you, what with all the long hours and alone time. You keep me sane, dog. Totally sane. Who's a good boy?

And to my readers and pals, you are the best. Thank you for your ceaseless enthusiasm for weird and creepy stuff, and for saving a spot on your shelf for my weird and creepy books. I'll continue to write them as long as you continue reading. And if you stop reading? Well, let's just say I *might* know where you live. Maybe. I mean, anything is possible . . .